Jackie FRENCH

The Lily and the Rose

Angus&Robertson
An imprint of HarperCollins*Publishers*

Angus&Robertson

An imprint of HarperCollins*Publishers*, Australia

First published in Australia in 2018
This edition published in 2019
by HarperCollins*Publishers* Australia Pty Limited
ABN 36 009 913 517
harpercollins.com.au

HarperCollins*Publishers*

Level 13, 201 Elizabeth Street, Sydney NSW 2000, Australia
Unit D1, 63 Apollo Drive, Rosedale, Auckland 0632, New Zealand
A 53, Sector 57, Noida, UP, India
1 London Bridge Street, London SE1 9GF, United Kingdom
2 Bloor Street East, 20th floor, Toronto, Ontario M4W 1A8, Canada
195 Broadway, New York NY 10007, USA

A catalogue record for this book is available
from the National Library of Australia

ISBN 978 0 7322 9855 5 (paperback)
ISBN 978 1 4607 0195 9 (ebook)

Cover design by Lisa White
Cover images: Woman by Ildiko Neer / Arcangel; coat and rose by
istockphoto.com; all other images by shutterstock.com
Author photograph by Kelly Sturgiss
Typeset in Sabon LT by Kelli Lonergan
Printed and bound in Australia by McPherson's Printing Group
The papers used by HarperCollins in the manufacture of this book are a
natural, recyclable product made from wood grown in sustainable plantation
forests. The fibre source and manufacturing processes meet recognised
international environmental standards, and carry certification.

To the hidden heroines of history —
and to all the women whose heroism continues

Chapter 1

When I was young on the North West Frontier men spoke of
'when the war is over'. War does not stop on the day of ceasefire.
Somewhere, always, the hounds of war snuffle in the gutters,
hunting for the next battle.

Miss Lily, 1914

THE BAVARIAN SOVIET REPUBLIC, GERMANY, 30 MARCH 1919

HANNELORE

The attic smelled of mouse and long-ago-eaten musty apples. Hannelore crouched behind the upturned bed, pistol in hand, and listened to the rats scrabble below. Bolshevik rats, hunting through the snow-slushed street.

Hunting her.

On the floor below her, old Anna screamed. She gabbled a plea. A shot rang out, so loud an icicle dropped, spear like, from the roof beyond the attic window. One shot. You did not need two to kill an old woman in her bed.

The pleading stopped.

Hannelore had counted three shots since the rebels broke down the door. Helga and Joseph must be dead too. She was alone.

Footsteps scrabbled upstairs. Rats in big boots. Well-fed rats, in this land of hunger. Yells, crashes, as doors were flung open.

A year ago she had been Prinzessin Hannelore von Arnenberg. She supposed she still was, though the revolutionaries had abolished titles and ownership of property through all the Räterepublik, the Bavarian Soviet Republic. You did not need a mob of men to hunt for one young woman, but it was worth it to capture a prinzessin.

Hannelore had always known she must give her life for her country. She had thought that would mean a diplomatically useful marriage producing more diplomatically useful children. That future was gone. The men would rape her before dragging her to the firing squad. Rape was what men did, in war. But she would not let them rape her. If men behaved like rats, they deserved to die like rats. The pistol felt warm in her hand, enamelled pink, inlaid with silver. A prinzessin's pistol, with six bullets.

The attic door crashed open. She waited till two figures stepped into the room. Two shots. Two bullet holes in two stomachs, the look of astonishment that men always acquired in that second when they realised their prey had won. Hannelore had nursed enough men in the war to know that a bullet to the stomach was lethal ... eventually.

Other men paused at the doorway now — bearded, filthy, in the rags of German uniforms, their red armbands showing they fought for the Munich Soviet, hungry, but for power, not food. The older ones pushed the most junior forward. The Soviets were all equal, except, of course, they weren't. Yet they still hesitated.

She managed to shoot four more of them. Six rats, bleeding, groaning on the attic floor now. Helga would have had to scrub away the blood, if they had let her live...

Her pistol was empty. But these fools obviously had not calculated how many bullets her pistol held, did not realise that she was helpless.

Which was exactly what Hannelore had hoped.

She was not going to let these men rape her, unless they liked to rape the dead. Even rats did not do that. Sometimes men did.

She stood so the bed no longer sheltered her and aimed her pistol at the door.

She felt the bullet that entered her heart as coldness, rather than pain. The one in her leg she hardly felt at all. Such foolish men, to waste a bullet in the leg.

She smiled as she fell. The Prinzessin Hannelore von Arnenberg was no use to the Bolshevik Republic now. And she had given her life for her country, as she had been bred to do, not this socialist republic but the earth, the trees, the people of her Germany ...

Sophie would understand that, she thought vaguely, as pain burned a thousand fires through her body. Sophie knew how one might love a country, but despair sometimes of its people. Dear, Sophie. Happy Sophie, safe home in Australien among her kangaroos ...

She never would visit Sophie now, Hannelore realised, as hands grabbed her, as cold turned to dark.

Chapter 2

For two years I created and managed three hospitals and a refugee centre. I was a person. Then the war ended. I became 'just a woman' again. No matter what society may decide, my dear, never think of yourself as 'just a woman'.

Sophie in a letter to her granddaughter, undated

LONDON, 1 MAY 1919

'Darling, you need a maid,' said Emily, Mrs Colonel Sevenoaks, gracefully lifting her tea cup in her most perfect drawing room, its walls covered in pre-war pale striped silk. Emily inspected Sophie's stockings, shuddered elegantly, and added, 'Desperately.'

Sophie reached for another apple tart. They really were excellent. A sponge cake crowned with sugar-dusted hothouse strawberries took pride of place on the top tier of the cake stand; small currant cakes, watercress or celery and cream cheese sandwiches the lower tiers. The maids of honour and the apple tarts, adorned with cream, were presented on matching platters.

On the footpath outside this house, a young man, legless, almost invisible in the yellow fog that licked the soot-stained buildings, sat propped up beside a sign reading *Wounded veteran*, offering boxes of matches for threepence to grey-faced passersby. Few stopped. Wounded veterans, legless, armless, or faces burned away by mustard gas, were commonplace these days. Down at Waterloo Station a torso with a face of desperation under his knitted cap waited helplessly for passersby to drop a coin into his cap. What if one day his wife, mother, sister, lover did not return to wheelbarrow him home. What then?

You had to shut your eyes to manage to smile in England now. Even Sophie, who all her life had stubbornly seen as much as she could. Even she could not bear to look too hard. How could you bear to see what you could not help? Or at least not enough to make a difference?

A few streets away she had seen children scrabble in the Thames mud, hunting for firewood, finding mostly what their fathers, brothers, uncles had found in the trenches before them: frostbite, hunger and mud. Sophie wondered if Mrs Colonel Sevenoaks had ever even experienced mud, except at a foxhunt, of course.

Prime Minister Lloyd George had promised England 'a land fit for heroes' in the last election. This Year of Victory 1919 had not seen that promise kept. A million men already were unemployed — naturally no one counted the women cast out of work with the end of the war, or the wan-faced women, in grey flannel, walking wearily to the grey jobs that soon would be returned to men, at man's wages, not the pittance given to women. Much of the army still waited to be demobbed; the government afraid of the growing desperation and violence if even more men were turned out to a land where no jobs waited. But did some employers want demobilisation delayed as long as possible, to keep wage costs down?

Britain, the colonies, had danced, prayed, laughed when the ceasefire had been declared. They had not understood. They still did not.

This was not the land of peace. The Peace Treaty with Germany had not even been agreed to, much less signed. Officially this was only a ceasefire, though most of Europe, America and the colonies tried to blot out the knowledge that the war — officially — was yet to be won.

Who still had the will to fight in 1919, when almost every country in the war was exhausted emotionally, economically, and by the influenza that had killed faster and more efficiently even than the guns?

Outside this drawing room widows, or members of the even vaster army of wives whose husbands had returned from the trenches mentally or physically unable to work, fed their families with a rind of mousetrap cheese, withered potatoes or a half a mouldy cabbage. There was little else to be had for the majority in this post-war England, still suffering from the German blockades, and the diversion of ships from food shipments from the colonies to the returning colonial troops home as fast as possible, before they too muttered rebellion.

One in seven men dead. One in seven too severely damaged in mind or body to work. A nation still on food stamps. Sugar, butter, even bread was severely rationed — but not in the home of Mrs Colonel Sevenoaks, or any of the 'upper 600' families who had estates to supply them not just with bread and cream, but hothouse pineapples.

Here, in this drawing room that smelled of pot pourri and apple wood, privation was for others. Mrs Colonel Sevenoaks would never be an 'other'.

Yet even Emily had spent four years wondering if the young man next to her at a dinner table might be alive the next week, the next month, and too many of them had not. Emily might be one of the few across Europe who had not missed a meal the entire war. But she too had scars.

Sophie bit a tiny portion of crust and apple, felt its buttery smoothness, and lost her appetite. She swallowed anyway. 'Why do I need a maid? I'm not arguing,' she added. 'But how did you know I don't have one?'

'Your right stocking seam is crooked. And white stockings! Darling, white went out an age ago.' Emily automatically stroked her own beige silk, the seams perfectly straight. 'Your dress is excellent —'

Sophie raised an eyebrow. Her wardrobe had been recently resupplied by the best private dressmaker in Paris, replacing the faded, louse-ridden garments of her war.

'— but there is a small stain on your collar,' continued Emily. 'And while your outfit was perfect for the sun this morning, it isn't for this afternoon's fog. A maid would have checked the weather forecast. She would also have advised you that with this year's short skirts, high heels are a necessity, if one is not to look as short-legged as a penguin.'

'Ah,' said Sophie, trying to imagine how she would have coped fighting a war and its ramifications in high heels. She inspected her seam, but didn't straighten it, in case Emily's butler entered with more hot water for the teapot, and his nose lengthened another two inches at the sight. But Emily — damn her slightly porcine aristocratic nose — was quite correct. Two years of running military hospitals and a refugee relief system in Belgium and France, two years nursing at Wooten Abbey before that, had made her temporarily forget the social necessity of a good maid.

'I don't suppose you could suggest one?'

'Darling, I'm not an employment agency,' said Emily sharply. Sophie's war service — and her failure to gain the prize of a good marriage, the ostensible aim of the debutante season that Miss Lily had prepared them for so well and so unconventionally — had let Emily forgive Sophie for being richer and more beautiful. But Emily was still ... Emily. 'It's almost impossible for anyone to find good servants.' She did not add 'especially for a colonial', but the implication lingered among the scents of buttered teacake and pot pourri.

'Munitions work has made girls think themselves too good for domestic service,' continued Emily. 'And why should Lloyd George give those ex-servicemen just lounging around the pubs an allowance when there are footmen's and gardeners' jobs going begging?'

Possibly because having spent four years in the trenches saving your life those ex-servicemen don't want to spend what is left of their own lives polishing your silver, thought Sophie. And alcohol dimmed nightmares — for a while — as well as provided camaraderie, with colleagues in the pub who understood all they would not repeat back home. But she didn't argue. The reconciliation with Emily was still too fragile, just like the ceasefire that had been prematurely called 'peace'.

And Miss Lily had also been correct. Women needed a network of other women, even in this post-war world where women over thirty had recently been allowed to vote, where women of good breeding might even visit each other, unchaperoned and unaccompanied even by a maid or footman, as Sophie was doing now. Although of course she was not well bred, just wealthy enough for that fault to be forgiven.

Emily reached for a currant cake. 'Surely Miss Lily could find you an adequate maid,' she suggested, just slightly too casually. 'Or is Miss Lily still ... absent?'

Did Emily care about Miss Lily? Or had her husband, now in the Home Office, an official reason for finding her? Miss Lily's covert efforts before the war to balance the power between Britain and Germany might now be seen as treason.

'As far as I know Miss Lily won't be returning,' said Sophie truthfully, 'but I don't think she took her maid with her. I wonder if she might be free.'

Green would be perfect. Discreet and deeply capable, thought Sophie. Green was born at Shillings; she had worked for Miss Lily for twenty years; and she already knew Sophie by reputation. 'I'll call Lord Nigel at Shillings and ask after her.'

Emily straightened in shock, though still swan-like, in her chair. Every girl who passed through Miss Lily's tutoring emerged swan-like, and gracefully flirtatious. How else could a woman influence a world that men ran both politically and domestically? Miss Lily's 'lovely ladies', were also — discreetly — intelligent. 'You've actually met the notorious Earl of Shillings?' Miss Lily instructed her pupils at the earl's country estate, but never when he was in residence.

'Notorious?' asked Sophie carefully.

Emily shrugged. No wrinkle appeared in the cloth of her embroidered blue dress — another benefit of having a maid who knew exactly how to iron and alter one's clothing so that it hung like an extension of one's body. 'He's never appeared in the House of Lords. Or anywhere in society for years. A total mystery. But you've met him?'

'I've met him.'

Sophie didn't add that Nigel Vaile, Earl of Shillings, had recently asked her to marry him. And that she had refused, not because she could not love him, but because he was too deeply bound to his land to let her be Australian.

It was time to return to gum trees, the blue gleam of the harbour, to darling Miss Thwaites, to the Higgs corned-beef empire and her father. She had a duty to do first, though.

Sophie closed her eyes briefly. She was so tired of duty ... just so tired. If only there could be true peace. A secure peace ...

'Where did you meet his lordship?' demanded Emily eagerly. 'What is he like?'

Sophie opened her eyes. 'I met him at Shillings, early this year. He was on leave, and invited me to visit.' Which was true, even if not the whole truth. She forced a little social vivacity back into her voice. 'He was weary, like so many officers. He spent nearly all the war with his regiment in France. Quite a 'lot of people met him there,' she added, slightly maliciously. Emily's husband had never seen active service. 'At the moment he's trying to get Shillings back on its feet.'

'A complete waste of his time, darling. I'm amazed he doesn't realise that. The old estates just aren't profitable any more, not with Land Tax and neglect during the war. More tea?' Emily poured more hot water into the teapot. 'Hubert is selling all but the Home Farm and the house to some Americans. We're keeping enough rough country for some shooting, of course. London property is more profitable and far less work.'

Income from property and country estates was socially acceptable, possibly because the owner of that income did not have to work for it, but could employ agents. The money from Sophie's father's corned-beef factories was not acceptable — especially as it was still being made by Mr Higgs himself. 'Old money', like Colonel Sevenoaks', no matter how it had been obtained, was superior to new money. Enough time made society blind to the source of money.

But Sophie's 'new money' was also large new money and a great deal of it had been spent by experts to make sure that Sophie was presented at court. Sophie was now 'presentable' in every sense. Except, she thought, for her crooked stockings, the stain on her collar, the incorrect shoes.

Emily sighed. 'Even the house needs a terrible amount of work to be livable again. The gardens were all dug up for potatoes and cabbages during the war, of course. It's going to take a regiment of gardeners to get them decent again. Everything has become so terribly shabby. I've convinced Hubert we really do need bathrooms now. It's not just that guests expect them — even maids these days object to carrying bath water upstairs. Those moving pictures have given them all quite ridiculous ideas above their station.'

Sophie put down her cup. 'I've really come to ask your help. I urgently need a secretary. I thought you might know of someone. Sorry to treat you as an employment agency,' she added.

'Darling, the season is nearly over! Why on earth do you suddenly need a social secretary now?'

'Not to keep my social diary.' Sophie took a deep breath. 'I've heard from Hannelore.'

Emily's social smile vanished. Her face looked carefully blank as she took another nibble of currant cake.

No need to tell Emily that the letter had actually been from Dolphie, Count Adolphus von Hoffenhausen. Dolphie was Hannelore's uncle but more like a brother, only a few years older than her. They had been brought up together. Nor was Sophie prepared to mention that she had last left Dolphie on the battlefield after shooting two of his men. 'Hannelore needs help. I'm still going home, but I need to go via Germany. I want to find Hannelore and take her with me.'

'A German.' Emily's face was still expressionless, but her voice sounded as if she'd noticed a fly in the sponge cake's whipped cream.

'Our friend,' said Sophie evenly. She put the uneaten tart back on her plate, carefully crumbling it so it did not look as if she had insulted her hostess by rejecting the quality of her afternoon tea. But she wasn't hungry. Had not been hungry now for months, or even years. Meals had been a necessary chore to keep up strength for the past four years, a matter of sawdust bread and potato and swede stew. Now, when the ceasefire and privilege put good food before her, she found it difficult to eat.

Emily considered her. 'Germany is still chaos, you realise. Hubert says there is a very real danger the communists will take over there, as they have in Russia. They've even established a soviet state in Bavaria.'

Emily had always been the most politically astute of Miss Lily's pupils. She took a watercress sandwich and added, 'Hannelore might even have been executed, like the poor Tsar and his family.'

Emily could have been talking about the weather, not the young woman she had briefly regarded as a friend, both at Miss Lily's and their finishing school in Switzerland.

'Germany will rise again, of course,' Emily added. 'Both economically and politically, especially as the country escaped the devastation of France and Belgium. But when? It all depends on how ruthless France is with the reparations when the peace treaty is finally agreed.' She looked thoughtful, nibbling her sandwich.

Emily is considering exactly how knowing a German princess might possibly be of future use, thought Sophie, once Germany has regained stability and power. But that was, after all, what Miss Lily had trained them all to do — to use their charms to be effective politically, though with possibly more compassion than Emily usually wielded.

Emily appeared to reach a decision. 'How can a secretary help you find Hannelore?'

'I need someone I can trust who can speak German. I thought a friend I worked with in France could help me, but she's entering Oxford now women can be granted degrees. I plan to make the expedition seem as if I am scouting for European agents for sales of corned beef, even possibly setting up corned-beef factories in Germany. That should mean I'm not suspected of being a spy, and am too valuable to shoot, with so much hunger.' Sophie smiled wryly. 'I may even succeed in getting new contracts, which might impress my father. My secretary needs to understand business and be ...'

Sophie hesitated. But this, after all, was Emily, who too had been taught that sometimes less ... conventional ... methods might need to be used to achieve a goal. '... broadminded. Intelligent. Willing to break with convention, if necessary, but able to be inconspicuously conventional too. And available to travel to Germany at short notice, despite the dangers, and then make her home in Australia.'

'Quite a list.' For the first time Emily's face showed a little of the strain women had lived with since the war began. 'Five years ago finding a woman like that would have been impossible. Now,' Emily gave her elegant shrug again, 'fortunes are gone. A whole generation of young men are lost. Titles have gone to second cousins. Too many women have no support at all ...'

Emily straightened. Was that ... relief on her face? 'I know someone who will suit you exactly.'

'You seem very sure of that.'

'She is my cousin.' A visibly grudging admission.

Ah, thought Sophie. A close enough poor relation for this unknown woman to be a nuisance. The English upper classes traditionally either supported or exported their poorer relatives. Australia would be a convenient destination. Assuming this cousin actually *could* speak German, and was capable.

'But with her background,' and yours implied Emily, 'she will need to be known as your companion, not your secretary.' A touch of the old Emily there, dictatorial and competitive.

'I don't care what she wants her job to be called, as long as she does it well enough to earn her wages. She speaks German fluently?'

'Just sometimes,' said Emily, 'your corned-beef roots still show. Her mother was Austrian.'

'*Was* Austrian?'

'Her mother died last year in the first wave of the 'flu. Her father, maternal uncles and two brothers were killed in the first and second offensives at the Somme. The title now rests with our second cousin, but we hardly know him.'

My word. 'Any other relatives?'

'Only myself. Her sister was a VAD. She caught consumption in Belgium but it was the influenza that killed her.'

My word, thought Sophie again. Emily could be describing the flower arrangements for her next dinner party, not the tragic family history of her own cousin, a girl she'd known all her life. But had Emily too been struck by these deaths, even if her well-bred face refused to show the pain?

Sophie retreated from obviously unwanted condolences to businesslike crispness. 'How old is she, where is she, what experience does she have, and what is her name?'

'She is twenty-four. She helped run the family estate during the war until Cousin Hartley returned from Palestine. Her name is Lady Georgina FitzWilliam and she is upstairs.'

Chapter 3

*A lady can still be graceful falling in a pig sty, and when she
rises, laughing, every man will see her as more beautiful than the
immaculate debutantes looking embarrassed. Grace can carry you
through small accidents or tragedy, my dears.*

Miss Lily, 1914

Emily departed in a swish of fringed pink silk. Sophie looked
at the apple tarts, the sponge cake oozing jam and cream, still
without appetite. How she'd have loved to feed her nurses like
this, and old Monsieur le Docteur. If only she could package
them up and send them to Belgium ...

'More tea, madam?' The butler appeared with a tray holding a
fresh teapot and hot water pot.

Sophie smiled. 'Thank you.'

She had already drunk an English Channel's worth of tea, but
Miss Lily had taught her never to refuse a gift of love. A dedicated
butler's service could be love. It could also be desperation for his
wages or self-importance. Who was she to know or judge?

She was staring at the sandwiches again, trying to convince
herself to eat one, for she had missed lunch and still had another
appointment to keep before dinner, when Emily appeared,
another young woman behind her.

Tall, bobbed hair, and wearing spectacles. No society woman
ever wore spectacles in public even if she was in danger of
mistaking the housekeeper for the door to the lavatory. The
spectacles alone were an indication of Lady Georgina's retreat
from good society. Her rust-coloured silk dress was fashionable,
but unsuited to her faded ginger colouring — Sophie guessed

that the dress was a cast-off from the darker Emily, worn once at a public affair and so not suitable to be seen in again.

'Georgina.' Emily made it clear in the order of introduction that, in need of employment or not, her cousin outranked Miss Sophie Higgs. 'This is my friend Miss Sophie Higgs. Sophie, Lady Georgina FitzWilliam.'

Etiquette required that Lady Georgina speak first. Etiquette, however, had not caught up with the possibility that a woman might employ her social superior. Sophie stood, as she had not politely stood when her 'social superiors' entered the room. 'It is a pleasure to meet you, Lady Georgina.'

'Thank you.' The voice was reserved, the face as carefully set in a smile as a footman might set a knife and fork on a blank white tablecloth.

Sophie sat. Lady Georgina and Emily sat too, Emily with a hint of annoyance that Sophie had not waited for her and Georgina to sit first. But this was, after all, a job interview, thought Sophie with a touch of malice. She inspected Georgina more closely, suddenly recognising the expression she had taken for resentment.

She had seen faces like this before: in men with shell shock, a term the military had banned in 1916, worried about pension demands when the war was over. What had this woman been through to look like this? The loss of her parents, her brothers, her sister? Yes, there'd be grief and shock from those, but not this look of emptiness, tinged with both distaste and desperation. This woman did not want this job, or perhaps any job. But she would take it, and not just because Emily's hospitality might be growing grudging.

'Emily has told you what the position entails?'

'Yes. It is very kind of you to offer it.' The words held no gratitude.

'No, it isn't,' said Sophie frankly. 'I want someone who can work hard, capably, discreetly and be utterly trustworthy. You will also possibly be going into danger. I have no idea what it will take to locate my friend, nor to bring her out of Germany.'

She did not mention Dolphie, who she hoped, just possibly, might also accompany her, not just back to Australia but also into a partnership of love. 'You might also find life in Australia ... limited.'

Lady Georgina hesitated. 'If I may also be frank?'

'Please do.'

'The connections to Germany and Australia are not a problem, but attractive. I gather we will set off soon?'

'Tomorrow if we can, though I think in three or four days may be more realistic, or even optimistic. My father's London agent, Mr Slithersole, is arranging connections for us on the journey. Part of your job will be to assist him. You will find him cooperative and efficient. You speak German fluently?'

'Of course.' Lady Georgina seemed to imply that a true lady did no less. 'I speak Hochdeutsch — standard German — and Low German. I also speak several dialects. My family spent a lot of time in both Austria and Germany when I was a child.'

'Going out to Australia doesn't worry you either? It can be ... brash. And insular.'

'I spent a year before the war in Ceylon. I doubt Australian society is more limited than the native colonies.'

'Excellent,' said Emily briskly. 'Sophie, if you will just ...'

'Just sign on the dotted line? Excuse my bringing the language of the office into your drawing room, Emily. But perhaps you can now tell me exactly what is going on? A woman of good family does not accept a journey into the various revolutions occurring in Germany, nor even to Australia, quite so readily.'

'An employee cannot have secrets?' enquired Lady Georgina, doing an excellent job of almost keeping the distaste of all that might be associated with Higgs's Corned Beef from her voice.

'No,' said Sophie. 'Or at least not the employee I need. I know that is neither polite nor discreet,' she added. 'But you will inevitably learn secrets of mine. Trust needs to be mutual.'

Lady Georgina glanced at Emily. Emily sighed. 'Sophie was still working in Belgium last year.' She turned to Sophie. 'I presume you didn't see the English papers?'

'I rarely had time to read more than the headlines.' Sophie did not add that even that was mostly in the trench latrines. She glanced at Lady Georgina. 'You were in the newspapers?'

'The gossip columns. Even in war there is gossip.'

'And what is this particular gossip?'

'I left my husband,' said Lady Georgina flatly. She waited for Sophie's horrified reaction. It didn't come.

'Did he beat you?' asked Sophie flippantly.

'Actually, yes.' The voice once again was unemotional.

She had been a fool. And a cruel fool. She of all people should know that Georgina's face of anguish turned to concrete, that desperate will not to feel at all, came from the same cause in women as it did in men. But the battleground that had caused this woman's wounds had not been in France or Belgium.

Georgina — it was suddenly impossible to add the 'Lady' — slid back one shoulder of her dress. The scars showed deep, ridged and red. Sophie had seen worse, but only as scars of war.

Georgina slid the neck of her dress back into place. 'He preferred a riding whip, but sometimes used a cane for variety. Never where it showed. Every Wednesday and Sunday evening — I was not permitted to accept or offer an invitation to dine on those nights. We always had roast meat on Wednesdays and Friday nights. Of course it was always tough, as it must be in Ceylon and so I deserved my punishment. It was our little ... ritual. And ... chastisement ... at other times as I deserved it.'

'You stayed a year with this man?'

'He is her husband,' said Emily. 'But of course, Sophie darling, you have no experience of the bonds of matrimony.'

Georgina regarded them both impassively. 'I stayed with William for two years, counting our time in England and the voyage out. I tried to do my duty as a wife as long as possible. And then it became ... impossible. And no, there was no hint of what his ... husbandly behaviour ... would be like until he legally owned me.

'In late 1914 after war was declared I took what I hoped was the last civilian boat home. The duties of war meant William was unable to follow me. He did, however, arrange an English court order for Restitution of Conjugal Rights. The matter was finally heard last year. I attempted to fight the charges. I lost,' said Georgina flatly.

'Of course you lost. You should never have made a spectacle of yourself ...' began Emily.

'I don't understand,' interrupted Sophie. 'Surely the court wouldn't order you to go back to a man like that.'

'A woman cannot divorce her husband because he beats her, nor even if he commits adultery. He must desert her too. William has no intention of deserting me. The gutter press was ...' Georgina paused '... avid, I think is the correct word. William is the only son of Baron Lynley.'

'I can imagine what the press made of it.' Sophie tried to make her tone as impassive as Georgina's. 'But you are here, not with him, despite the court's judgement?'

'It is still not easy to get a passage to England from Ceylon. Even the court cannot order the war office to find a berth to Ceylon for a deserting wife. William arrives in England in three weeks' time. I planned to leave before then, for France perhaps. But he has friends and connections in France.' She smiled slightly for the first time. 'He will not think of looking for me in Germany or Australia.'

'Why doesn't he let you go? Excuse me,' Sophie added, 'that is impertinence, a curiosity that is personal and not that of an employer.'

'He is not particularly interested in me at all. He wants his son, Timothy. I was pregnant when I left. I had,' said Georgina expressionlessly, 'miscarried twice during our marriage, both after severe beatings.'

'The court did not take the miscarriages into account?'

'Legally it is of no account. The gutter press, however, found it of vital interest.'

'Where is Timothy now?' asked Sophie gently.

'Being cared for. William of course was granted custody of his son. A wife who deserts her husband has no right of access to her child. But William has to find his son before he can claim him.'

'Georgina does not care to let even her family know the boy's whereabouts,' said Emily curtly, helping herself to sponge cake.

Sophie glanced at Emily, successfully hiding her anger by gracefully forking up the sponge cake. One could not gracefully fork cake and look annoyed. Miss Lily had taught her charges well. Emily had not even bothered to mention the boy's name. To Emily the boy was a problem — a major one — rather than a person.

No wonder Emily was keen to move her cousin to the other side of the world. Even with a different surname, last year's publicity must have been detrimental to Emily's husband's career. Her Majesty's public servants, and their relatives, appeared in *The Times* only under Hatch, Match and Dispatch, or for honours received. Never, under any circumstances, in the Divorce Courts, or the front pages of the gutter press.

'Georgina,' Sophie tried to keep her voice steady, 'we can't take a young child with us into Germany. But Timothy could join us in Australia —'

'Timothy is safe where he is now. He will remain there till he can join me. I can't risk him leaving his refuge now. Once his father has physical as well as legal custody of him I would no longer be allowed to see him, even communicate with him.'

Georgina closed her eyes, as if to try to block out the vision of what her son's life might be with his father. 'Timothy is his father's heir, of course, but once he is twenty-one his father will have no power over him, not even financial power — I have money of my own. I only need to keep him safe till then. When Timothy is an adult ...' Georgina took a deep breath, 'he can face his father on an equal footing. William enjoys hurting people, but only those who have no power to protest. He is extremely charming to his equals and betters. The native workers were terrified of him. He said it made them better workers.'

And those workers needed their jobs. Timothy must be four or five years old now, Sophie calculated. Not quite old enough to understand why his mother had abandoned him — if she had. Sophie strongly suspected Timothy was either in London, or, more likely, within a few hours' train ride, where his mother could visit him. But that must be discussed in private. Like Georgina, she did not trust Emily, who so obviously believed that a man must not be separated from his son and heir — or at least not if it created unfortunate publicity.

She stood. 'I can offer you a salary of a hundred pounds a year, to be reviewed after three months. Could you move into the Ritz tonight? I will inform them I need another room. Ask for me — there is no need to give your own name. In fact when we begin our journey perhaps it will be best if you assume another name. Smith would be adequate but possibly too common to avoid suspicion. You could be Mrs Wattle, perhaps.'

'Wattle?' Georgina sounded dazed, the first emotion she had shown.

'An Australian flower. There is no reason your husband should ever discover that a Mrs Wattle in Australia is Lady Georgina FitzWilliam.' Sophie would hire two rooms at the Ritz tonight, one in the name of Mrs Wattle, that Georgiana would most definitely not occupy. But the misleading name might divert Emily's bloodhound instincts until they had left England.

She scribbled a second name on Mr Slithersole's card and handed it to Georgina. 'Here is your new name, in case you forget it. Telephone Mr Slithersole from the hotel. I will leave it for you and Mr Slithersole to finalise the business contacts we need to make in France, Belgium and then hopefully in Germany.'

'You're not put off by my notoriety?'

'On the contrary. It demonstrates you are determined, capable, can be discreet where possible but do not value discretion above love, and have every reason to stay in my employ. And no scandal is attached to Mrs Wattle in Australia, so you will not embarrass me or the firm of Higgs's Corned Beef. I may be back late tonight. We will meet for breakfast in my suite at eight am.'

'Yes, Miss Higgs.' Was that a smile?

Sophie stood. 'I had better see about getting that maid. Thank you for your help, Emily. You have been magnificent, as always.'

Emily gave her the smile that said, Miss Lily taught me too to use praise as manipulation. But she seemed sincere when she said, 'Give Hannelore ... my best wishes.'

Chapter 4

A man dresses to impress others, or please himself, or simply to stay sufficiently warm and decent. A woman should dress to give others pleasure in her company. Never dress to intimidate, to say, 'See, my wealth and diamonds are greater than yours.' Your companions should be slightly happier each time they look at you.

Miss Lily, 1914

Sophie drove herself back to the Ritz — a failing the doorman forgave when she pressed a half-guinea into his hand and asked him to park the car for her. She had learned to drive competently in Belgium, but navigating through a foggy London night would tax a far more experienced driver.

She was so tired of the grey of London days, the evening snuffle of the yellow fog, the river stench suddenly shivering its varied smells into unexpected places, so a dining room might smell of river mud, or a flower seller's basket of dead eels. She had exchanged the smoke-tinged sky of war and Belgium for low grey cloud, coal smoke and the chattering of shattered people trying to forget.

No, this was not yet peace. But it was time that she went home.

She telephoned Shillings from her suite. To her relief Jones answered.

'Shillings, his lordship's residence.'

'Jones, it's Sophie.' Jones would not use her Christian name, but nor would she call herself Miss Higgs to him.

'I thought you had left for Australia, Miss Higgs.' It was good to hear his voice.

'I was delayed. How is Nigel?'

'His lordship is at the Home Farm. I will ask him to call you —'

Which was not what she had asked. But she did not have time to press Jones to give more details now. 'Jones, forgive my urgency. I need a maid, preferably by tomorrow. I have had a letter saying that Hannelore, the Prinzessin, is in trouble.'

Jones knew Hannelore well, from her time in Miss Lily's care at Shillings, when Jones was butler there, and not Nigel's secretary. 'I'm going to Germany to try to find her before I go home. I wondered if Green ...' Her voice faltered.

Green had not been needed as a maid since Miss Lily's disappearance. 'Does Miss Green still work at Shillings?' she asked cautiously.

'Miss Green took up ... war work. She is now employed in a London household, but I believe the position is not congenial to her. May I ascertain her wishes and telephone you back?'

'You may, Jones,' she said gratefully. 'It's the Ritz.'

'Of course it is, miss,' he said, in tones that were almost accurate for the perfect butler.

'I don't suppose you know a chauffeur too, who might take us to Germany? Preferably one who won't make anti-German comments and who will be polite, who can use a pistol and his fists, and might pass at a pinch for German even if he doesn't speak the language.' Most Tommies had picked up a few words of German in the trenches, as the enemy had learned a little English too. 'The job will only be for two or three weeks, but I will pay well.'

'I will ascertain, Miss Higgs.'

She changed into evening dress as she waited for the call to be returned. Claret silk, low necked — James might ask her to dine after their discussion. A dinner that would have been impossible for a single woman and a widowed man before the war was now not even mildly scandalous. The hotel maid had arranged her stockings but included one with a ladder, and the colours did not quite match, which would be noticeable with the shorter hems worn since the war. She scrabbled among the silks trying to find a pair that matched.

The telephone jangled. 'A call for you, madam,' said the woman at the switchboard.

'Jones?'

'Miss Green will be with you this evening, Miss Higgs. I believe his lordship can provide the driver that you need too. I hope you do not mind my informing his lordship when he returns.'

'Of course not. But I have to leave for an appointment. If his lordship would like to telephone me, it needs to be later tonight ... No, please tell him I will call him at ten o'clock tomorrow morning. Would that be suitable?'

'I believe so, miss.'

There was no one to hear her, except the switchboard operator, who might be listening in. And the operator at the Shillings exchange too, who almost certainly was listening and would pass on any drops of gossip from this call. But nonetheless she said, 'I won't have time to return to Shillings before I leave for Germany. Give Nigel my love. And my love to you too, Jones.'

Could a blush be felt across telephone lines? But his voice held no embarrassment as he said, 'I wish it were not Germany, Miss Higgs. I am sure his lordship will feel the same. May I wish you Godspeed?'

'You may. Thank you, Jones. For ... for everything. Look after Nigel.'

'I will, miss. Take care.'

It seemed Jones too felt on this occasion they might forget about who might be listening. Two such loving men, Jones and Nigel. It would be so easy to marry one, to be cared for by the other. She might even have the company of Miss Lily again sometimes, despite Nigel's assurance Miss Lily would never hold her 'classes' for young ladies of political promise again. To live among quiet English fields ... and perhaps play a part in the challenge of world affairs too, performed on a stage far away from Sydney, for surely Nigel must now take up his seat in the

House of Lords. No man with his sense of duty could confine his interests to his estates.

But England did not have gum trees. Nor did it have her father and Miss Thwaites and Thuringa, nor blue hills nor eagles balanced on the wind's hot breath. Nigel was as bound to Shillings and England as she was to her own country. Love for Nigel was complicated, and always would be. Sophie Higgs could manage hospitals and refugee centres, but she was not sure she could cope with such complicated love. Not now, when so much emotion had been leached by war. Possibly not ever. And marriage, as poor Lady Georgina had found, was a bond for life.

She found she was crying as she put the receiver down.

Chapter 5

The human body can survive a surprising time with no food. But without love we are not truly human.

Miss Lily, 1914

THE BAVARIAN SOVIET REPUBLIC, 1 MAY 1919

HANNELORE

She was not dead.

Her body hurt, so this was not Heaven. Nor was it constant agony, so it could not be Hell. Her body existed mostly as a problem: try to will away the pain with unconsciousness or sleep.

Her body was in a bed (small, hard), on a mattress stained by body fluids, most of them — probably — hers, under a duvet of feathers stuffed into sacking. The rough hands that intermittently tended her were male, shoving a salty liquid into her mouth or changing bandages that were stuck to her wounds so clumsily that she, thankfully, fainted again while they worked.

The male hands meant that she was — probably — captive. So the revolutionaries did not want her dead, though this was not through any compassion or charity or there would have been women's hands to help. They had raped her, after all, if a bayonet counted as rape, the perpetrator laughing that he was ensuring no little aristocrats would ever be bred from this one. But after that they seemed to have made some effort to keep her alive. Even the pads they placed between her legs were almost blood free, now. She had to force herself to look at them each day, to assess her health, her chances of survival. But she had nursed enough Belgian refugee women to know that while such injuries healed surprisingly often, it was unlikely now that she could ever have a child.

She had never particularly wanted children, just accepted with some degree of happiness that they would be part of her life. The knowledge that children were now an impossibility was too great an agony to dwell on.

She had to think of now, not of what might have been. She HAD to think, or she would not survive.

Was she being held as a hostage, to exchange for socialist prisoners? Or till she was strong enough to stand and be publicly executed? The latter was more probable.

But it was so hard to think.

Mostly she did not care. Why should she?

It would not matter to anyone in particular if she died. Dolphie had affection for her, she knew, but she was also a problem for him. She was, after all, a traitor to her country, though that was probably not widely known.

The prinzessin had once had many friends. Hannelore had known only two. Her first had been Emily Carlyle, who she had met at school in Switzerland, and stayed with at Miss Lily's very different kind of school at Shillings. Emily had dropped her acquaintanceship the very minute intimacy with a German became embarrassing.

Which left Sophie. Toasting crumpets with Sophie, Alison, Emily and Miss Lily at Shillings, and spreading them with honey. Pretending with Sophie that one day she might escape to the sunlit land with kangaroos called Australia.

Australia so wonderfully did not matter — except as a source of raw materials, wool, wheat, men — to England. It was almost a play place, with its hopping animals and trees that Sophie said looked blue from a distance. If she had visited there, she might have been, just for a little, only Hannelore, with no duty to follow.

Was Sophie there now, among the kangaroos? With children, perhaps? Sophie and her happy family. Something to dream about as Hannelore's life faded with the light. Something, at least, that was good.

Kangaroos and crumpets ...

Chapter 6

Dusk is the time of most potential. Life changes at dusk, just like the light. A work-worn woman becomes glamorous, a tired man eager for what the night may bring. Every dusk may be adventure.

Miss Lily, 1914

1 MAY 1919

SOPHIE

James Lorrimer had responded to her request to meet him with an invitation to his London house at five pm, too late for afternoon tea, too early to dine.

Sophie had never been to his house, not even in her debutante year when James had courted her because, as a widower, he did not entertain. Since then their wars had been spent mostly on different continents, as James did his best to urge the USA to join the Allies, and then to negotiate the even greater diplomatic problems when it did.

A good house — a plain Georgian façade opening onto a street, a gated park opposite, for the use of the street's inhabitants only.

She knocked. James opened the door himself, though a butler hovered behind, retreating as James took her hands in greeting as she smiled up at him. 'Sophie, it's an unexpected pleasure. I didn't hope to see you again for years.'

Or ever, possibly. Less than two months earlier she had refused his offer of marriage and declared her need to return home. There was little chance that James Lorrimer, His Majesty's dutiful public servant and guardian of His Empire, would ever go to Australia, even if the Prince of Wales was soon to make a ceremonial visit.

'Come into the study. Sherry? You said you needed my help.'

'Sherry is perfect at this time of the day, isn't it?' The first two rules of manipulation, Miss Lily had taught her and the other girls, before the war. Smile, so they smile back at you, and then make your companion agree with you.

'Exactly.' He handed her a small glass of the pale liquid.

'What kind is it? I am astonishingly ignorant about sherry.'

Rule three. Ask a question they can answer.

'Amontillado.'

She smiled at him again over the rim of her dainty glass. 'It's wonderful. Thank you. Sherry, all this ...' she gestured at the fire (expensive wood, from his country estate, not coal), the book-lined walls, the heavy velvet curtains '... it is so peaceful after the world of war.'

She sat, in a deep leather chair.

He sat opposite, studying her as she sipped her sherry. 'I think perhaps you had a harder war than I did,' he said at last.

Perceptive. Few men, even now, would admit that without the work of women, the war would have been lost by that first Christmas. She would reply in kind. James responded best to honesty.

'I don't think it is possible to measure that. I ... I've come away unscarred, mostly. And much of it was challenging. I enjoyed the challenges, even if not the circumstances that made them necessary. I feel a little guilty about that. How much I relished challenge. How comfortable my life is now.'

He smiled at that. 'I feel the same.'

'If I am to be truly honest — for some reason I *am* honest with you — what angers me most about the war isn't the loss, or the tragedy. It was the sheer inefficiency. Twenty thousand men sacrificed for a single hill. An entire campaign like Gallipoli ordered with no thought about how to supply an army with water on a dry peninsula. If those men had had a proper water supply, they might have taken Constantinople and the war would have been almost won. If my father ran his factories like our leaders muddled the war, he'd never have made his first sixpence. And I am being deeply insulting,' she added ruefully, 'as you are one of those leaders, and an extremely able one.'

'Which means I agree with you, but can never say it beyond this room. Sophie, how can I help? I presume you do need help?'

She had prepared what she had to say — and what she needed to leave out — carefully. 'You remember my friend Hannelore, the Prinzessin von Arnenberg? She was at the Carlyles' country house the day we met.'

'I remember her well. And her young uncle, the count.' Within an hour of their first meeting James had asked her to discover whether either Hannelore or Dolphie knew the route Germany planned to take to attack France. If either knew, Sophie had not found out. Hannelore had seen through her attempts at once.

'I've had a letter. She's in trouble. We were very close, in that summer before the war when I needed help to be accepted in society. Now it is my turn to help her. I plan to motor to Germany, using the excuse of ...' she smiled at him '... corned beef. My father's English agent is arranging meetings with businesses that might take out new contracts in France and Belgium. Hopefully one of them may have a contact that will give me an excuse to go to Munich.'

'Munich! Sophie, are you insane? There is a revolution there. They've proclaimed a Munich Soviet. Every car has been commandeered, the houses and property of the well-to-do confiscated, profiteers shot. You have no idea what you are getting in to.'

'James, I have just spent two years in a war zone.'

'War is more predictable than revolution. War is mainly directed at soldiers. Revolution affects everyone. Possibly particularly corned-beef capitalists in expensive cars. Does your father approve of this?'

'Of course he wouldn't. He doesn't know about it.' She thought of the starving, empty-eyed refugees she had worked with, the homes that were rubble, the farms turned to mud. Only a man who had spent most of the war in boardrooms and committee meetings could think war affected mostly only soldiers.

But she felt reasonably sure she — and her companions — would survive a few days in Germany. Miss Lily had taught her how to be noticed, socially and politically. War had shown her when, and how, to be inconspicuous — and how those with access to almost unlimited corned beef might be very valuable to both sides in a conflict.

James gazed at her. 'You must have been very ... persuasive ... with Higgs's English agent for him to follow your orders, and not ask permission from your father.'

'We know each other well by now. Mr Slithersole was invaluable through the war and my father is not well. Mr Slithersole agreed we should not worry him. I hope to be out of Europe and on a ship to Australia with Hannelore within three weeks.' Once again she did not mention her hope that, just possibly, an Australian corned-beef heiress and a German count might make a life together in Australia.

James sat back in his leather chair. 'You still will not marry me, Sophie?'

She blinked at the change of subject. 'No. I'm sorry, James —'

'Then perhaps we might start our relationship on another footing,' he said softly.

She looked at him, startled. 'What do you mean?'

He lifted a folder from the table by his chair, and opened it. She hadn't noticed it until this moment. He smiled at her, a very different smile from one she had ever seen him give, glanced at the words in front of him, then back at her. Suddenly she saw the core of duty and capability she had only glimpsed in him before.

'In May 1917 a Miss Sophie Higgs arrived at Cambridge with an enigmatic note she claimed had been sent by a German acquaintance,' he said quietly. 'It contained a formula for mustard gas and the date and place where it would be first used by the Germans on our troops at Ypres. Miss Higgs was instructed by the officer in charge to keep the matter secret and return at once to Wooten Abbey. Miss Higgs agreed to do so, but did not. Her disobedience might have resulted in criminal charges being laid. For ... various reasons including her social and family connections, they were not.'

Sophie watched him, silent.

James's eyes evaluated her calmly as he continued. 'Instead, Miss Higgs travelled to France. She somehow enlisted the help of a French Général, now deceased, and a Captain Angus McIntyre. Her intention appears to have been to inform the British troops at Ypres of the impending attack —'

'Which the British High Command would not do, as they intended using the formula themselves.' Sophie's voice was as quiet as his.

'Decisions of that kind must be made in wartime.' James looked at her steadily. 'No one seems to know what happened after Miss Higgs left with Captain McIntyre. The Captain was severely injured soon after his return to his duties and claims to have no memory of the events preceding it.'

Thank you, Angus, thought Sophie. Though she wished he had told her he'd been questioned by Army Intelligence. But Angus also thought she was immediately going back to Australia — he probably assumed there would never be any repercussions, once she was leaving England.

James Lorrimer still spoke quietly. 'Miss Higgs was next observed a month later ...' by whom, she wondered '... running a hospital near Ypres. Her work expanded into three hospitals, specialising in what is popularly known as shell shock, as well as a chain of refugee shelters. Have I left out anything pertinent, Sophie?'

That I killed a man and severely wounded another, and that still haunts me. That I left Dolphie wounded and helpless in No Man's Land, when he too was trying to stop the atrocity or warn those who would be gassed. That my warning came too late, and men died in agony. That those who survived that gas attack and others, German and British, are still in agony — blinded, voiceless — will be all their shortened lives.

'I think that is a concise summary,' she said.

'Did the information about the mustard gas come from the prinzessin?' asked James.

'Yes. England owes her for that.' Though it had not proved the decisive weapon both sides had hoped it might be. Mustard gas was agony for those who touched or breathed it, but it could too easily blow back on those who had released it, and it pooled into hollows, where the sharp eyed — or lucky — might avoid it.

'And yet at the Carlyles the prinzessin seemed extremely loyal to her country. Was she a traitor?'

Again, honesty would work best. 'I think she truly was loyal. But that weapon ... I saw it used, James. Mustard gas did not shorten the war. It simply made it more barbaric, and the weapons of any future war will rise from the shoulders of that barbarism. That is what I wanted to stop. I think Hannelore did too.'

'Do you too put your loyalty to humanity above loyalty to your country?' His voice sounded merely curious. She was aware, however, that her words might be enough to convict her as a traitor. Traitors were shot, though possibly not if their fathers provided most of England's corned beef.

And if words in this room were not repeated.

'No,' she answered truthfully. 'But true loyalty to my country — which, after all, is Australia, though I am loyal to the Empire too — means I do not want it to be barbaric.'

'Ah,' he said, 'a good answer. What do you want from me, Sophie?'

'Information. The safest route to Munich, to keep away from the areas of revolt — I'm not stupid, James. I know how dangerous and unpredictable revolution is. I need to know what train systems are working. Can I get a train to Munich? Is train travel through the rest of Europe safe? Can a car or horse and carriage be hired in Munich? Yes, I already knew that any private car would be confiscated by the Soviet government there. What would be the safest route from Munich to the best port to board a ship for home?'

He looked at her, this new James who was, somehow, even more himself than the James she had known. This was the professional, not the social man. 'That information might take some time to assemble.'

'How long?'

'Overnight, if I ask the right people for it. Months, or never, if you do not know exactly who to ask.'

'Will you ask the right people?'

'Will you show me the letter? Not the one about Ypres, the one asking for help.'

'It is personal.'

'It might also,' he said, 'be a trap. Have you considered that? Revolutions need money. Kidnapping an Australian heiress for ransom might buy a lot of weaponry.'

'And corned beef? Germany is said to be starving.'

'Northern Germany supplies the rest of the country adequately. Or almost adequately. Yes, there's hunger, but no more than in England. Belgium and France are suffering far more. After all, they were the battlefields. It was their farms that were turned to mud and rubble not Germany's.'

'I imagine it is even more difficult to distribute food in times of revolution than during a war, when one knows more or less where the front lines are,' Sophie said dryly. 'It's possible there's far more suffering in Germany than you are aware of. I have probably seen far more of … disrupted society than you.'

'An excellent observation. I have always admired your ability to observe, and to analyse. May I offer a partnership, Sophie? I will give you the information you need in exchange for your … observations … while you are there.'

'You want me to spy for you?' she asked slowly. 'James, I am carefully assembling a corned-beef mission through war-torn Europe so I will not be taken for a spy. Now you want me to become one.'

His smile appeared again. 'No. A spy is covert. You will be extremely obvious and your telegrams and letters will almost certainly be read by others before they reach me. We cannot risk anything that hints of covert communication. There will be a need for code words for certain issues of … interest.'

'What issues are those?'

'The Kaiser, to begin with. I know he wishes to return to Germany from Holland. King George has refused him the refuge he demanded in England, but he still plans to try to return to power. Is there any support for him among the officer class?'

'If the revolution spreads beyond Bavaria, the officer class won't have the power to give the Kaiser back his throne.'

'I believe there may be news about that revolution tomorrow.' James smiled at her surprise. 'I do have extremely good contacts already, Sophie. According to my informants, the Freikorps plan to attack the Munich Soviet tomorrow, in large numbers. The Freikorps are well funded and are expected to be … savage. By the end of the week the Munich Soviet rebellion will officially be over. By the end of the month it probably will actually be over — it will take time to mop up the remaining rebels.'

Sophie stared at him. 'Your sources of information must be very good indeed.'

'They will be even better if you join them. You will meet people my contacts have no access to. You also have the commercial experience they lack. I need to know how the businessmen of Germany see the future. Businessmen are often better judges of political stability than politicians, who tend to believe their own propaganda. A good businessman cannot afford the luxury of illusion. Any businesses that have survived the last few years are undoubtedly run by extremely capable men. I also need to know what links the German soviet movement has to Russia, or to England,' he added. 'But unless you happen to be in conversation with German revolutionaries, which I profoundly hope you won't be, I don't expect you will learn that. But you might perhaps hear something about Bolshevik sympathisers here in England.'

'England? Surely not.' She suddenly remembered Lady Mary, and the Workmen's Friendship Club she joined just before the war, feeding the unemployed in the East End. Surely that was *noblesse oblige*, Fabian socialism, not Bolshevism and revolution. And yet there were a million unemployed people in England, and more troops still to be demobilised, hunger, even starvation, and desperate powerlessness, the fodder on which revolution had grown so swiftly in Russia.

Did the Workmen's Friendship Club offer revolutionary propaganda now, as well as bread and stew?

James still watched her. Yes, she thought, he knows that I visited the Workmen's Friendship Club. That was where she had met Dodders, who had later become an ambulance driver on the front lines, and then a nurse who had learned her skills on the wards, because there was no one else to do the job. Darling Dodders, dead now, like so many other friends, in Belgium.

'Sophie, I am going to trust you with information that has not been made public, under the Defence of the Realm Act. It must not be made public. Do you understand?'

'Yes.'

He smiled once more at the promptness of her reply. 'And do you agree to keep it secret?'

'Yes.' Don't trust me, James, she thought. I lie. We may both be loyal to our countries, but my idea of where that duty takes me may be different from yours.

Except, of course, James Lorrimer knew that already.

He smiled at her, as if he had guessed her thoughts. 'Very well. In January more than two thousand British infantry at Calais formed a soviet modelled on the Russian ones.'

'British *soldiers*?!' She knew there was deep discontent. But not a British soviet!

He nodded. 'It has been kept from the public, of course. The men refused to work, or take orders. Their so-called revolution was settled without bloodshed — mostly the men just wanted to be demobilised and sent home. But only two months ago an English soviet was proclaimed by five Guards units in Sussex, with over two thousand men. They marched into town where they were greeted with cheers by the watching crowds. Luckily the mayor acted swiftly and sympathetically. That revolution too was put down before it could grow larger, the men separated and demobilised.'

'I had no idea,' Sophie said quietly.

'Few people have. Nor can this be made public. Once the British people believe revolution is possible, they may act on the idea. Especially if they are cold and hungry and hopeless, and have had their normal social patterns disrupted by a war.'

'Disrupted' was such an inadequate word for the millions of family tragedies across the world, but she did not correct him. 'Do you really think England is in danger of a revolution, like the Russian one?' It was impossible to think of the English executing the extremely likeable King George and Queen Mary, much less dispossessing aristocratic landowners like Nigel. Yet the Tsar and his family were likeable, and had been executed in Russia. Germany had thrown out the Kaiser, though few seemed to mourn his loss as they did the Tsar and his family.

'I think we can keep England free of revolution, but only if we can keep all possibility of bolshevism out of the press for the next six months or so, until the army is demobilised and food and coal production begin to be stable again. And to do that we need to know who might be the leaders of revolution here, particularly those with wealth and connections to the press and sympathetic politicians. I think the British troops would prefer jobs and family life to soviet rebellion. The English working class has opportunities now they could not have dreamed of in Marx's time. I suspect we may even see a Labour government within the next decade. As far as I know, the communists in Britain could hardly rustle up a party of three balloons and a cake right now, much less a soviet state. But more information on their activities would be useful.'

'I can see that,' she said slowly. What was Lady Mary doing now? She might be able to find that out, at least, before she left for Europe.

He looked at her keenly. 'There may not be any real immediate danger of revolution in England now. But there would be if the soviet movement spreads in Europe, even just in Germany. A communist Germany allied to a communist Russia would be dangerous, not militarily — they are too busy fighting among themselves — but socially. Communist sympathy in England would encourage more strikes, especially among the coal miners, just when we need that coal to get British industry back on its feet and men employed in it, and more trade unionism, which would be unsettling too.'

She raised an eyebrow perfectly. Miss Lily would have approved. 'We've never had a strike at a Higgs factory. If you pay decent wages, and give good working conditions, there is no need for any of your employees to strike.' Though one of the first things she must convince her father to accept when she returned home was to increase wages even further, which her father had always been reluctant to do in case the other factory owners retaliated. But since the war Higgs's Corned Beef industries could surely ignore the great fraternity of factory owners and their determination to keep wages at near starvation level.

James did not seem to be interested in the connection between wages, starvation and strikes. 'Sophie, we need to know just how powerful the soviet movement is in Germany, what the local people — the workers, the business people — think about it.'

'I have a feeling that your work in the past few years may have had a little more to it than you mentioned in your letters. James, I'm not cut out to be a spy.'

'On the contrary, you are ideal.'

'No. I'm like millions of other women. And men too. I want to leave the war behind. Enjoy the peace, and find my life again.'

'You will. Once you return to Australia you will be of no more use to my ... networks.'

She should be insulted by the implication that her country was useful for providing only food, troops and cricketers. But she accepted his assessment. Despite the sacrifice of sixty thousand Australian soldiers, her country had little say in the affairs of the world.

'All I am asking for is a few discreet letters and telegrams in return for the information that you will certainly need. Now, may I see that letter?'

She hesitated again. But she did need the information, even more than she had realised when she'd arrived. She pulled it from her handbag. He read it, not even raising an eyebrow at the opening line.

> *Liebe Sophie,*
>
> *I write to you for Hannelore, who will not write. Do not worry.*
>
> *She is safe and well, or safe for a time and well enough, though far too thin. But then I do not think there is a person of plumpness in the whole of Germany.*
>
> *Hannelore's estates are in Russian hands now, as are mine. I cannot help her, as I would wish to do, not just because of the loss of fortune, but because of other matters of which I may not write but which, perhaps, you will understand.*
>
> *I write to you as her friend, knowing that you will still be her friend, and not her enemy, and can offer her a home, a future, in Australia and its sunshine perhaps, as you once promised, far from the starvation and misery of Germany. You may start with the address on this envelope. She is not there, but the people will know where she can be found.*
>
> *I remain yours faithfully, as I always have been, and will always be,*
>
> *D*

'So,' he said, looking up. 'It is the count who asks, not your friend?'

'Yes,' she admitted, flushing.

'Sophie, *I* am speaking as your friend now. The friend I hope I will always be, no matter what other paths we take in our lives. You seem to have read this letter as an appeal to gallop across to Germany and save your friend.'

'Isn't it?'

'Possibly. It could also just be a ... tactful ... request for money, for both the count and his niece, accompanied by a letter of invitation to her to join you in Australia.' James smiled once more at her expression. 'You really didn't see that, did you? You are the Sophie Higgs who dashed into a war zone to save ten thousand British troops from mustard gas. The count would not expect you to go to Germany. No man would expect a woman to risk herself like that.'

There was no reason not to tell him now. 'Dolphie ... the count ... would expect me to do just that. I met him on the way to Ypres. He was the one who gave the information to Hannelore. He was trying to stop the gas attack too.'

'What? Impossible.'

'Well, warn the British then.'

'A German officer warning the British? Sophie, are you sure of this?'

'Yes. No.' Dolphie had never actually said that was why he was so near to Ypres. But why else would he have been there, with so few men? How else had Hannelore got the information to pass to her?

'I think Dolphie may value humanity above patriotism too,' she said.

James glanced at the letter again, then handed it back to her. 'You may have a chance to find out. Sophie, as your friend, I advise you to send them money, and tickets to Australia. Sail home and forget the war and live your life.'

'Only after I know Hannelore is safe. And have seen her, in Germany.'

Yes, this was the James Lorrimer she liked, could even — almost — have married. Because he did not argue with her. Instead he said, 'Very well. I'll have the information for you tomorrow. I will make the phone calls now.'

'Thank you. And I will ask your questions, and send you as much information as I can.'

He nodded his acceptance of their contract. 'Will you stay to dine?'

She must have looked surprised. She had thought they might dine together, but not at his house, unchaperoned.

'My aunt is now my hostess,' he explained. 'I'd like you to meet her.'

She had dressed to dine with him, had even hoped he might ask her. But she had too much to evaluate now — and to do. She stood. 'Another time. I've arranged for a new lady's maid to meet me at the hotel — she used to work for a close friend. I will need to ...'

'Explain that her duties include a short journey into enemy territory?'

She met the smile, this time. 'Exactly that.'

James took her hand in its kid glove and kissed it. 'Keep safe, Sophie. Please don't stop writing to me even after you leave Germany and have no official information to send. I have ... valued ... your letters for four years.'

'Even though there can never be anything of interest to the Empire in Australia except our wool, wheat, corned beef and cricketers?'

'There will be Sophie Higgs. That is interest enough.'

Yes, she liked him. Even with this new knowledge of him — perhaps even especially with this new knowledge — she suspected that marriage with James could be both interesting and happy.

But she would be sharing his life, not creating her own. In this world after the war, where women had tasted challenge, that would never be enough.

She remained thoughtful as she walked through the doors of the Ritz, smiling automatically as the doorman held them open for her. Was James correct? Had she misinterpreted Dolphie's letter? Was the expression 'I remain yours, always' not an expression of love but just Continental chivalry?

Was she charging futilely into danger, as she had two years earlier? No, that had not been futile, for even if she had not been able to protect the men from the gas, she had achieved a lot in France and Belgium. She had also found herself, her father's daughter, at heart an organiser, a businesswoman. And a good one.

She stood at the hotel counter in the lavish lobby, waiting for her key. A young man glanced at her, then smiled. She smiled back, automatically, the slow smile that began with the eyes then quirked the lips: another legacy of the months with Miss Lily. The young man wore evening dress, with one of the 'King George' short beards newly fashionable after years of regimental shaving in the trenches. She tried to think where she might have met him. Probably he hadn't had the 'beaver' then. The young man held out a silver cigarette case. 'Gasper? Only stinkers, I'm afraid.'

She shook her head. 'I don't smoke, but thank you.' She still couldn't place him. She waited for him to remind her when they had met. In France, or perhaps he had been a patient at Wooten ...

'Sensible girl. I say, would you like to join us for dinner? A rum crowd, but great fun.'

She blinked, startled. He was a stranger. Had he taken her for a woman of easy virtue? Surely not in the Ritz. She was used to men speaking to women without an introduction these days, but not offering an invitation to dine. Surely manners had not relaxed that much with the war!

She really did need a maid *and* a companion, to ward off attentions like these.

The young man was waiting for an answer. What was the etiquette? She settled on a smile, trying to make it businesslike, not feminine. Maybe she needed lessons now in how *not* to be beautiful ... 'No, but thank you.'

'Hope you don't mind my asking.' He looked slightly anxious.

'Not at all,' she lied. She watched him saunter past the pillars to the dining room, then noticed the man behind the counter holding out her key. 'Miss Higgs, if you will pardon me, I am sure the young gentleman meant no harm. Modern manners, you know.' The receptionist lowered his voice discreetly. 'Sir Humphrey Teaser's son. A good family.'

And regular guests here, obviously. Would Lady Georgina know how one was expected to behave in this new world of peace? But possibly, probably, it would be all quite different again back in Australia.

'Oh, and Miss Higgs, there is a visitor in your sitting room. The Earl of Shillings. He said he was expected.' A note of concern now. Sophie wondered if the Ritz would evict a male visitor — even an earl — if she looked shocked and said, 'I cannot possibly meet a man alone.'

Pleasure fizzed through her. She had assumed she wouldn't see Nigel again until … until … no, there was no 'until', for just now she could not imagine visiting Europe again, not for many years and then both their lives would necessarily be so different …

He must have motored up to town as soon as he had heard her plans, she thought, as she hurried, still swan-like, along the corridor. Had Nigel come to dissuade her? She unlocked the door, then stared at the figure in the armchair.

'Miss Lily!'

Chapter 7

I once met a woman who had a nose like an eagle, a squint, and a complexion like crocodile skin. Yet she was beautiful, as soon as she met your eyes, or smiled.

Miss Lily, 1914

She looked exactly the same — the soft gold hair, still worn in a loose chignon, a long closed blue-grey silk evening coat with a matching chiffon scarf at the neck, sapphire earrings glinting in the firelight, her posture inexpressibly graceful in the chair next to the fire. But as the shock ebbed away Sophie realised Miss Lily had once again sought out the shadows of the room, the flickering firelight to smooth reality: the shadows under the eyes, the weariness the smile could not disguise.

The slightly anxious smile. The Miss Lily she had known before the war had never seemed anxious.

'Sophie, darling, I hope you don't mind.'

'Mind? No. It's wonderful to see you. I was so afraid I'd never see you again! I've missed you so much. So incredibly much.' Without realising it she had already run to the chair, bent to kiss the smooth cheek, smelled roses and lavender and the scent that was Miss Lily's own, felt Miss Lily's graceful gloved hands hold her close.

Then let her go.

Sophie stepped back reluctantly, found a chair, sat. She stared at the woman in front of her. Miss Lily had vanished in 1914. Her attempts to keep the balance of power equal between Britain and Germany and stop any war between them had become treason once battle began.

Nigel had said Miss Lily had gone forever. Why had she returned now? And in Sophie's hotel suite?

'Jones is downstairs with Green.' Miss Lily smiled, still nervously. 'You needed a driver.'

'Jones? But can you spare him?' She didn't mean from his job as Shillings's butler, or even as secretary, whichever Jones was now.

'If you need protection, there is no one I trust more than Jones.'

The kindness and the generosity almost made her cry.

Miss Lily seemed to regain her confidence and her composure. 'I also have contacts throughout Europe that may be useful, especially in Germany.'

'Of course,' said Sophie slowly. Miss Lily had been training her 'lovely ladies', from the most influential families of Europe, for many years. Hannelore's aunt was — or had been — one of her close friends.

'May I see the letter from Hannelore?'

She had hesitated before showing it to James, but even now the habit of obeying Miss Lily was strong. She took out the letter again. 'It is actually from Hannelore's uncle,' she admitted. 'James Lorrimer — I've just seen him — says it is really a politely veiled request for money and an invitation to Australia. I ... I'm not sure any more.'

Miss Lily took the letter. She read it wordlessly, then looked up. 'I think it leaves the course of action up to you. But one can deduce something more from the wording.' She smiled at Sophie, the old Miss Lily smile of charm and understanding. 'The man who wrote it loves you.' She paused. 'Or wishes you to believe that he does.'

'You ... you think so too?' It should be incongruous discussing Dolphie's feelings for her with Miss Lily, of all people. But Miss Lily made all confidences possible.

'Of course.' Miss Lily watched her intently. 'You knew the count before the war, didn't you?'

'Yes. Then Dolphie and I met again in Belgium in 1917,' said Sophie quietly.

Miss Lily raised the perfect eyebrow that Sophie had imitated a few hours earlier. 'In a war zone, in the middle of war with Germany? That, perhaps, is a story for another time. Sophie ...' No one says my name quite the same way Miss Lily does, thought Sophie, 'I think we can assume that this ... Dolphie ... of yours does, indeed, have feelings for you. You are extremely lovable, despite your fear that it was only your father's wealth that was attractive.'

'I think you cured me of that,' said Sophie, smiling. She had not felt like this since before the war, she realised, this feeling of a world of two, her and Miss Lily.

Miss Lily regarded her. At last she said, 'I do not have the right to ask you what you feel for him. I suspect, despite whatever meetings you may have had, you do not truly know. War is — a different time. Its emotions are not necessarily the ones you may feel in peace time. I know too well ... and that too is a story for another time. Shall we just say that a German count and a colonial ...' She hesitated.

'Corned-beef heiress?'

'As I have told you many times, do not define yourself by corned beef. I know the Count von Hoffenhausen's family very well indeed. His expectations of life, and yours, may not have been the same, even in 1914.'

'His life is gone now,' said Sophie. 'His estates. The whole of the Germany that existed before the war.'

'Perhaps. And for a time. As you know, Germany was not defeated militarily, but by its own revolutions at home and in the trenches. Germany accepted the ceasefire, thinking it was simply an end to the war. Now it is France that is war-like, demanding conditions and reparations impossible for Germany to fulfil. If Europe is to have a lasting peace, Germany must have a prosperous peace too. But we shall see.'

'Miss Lily, there is one thing I do finally understand.' Sophie met Miss Lily's eyes, those kind, wise eyes. 'I *am* corned beef.' She laughed at the ridiculousness of her statement. How long had it been since she had laughed so freely? 'No, I don't mean

I am made of it — I have eaten less corned beef in my life than possibly anyone else in Europe. Even in France when corned beef was all we had, I rarely ate it. But at heart I am a ... a purveyor of corned beef. I like feeding people. Organising people. I will be representing Higgs's Corned Beef in Europe and in Germany too. It's not just a cover. I hope to persuade my father to let me take over the business when I return.'

Sophie felt the smile flow across her face again. 'Dad hoped my husband would do that. But if I can't present him with a husband, perhaps he will accept me in his place. He knows the work I have done in France, and approved of it ... and me.'

'Running hospitals is perhaps more womanly than managing factories,' said Miss Lily dryly. 'Though both require similar aptitude and skills.'

'Perhaps. I can only try.'

With relaxation had come tiredness. Sophie had not realised until now that she had not really rested for five years. The voyage home booked for the previous week, before her sudden change of plans, would have meant six weeks of quiet routine, with nothing, absolutely nothing, to organise. Not the war-wracked Shillings estate, neither Wooten Abbey nor hospitals nor refugee relief ...

'Have you dined?' asked Miss Lily softly.

Sophie shook her head. 'I'm not really hungry. But you must be.'

'I will ring for crumpets,' said Miss Lily. 'The Ritz should be able to supply crumpets and honey. Not Shillings honey, of course, but I am sure it will be good.'

Tears stung Sophie's eyes again. Crumpets and honey and Miss Lily had been her dream of comfort all through the war. And here they were again, and yet, not quite ...

Miss Lily gazed at her with sadness and perfect understanding. 'But as it was the earl who entered your suite, perhaps it should be the earl the chambermaid sees.' She stood, pulled the bell for service then looked at Sophie with an expression hard to read. 'May I have one last embrace, my dear?'

'Of course.' Once more the feel of Miss Lily's arms, the breath of her perfume. Then Miss Lily stepped back.

'You may prefer to look away.'

'No,' said Sophie quietly.

'You're sure? Very well then.' Miss Lily removed her earrings, and then her evening coat, showing the shirt and waistcoat and the trousers held up by garters beneath, incongruous over silk stockings and women's shoes. The gloved hands removed the high heels, the garters, pulled men's shoes and socks and jacket from behind the chair and put them on. The gloves went next, and then the wig ...

'And just in time,' said Nigel quietly, at the knock on the door. He went to answer it, speaking softly to the chambermaid. He shut the door again and looked at Sophie. 'Well?'

She didn't know what to say. Nor what to feel. For the last twenty minutes she had been with a woman — a woman who she loved and felt she knew as deeply as anyone on earth. And now she was with a man, who she also loved, but in a different way ...

'You've plucked your eyebrows,' she said inconsequentially.

She should be feeling shocked. But she had seen a man die hand in hand with his friend who was not 'just a friend', both admitting only in those last minutes the love they had kept hidden. She had seen women run through mud where shells still burst in flowers of shrapnel, to fetch wounded men that they had never met. That was love too. She had known a million kinds of love, the last few years. How could she not love a man who admired women deeply, who felt pride in feeling that he, too, was female?

And yet, of those million kinds of love, how many were the basis for a fulfilling marriage, or even one that society would allow?

She did not know. She did know that just now, physically and emotionally exhausted, she could not face a ... complicated ... love. And yet wasn't that exactly what Miss Lily had warned her she might face with Dolphie.

Nigel carefully did not meet her eyes as he crossed back to the armchair. He shrugged, as he sat in its shadows again. A very different shrug from Miss Lily's. That was where the true difference lay, Sophie realised. It was not the clothes or make-up, which she had suspected Miss Lily of using discreetly before. The man in front of her wore none. Even the eyebrow plucking was subtle, a mild shaping that didn't look incongruous on a man's face. It was the tilt of the head, the position of the hands, the way the body flowed, the confident posture that said 'This is who I am, and happy with it' that created the image of male or female, young or old, beautiful or ugly.

'Shall we go over your plans?' asked Nigel quietly, leaning back in his armchair. 'I can see then where possibly a note to my friends may help you.'

Miss Lily had assumed she would be indispensable. Nigel did not know.

She longed to comfort him. Reassure him that the Earl of Shillings would find a place in this new world, where he might find both duty and fulfilment.

'Of course,' she said. 'There are no words to say how grateful I am. For everything.'

That was the only reassurance she could give.

Chapter 8

What is love? Simply caring for another person, or even a place, so deeply that you never count the cost of helping them.

Miss Lily, 1914

2 MAY 1919

HANNELORE

The shots woke her. Distant shots and screams.

And silence. She hadn't realised there had been a constant drone of voices nearby, the clop of hooves, the occasional stutter of a motorcar. Now even the pigeons had retreated.

Or hidden. For suddenly the building erupted around her ... more shots, yells, the descending scream that meant a man was dying. More footsteps on the stairs. But this time, when the door was flung open, no gun was pointed at her. A voice said, 'Just a woman.'

The steps retreated. And again there was silence.

The silence continued. Not even a floorboard creaked indoors. Outside gunfire sounded spasmodically, and more cries of terror, agony or triumph. She was, however, very clearly the only living person remaining in this building.

But how long could she survive? She would have laughed, if she'd had the energy. Because only her captors had known she was here — had known that as a prinzessin she was of value, to someone, somewhere, even only as an example when they took her life.

If she wanted to live, she had to find help. No one would come for her. Whatever revolution was intensifying outside it would be days, weeks, months or even years before order was restored; it would be months, perhaps, before anyone even thought to look up here, and found her decayed body in the bed. She had always assumed her eventual death would be accompanied by a mahogany coffin, with flowers, and burial in the small, walled open-air crypt, dappled with ferns and age, where five centuries of her ancestors rested.

She did not want to die there, bloated, rat-eaten. She did not want to die there, alone.

She did not want to die at all.

She passed her hand carefully over her two wounds, the one where a bullet seemed to have passed through the side of her breast, missing her heart; the second where one had lodged in her leg and, she thought, had been dug out, though she had lost consciousness at the beginning of the procedure; nor had her captors informed her if it had been successful. Both bandages were dry, but the pain surrounding them suggested both injuries would bleed again if she tried to move.

She slid from the bed and found herself collapsed on the dusty floor. The bandages were already spreading with bright red. She felt no pain. This agony was too great for a body to comprehend, just sweat and trembling shock.

She could lie there and die, or continue.

She crawled, stopping only when the world grew too cold and black, continuing as her vision cleared.

Did the journey take minutes, hours or days? The door was the first objective and then the stairs, rough wooden stairs, taking them one by one, hauling her body *bump*, *bump* from one onto the next, pausing to catch her breath at every one, one flight, and then another. On the second landing a man leaned against the wall, staring at her, blood still bubbling from his mouth.

She fought back an urge to say, 'Guten tag, Comrade,' to him, another member of the brotherhood of the bleeding. But that would waste precious and ebbing energy.

One more flight of stairs. She could see a doorway now. Daylight. It took ... time ... to get there. Pain, as she tore her fingers and bare toes to propel herself down and forwards. The wounds themselves stayed beyond pain, which was useful, though she knew she teetered on the edge of consciousness. She left a trail of blood behind. Vaguely she wondered how much more she had to lose.

And then she reached her target. The door, and blessed sunlight, and air that smelled of gun smoke and the tang of blood. A thrush sang above her. She almost smiled. How much better to die under the gaze of sunlight, and with a thrush's song.

But she still did not want to die.

She crawled from the door, down two more stairs, onto a footpath. Leaflets everywhere, crumpled, dirty, windswept into piles by the wall, trodden into mud. Hundreds of them. Thousands.

Shots in the distance, not just the sporadic shots of fighting, but the orchestrated volleys that meant execution squads. She heard boots, *tramp*, *tramp*, *tramp*, then saw them, boots that might have once been issued by the German army.

'Helfen mir, bitte,' she murmured to the boots.

The boots did not stop. Why should they? The city must be littered with bodies today. She must do better.

More boots. More than two, less than a regiment. She summoned every ounce of the authority of her ancestors, the last rags of energy, and looked up from boots to faces. 'Ich bin Hannelore, Prinzessin von Arnenberg. Helfen, Sie mir!' I am Hannelore, Princess of Arnenberg. Help me!'

She did not add 'bitte'. Please.

The boots stopped.

Chapter 9

Coffee sharpens the brain; tea relaxes it, but leaves you alert.
You can deduce much from which your companions choose. If they
choose tea, they are relaxed; if they choose coffee, then they want
something from this meeting — status, information, or possibly just
your friendship. Remember, when serving, that tea always outranks
coffee. Leave the teapot for the most senior woman present to pour.

Miss Lily, 1914

They all breakfasted in her suite: Sophie, Nigel, Jones, dressed
in a pre-war chauffeur's grey uniform that almost fitted him,
Georgina in plain black and perfectly ironed linen, as if she had
costumed herself as the insignificant 'ladies' companion' she was
now to be and, at Sophie's insistence, Green.

Green was a small woman, and wiry; her grey hair was cut
short, stylish but not overly so. She wore no cap, just a grey serge
dress, shoes so sensible they could balance the national budget,
and a white apron. She was totally forgettable, until you saw her
eyes and realised forgettable was exactly what Green wanted you
to think she was. The ambition of a good maid? Or something
more? There would be time to find out.

She would also find out why Jones and Green were so carefully
casual about the way they looked at each other.

'This is a strategy meeting,' said Sophie, as Green made her
selection from the dishes in their warming trays on the buffet (no
post-war austerity at the Ritz), rejecting the kedgeree, bright with
curry powder and yellow smoked fish, the bacon, fat sausages,
the luxury of grilled autumn tomatoes weeping red juice, the
porridge, and selecting devilled kidneys, scrambled eggs and

54

toast with the enjoyment of someone who had worked in a good as well as 'great' house, where servants automatically ate much the same food as 'those upstairs'.

Nigel ate sparingly; Jones consumed his meal with the dedication of a former army batman who was never sure of the next one. Georgina filled her plate with kedgeree, then liberally spread three slices of toast with butter and marmalade. Sophie wondered if perhaps her place at Colonel Sevenoaks' table had been a somewhat grudging one and had unconsciously restricted her helpings to suit, especially of food like marmalade with its rationed sugar content.

Sophie tried to make herself feel hungry. This would possibly be the last kedgeree she saw till she could instruct a cook in Australia on the intricacies of richly buttered rice, fish and curry powder and the vexed question of whether to add chopped hard-boiled egg ... or not. But though she had devoured the previous night's crumpets and honey, once again her appetite had crept away.

Sophie handed James's copious notes, some written in several hands, others typed, to Nigel. They had been delivered to her bedroom at seven am by the chambermaid, with apologies for the early intrusion.

Green had magically appeared two seconds after the chambermaid to take the notes before the woman could cross the room to Sophie's bed; had handed the notes to Sophie herself; ordered tea, biscuits and a pot of hot chocolate from the chambermaid; then had laid out a freshly pressed green linen dress. Green had also somehow procured fashionable beige stockings overnight, though not, thank goodness, high-heeled shoes.

Sophie's short hair, usually flying in at least two unwanted directions, behaved itself as soon as Green touched it with a comb. Green fixed a silver bandeau across her hair and forehead, provided in Paris by the dressmaker at the same time as her other clothes, but which Sophie had never bothered wearing. Green must have already sorted through her clothes most thoroughly to have found it. A touch of powder; a few dabs of almost invisible lipstick in the perfect shade. Green must have remembered her colouring from years before, and, somehow, found time last night to acquire the necessities of a 1919 ensemble. Sophie relaxed as pearls, perfect for daytime wear, were draped around her neck, then matching earrings. Green fastened the buttons at the back without Sophie having to imitate an orangutan or discreetly find another woman to help. Being tended to once more made the world of peace feel closer, almost possible.

And I am about to leave it deliberately, she thought, sitting at breakfast in her most suitable green, a damask napkin on her lap, nibbling a corner of toast, for a land of revolution.

Nigel flicked through the pages of notes. He glanced up at Sophie. 'Lorrimer's conclusions?'

Ah, she thought. Nigel — or Miss Lily — does know James, or at least his reputation. She had suspected they might. 'He has obtained train timetables for us — or rather, the times the trains are most likely to really depart. He suggests we travel mostly that way — less chance of being caught up in civil unrest — and that we stay at hotels near stations, hiring taxi cabs where necessary, though the businesses we visit may well send a car for us. Mrs Wattle, do you have anything yet from Mr Slithersole?'

'Mrs Wattle', who until last night had been Lady Georgina, pulled a sheaf of papers from her handbag and handed them to Sophie. 'A list of potential clients, Miss Higgs. Mr Slithersole asked me to express his continued best wishes and the news that "Johnny has been demobbed".'

'His son,' explained Sophie.

'So I gather. I have drafted a telegram and following letter to each of the contacts. With your permission I will send them after we have finished here.'

Efficient, thought Sophie. But perhaps not so surprising, as Georgina was used to estate management. 'Well done.' She took a forkful of kedgeree. It tasted excellent, and rich. She felt no temptation to take another. 'Please proceed as planned.'

'Jones has letters of introduction,' said Nigel. 'You may not need most of them, or any of them. But it is useful to have contacts. Telephone Shillings of course, or telegraph, if I or my cousin can be of service.'

His cousin? Sophie realised that of all the people at this table, Georgina was the only person who did not know Nigel and Miss Lily were one, or rather two who could not exist at the same time.

'Very well,' said Sophie. 'Green, would you mind obtaining, well, whatever you think Mrs Wattle and I may need? You too, perhaps, Jones?'

'Pistols, ammunition, maps, bandages, disinfectant,' said Jones, helping himself to more toast.

Sophie pulled the bell to ask for more. 'I'm glad you can joke.'

'I wasn't,' said Jones, spreading strawberry jam.

'Several lengths of wire,' said Green, sipping tea neatly. 'You can do many things with a length of wire, and more quietly than a pistol. And two pairs of metal knitting needles, as thin and sharp as you can find them, and four balls of brown wool.'

'Noted,' said Jones, flashing her a quick grin. Green grinned back fleetingly.

Sophie stared at them. Lengths of wire? Sharp metal knitting needles? Who WAS Green? What exactly had her 'war work' been? And what *could* you do with lengths of wire, and why should Green want to?

She had accepted the different roles Jones played in Nigel's life: batman, then butler; batman again and now secretary; and always friend. Jones was the first person she had met at Shillings, and a constant presence there. She had only glimpsed Green twice, down in the servants' hall, for none of the 'lovely ladies' had been admitted to Miss Lily's private wing where Green had tended her mistress.

She had always thought of 'Miss Lily and Jones', or more recently 'Nigel and Jones'. For the first time she realised Jones, Green and Lily/Nigel must have been a threesome. Or had it been 'Jones and Green' with Miss Lily? Then why weren't

Jones and Green married? Butlers and ladies' maids rarely were permitted to marry, but surely Nigel would have allowed it, even encouraged them. What *were* the relationships? Had Jones and Green been together once, and quarrelled? What had the three of them been doing, in all those years before she met Miss Lily?

And the last four years? Nigel and Jones had spent the war with the county regiment, in France, where so many boys and men from Shillings had been lost. Had Green been a VAD? Sophie observed her across the table. Green might be a ladies' maid, but someone who had been maid to Miss Lily possibly would not want to endure the rigid subservience of a VAD ...

'I must head back to Shillings,' said Nigel, breaking into her thoughts. He smiled at Sophie's unasked query. 'I am quite capable of driving without a chauffeur.'

She had hoped he would stay until she left, that Miss Lily might even reappear. She wanted to ask him a million questions, not about the journey, but himself: how was he faring; and did Miss Lily return, just sometimes, in the solitude of Shillings, as she had here the night before?

She looked at him across the table — those kind, sad, intelligent eyes. Had part of her reluctance to marry him been because of the risk she would always be slightly the outsider, tacked on to her husband's profound friendship with Jones? Had she been mistaken? She wanted to cling to him, to take his hand and not let go, to ask him about the almost twenty years of which she knew almost nothing, except Miss Lily and her lovely ladies.

But she was committed. Committed to going to Germany, and then home. She forced herself to smile back at him. 'Thank you, more than I can say. For everything.'

He stood, bent, and kissed her cheek. A hint of Miss Lily's perfume lingered under the bay rum in his hair. 'Travel safely,' he said quietly. 'Telegraph me, if you have time, so I know you are safe.'

She imagined Jones would report as well. 'Take care too,' she said. She would have liked to add, 'I love you. No matter who we are or in what kind of way, I love you.' But not with the others listening. It seemed Nigel was deliberately not giving her the time or privacy to say more.

Georgina stood too as the earl departed. 'I'll send the telegrams.'

Green followed her, with a bob to Sophie that was the post-war replacement for a curtsey.

Which left Jones.

'Good sausages,' he said, as the chambermaid appeared. 'More toast, please,' he requested, sounding suddenly like a gentleman who often dined at tables like the Ritz. He glanced at Sophie. 'And more coffee?'

'Please,' said Sophie. She needed it.

Jones waited till the maid had left. 'Eat some toast,' he ordered her. 'You've eaten almost nothing. You're getting far too thin.'

Sophie blinked. She was not used to servants giving her orders. But then Jones was ... Jones. The maid arrived with fresh toast, another silver coffee pot, gently steaming. Sophie let her cup be filled again, added milk, then obediently took a slice of toast, avoided the butter, and spread on chunky marmalade.

'We'll have to put you on one of those fattening diets if you don't watch out,' said Jones. 'She wanted to accompany you to Germany, you know,' he added while applying brown sauce to a second helping of sausages.

'Miss Lily?'

'No, Queen Adelaide. Of course, Miss Lily. She came ready packed to do so.'

'But why didn't she?' Surely I made her welcome, thought Sophie. And to have Miss Lily back, for weeks ...

'Because you are going to meet this Count von Hoffenhausen,' said Jones. 'Nigel wouldn't want to play gooseberry. Or see you with another man either.' He seemed to have no trouble talking about his friend, companion and employer as two people, not one.

'I ... I didn't realise.'

'There's a lot you don't,' said Jones. 'He does love you, you know. And Lily does too.'

'I know. And I love them both. But can you see either Nigel or Miss Lily living in Sydney?'

'Nigel? No. Not while Shillings needs him. And the estate needs him now, if it and the farms are to continue. Miss Lily,' Jones chewed his sausage thoughtfully, 'perhaps.'

Sophie had never considered that the colonies might suit Miss Lily. Miss Lily had wanted to be at the centre of political Europe — even if it was a discreet and mostly hidden centre, directing events off stage. Maybe now, like so many others, she merely wanted refuge.

But Nigel's life was Shillings, its people so devastated by war. Nigel would not abandon his duty. There was no way to free Miss Lily now.

Chapter 10

A gentleman stands when a woman enters the room. He is silent when she wishes to speak. Of course that does not mean that he will listen.

Miss Lily, 1914

Sophie managed a conversation with Georgina that evening. Jones had tactfully refused an offer to dine with them: he and Green would have dinner together. Sophie realised that her presence would inhibit conversation — and possibly more — between the two old friends. Though if they were more than friends, why hadn't Green gone back to Shillings after her 'war work'?

Which left Georgina. One dined with one's 'companion', though not necessarily with one's secretary. Possibly Georgina too would prefer solitude to forced conversation with her employer each evening. She would need to be carefully given the choice.

Tonight though, there were matters to discuss.

It had been a long time since Sophie had automatically changed for dinner. Tonight Green laid out a low-cut burgundy silk, trimmed with crystal beading, and a necklace of small diamonds to be twisted into the modern style of double strand bracelet. The new style left more of her back and shoulders bare than she was used to, as well as showing a lot more of her legs. With the weight of hair and petticoats gone it felt curiously and enjoyably liberating.

The table in the living room had been set for two, the silverware gleaming. Sophie offered the hotel menu to Georgina, who shook her head. 'You choose, Miss Higgs.' She too wore evening dress; a rather dismal grey silk, just low necked enough for it not to be dowdy.

Sophie felt like saying, 'Choose your own meal. It's your stomach.' But this scene must be humiliating enough for Georgina without offering an uncouth comment that Georgina could not respond to. Yet, thought Sophie.

It would be impossible to live with a 'companion' who did not become a friend who could speak up honestly. If friendship were impossible, she would have to find another solution for Georgina in Australia — and for her son.

The footman knocked and entered to take their order. Sophie consulted the menu quickly. 'Consommé royale. No fish, I think, unless you would like it, Mrs Wattle? No? I think we will pass on the game course, as well. Chicken cutlets, asparagus with Hollandaise —' it would be forced hothouse asparagus, of course, in May, and possibly the last she'd have till she could arrange for the delicacy to be grown at Thuringa '— and potato soufflés. Prunes on horseback for a savoury, oh, and Bombe Imperial.' Surely ice cream would spark her appetite. 'Could you bring all but the ice cream at once, and we will serve ourselves?'

'Of course, Miss Higgs. Cheese and biscuits, Miss Higgs? Coffee? And to drink?'

'Champagne,' said Sophie, who knew nothing of wine beyond the *vin ordinaire* of the villages she had lived in, and the champagne she had drunk for celebrations. Tonight did not qualify as the latter, but the talk would flow more freely with some alcohol. 'Cheese, yes please, but no Stilton.' They served it almost rancid there. She did not think she could bear the gangrenous smell. 'And coffee.' Which she would not drink, but Georgina might wish to.

They talked of inconsequential matters till the champagne was poured and the meal delivered. Sophie held up her glass in a toast. 'To the future.'

Georgina hesitated. 'To the future,' she repeated, then drank.

Sophie put down her own glass, and regarded her. 'Do you resent me terribly?'

Georgina glanced up from her consommé. 'Of course.'

Sophie nodded. 'I am far from your social equal; I suspect you have no need of the salary I will pay you, but take it so you have the protection and camouflage of being my employee. If I were you, I'd be steaming.'

'I can't afford to steam. May I be frank?'

If you can't afford to steam, you can't afford frankness, thought Sophie, sipping soup then rejecting it. Instead she said, 'Please.'

'You and my cousin are exactly the kind of women I despise. You play with the world. And, yes, you do good works, but only because you enjoy it. You are even enjoying this escapade into Germany.'

'Really?' responded Sophie, trying to subdue her anger. What did this young aristocrat know of her beyond her wealth and connection to Emily? She doubted that Emily had thought to mention Sophie's wartime achievements. Yet she was also honest enough to acknowledge that despite her longing for home, part of her did relish the sense of 'one more adventure'. She put down her soup spoon. 'If your husband had been a better man, would your works have been so much more useful that Emily's or mine?'

'Yes. I'd have helped my husband manage the plantation, a job that actually produces something, not playing politics and jockeying for position.'

'And Higgs's Corned Beef is a less valuable product that ... what was it you grew? Rubber? Coffee? But I am forgetting, aren't I? Those are respectable crops, like wool, or cotton or even beef. Corned beef is not.'

'You don't run the factories, or the farms. You just spend the money.'

A good point. 'I hope to play a part in running the business when I get home. And yes, I do spend the money, but in the past four years I have spent it on very good causes indeed. You really know very little about me. Do you really think I'd risk you all on this journey into Europe just for fun?'

'Not for fun, perhaps. But I believe you do regard this expedition as an adventure. So does that man Jones, and your new maid. Am I now fired?'

This woman was perceptive. 'Do you want to be?'

'Probably, or I wouldn't have said so much. But I can't afford to be.'

She did not, however, apologise, Sophie noted. Georgina must have been holding in her resentment of Emily for a long time. Now she had been expected to be subservient to a brash colonial commoner, as well. Lady Georgina, employed by a Miss Higgs, had not managed subservience.

Sophie looked at her thoughtfully, giving Georgina time to regain her temper — if she wished to. 'You need me, at least at the moment,' she said at last. 'So let us get a few things clear. I do need your services for the next few weeks. I can't appear as a respectable businesswoman in Europe if I am accompanied only by servants; nor do I speak more than a few words of German. But once we reach Australia I can easily obtain another secretary. You can stay in my employ in my home, or in your own house, or I will help you establish another identity. After that, if you wish, you may have nothing more to do with me, or Higgs's Corned Beef.'

'That is ... kind.'

'This is in my interest quite as much as yours,' acknowledged Sophie dryly. 'Now, your son ...'

Georgina laid down her soup spoon. 'My son is not to be discussed.'

'Because you do not trust me?'

Georgina's eyes turned to granite. 'My dear cousin, and your dear friend, has tried to have me followed every time I have visited him. Once his father has custody of him, any potential embarrassment to her vanishes. Emily did not succeed. Neither will you.'

'Emily is scarcely my dear friend. She regarded herself as

my enemy until I redeemed myself with hospitals and formal recognition from both the French and English governments. But that is irrelevant. Do you really think that if I wanted to inform Emily of your son's whereabouts I wouldn't find out where he was once you have brought him to Australia? My family has contacts across the country. You don't.'

She saw the flicker on Georgina's face. 'Ah. You intend to vanish before we reach Australia. I should have guessed. South Africa? Gibraltar?'

Georgina was silent.

Sophie was growing tired of this. Or rather, she was growing weary generally. The brief peace she had felt in Miss Lily's presence had vanished. 'Very well. Shall we make a deal? Or rather, I will make an offer that you can choose to accept or not. I have asked Mr Slithersole to book us passage on a ship from Naples in a month's time.'

Sophie smiled. 'There are no passages available, of course, but passengers can be persuaded to postpone their voyages for the right price, especially in times like this. If necessary, he will arrange a passage on another ship, if we are delayed or choose to leave earlier. He will arrange an extra carriage be added to trains for us where necessary too.'

'How convenient to be able to buy whomever and whatever you like.'

Definitely Emily's cousin, thought Sophie. Why ever had she thought Mrs Colonel Sevenoaks might provide her with someone congenial? She should have asked Ethel to recommend someone, or Sloggers might have known a friend who needed a few weeks' work, even if she could not afford the time away from Oxford herself.

'Mr Slithersole will book two extra passages for a "Mrs Smith and her child". I presume your son is in the charge of a woman who will bring him to you? And that she will not mind using an alias? No need to answer that. If you learn to trust me in the next week or two, you may be able to arrange to have them meet the ship. I am trustworthy,' she added. 'Uncouth and impulsive, but I always keep my word.' Except that once, she thought, when I lied to Dolphie on the battlefield …

'You're not uncouth. Your manners are surprisingly good.'

'I will forgive the "surprisingly". I was well taught, by a dear friend, when I first came to England.' Sophie stood, and gathered the soup plates.

'I suppose I should do that,' said Georgina.

'Nonsense. Put it down to the ingrained tendency of my class to tidy up. Both the table and the world. But you may serve yourself the cutlets. I seem to have lost my appetite.'

Chapter 11

Bathing is not just a way to cleanse. It can be a quiet time to repossess your body and your mind. You find your true self in the silences.

Miss Lily, 1914

SOPHIE

Green had laid out her nightdress, a new one in eau-de-nil silk; and her bath was already steaming, scented with roses. The fire burned in the fireplace, wood, not coal, and a luxury.

'Green, you are a treasure. I adore the nightdress.' She had forgotten the enormous security of having someone wait for you each night, of letting someone unbutton your dress as you stood childlike and being tended.

'I took the liberty of buying new undergarments too, Miss Sophie. You did tell me the clothing allowance was,' Green permitted herself a hint of a smile, 'unlimited. You will need more formal dresses for the ship. I will ensure that they are waiting for you there.'

'As I said, a treasure. It is possible though we may not make the *Rosanna*.'

'I will order the trunks to be stored, and released to the ship on my telegram.'

'A triple treasure. Please order whatever you need for yourself too, before we leave.' Green must have travelled extensively with Miss Lily, but her clothes would be pre-war, and probably worn too.

'Thank you, Miss Sophie.'

'And do yourself proud. Dresses for your day off and evening dresses for aboard ship. You won't want to dine in uniform.'

Green smiled. 'I wouldn't want to stand out from the other maids. But a few pretty dresses ...'

'As many and as pretty as you like.' She added casually, 'I imagine that when you travelled with Jones and Miss Lily, you had a first-class cabin too.'

Green hesitated. 'Sometimes. I would not want you to think I was presuming, Miss Sophie ...'

'Presume away. I won't be the one making the bookings. We may have to take what we can get — maybe we'll all be in steerage. But make sure you have the right clothes for first class too. By the way, I was too tired to thank you last night. I hope there was no trouble resigning from your last job. Please let me reimburse you if you had to forfeit wages.'

'If you will excuse me saying so, Miss Sophie, it was a pleasure to tell the lazy chit I worked for to get out of bed and fetch her own chocolate creams. She had as much need of an experienced lady's maid as I have of a third leg.' Green considered. 'Though a third leg would be useful when the other two get tired.'

Sophie laughed. 'Feel free to tell me whenever I need to get my own chocolate creams. Good night, Green — I can take care of myself from here.'

'Are you sure, Miss Sophie?'

'It's been more than four years since I've had the gift of a maid. I am not quite as helpless as I once was. Oh, if you are buying hats for me, choose at least three for yourself. You will need them in Australia.'

'I know. I have been there before, miss. Good night, miss.'

So, thought Sophie, as she slid into the gloriously scented water and reached for the perfumed soap. Nigel ... or Miss Lily ... had perhaps visited Australia too. Perhaps one day Green would tell her, or Nigel, when she wrote to him. Dear Nigel ...

No regrets, she said to herself. You are going to find Dolphie and Hannelore, then you are going home.

Chapter 12

Grace is a luxury, my dears. A charlady, bent from work, cannot be graceful. Never forget you are privileged. Always give back what you can.

Miss Lily, 1914

The baby's body lay half hidden by long grass in a storm-water ditch. In the glimpse as the train clattered by, Sophie thought it still lived, then saw the rat bites on the cheek, through the porcelain flesh.

The length of the grass must make it easy for passersby to pretend the baby's body was not there. This was time to help the living, not waste strength on the dead.

Sophie forced her eyes away as the train chuffed past. What should she do? Pull the cord to stop the train, to bury one small body? She glanced at Georgina, but her companion looked lost in memories or, possibly, plans. Green and Jones had refused to travel with them in first class. 'Appearances are important,' said Jones, which settled the matter.

The France of peace was strangely different, and yet still the same. The same men in uniform, but now instead of lounging against walls smoking, they crouched on pavements, medals bright and eyes dull whenever the train stopped long enough for her to see them properly. The same black-clad peasant women with thick, veined ankles carried scavenged firewood, or drove bullock ploughs. Glimpses of blackened battlefields, still mud and blood, but fringed with green. The same pigs, rooting in their sties, stared indignantly at the train that passed above them. Every scrap of ground along the railway line grew vegetables or held geese tended by thin children.

Even the train was still filled with French and English soldiers, except in first class, where the few officers tended to congregate in the same carriage. Despite the looming demobilisation, the English ones had been sent for some unknown and possibly senseless military reason back into France; they were joking, singing, sometimes drunk, their eyes still shadowed with what they had seen and the unknown to come. Even if the new world of peace proved a good one — unlikely — the whispers from the dead and missing would be with them always.

There was still no dining car, or not on this train, but Green appeared at each stop with a hamper, with everything from Thermoses of coffee or bouillon to smoked cucumber and salmon sandwiches and rich dark fruitcake.

Their first stop was Paris, staying at another gloriously unchanging Ritz, and Sophie negotiated her first corned-beef contract, 'Mrs Wattle' sitting beside her neatly taking notes, Jones in his chauffeur's uniform, Green back at the hotel organising meals as well as clothes and the next day's transport.

Georgina proved efficient and capable, if still taciturn. Green, however, was exactly the treasure Sophie had expected. She had telegraphed Sophie's measurements from London to a private Paris fashion house, extending Sophie's still-limited wardrobe. The order arrived with assurances that they would be delighted to continue to supply Mademoiselle Higgs with garments of the most fashionable once she had crossed the ocean to Australia, from underwear to ball gowns to outfits *le sportif* if Mademoiselle Green would correspond with any changes in measurements. They even recommended a dressmaker and milliner in Sydney who would be suitable for alterations, if necessary; and a shoemaker who worked from the latest Paris designs, with a quality *assez tolérable*.

The Parisian corned-beef contract was a good one. Sophie had assumed it would be, no matter how inexperienced she was at negotiating orders. France still starved, its farms turned to battlefield mud, its men dead or crippled; and land deeply tired both physically and mentally after being the ground on which so many countries had fought.

Dad will be glad of another market, she thought. He was an accidental war profiteer — as an ex-soldier he had never rejoiced in war. This war had made him far, far richer, but now, without the contracts to feed the troops with bully beef, Higgs's Corned Beef faced a leaner future unless they obtained new commercial opportunities.

This contract, like all others, must officially be negotiated as an export from England, via Mr Slithersole. Australia was forbidden from selling to any nation other than the Motherland. The transport to London and then back to Paris would put an extra halfpenny on each can, which the customers could only just afford. But that was one of the conditions the English government demanded of its loyal colonies.

They travelled from Paris to Lille, Green and her hamper still magically supplying the Bath biscuits she had discovered Sophie would nibble with coffee even when she had no appetite. They stopped twice to meet businessmen who politely pretended not to be shocked at discussing terms with a young woman in a dark blue linen suit, creamy white blouse and a ribbon at her neck comfortingly reminiscent of a man's tie.

These contracts did need firm negotiation — unlike the more experienced Parisian wholesaler, the provincial merchants seemed to feel a woman would sign away any rights, even keeping the present low price unchanged indefinitely as France's prosperity returned in the years to come. Sophie swiftly disabused them.

It was difficult, however, to focus on these small-town men, with their small mentalities, when outside wounded veterans begged on street corners or sold home-made brooms with a mixture of desperate hope and crushing despair, when children sat on crumbled walls, hollow cheeked and without even the energy to play.

Even the Higgs fortune could not help them all, or even a noticeable proportion of them. It could, however, provide food and eventually jobs to some. Each to their own duty, thought Sophie. This will be mine.

They stayed at railway hotels, as James Lorrimer had suggested. These too had changed. Not in their comforts, nor their menus — somehow, throughout the war, the Mesdames of the kitchens had managed to procure pheasant or wild boar for their favoured customers or even venison hit by a train, butchered by the guard and bought for a ruinous price their more wealthy customers happily paid. The hoteliers had cultivated their own gardens of endive or lettuce, asparagus, artichokes, carrots and new potatoes, and still did. But now the clientele was mostly commercial — as we are, thought Sophie — and, like her, hoping to make money from feeding a land whose chief crop for four years had been battles. Would blood make good fertiliser for France's fields?

Most startling was the loss of the 'unknown army' of women, like Sophie, who had volunteered for the duration, manning ambulances, first-aid stations, refugee relief booths, uncounted and unacknowledged, the vastness of their numbers an embarrassment, for to acknowledge them would be to admit that none of the warring nations, except the United States of America, had been able to feed, clothe or transport their troops efficiently, or provide for the wounded. These had been the women who had automatically recognised each other, supported each other, provided anything from a dress to food or transport or advice regarding which colonel had roving hands and should be avoided, or which casualty posts had the best or most compassionate surgeons.

They had been her friends, her colleagues, her support. Now they were gone, dispersed back into the land of peace, and the men who controlled it. Sophie suspected that most, like her, could no longer be entirely controlled.

Yet still, as the train steamed its way to Lille, Sophie found herself watching for ambulances driven by women in jodhpurs;

bullock carts filled with wounded men guided by peasant women in black; or small tribes of village women bringing pots of hot soup to marching men.

All she saw was ghosts and memories.

They stayed two nights and a day at Lille to complete Sophie's business dealings, in an office above a warehouse empty of all but rats, where a small cadre of ex-soldiers boiled water in a can above a tiny fire in a courtyard.

The next train took them to Brussels, pausing at the border for the passengers to produce the new documents of identity now required to enter another country. Sophie wondered how much use this was in keeping out refugees, or even anarchists with bombs. After all, a simple photograph, physical description and signature had converted Lady Georgina to Mrs Wattle.

Brussels bustled, like London, with post-war urgency. It was only when you looked that you saw the beggars, and the painted women desperate, loitering in the alleys, trying to smile.

Sophie gave the first band of begging children francs, and the word must have spread quickly, for after that they were invariably followed by more. Georgina and Green were charged with doling francs out to each of them. There were worse fates than begging for a child in times like this.

But the office she visited stood well above the poverty in the streets. The furniture might be old, but it was dusted and polished; the rugs were threadbare but well beaten. Monsieur Gabelle signed contracts for five years' supply, with an option to renew. Sophie suspected that the wholesaler would have signed without her visit, but the appearance of the daughter of the firm undoubtedly added a personal note and possibly made renewals more likely.

Even better, Monsieur Gabelle had a brother-in-law in Munich ('One can confess these things now the ceasefire has been signed, can we not, mademoiselle?') who dealt in wholesale grocery. Monsieur Gabelle would telegraph Herr Feinberg to ascertain his interest in Higgs's most superior corned beef.

Herr Feinberg's telegram in return assured them he was indeed most interested in corned beef, if an acceptable price could be arranged. He wished to assure Fraülein Higgs that while parts of Bavaria were 'troublesome', order had been restored under the Freikorps in Munich itself. It was not perhaps recommended to drive to the city, but the train from Stuttgart was 'almost regular' now and, she would find, well guarded. He was her devoted servant ...

Sophie grinned as her companion translated the telegram. Georgina grinned back, before she remembered to hide her expression once more.

Sophie had her Munich contact.

Impulsively — for she had sworn to herself she would leave her own land of war behind, and now that she had the contact she needed in Munich there was no excuse for delay — she asked Jones at dinner that night if he would mind hiring a car for the afternoon, and driving her back to the village she had made her headquarters during the war and where she had established her first hospital.

He looked up from his *potage bonne femme* with the eyes of one who had an excellent idea of what those years had been like for her. 'Of course.'

'Do you wish me to accompany you, Miss Sophie?' asked Green. She added hesitantly, 'I have ... a place ... in Brussels I would like to visit.'

Sophie restrained her curiosity 'Of course, please do take the day off.'

'May I accompany you instead?' asked Georgina.

Sophie looked at her in surprise. 'Of course,' she repeated.

The journey was as emotional as she had expected, daggers piercing her with each vista. Even the picnic basket in the back reminded her of the desperate journey with Angus, skirting the front lines all the way to Ypres.

She hoped Angus was happy and would soon be settled enough to ask that admirable young lady to marry him, a woman who would never demand he risk his life to save men from a poisonous gas attack, who would never shoot a partridge, much less a man.

The land was so strangely familiar, yet so altered already too. Surely that vineyard over there had been the mud of No Man's Land. She'd known the skeleton of that tree, now sprigged with green. And the vines must have grown back up from their stumps. Such hardy beings, grapevines. She hoped those who tended them had fared as well.

They stopped twice to give part of the contents of their basket and some money to families sitting vacantly on the roadside as if they had no will or strength or purpose to go further. But the village, at least, had no women clutching babies, begging from shop to shop, holding out translucent hands while their infants tried to find the energy to whimper. The main street smelled of baking bread, though that bread was probably still mostly potato or acorn flour and sawdust. It even had a café now, where there had been ruined walls only months before. Old men with pipes and glasses of wine sat outside.

Here, at least, and partly with her help, both financial and organisational, mud had become farms, fields green with cabbages, leeks, potato plants and trellises of peas. Tethered oxen munching the roadside grass glanced suspiciously as their vehicle approached, wondering if these humans expected them to leave their well-earned leisure to plough, then bent their heads again as the car passed on.

Her hospital had a new rose garden out the front, planted, she suspected, by Madame Printemps, whose menfolk bred roses and who had protected cuttings in her cellar when the shelling was bad, and collected rose seeds from briars so that the family business might survive when her men came back from war. Sophie did not call in at the hospital, although she longed to, in case the sisters who ran it now felt that she had come on a mission of inspection.

Instead she had Jones drive to the farm of her small helper, Jean-Marie. He had grown a foot taller and sported a crop of pimples and a grin. She missed the small boy he had been;

she was glad of the young man he was becoming. His relations with the papa he had not seen for most of his life were now affectionate and casual.

Charlie bounded joyfully around her. He had become a father of six multi-coloured and multi-breed puppies, their mother being a miniature poodle belonging to Madame of the bakery. Jean-Marie's parents insisted on feeding Sophie and her two companions a late afternoon meal of roast chicken, from the brood that pecked outside the new back door, with home-grown potatoes and peas followed by apple tart. It was the first meal Sophie had truly enjoyed since the crumpets at the London Ritz with Miss Lily.

They were finishing their chicory and roasted acorn coffee when Jean-Marie ran to answer a knock at the door. Strange, thought Sophie, seeing Charlie snooze unconcerned before the fireplace, to be in a France where one no longer had to fear a knock at the door, or those who arrived and failed to knock.

'Sœur Claire et Sœur Anne-Marie, mademoiselle,' Jean-Marie announced, ducking his strangely long new body under the low lintel.

Sophie stood to greet them. 'Mes bonnes sœurs! I must apologise for not calling on you at the hospital this afternoon.'

Sœur Claire smiled, her withered apple face falling into wrinkled pleats, as Sophie introduced 'Madame Wattle' — Jones had tactfully retreated to the kitchen — and Jean-Marie's mother left hurriedly to put on more 'coffee' for the honoured visitors, and to bake a fast batch of crisp 'chat's tongues'.

'News of your arrival spread within five minutes, my dear Sophie,' said Sœur Claire, spreading her dark skirts as she sat. 'But we have come to ask for assistance.'

'But of course.' Sophie reached for the chequebook she had secured from a bank in Brussels. Higgs Industries already sent the hospital a monthly stipend, but she could well imagine there had been unexpected expenses. The guns might have stopped firing, but the war would not truly be over till millions of displaced persons had lives and homes and food.

Sœur Claire waved the chequebook away with a cracked and reddened hand. 'It is advice we want.' She glanced at her companion.

'We wish to build a factory,' said Sœur Anne-Marie, as calmly as if she had said they wanted to wash the linen. She had been the youngest of the sisters, widowed in the first month of war, still a novice when Sophie had met her. Sophie had wondered if she might regret abandoning the world for the cloister as her grief faded. But it seemed from the dark habit that Sœur Anne-Marie had not only taken full vows, but was solving the problems of the world too, or at least the world that touched the sisters' lives.

'A corned -beef factory? Here?'

Sœur Anne-Marie laughed. It was so good to see her laugh. 'I do not think the local farmers would care to give up their precious oxen for corned beef. And one needs good teeth to eat an ox at the end of its working life. No, we wish to can soup. Potato and leek to begin with, but perhaps wild mushroom, or mushroom and barley. Am I right in thinking the process is much the same, no matter what one cans?'

Sophie nodded. 'Basically you prepare the product, then place it in the cans. The sealing is the most complicated part, and then the cans must be boiled, which takes time and fuel. I don't know how long different soups would need to be boiled to make them safe to store, but it should be easy to find out.'

'A cannery would not just provide funds for the hospital,' said Sœur Claire, 'but security for the farm families. We could offer guaranteed prices for their crops. And if there is a wet summer and the potatoes fail,' she shrugged, 'then there will be wild mushrooms.'

'You need a building.'

'We have volunteers enough to build one, and landowners who will donate the wood to boil the cans. We thought each family might lend its copper, except on wash days, for the boiling. But we need to know about the canning machinery needed and where to buy it, how to install it and agents perhaps to buy what we produce.'

'Of course.' Sophie felt slightly stunned by their industry. But they were correct in all their assumptions. 'Madame Wattle, could you write to Mr Slithersole? I think perhaps this is a project his son would love to supervise. Higgs's Corned Beef will of course cover all costs,' she added to the sisters.

'You are too generous. But we have most excellent engineers back among us now. I hope the cost will not be too onerous. And the recompense for our community will be great.'

'It is an honour to help,' said Sophie. She found Georgina looking at her strangely. Was she worried about getting to the train station in the dark? The car's battery was possibly not reliable enough for headlights.

She glanced at her watch and stood, suddenly reluctant to leave. This village — or its battle-worn skeleton — had been her home for eighteen months. This had been her community, the exigencies of war bringing them closer than any she had known in times of peace.

But duty — and life, she reminded herself, weariness descending again — lay in front of her now. She began the farewell embraces.

It was late by the time they reached the hotel. Georgina had been quiet the whole journey. Even her 'Good night' was soft on the stairs.

Sophie opened her bedroom door. Green sat by the fire, knitting the dull brown wool with the needles Jones had found for her, but she stood as Sophie entered. Sophie took in her nightdress warming on the rack by the fire; the bulge of the warming pan in her bed; and the faint, already familiar scent of roses: Green must throw a little pot pourri on the coals to scent her bedrooms. 'Thank you, Green. I hope you had a good day.'

'It was ... satisfying, thank you, Miss Sophie.'

'What are you knitting?'

'Memories,' said Green briefly. It was clear she wished to say no more.

'Did you visit friends? Are they ... well?' It occurred to her that perhaps any friends might need assistance in this world where war's breath lingered.

Green smiled grimly. 'As well as can be expected. I visited their graves, Miss Sophie. But they are well tended.'

'I ... I'm sorry.'

'So am I, Miss Sophie,' said Green, in the tone of one who does not want to answer questions.

Green's wool. Her knitting. Suddenly Sophie remembered the elderly refugee patient last Christmas Eve, who had died as Sophie kept her company by her bedside. The old woman had knitted, knitted, knitted, her fingers growing more and more feeble as the scarf grew. The knitting had held messages that must be sent to her family and colleagues. Spies, as that old woman had been, the knitting a code used to transmit information across occupied Europe.

Sophie had not known the code; had not even known till that night that such a knitted code existed, or of a resistance movement that covered all of occupied Europe. La Dame Blanche, mostly old or very young. An old woman and her grandchild could blow up a railway then look innocent when the Germans arrived, and say, 'We saw nothing,' and be believed, for what soldier would suspect an old woman or a girl could blow up a railway?

Nominally under British control — or at least the British sometimes believed it was — La Dame Blanche had many rules, but one unbreakable code. Courage under fire or torture till death, and a total refusal to betray their friends.

Sophie had made sure the scarf was delivered to the right person that Christmas. Her world view had changed a little that night. Miss Lily had taught her the political and social skills that upper-class women might wield. But here were women, unknown, anonymous, providing almost all the intelligence that gave the Allies the chance to defeat Germany.

And never once had they publicly been given credit, just as the majority of female-run hospitals like her own, as well as ambulances and medical teams operated or organised by women, were ignored in official reports. Even the Red Cross did not officially acknowledge them.

Sophie sat on the edge of the bed and stared at her quiet, wiry maid. 'I have heard of La Dame Blanche,' Sophie said softly.

Green looked up at Sophie in shock. 'An old woman in one of my hospitals knitted as you're doing. She died,' added Sophie briefly. 'An intelligence officer explained the code to me. How did ...' She stopped. Those questions were for another time — and only if Green chose to talk about them.

But Green answered anyway, 'Two Belgian refugees, sisters, were billeted in Shillings village at the start of the war. They returned to their own country to fight the invader two years later. I joined them, later,' said Green simply. 'The English needed liaison with the Belgian women — it all began here in Brussels, you know. The English men liked to think they were in control, but actually they knew little of what was really going on. Finally someone in authority had the sense to send a woman over, not a man.'

'Not James Lorrimer, by any chance?' asked Sophie.

'I have no idea. I was asked to visit a small shop in London. I did ... and ended up here in Brussels.' She smiled reminiscently. 'The other woman began to trust me soon enough. Within months we had a woman knitting on every railway platform. So much information in every scarf, or pair of socks. So many knots, or a slipped stitch, or a twist in the wool — they told which were army trains, troop numbers, armaments. Most of us survived, you know. Men so rarely truly look at women. But today I wanted to farewell those who did not.'

'You were amazing,' said Sophie softly. 'But no one even mentioned La Dame Blanche.'

'I expect when they write the histories of the war they won't mention your hospitals either,' said Green dryly. 'Nor the girls in their home-made ambulances. We won the war for them. But wars are supposed to be won by men in uniform, with a few lasses in uniform helping now and then. We did too much, that was our trouble. Now they need to forget us.' She considered. 'And maybe a good thing too.'

'Why?' asked Sophie.

'This isn't the end of the war. Even signing the Treaty won't be the end. It's just a pause ... till both sides have enough energy to be at it again. Best La Dame Blanche and our codes are forgotten, till we are needed again.' She looked consideringly at Sophie. 'I'll teach you, if you like.'

'I've always been a terrible knitter. I suspect you need to be a good one to deliberately make mistakes.'

Green smiled. 'We'll see. It may be useful.'

'Your friends.' There was no tactful way to ask this, thought Sophie, thinking of the graves Green had mentioned. 'The ones you met at Shillings. Did they survive?'

'No,' said Green, almost, but not quite, matter-of-factly. 'Five of us were captured. The others were executed, but I was kept because I was English, and so might be valuable in an exchange of prisoners. His lordship used his influence ... It is good to work with a woman again, a woman who does things, who chooses her own path in life. I am proud to work with you, Miss Higgs.'

'I am proud to work with you, Miss Green of La Dame Blanche.'

Green reached to slip off Sophie's coat, once more a lady's maid.

Sophie let herself be tended, saying nothing. For what more was there she could say?

Chapter 13

All life is a journey. If one is lucky, determined and skilled, one may even choose the destination. Whenever possible, enjoy the view.

Miss Lily, 1914

The train journey from Stuttgart was indeed 'almost reliable'. The revolutionaries had melted like the winter snow. Spring had budded the trees lime green, though the firs wore their usual dark frown. Children looked ragged; groups of men wearing part uniform, part civilian clothes muttered at the edges of the railway stations.

The first-class carriage was comfortable, even if the leather seats were worn. A dining car held customers of comfortable build too, and elegant or even opulent dress, and offered a menu of almost pre-war choice, pheasant, venison, choucroute, and an astounding range of tortes of elaborate colours and construction. Sophie remembered Dolphie's remark about his sister-in-law, the Krupp heiress, and her moustache, but none of the women tucking into three-layer chocolate cakes 'mit Sahne', apple Zwieback torte, Pflaumenkuchen or sugar-coated Springerle seemed particularly hirsute.

They sat together, this time. Security was more important, with revolution in the dark woods and dappled fields around them, than 'social convention'. Green taught Sophie the knitting code, in between glances at the scenery, making it seem that she was merely showing the younger woman how to improve and vary her stitch. Sophie doubted she would ever use it. But it linked her to thousands of women resistance workers, as well as that lonely figure in her hospital last Christmas, a link to all the 'roses of No Man's Land', who must be so carefully forgotten now the firing had ceased. And perhaps Green was right. If 'normal' was to begin again, women must go back to the kitchens, and tending children, and the myth that this was all that fate ever intended them to do.

The air as they stepped from the train onto the station platform smelled, like every railway station's air, of coal and steam and travel-worn clothes, but above that was the cold tin of melted snow and pine forests. The meadows they had passed had been lit with alpine flowers and the flash of red deer.

On Herr Feinberg's advice they stayed at the Bayerischer Hof on the outskirts of the financial district; the hotel was now under new management and awaiting refurbishment and extension, but those elite customers recommended by Herr Feinberg were still welcomed. It was comfortable, if not luxurious, although Herr Süss promised that when they next returned his hotel would be opulent once more. They stayed in adjoining rooms, and ate together too. This seemed a world of peace, yet shadows twitched around each corner. There was reassurance in staying together, and if sometimes she heard Jones's voice in Green's room next door, it was no business of hers.

She listened carefully, anyway, but heard too little to draw definite conclusions.

Dinner was local trout 'a bleu', dropped into its poaching liquid at the moment of its death so it arrived still twisted from momentary agony, and sweetly succulent; roasted venison, with a sweet berry sauce; Schmandkuchen, a sour cream cake, and a choice of local beer or a dusty bottle of wine from the cellar. Breakfast was extremely good coffee, not the acorn and chicory substitute she was used to in France, even in good hotels, though beer was offered too, and a selection of croissants, light and flaky, as well as the Bavarian almost black rye bread.

Sophie forced herself to eat a croissant, then stepped into the car that Herr Feinberg had sent for them. All cars had been confiscated by the Soviet leadership, but the new coalition government seemed happy to hire, or sell, cars to wealthy citizens, especially those who, like Herr Feinberg, might keep their troops and citizens fed.

The car took them to a private home, not an office. Frau Feinberg herself let them in, apologising for the informality of doing business away from an office. 'The troubles ...' she said, waving plump hands vaguely, as a maid led Jones to the kitchen and Herr Feinberg emerged from his study to welcome Sophie and Georgina.

They were offered coffee 'mit Sahne', the cream thick on top of their coffee cups, a three-layer nut cake, again 'mit Sahne', and an even more excellent contract, larger than the French and Belgian ones, and this one definitely all hers, not thanks to Mr Slithersole's connections.

'But I must acquire the agreement of my colleagues,' said Herr Feinberg in English, sampling his cake. Sophie had hardly needed Georgina's German, even at the hotel, but it was still useful to have her take notes of the meeting. 'A small consignment I can take regularly, but if we all order together it will be more efficient I am thinking.'

'Indeed, Herr Feinberg.' She sipped the coffee, forced herself to take six polite bites of cream cake with apricot jam, and promised the initial agreement with Herr Feinberg could be extended to his colleagues — it was not as if Higgs's Corned Beef would have a shortage with the army contacts ending.

She and Georgina settled back in Herr Feinberg's motorcar, Jones sitting next to the driver. Sophie allowed her eyelids to close. She had not been sleeping well ...

The car braked suddenly, hurtling her forwards.

'Are you all right?' demanded Jones, just as the driver said, 'Schau nicht!' Do not look ...

Sophie looked.

Eight men in assorted uniforms blocked the road, holding rifles. Three men and a woman faced them, their hands bound. A volley of shots, and the prisoners fell to the pavement. One of the uniformed men strode over to the car and thrust his rifle at the driver.

The driver unleashed a torrent of words, gesturing at Sophie and her companions.

'He is saying you are an important supplier of corned beef,' said Georgina softly. 'That we will leave Germany tomorrow or the day after, have no interest in politics, that we saw nothing, will never speak of this. Have you money?' she added urgently.

Sophie held out a bundle of marks. The man took them and began to count. One of his colleagues strode towards them.

'Tell the driver to reverse away slowly,' said Jones quietly. 'Stop only if they order him to do so.'

Georgina spoke clearly and precisely The driver glanced uncertainly at Jones, who nodded. The driver then put the car into reverse. The uniformed man said something sharply, but it did not seem to be a command.

'Tell him to accelerate if I yell "Schnell!"' said Jones, pulling a pistol out of an inner pocket of his coat. Sophie reached for hers too. Georgina stared at it, but to Sophie's relief, quietly relayed Jones's order to the driver.

Their car turned the corner. They were free.

Chapter 14

How will you deal with tragedy? For you will all face it, my dears.
Everyone who loves must face loss too.

So hold loss gently, and tragedy as well. Hold it out as if it is a
ball in your hand, so that you can also see the beauty all around.
For even at the worst of times there is beauty. And when the senses
are sharpened you may see it even more wonderfully than before.

Miss Lily 1914

They did not refer to the incident when the driver left them at the hotel, both pistols hidden again. Sophie tipped him well.

'Coffee,' she said.

'Brandy,' said Jones. 'Or schnapps or whatever it is they drink here.'

Sophie nodded her agreement. She sipped the small glass of clear liquid, and forced herself to eat a ham sandwich — thinly sliced ham, pungent mustard, rye bread with caraway seeds — as she studied the map of Munich's streets that the proprietor, Herr Süss, had given Jones, her heart beating not just from the shock of what she had seen, but what she must do that afternoon.

It was time to call at the address on the envelope of Dolphie's letter.

But first she must write to James Lorrimer, keeping the bargain they had made. She knew now, even more than before, how dangerous this quest might be. If she did not return from the afternoon's walk, James must have his letter.

The hotel ink was thick, probably pre-war, and blotted easily, but the pen nibs she had brought from England were still sharp.

The hotel notepaper was pre-war too, thick and only slightly yellowed.

> *Dear James,*
> > *I hope you are as well, as we all are.*

She paused, trying to find phrases that sounded casual, but would still convey her meaning.

> > *We have been having a surprisingly excellent time. Everyone here is friendly and hospitable now the recent troubles are over, and especially anxious to begin trade again and establish good relations with England. Higgs's Corned Beef seems more important than any politics, and likely to remain so.*
> > *Have you heard how Uncle Alec is?*

(This was the name they had chosen for the Kaiser.)

> > *I've have had no news of him, or cousin Hannah. I hope he has recovered from the influenza — it can be nasty for a man of his age.*

(She hoped James would not read anything into what was purely a desire to pad out the letter with inconsequentialities.)

> > *I know you said that he'd like to come home, but I'm fairly sure he'll stay at the seaside now he is there and settled reasonably comfortably, where the air is far better for a man of his age and health. Your idea of a comfortable seaside resort and mine though differ considerably — I wish you could see our (warm!) Australian beaches! I am looking forward to my first swim at home.*
> > *My meetings have all been good. Everyone, it seems, is as anxious as Higgs's Corned Beef that life resume normality, and each contract has been most satisfactory.*

(A way to tell him, she hoped, that the hunger in Germany was indeed as bad as that of France and Belgium.)

> *Each has been for five years, with an option of indefinite*
> *extension, which I am reasonably confident will be taken up.*
> *Munich is most interesting.*

(For surely any reader would expect her to mention some politics at least.)

> *Much is happening here, for it is said that the situation in*
> *Berlin is too volatile for political negotiations to take place there,*
> *and Munich offers the stability the capital lacks. It is so beautiful*
> *too! I hear that Herr Ebert advocates reform not revolution.*
> *Imperial Germany has indeed gone, and in its place will be*
> *a democratic, not a socialist, state. This promised stability is*
> *comforting to those of us who are doing business here.*
> *No more news now! I will write from the ship, if not before.*
> *Always yours,*
> *Sophie*

She handed the letter to Georgina to post. It was as true an assessment as she was able to make. Things did indeed seem stable, despite the incident that morning. Europe had experienced four years of killing without the formalities of a trial, and Munich had also just had a revolution, but its people wanted the rule of law again, wanted prosperity. This was the tail of chaos, with a new political animal entirely emerging, one plump and content on schnapps and cream cake, or at least sausage and beer.

And yet ... and yet ...

The crags above Munich were cold and so were its streets, despite the coming of summer. She imagined that before the war, or even before the revolution, the city had been bustling — their hotel was on Promenade Platz, but no one promenaded now. Was it hunger or caution, as the inhabitants waited to see how stable their new government may be, and if the proposed elections actually happened, changing Germany from a monarchy or soviet state into a mildly socialist democracy, promising reform of the gentlest and most needed kind, not revolution, confiscation and execution?

And each night too, and even through the day, you could hear short volleys of shots. How many communists must be killed, she thought, before the new regime felt stable? Surely true normality would begin soon, if the eagerness of Herr Süss and Herr Feinberg were a guide.

She rang a bell for Green.

'Inconspicuous clothes, I think,' she said.

Green nodded. 'I took the liberty of bringing an old trench coat I used to wear, miss, and boots a little worn. With a scarf you should not be noticeable. I put knitting needles and wool in one of the pockets. No one questions a woman dutifully knitting socks or an undervest. But a knitting needle can be a useful weapon. Go for the eyes if you can, or the kidney, or about three fingers down from the breastbone, angled upwards. But the last two need strength and practice.'

And a degree of ... determination, thought Sophie, that Green assumed she possessed. Did she? On reflection, probably yes.

'You may also leave messages in lengths of knotted wool, the kind of scraps that might be moth eaten and discarded.' Green hesitated. 'I have similar clothes for myself. Two women are safer and less conspicuous than one alone.'

Sophie was touched. 'You are very kind.' And four knitting needles more potentially lethal than two. 'But Jones will follow me. And this is my duty, not yours.'

Green smiled. 'You are my duty now.' Another pause. 'Miss Higgs, I am afraid that Mr Jones may not have given you my ... full ... background when you hired me.'

Sophie stared. 'You were born on the Shillings estate, became Miss Lily's maid and then worked for La Dame Blanche ...' And I am fairly sure you spend your nights with Jones, and not playing tiddlywinks, she thought. 'I'm not doubting your ability. But I don't have the right to risk your life a well as my own.'

Green met her eyes. 'But I have the right to risk my life if I wish to. The war was not my first experience of ... challenges.

Some of my times with Miss Lily were more … varied … than a lady's maid is usually exposed to. I believe I might be of help if the situation becomes difficult,' said Green calmly.

No wonder Green had not hesitated to leave what might have been a well-paid job as a lady's maid, and agreed to live across the world. She had lost her position at Shillings once Miss Lily … retired. Sophie was sure Nigel would have offered her continued employment, but there was no other suitable job at Shillings with the same status for a woman like Green, apart from the already filled job of housekeeper.

The war had given Green another life, and other companions in it — and then she had lost them. She was possibly as eager as Sophie to leave the war behind — and as unwilling to accept the potentially stultifying roles to which women were expected to return. And if Green wished, for whatever reason — loyalty, friendship, adventure — to be part of the search for Hannelore, Sophie had no right to prevent her.

'Ask Jones if you can walk with him, innocently arm in arm, staying well away from me,' she said. She tried to grin. 'I am just going for a walk. If you two care to go for a walk together, who am I to object?'

'Our employer,' said Green dryly.

'There is that,' said Sophie. She held out her hand and took Green's work-roughened one, like hers scarred from so many infections during the war. 'When your youngest sister Doris was my maid I think we became friends. I would be honoured if one day we might become friends, as well. I know as an employee you can't very well refuse,' she added. 'Or maybe Miss Lily taught you how to do that? Perhaps you have a tactful way to repel advances of friendship from an employer.'

Green smiled. 'Perhaps I have. But in this case, I don't want to use them.'

Sophie noticed she did not add 'miss' or 'madam'. 'Time to go,' she said.

Chapter 15

You may know someone for ten years, then suddenly realise, 'They are my friend.'

Miss Lily, 1914

The house was built in a style that in England she would have called Tudor: wood and plasterwork, the latter once whitewashed but now dingy with the last of the winter mould. The doorstep too had not been recently scrubbed, as respectable doorsteps had been each morning before breakfast, before the war. She knocked, aware of the shadows, the unlit cobbles, glad of Jones and Green walking casually along the street behind her.

The door opened. A woman stood there, sunken bodied, her dress loose on what had once been sturdy shoulders, her head covered in a peasant's scarf.

'Entschuldigung,' said Sophie, hoping she was remembering Georgina's language lessons properly, 'Ich bin Fraülein Sophie Higgs. Meine Freunde Hannelore bleibt hier vielleicht?'

The woman looked at her with blank-faced suspicion. 'Sie sind Englisch?'

'Nein. Ich bin Australien.'

'Ah.' The woman's face relaxed into what might be its normal expression, a combination of fear and sadness. The question had been a trap.

So friends had been there before — or not friends — looking for Hannelore. And this woman knew Hannelore had an Australian friend, a fact only those who knew her well might have been told.

'Kommen Sie bitte herein. Schnell,' the woman added in a hurried whisper.

The door shut behind her, bringing her into the scent of old cabbage and fresh mouse.

'Do you speak English?' asked Sophie hopefully. If Hannelore was not there, there was no way she could follow instructions in German, and yet this woman might well hesitate to write them down.

The woman looked at her consideringly in the dim light coming through the single window above the door. At last she admitted, 'I am speaking some English. You wish to know where your friend is?'

'Yes. Please! Is she here? Is she all right?'

'I cannot tell you.'

'Please! I truly am her friend. I wish to help.'

'I *cannot* tell you,' the woman emphasised. 'I do not know. But I can perhaps be finding someone who does know. You are staying where?'

'The Bayerischer Hof, on Promenade Platz.'

'That hotel I know.' She appeared to calculate again. 'Tomorrow afternoon at two o'clock, walk along the promenade. A man will come. You will go with him, and he will take you to ... your friend. If no one comes, it means she is not to be found, or does not *wish* to be found, or it is most unwise to find her, and you will leave München. You are understanding?'

'Yes.' Though Sophie certainly would not leave Munich if this approach failed, but would try to find Hannelore's aunt or old army colleagues of Dolphie's ... 'There will be three of us.' She would not risk Georgina, and risk leaving her child motherless; nor was this Georgina's quest.

'No. Only you must go.'

'I must insist.' And Green and Jones had far more experience, it seemed, than she did.

The woman stared at her. 'Your friend is in danger. You understand? Dangerous to know. The communists wish her dead as an example. The Freikorps ...' The woman shrugged. 'Who are the Freikorps? Do they even know, except that they are not communist? Do they wish aristocrats like the Kaiser dead too? So many blame the aristocrats for the war, and for agreeing to end it too, when we might still have won. To you, your friend is just a friend. To others she is,' she shrugged again, 'I do not know the word.'

'A symbol?'

'I do not know what that may mean. Perhaps soon, your friend may live in safety. But now, yes, even to be knowing her is risky.'

'Then she is safe?'

'I told you, I do not know. If she is alive, she is risky. Danger for her, danger for you. You still wish to see her?'

'Yes.'

'Tomorrow afternoon, then. Be on the promenade at two o'clock, for they will not stop. Now, please to go, and quickly from the door.'

'Why? Is it forbidden to speak to foreigners?'

The woman stared at her. 'Forbidden? Of course it is not. But we have been at war with Engländers for four years, have now been betrayed by Engländers to the French. I do not want my neighbours knowing an Engländer has been here.'

Or an Australian, thought Sophie.

'Thank you,' she said. She pressed a roll of money into the woman's hand. Probably, hopefully, this woman had been and still was loyal to Hannelore. If not, well, need was still need.

Chapter 16

*Never use commercial rouge, unless you wish to look like an
actress or a woman from a bordello and wish to signal that a quick
seduction would be welcome. But a small amount of raspberry
juice — never beetroot — mixed with almond oil and beeswax and
rubbed into the highest point of your cheeks will take away years
or the marks of sleeplessness or worry. Your maid will make it for
you, but all women should know the recipe, and how to apply it
themselves if necessary.*

Miss Lily, 1914

'I am coming with you,' stated Jones, as they sat with her in
the garden, Green joining them now as she always did for what
Sophie privately thought of as tactical discussions. 'His lordship
would never allow —'

Sophie shook her head. 'The contact will leave without me if
anyone else appears.'

'They could be taking you for ransom,' Green pointed out.
'Or as a hostage.'

Sophie thought of the rag-tag soldiers today. One of them
could have followed their car, asked where the strangers were
staying. A wealthy foreigner would indeed be worth ransoming.
But they would not have known she would go to that particular
house ... only Dolphie would have known that — or someone he
had told, either willingly or because he had been tortured. Or,
just possibly, to exchange her money for Hannelore's life.

And what were her options? To ask Herr Feinberg and his
colleagues how they might find Dolphie? As an army officer
there should be a record of his whereabouts or, if he had been

94

demobilised, an address. But that address was most likely in Berlin, and Berlin was just as dangerous as Munich, probably even more so than here, where at least one party seemed currently to be in control.

And what was Dolphie's status now? He had implied he had neither the money nor position to help Hannelore. Was he disgraced? Had his wound left him crippled? Asking about him might be dangerous for him as well as her, revealing that he had enemy connections.

The longer they stayed in Germany, the greater the risk to herself, and to others. This was her search; and tomorrow, she alone would have to take the greater risk.

'If there is no message from me in twenty-four hours, you are to leave for Naples. Jones, take Georgina and Green to the ship as planned. After that,' she shrugged, 'it is up to you, or you and Nigel.' Nigel's orders would always supersede hers, for Jones. And Jones would trust his own judgement, she suspected, even above Nigel's.

'Yes, Miss Sophie,' said Green. She gave a small, silent nod as her eyes met Jones's.

Sophie smiled wryly. Green, too, would prefer her own judgement to orders. But at least she and Jones kept up the pretence of deferring to their employer.

Her clothes were laid out on the bed; respectable coat and jacket, the 'trench coat', and next to it, the knitting needles again, this time with a bunch of tufts of brown wool as well as the ball of wool and beginning of a knitted scarf — all Sophie could believably manage.

Sophie glanced at the brown tufts, then looked questioningly at Green.

'Drop one tuft of wool at each turn,' said Green. 'They're inconspicuous. Tie a small knot if the enemies are armed; a knot on two strands means ten to twenty enemy. Three strands means forty to eighty...'

'I'm supposed to be meeting a friend. Or friends.'

95

'Who may be enemies,' said Green quietly.

Sophie did not reply. But she put the strands in her pocket.

The morning was grey, looking heavy as snow clouds, though only a grey drizzle fell in the warmth of late spring. The affable Herr Süss kept offering coffee, schnapps, strudel mit Sahne, and his plans for the renovations of his hotel. 'The most splendid in Europe it will be, Fraülein Higgs. You must bring all your friends to visit.'

She agreed it would be a most glorious hotel, then pleaded a headache and the need to stroll, which he accepted, managing to refrain from asking her to be careful, which might have ruined his reiterations of the safe and peaceful present as well as future of his city.

At one-forty exactly she began to walk along the promenade then back again, wearing the same gabardine trench coat, once made popular by officers early in the war, and recently adapted for women's wear, and a woollen scarf about her hair and neck. She wished she could wear trousers, but although she did own a pair they would make her more conspicuous on this city street.

Her pistol lay in one pocket, hidden she hoped by the wool; extra ammunition in another, along with the knitting needles, her billfold holding an unwieldy lump of bills, and the Brussels chequebook — Munich banking was still too unstable to risk setting up a local account, but she expected a draft on a Brussels bank would be acceptable here, if it was a large enough amount to be worth a journey to cash it in another country.

A car passed. She looked up, trying to meet the driver's eyes, but he passed on. A cart full of potatoes and cabbages stopped, but before she could reach it the driver headed for the hotel kitchen. He returned only to lug the sacks to the hotel, then jig the reins of his thin horse.

She walked again. Herr Süss would think this a most peculiar headache.

Another cart, this time with empty sacks, its load sold. The horse was even thinner than the one before, blind in one eye and lame, the driver muffled in a sacking coat, with scraps of the same hessian draped around his head and throat. She waited for this cart too to pass.

The cart stopped next to her.

Dolphie's voice said, 'Sophie!' and then, 'Climb into the back. Quickly. Hide under the sacks as soon as we are out of sight of the hotel.'

She obeyed without speaking, her heart beating louder than the limping clop of the horse, for the cart moved on within seconds. She realised it would have blocked the view of anyone looking from the hotel, and the footpath and road had been clear, the Munich streets still eerily empty even during the day.

The horse kept shuffling on, its uneven hoofbeats hollow on the cobbles. Dolphie didn't speak.

The road rose. The cart turned a corner, bumping now on a rutted surface. Sophie could smell cows and mud above the scent of old potatoes and dusty jute.

Sophie hesitated. This was Dolphie. She trusted Dolphie. And yet she threw out one of the tufts of wool, watched it float down to the ground between the cracks in the floor of the cart.

An hour passed, or more. It was impossible to see her watch in the dimness under the sacking; nor did she want to risk moving in case she was seen. The cart turned again. Once again she pushed a tuft of wool between the cracks. She could smell something new, both old and familiar ... Swans, she thought, just as Dolphie said, 'You may come out.'

Or swan dung. For as she thrust the sacks aside she could see a lake and a muddy stream leading to it, with white birds ducking their necks hopefully into the water. A black-green forest of tall pines slithered down the mountains to the lake and behind them too, except for the track they had come along, but here two pale brown cows cropped short grass. A small turreted building, a bit like a palace that had shrunk several times in the wash, sat with its back to the forest.

Apart from the cows and the swans and Dolphie, the land was lifeless.

She clambered stiffly from the cart, trying not to ladder her stockings. Dolphie had already got down and was unwrapping his sacking scarf. He did not offer her his hand.

She stood and stared at him, unable to move. Both his arms worked — she had been terrified his wound in France might have become infected, that he would have lost his arm, or at least the use of it. He was thin, with the sunken eyes most ex-officers had. He wore uniform trousers, but a jersey over a civilian shirt with a soft collar.

'Sophie?'

She nodded, unable to find words. She should drop another tuft of wool, in case they moved again. Dolphie wouldn't notice, or would think it was just some sacking she needed to brush from her clothes. But she could not.

'I knew you would come,' he said stiffly. 'Sophie Higgs would always come if she was needed.'

'Hannelore?' she whispered.

'I will take you to her.'

'She is alive?'

He nodded.

'I ... I was so afraid. Afraid for you too. I am so sorry. There is no way to say how much I am sorry.' How could you apologise for lying to a man, shooting his men, leaving him wounded, stranded, near the front line?

It was impossible. She should not even try. She stared at him, trying to find something, anything, to say next.

'Oh, Sophie.' He stepped towards her. Suddenly his arms were around her, and hers around him. Their lips met. His were cold and firm, and only slightly desperate. His body fitted against hers, smelling of sacks and old potatoes and horse and man.

Time and place vanished. She had never felt like this, not with Angus, or Nigel. It was as if Dolphie too needed the world to vanish, or shrink till they were the only creatures in it.

She did not know a kiss could last so long. Or perhaps time had simply stretched, or they had moved to a world where there was no time ...

She stepped back, smiling uncertainly, saw his smile, just as uncertain. She gave a cry of joy and clasped him again. Nothing mattered, not the danger nor the strangeness, just the beat of his heart, the warm male smell of him …

… and Hannelore.

She looked up at him. 'Hannelore?'

He blinked, as if finding himself again after the kiss. 'She is recovering.'

'Recovering?' The world returned. 'From what?'

Dolphie gave a shaky laugh, one arm still around her waist, as if he could not bear to let her go. 'From war, from revolution, from influenza … Where should I begin?' His voice grew emotionless. 'The rebels stormed our aunt's house. They killed our aunt, and the servants who had stayed loyal. Hannelore and Old Pieter, the gardener, carried Grossmutti to safety in another house, but someone must have tipped off the rebels. They killed Grossmutti and the servants, and shot Hannelore, but decided to try to keep her alive, for ransom or public execution, I do not know. She thinks the Freikorps must have killed her captors. She asked a group of Freikorps for help. Many of the Freikorps know me.' He shrugged. 'I brought her here.'

'Where is here?'

'My uncle's hunting lodge. It might be mine, for he died last year and his sons perished in the first year of the war, but without a government to manage land titles …' Dolphie shrugged again. 'Who knows who we are, or what we own? But the farming couple who live here have a garden and an orchard and cows. There are deer in the forest, mushrooms and berries and fish. We have managed, Sophie. And in a few weeks it may even be safe again to be a count and prinzessin in Germany.'

'And now I am here perhaps you can do more than manage. Please, may I see Hannelore?'

'Of course. Sophie, there are no words to thank you for coming here.'

She looked at him sombrely. 'There are no words to apologise for what I did, back in Belgium.'

'You did what you had to, and with courage. I have never admired a woman more.'

Angus had been intimidated by a woman who would shoot an enemy for the sake of ten thousand other men. She did not know what Nigel — or Miss Lily — would have felt. But the hard core of shame at her own actions, which she would do again if faced with the same circumstances, began to melt.

'Come and see Hannelore,' he said, taking her hand.

Chapter 17

A perfume for the boudoir:
*   1 tbsp candle wax*
*   1 tbsp almond oil*
*   6 drops gardenia oil*
*   1 drop oil of Bulgarian roses*
*   Melt the wax in the oil over a candle. Take off the heat. Pour*
into a small jar and add the perfumed oils. Keep well sealed. Apply
to the hollow of the neck and to the wrists.

Miss Lily, 1914

Three broad steps led to a stone portico. The swans glanced at them from the lake, evaluating their potential as threat or perhaps throwers of bread — more likely the former, as there'd have been little bread spared for swans over the past four years, and meat had been scarce.

The front door led to what was evidently the main room, a vast fireplace meant to hold whole logs, smelling now of old damp ashes; a long table that could have held a banquet for Henry VIII. The heads of deer, bears, wolves and tusked boars stared down at her glassy eyed. It was unnerving, being watched by generations of dead animals. The flagged floor breathed cold. But Dolphie's hand was warm in hers.

He opened a small door behind a dusty curtain, a servant's door, meant for serving the master inconspicuously. A narrow passage between stone walls was lined with doors carved with more animals among scrollwork. Dolphie opened the second door along and gestured to her to go inside.

Warmth and shifting light reflected from the lake through an uncurtained window — the curtains were piled on a bench next to the wall. And then she realised it was a bed, not a bench, and the curtains had become blankets. Hannelore's white face gazed at her from the nest of velvet. 'Sophie,' she whispered.

Sophie ran to her. 'Hannelore! I am sorry I've been so long.'

'Three weeks since I sent the letter,' said Dolphie behind her. 'That is fast indeed, even for liebe Sophie.'

Sophie took Hannelore's hand, automatically feeling her pulse. Too fast, but steady. 'You were shot? Let me see the wound.'

Hannelore laughed weakly. 'No social pleasantries! Darling Sophie. Miss Lily would be appalled that your manners have deteriorated so. I am shocked!'

Sophie managed a smile. 'It's terrible weather, isn't it? Do you think it will be fine tomorrow? Your ... blankets are most colourful. I have never seen green velvet blankets before. Now may I see your wound? I have been helping to nurse for four years,' she added.

'Then you may replace the bandages. If you do not mind,' added Hannelore. 'Helga's ointment is good but she does not see well any more and, well, your hands will be gentler. Dolphie, bandages?'

'You see how she orders me about? A general would be less demanding!' Dolphie sketched a salute and closed the door behind him as he left.

'He has been so good to me,' said Hannelore quietly. 'He should be with his friends, finding a proper position in the new government. Instead he stays with me.'

'You have me now.' I will send a message to the hotel, Sophie thought. If Hannelore was not well enough to travel yet, Jones and Green and Georgina could stay here too and help. Dolphie would not object once he knew they could be trusted. Georgina would have to contact Mr Slithersole to delay their passages home.

'Dolphie said you would come. He was so sure.'

'Hannelore, don't cry. Please. Of course I came. You should have known I would.'

'When the soviets held me, I dreamed of you, and kangaroos and sunshine. But you might have been back in Australia already. It could have been months before you ever saw his letter ...'

'I nearly was on the ship to go back home. I am so incredibly glad I wasn't.' She stopped as Dolphie came in again, carrying a tray with two steaming bowls on it, and a sticky-looking jar. An old woman — no, not old, just bent and careworn so she might have been forty or eighty — followed him, carrying what looked like freshly boiled, ironed and rolled bandages.

'This is Helga,' said Dolphie. 'Helga, this is our most dear friend, Sophie, who has come to bring beauty and happiness to us again.'

It was perhaps the most wonderful thing anyone had said of her. Sophie flushed, then took the tray and put it on the floor by the narrow bed.

The old woman curtseyed low to Hannelore, then to Sophie, then handed Sophie the bandages. She said something in German, too fast for Sophie to catch a word of it, or possibly she spoke in dialect. Dolphie answered in the same fast tongue. Helga smiled, curtseyed again to Hannelore, to Sophie and then to Dolphie, and backed out.

As if we are royalty, thought Sophie, and then realised, slightly stunned — Hannelore *is* royalty. She had never quite understood how much that would mean in Hannelore's own country. And in Australian society too. Being a princess would far outweigh being a former enemy.

'Out,' she said to Dolphie.

'So I am to be ordered around by two women now? Will it be this way all my life? I can see it now. Bring the coffee, Dolphie, fetch the footstool.'

Hannelore managed a weak laugh again. 'Dolphie, go.'

He did, with a small intimate smile for Sophie.

Sophie lifted the curtains from Hannelore's body. They smelled clean, not even musty. Hannelore wore only a man's soft shirt. Sophie lifted it, carefully keeping her face expressionless.

Two wounds. No sweet corrupt smell of gangrene, no ominous red lines that meant blood poisoning and certain death. She unwrapped the bandage on Hannelore's leg first. The flesh around it was swollen, so there was some infection, but the granulation meant the wound was healing, Hannelore's own body keeping the toxins under control.

'Well?' asked Hannelore, only the sweat on her forehead showing her pain as the wound was disturbed.

'Healing well.' Sophie bent and sniffed again. A herby smell …

'Helga has been putting her cream on it. She makes it herself. Beeswax, comfrey, calendula, chickweed, some names I do not know in English, a sort of cactus plant. I think it must work, if the wound is healing.'

Sophie thought of Monsieur le Docteur at her first French hospital, with his maggots, and the herbal cures the village women had provided that did indeed help, and gave her hospitals a far higher recovery rate than the official army ones.

'This will hurt. Do you have anything for the pain?'

'Laudanum just makes me ill, and we have only a little. It is best kept for emergencies … schnapps does not touch the pain. It just makes it harder to cry out. Change the dressings, Sophie,' she said quietly. 'I am used to pain.'

Sophie washed her hands carefully in one of the bowls — a rosemary and lavender tea, she thought. She dried her fingers on a cloth, applied the cream as gently as she could, then bandaged the leg again.

The wound should have been stitched long ago. The scar might stretch and tear later, but it was too late to disturb it by trying to stitch it now. Now for the one on Hannelore's chest …

To her relief that one was nearly healed and had scabbed over, just needing more cream and fresh bandages.

Hannelore looked even whiter when she had finished. Sophie sat, holding her hand, wiping the perspiration from her forehead, until the shock of the pain subsided.

The door opened. Dolphie appeared again and Helga was holding another tray. She placed it on the floor and then took the soiled dressings and bowls, again curtseying deeply, then backed out of the room with a muttered farewell.

Sophie looked at the tray. Three bowls of a soup-like stew, with meat and potatoes and swede. The food in one of the bowls had been puréed into a pale brown slop, presumably to make it easier for Hannelore to eat.

'The last of the venison,' said Dolphie. He picked up Hannelore's bowl and began to feed her, spoon by spoon. 'Eat while it is hot,' he advised Sophie. 'Heat is its best characteristic.'

Sophie obeyed, suddenly desperately hungry. The stew was filling, though for her taste the venison was beyond its prime and had a faint taint of rot. But perhaps, like game in England, venison there was not eaten till it had hung so long it had a pale green surface and an Australian cook would have thrown it out or at least steeped it in vinegar for a day.

'I will check the rabbit snares tonight,' said Dolphie, pausing to eat a spoonful of his own stew. He smiled at Sophie. 'I am becoming a poacher on my own land, setting snares and traps. Shots would attract attention.'

'How much danger are you in?'

'And you, from being here? I do not know. A week ago, much danger from the soviets, but now the city is under Freikorps' control the only danger comes from rebels who have not yet been rounded up, and deserters from the army. But there are still many of both, I am thinking.' He fed Hannelore another spoonful.

Sophie thought of the men and the women killed by the firing squad in the street. Perhaps they had been the ones who had captured Hannelore ...

But she also suspected they had died without trial. As James had said, revolutions were not ... tidy, with the two sides carefully demarcated by uniforms.

'You must know this land well,' she said, thinking of trapping deer and rabbits. Once, in that far-off land of Before the War, he had wanted to show her the forests he loved.

'Hardly at all, or at least that was the case two weeks ago. My other properties, the estate I grew up on,' he raised his hands, 'were captured by the Russians. Hannelore's inheritance is in Russian hands too. This place was my mother's brother's — my mother was from Bavaria. We came here a few times when I was a child. The woods belong to the estate, for hunting, and the farm to supply the lodge. Now it is all I have.'

A large house, and a farm that could one day be good, that was probably several hundred acres, even more, and woods for hunting. Many would have thought it a fortune. But not for a count and a prinzessin.

She put her empty bowl on the table and glanced outside. The shadows were growing longer. The swans had vanished, the water a dark reflection of the trees.

'Sleep, Hannelore,' said Dolphie gently. He turned to Sophie. 'Helga will make you up a bed here. That is, if you are staying?'

'I am staying.'

'I thought perhaps you would. Helga will keep the fire lit. I have asked Helmut, her husband, to light a fire in the hall too, just for tonight. We must celebrate your arrival, liebe Sophie.'

'I need to send a message to my friends.' Jones and Green might already have picked up her tufts of wool, she thought. Should she tell Dolphie they almost certainly knew where she was? She was about to speak when he added:

'Helmut has sent a message to say you are safe, and will send them a note in your own hand tomorrow.'

She bit back the words. Dolphie should have told her about the message before he sent it; given her a chance to send a message too. Now, and not tomorrow. Was he simply used to taking charge, or was there a reason he wanted her alone, tonight? It was true; she did not really know him. And yet, in a way, she felt she always had.

Dolphie bent and kissed Hannelore's cheek. 'I will come in to say good night, and to deliver Sophie to you. And I will take most good care of her now.'

Hannelore met his eyes in an unspoken communication. 'I am glad,' she said as she curled onto her good side to sleep.

Sophie followed Dolphie out into the hall. The fire had been blazing for some time, for already coals glowed in the hearth. The hall was almost warm, and it was actually hot at the table to which Dolphie led her. A bottle and two glasses sat there, and a plate with eight woodland strawberries on it.

'The best we have to offer,' said Dolphie, with his first trace of bitterness.

'You should give the berries to Hannelore.'

'She had a bowlful earlier. These are my small share.'

'Then thank you.' They were richer in flavour than any she'd known, and welcome to take away the slightly rancid taste of the soup.

'To the future, to the magnificent Sophie ... and to no more misunderstandings.'

She smiled, despite the strangeness. Dolphie could always make her smile. 'No more misunderstandings. Dolphie, you were right when you said you and I have never really understood each other. We need to put that right. We need to ...'

'Shh.' He put his fingers lightly on her lips. 'Let us not talk of the past. We have the present, and the future.'

She nodded, unwilling to spoil the moment, and sipped her wine. It tasted of flowers, and was stronger than the wines she'd become used to. Her head swam after only a few sips.

He took her hand again and kissed it, first the palm, and then her bare ring finger. 'I thought you would be married. Engaged at least.'

'No.'

'But men asked?'

'Yes,' she said honestly. 'Men I liked, even loved. But I'm not the girl I was in 1914, content to share a man's life. I need my own challenges.'

'So I saw, at Ypres.'

'Dolphie, I am so sorry,' she repeated. 'What happened to you, after I left you?'

'A party of our troops came soon afterwards. They missed you by perhaps ten minutes. I was the highest-ranking officer, so there were no questions. I think the men were glad to have a commander again. I was recalled to Berlin soon afterwards, to help try to persuade the Kaiser to abdicate.'

Dolphie shook his head. 'He was so very much out of touch, so dangerous to the future of Germany. But he could not see it. To him it was God who had put him on the throne. He did not see he had a duty to keep that throne safe for future generations.'

'And now he has gone.' She thought of her promise to James. 'Will the Kaiser return?'

'No. Oh, he wants to, will try to, I am having no doubt. But he has no support, not even from the Junker class — the true aristocrats. The people, they blame him for the surrender and their pain and poverty, and they are right to do so, to have been so taken in by President Wilson that he accepted a truce without truly reading its terms. We agreed to a ceasefire, then found ourselves betrayed. But enough politics. What happened to you after you left me that day?'

'I arrived too late to warn anyone that the mustard gas would be used. It was … bad. I stayed, helped the women in the ambulances for a few days, then found a building that was not too badly damaged and opened a hospital, then later on two more, and then places where refugees might spend a night or two and be fed and rested on their way home, or as they travelled to Red Cross camps.'

'And now, as soon as the British blockade has ended, you are selling us your corned beef.'

'How did you hear that?'

He looked at her seriously. 'I am isolated here for Hannelore's sake, till she is stronger. But I have friends in Munich who know what is happening and who send news to me.' He shrugged. 'There are many counts, but few prinzessins. I am afraid, also, that those Hannelore can identify may try to silence her if they know she is alive. But each day makes that less likely.'

Sophie thought again of the execution on the street.

He lifted her hand to his lips again. 'No more sad stories. Drink your wine. There is something I have wanted since the first evening I met you, at your debutante dance.'

Suddenly she was back at Wooten House, 1914, trembling with joy and anticipation. Alison, she thought, darling Mouse who had shared that party with her, who had been her dearest friend, who had died as much from the war as childbirth.

And then, coming back suddenly to the present ... does Dolphie mean he wishes to sleep with me? Before the war that would have been impossible, but here, and in this lonely place ...

Instead Dolphie stepped over to a table. He turned a handle round and round. Suddenly music crackled from an elderly phonogram, filling the room with the Blue Danube Waltz.

Dolphie bowed. 'Miss Sophie Higgs, will you waltz with me?'

The music filled the room. 'With all my heart, Dolphie.'

'And my heart is yours.'

His hands touched her lightly, one on her waist, his other hand in hers. He had worn gloves when he had danced with her in England, she remembered. His bare flesh was warm. Instead of the small steps of the modern waltz he drew her into an old-fashioned one, whirling in a vast oval about the hall, as if a hundred dancers were there with them. The music, rough and hiccupping, still swooped and soared.

Sophie laughed with the sheer joy, the giddy unexpectedness of it. She could have been in a ball gown and Dolphie in evening dress. Behind them there was a banquet laid out with pheasant in aspic and meringues ...

The phonogram music ground to a halt. Dolphie swung her around one last time, but did not release his hold. 'Sophie Higgs,' he whispered, 'will you do me the honour of being my earthly joy? Will you become my wife?'

'Yes,' said Sophie. She smiled at him, trembling slightly. 'I should have prepared poetic words too.'

'That one word is all that you must say. Always, always yes.' He kissed her again, more gently this time.

We have our whole lives to talk together now, thought Sophie, and then was lost in the feel of him, the heat of him.

Once more it was he who broke away. He shook his head, as if to clear it, then laughed. 'We must tell Hannelore. She has longed for this. Before the war, as well. But she agreed it could not be, not when our countries were enemies.'

He took her hand, and led her down the corridor again, then opened the door quietly. The room was now lit by a single candle that smelled of fat, not wax. Helga sat on a corner of the bed sewing. Hannelore nodded to Helga to leave. She waited till the door was shut, then smiled at them, her eyes sparkling. 'Do not tell me. You have asked her and she has said yes.'

'Yes,' said Sophie.

'I ... I am so happy. All was grey and then Sophie appears and now there will be sunlight.'

'Hannelore, darling, don't cry.'

'I have not cried enough. Now I can, because I know there will be happiness. Dolphie, give me your handkerchief.' He handed it to her; she wiped her eyes, then blew her nose. 'I will cry again at your wedding, but that will be of happiness too. Your marriage must be soon.'

'It had better be,' said Sophie, thinking of the way her body responded to Dolphie's kisses. 'We can honeymoon on the ship.'

Dolphie smiled at her. 'I do not think this is the time for a honeymoon cruise. On our fifth anniversary, I promise you, we will sail down the Danube.'

There was a moment of silence. Sophie looked at him, puzzled. 'The ship to Australia,' she finally said. 'Dolphie, your letter asked me to take Hannelore to Australia.'

He nodded. 'But there is no need now. You are here, and the communists have been defeated.'

He put his arms around her shoulders and looked deeply into her eyes. 'You will have all the challenges here you have ever needed, Sophie. You can trust that I am not a husband who expects only Kinder, Küche, Kirche from his wife. Germany needs a Sophie Higgs.' He smiled. 'Or a Countess von Hoffenhausen. Build us your factories, establish hospitals.'

She stepped back. 'Here? Dolphie, your country hasn't even begun to pay war reparations yet. Surely you can see things here will get far worse long before they start to improve?'

He straightened, soldier-like, and stared at her. 'And because of that we must leave?'

'I ... I thought that was what you wanted. That you might come to Australia —'

'And run a corned-beef empire?' She was startled at the incredulity in his voice.

'Perhaps,' she said quietly. 'I happen to believe that producing corned beef is better for the world than Krupp armaments. But there is the Thuringa estate to manage. Other challenges a man like you might create.'

'The world needs both corned beef and armaments,' put in Hannelore diplomatically.

'Perhaps.' Dolphie did not look at her. He took Sophie's hand again. 'You do not understand. The more my country needs me, the more I must stay here. And Hannelore too.'

'But you asked me to take her to Australia!'

'For a time only. Until the world settled, until she could be safe.' He met Sophie's eyes. 'And to come back when she was needed by her country again.' His voice rose. 'Germany has not been defeated. No enemy army even set foot on German soil!'

Except the Russians who took your estates, she thought. 'There is no need to lecture me —'

'Is there not? You do not understand, I think. How could you? I am sure your government does not tell its people the truth.'

'I know that.' She thought of James Lorrimer, the secret British soviets that had been destroyed. 'I know more than you think.'

'Do you know that our armies still outnumber yours, and all of America's too? Your empire did not win the war. We were betrayed into a false armistice, by the lies of Woodrow Wilson's so-kind list of fourteen conditions. By the time the true terms had been drawn up ... such a coincidence ... it had all changed. Germany must give up our lands, our money, disarm. And by then our army had been disbanded and your blockade was starving us.'

'Dolphie ...' She held up her hand to stop the flow. 'I agree the terms are not fair. England thinks so too, but Clemenceau insisted. England owes war debts to the Americans too. Seven and a half billion pounds.'

'And we must pay ten times that!'

Sophie bit back the childish phrase, You started it. You destroyed other people's countries. You are even proud that none of the fighting damaged your own. She forced herself to sound calm, 'I don't want to live in Germany, Dolphie. Or England, for that matter. I don't even want to live the life of a Countess von Hoffenhausen. I hoped we might build lives of our own, with Hannelore.'

'In Australia?' Dolphie made it sound as if she had suggested housekeeping on an iceberg. One infested by cockroaches, thought Sophie.

'A land of convicts and savages —'

'Don't forget the kangaroos,' said Sophie bitterly. 'Dolphie, I'm sorry. I can't marry you. We have ... misunderstood ... each other again.'

'No!' said Hannelore desperately. 'Sophie, you do not know us. Truly. When you have spent a few days here, seen the flowers in the meadows, walked the woods, you will feel differently. This is very much an easy country to love.'

'I'm sorry,' said Sophie gently. 'I know it's beautiful. I'm sure I could learn to love this lake, your forests, just as I learned to love those in England. But it still wouldn't matter. My country is Australia.'

'As mine is Germany,' said Dolphie.

Sophie nodded. 'I thought that when you gave the formula for mustard gas to Hannelore, the date and place it would be used, it was because you put humanity above nationalism. You risked your life to stop that gas being deployed. But we are still of our own nations, aren't we? Germany and Australia.'

Dolphie stared at her, his body motionless. At last he turned to Hannelore. Once again Sophie had the feeling that they communicated without words.

At last Dolphie said stiffly, 'You are mistaken. I am sorry, Sophie. Your coming here, it was in error. You took me for a traitor. Fell in love with me, perhaps, because you thought I was a traitor. But I love my country.'

'But you were going to Ypres —'

'To see the effect of the gas. Not to stop its use, or to warn the enemy. I and my men were to make notes about how well it spread under battle conditions. Sophie, our men had been waiting with the gas for three weeks for the perfect day to use it, one with no wind to blow it back on them, enough breeze to carry it to enemy lines.'

'And yet on that day when the order finally came for it to be released, the gas hardly travelled at all,' she said steadily. 'That attack failed.' At least as an effective weapon of war: it had destroyed men, lives, dreams, families, most efficiently. It had even warned the Allies of what was to come even more efficiently than she might have done ...

It had been, perhaps, the worst possible day to launch the new attack. Why release it on that particular day? Accidental? Deliberate semi-sabotage? And if the sabotage deliberate, by whom, and why ...?

'I ... I don't believe you were there just to gather information.' She had been sure, back then at Ypres, that she had seen sorrow and compassion and desperation in his face.

She turned to Hannelore. 'Dolphie wouldn't have given you the coordinates and formula to give to me if he didn't want to stop their use.'

'That is not so.' Hannelore's voice was cool and precise, though she did not meet Sophie's eyes. 'Dolphie could not know you had a way to understand the formula, much less know what it would do. A debutante, knowing that much chemistry? It was meant as a taunt, once the gas had been released. The English would soon have worked out the formula themselves once it had been used.'

It did not quite fit. Almost ... but if she was not supposed to have found a way to decipher the formula, how could it have been used as a taunt? And she had not mistaken the nuances of Dolphie's letter, hoping she would come in person to Germany.

She did not think she had misunderstood Hannelore's wartime letter either, nor Dolphie's mission at Ypres.

But she did understand this: that if she would not agree to marry Dolphie, to stay in Germany, she could not be trusted with the knowledge of what they might have done during the war. Just as they had not entirely trusted her with this location.

Dolphie had once accused her of not understanding him, but he had also said, 'But I made sure that you did not.' He had played the aristocratic playboy, before the war, hiding what had almost certainly been a diplomatic or espionage mission to England. She wondered what role he played in Germany now. What was his standing in the Freikorps that had rescued Hannelore?

What standing might he hope to have in the new government, with the Higgs fortune behind him?

'Hannelore, will you at least come home with me? Just for a few months, or a year? Till you are strong again.'

Hannelore shook her head. 'I would love to. But now the revolution has been suppressed my duty is here too.'

'I see. I'm sorry. More than sorry. Dolphie, will you have the cart brought round? There is no point my staying longer.'

He shook his head. 'It is too dark for the horse to find its way without a lantern. And a lantern might be seen. There are not just soviets wandering around in the woods, but stragglers from the army. It is not safe to go tonight.'

'My friends will be worried.'

'I sent them a note. I told you.'

'You were so very confident I would stay.'

'Sophie, you need to stay, a few days only. We need to talk again.' He spoke as a count, a man used to being obeyed.

'And I want to leave, now.'

'It is not safe to use a lantern!' he repeated.

She forced her voice to stay steady. 'I don't need the cart or a lantern. I am used to riding by moonlight. The horse will follow the track and road.'

'Sophie, you must accept that I have to protect you —'

'And you must accept that I will make my own decisions.'

He did not answer. Hannelore said nothing, lying on the bed, but an expression impossible to read flickered in her eyes.

Sophie stepped towards the door, then stopped, as Dolphie blocked her way.

She had never been truly frightened before. Not even under fire in Belgium. She had been scared then, but mostly that she could not carry out her mission, not for herself.

She was scared now. She was not even sure what she was scared of — the foreignness of the lodge, the desperation in Dolphie's eyes, which she had seen in almost every man who had fought, who had learned to make little of the loss of life, who was used to the strange moralities of war. Perhaps she was most frightened of her own feelings.

Nigel had been right. This land was so much more foreign than England. She had not understood. Worse, she still did not understand. It was not safe for her to stay, even for a few days, in case she blundered again ...

'Do you give me your word you will take me back as soon as it grows light tomorrow?'

'Sophie, Hannelore needs you.'

Hannelore pushed herself painfully up on her pillows. 'Sophie, do not listen to him. Yes, I need you. I need to think of you being happy. And if that is with your kangaroos ...' she attempted a smile '... then that is what it must be. You have seen my wounds are healing. Helga nurses me well.'

Dolphie looked at her sharply. 'Hannelore, I think you need to consider what you say. Sophie, Helga has made up the bed for you here. You and Hannelore can talk, remember past times.' He tried out a smile. It did not quite work. 'She can tell you what life is like, to be an aristocrat in Germany. My lands may be taken, but not my title, nor hers. Once Germany is stable again you will have opportunities here no amount of money from corned beef could ever give you.'

My money in exchange for your title, thought Sophie, and the deference due to an aristocrat. She met his eyes. 'I think

Hannelore needs to sleep, not talk. And you have not given me your promise to take me back.'

'Hannelore —' he began.

'— was a nice little ruse to get the Higgs fortune to Bavaria?' The voice behind them was soft. Sophie hadn't even heard the door open. Jones stood to one side, a pistol in one hand, a lantern in the other. 'No point calling for the servants,' he added. 'They are a little … tied up at the moment. Miss Sophie, would you mind opening the window?'

'This is an outrage —' began Dolphie.

'I reckon luring a young woman into a revolution so you can get her money is a bit of an outrage too,' said Jones, as Sophie opened the window. A figure moved out of the bushes. Green, also with a pistol in her hand.

Jones gave Sophie a wolf-like grin then turned a harsher countenance on Dolphie. 'You didn't think we would let her go into the unknown, did you? That horse was so lame I could hardly bicycle slowly enough to stay out of sight.' He did not mention the tufts of wool along the road.

'And you will carry her away on your gallant bicycle now?' demanded Dolphie.

'In a car, and we won't be stopping either, so don't bother sending messages to your pals to grab us.'

Dolphie looked at Sophie. 'Sophie, you truly wish to go?'

She longed to stay to tend Hannelore. She wanted to keep arguing till she found out the truth about the information she had been sent about the mustard gas and Ypres, for she did not think she had found it yet. Nor did she think Jones's assumption was correct — that Dolphie's letter had been a trick to get her here so he could seduce her, marry her, re-establish himself with her money. Or at least, not entirely.

But she spoke the truth when she said, 'I don't want to live in Germany. Or — forgive me — marry someone who hopes for a future where he may be an enemy of my country again. Hannelore, may I at least give you money? I brought a draft from a Belgian bank.' She reached into her bag just as Dolphie grabbed her arm.

'We cannot afford for you to leave now. Someone may see the lights! Cars must always be a curiosity at this time.'

'It's bright moonlight,' said Jones. 'I'll drive without lights till we are far from here.'

'You will put us in danger! I cannot allow you to do this.'

'Sorry,' said Jones, not sounding sorry at all. 'But I don't take orders from you. I'm taking Miss Higgs with me.'

'And I will shoot Miss Higgs if you try,' said Dolphie, the pistol in his hand pressed into her back.

Sophie was not sure whether to laugh or cry. Of course Dolphie would not shoot her, just as he had not when they met at Ypres. She straightened, tossed the bank draft onto the bed, then turned slightly so that her own small pistol touched his stomach. A pistol she would not use any more than he would his. But this farce needed it, if she was to leave tonight.

Would Dolphie have taken her pistol, if he'd guessed she had one? Would he have left the knitting needles? Why was it so much easier to imagine shooting a man, than stabbing him with a long metal needle ...

'Are you hoping for a suicide pact where we die in each other's arms, Dolphie? You will need to crank up the phonogram again so we can do it properly, singing an aria. Or you can let me go.'

He glanced down at the pistol in her hand, pressed now to his side. 'This is becoming a habit, Sophie,' he said, almost sounding like the Dolphie she knew.

I must tell James about the bitterness I have heard today, she thought vaguely. There is much in this that the British government needs to understand. The war continues ...

Dolphie released her arm. Hannelore still had not touched the bank draft.

'Miss Higgs and I will walk out of here while Green keeps you covered,' said Jones. 'She can shoot a pheasant at a hundred yards, so I'm pretty sure she can shoot a Hun at five. Or a prinzessin. Excuse my not bowing,' he added to Hannelore.

Hannelore must recognise him from her time at Shillings, thought Sophie. Though Jones had never spoken like that when he was the butler there. Perhaps there is nothing she wishes to say.

'Goodbye,' she said, lost for any other words, or for enough to make sense of everything she felt. 'Take care, both of you.' She was about to add that Hannelore had her address in Sydney and Thuringa. But suddenly she wished to say goodbye forever to this land of war and revolutions.

A thought struck her. She turned at the door, and looked at Hannelore, watching her wide-eyed and silent from the bed. 'Use the money to start a factory selling canned soup. That may be beneath the dignity of a prinzessin, but it may also be the best you can do for your country now.' She did not glance at Dolphie as she walked out the door and into the passageway.

Jones walked behind her, still holding his pistol, as she held hers. But there was no pursuit, just as there had been none near Ypres, more than two years earlier. Even when Jones started the car, the headlights off as he had promised, there was neither light nor movement from the lodge.

Within half a minute it was lost behind them, behind the trees.

Chapter 18

Portable Soup

> *Excellent for voyages of the physical, not emotional kind.*
> *1 lb mushrooms*
> *10 lbs carrots*
> *10 lbs cabbage*
> *10 lbs tomatoes, if obtainable*
> *10 lbs celery*
> *1 gill sugar*
> *10 lbs chicken bones*
> *Cover in a scrubbed copper with water. Boil for five hours,*
> *adding water as necessary. Strain. Boil the clear liquid till thick.*
> *This may take overnight, on a low heat. Allow to set into a dense*
> *jelly. Cut finger lengths and wrap each piece in greased paper, and*
> *then oilcloth. Keep cool and in as dry a place as possible, preferably*
> *in a metal-lined chest, with sachets of raw rice to absorb the moisture.*
> *Dissolve one square in a bowl of boiling water and drink hot.*

Miss Lily, 1914

They drove through darkness, but the cart tracks showed white even in the blackness under the pines. Jones waited until they were several miles down the road before putting on the headlights.

Sophie sat silently in the back scat with Georgina, Green in the front with Jones. Their luggage was strapped behind them.

Sophie did not speak. In truth, she did not know what to say — to thank Jones for her rescue? To reproach him for not following her orders? She was not at all sure she had needed to be saved. The high-pitched drama might have been unnecessary.

Or it might not.

Nor had Jones ever agreed to follow her orders. He obeyed Nigel, if he obeyed anyone at all. It had been a mistake to think that although he played the role of butler and batman, who served both his master and his country, he was their servant in the sense of unquestioning obedience. Nor was Green simply her maid. She had accepted that implicitly when she had heard Green's story. Jones and Green — and Miss Lily — had been involved in 'challenges' long before Sophie Higgs had come to Shillings.

It did not matter. He and Green had extricated her. The job she had come to do — find Hannelore, help her, to see if she and Dolphie might make a life together, was completed.

It was time to go home.

They drove through villages, strangely intact after the rubble piles of Belgium and France, through fields and forests. Georgina dozed, not even waking when Jones stopped to refill the car with cans of petrol fastened at the side. Green took over the driving while Jones slept beside her; he had the talent for sudden deep sleep that those in the trenches achieved — or soon died when weariness made them inattentive.

Sophie slept as well. She woke to pale gold morning light, an alpine meadow, an inn with wooden fretwork and the scent of coffee, horse droppings and frost-rimmed cabbages from the field behind the inn.

'Breakfast,' said Jones, briefly.

'Thank you,' said Sophie, just as briefly, to him, to Green, and then to Georgina. 'I'm sorry. This has not been ... pleasant.'

To her surprise Georgina smiled. 'You never promised me a pleasant journey. Look at the sunrise.'

Sophie looked. Cream and gold rising above an alpine skyline where snow shone vivid pink. Gaudy. Postcard. Almost heartbreaking beauty.

'And there is a sunrise every day,' said Georgina softly. 'No matter how hard the night. An old native woman told me that.'

'She was wise,' said Sophie, then followed Jones and Green to the scent of coffee, to wide, bowl-sized cups of hot chocolate and rye rolls with caraway seeds hot from the oven, spring butter still dewy from the dairy, none of which she could eat.

Chapter 19

It is easy for me to sit here, comfortably giving you advice. It is
harder to remember advice, even one's own, when one is in pain,
either of the body or the heart. But that is when you need to find
your wisdom most.

Miss Lily, 1914

HANNELORE

Breakfast was potatoes, cooked with milk and butter, served in a
cracked porcelain dish, with a well-polished silver spoon.

Hannelore dismissed Helga with a carefully placed and
grateful smile. Despite the drama of last night she felt stronger
this morning, as she had each day since her rescue. Today she
would feed herself.

Dolphie had not yet appeared. She did not know if he was
trying to follow Sophie, or swallowing his failure by checking
his snares and traps in the woods. She had nearly finished her
breakfast potatoes when he opened the door.

She put the bowl down. 'Sophie?'

'Gone. I walked along the road to check they got away safely.
They have.' He sat on the hard, wooden chair by her bed, his
voice emotionless, the shadows black under his eyes.

'Why did you say those things last night?' she demanded
in sudden anguish. 'You could have compromised. Allowed
me — and her — to spend part of each year in Australien. So
many wives spend a part of the year in their own countries, in
Denmark, in Switzerland. No, you could not have become an
Australian factory manager. Never! But she is Sophie! She would
have accepted that!'

'You do not understand.'

'That is right! I do not!' She had dreamed so long of having Sophie as a sister, or technically an aunt. Yes, Germany must always be her duty, but a little time in Australien, far away from hardships and winter — could she not have had that?

'What of the next war?' asked Dolphie quietly. 'Hannelore, you know, as I know, that there must be another, if Germany is to rise again. Germany cannot prosper without the industry of the Ruhr, without the land the French wish to steal from us, if we cannot pay what it is impossible to pay. It may take us ten years, or twenty, but Germany must fight again. And Sophie would be our enemy.'

'But her children would be German. And what could one woman do …?' Hannelore became silent as she remembered exactly what one woman might do, what she had once dreamed of doing, what Sophie had already achieved.

'Perhaps she would do nothing, by the time that day came. Could do nothing, made helpless because she could not be an enemy of her children's homeland. And that would be the worst of all. I could not do that to her. Not to Sophie.'

She would not cry. Her body had learned that tears did nothing but pass the time. She'd had such dreams, until today, till Dolphie and Sophie had shredded them, as cleanly as an assassin's bomb would have turned her parts into splatters of bone and flesh.

Perhaps that would have hurt less than this. At least, she thought drearily, it would have been quick.

'May I have more potatoes?' she asked quietly. It was the only thing she could think of to get him to leave.

He looked at her in surprise. 'Of course.' He slipped out of the room to fetch them.

Hannelore gazed at the peeling plaster of the ceiling. What could she replace her dreams with now?

Chapter 20

I recommend you always travel with Bath biscuits. They settle the stomach, and survive everything from a ship voyage to a camel trek in the Hindu Kush.

Miss Lily, 1914

Sophie forced herself to drink soup on the train two nights later, as well as dutifully eating on the Bath biscuits Green handed her throughout the day, knowing that food meant energy and she must keep hers.

There had been no pursuit, had perhaps been no risk of any; nor had they come across gangs of desperate men, though there had been distant shots during both the days and nights, hunters after deer or rabbits, or men. Once she had seen the decomposing bodies of two hanged women, dangling, heads down, from some trees: a warning or retribution to be killed so publicly then left. She knew from her time in Belgium how long it took a body to go from white to pink to purple to grey then black.

It seemed Jones had purchased the car in Munich. Sophie did not ask from whom, or how; nor did she ask how he disposed of it once they reached Switzerland and took the train to Naples, green meadows around them, white-dressed alps above, leaning cliffs of snow that gleamed icily and seemed about to fall.

The train was Italian, old-fashioned, bare brown varnished wooden walls and pale creases in the brown leather seats, and a single restaurant car where they ate at a white-clothed table, Jones and Green now automatically sitting themselves with Sophie and Georgina. Those in second and third class ate in the same dining carriage, but at the other end, on bare wooden benches, bringing their own cold sausage and bread and ordering big straw-wrapped flasks of a rough red wine to go with them.

Sophie ate little: radishes with butter and a few green almonds. She shook her head at the offers of omelette and braised rabbit.

But it seemed they were not to go to Naples. They left the train on Jones's orders soon after crossing the Italian border, where another chauffeur awaited them.

The chauffeur, a thin intense man with no English beyond 'Good evening', even though it was ten in the morning when he collected them, drove them to the coast in a low-slung green car, onto the back of which their luggage had to be strapped in an unsteady pile.

A rowing boat waited, tied up by the long boardwalk. It carried them, two by two, out to a waiting yacht. Jones, Nigel, James Lorrimer or even Mr Slithersole had decided they would take ship for Australia from Gibraltar, not from Naples, though it had almost certainly been Nigel's contacts — or Miss Lily's — who had provided the yacht on which they were to sail there.

Sophie was seasick, which excused her from meals, decisions or trying to make sense of the past weeks. Georgina and Green spent most of the time up on deck with Jones, looking in on her every half-hour to make sure she had sipped from her glass of water and nibbled a dry biscuit, both of which she managed without heaving.

She, who had once longed to see the world, was content now to face the wall and try to ignore the sway of the yacht. And then at last the yacht stopped, but not for the day and night's respite on dry land that she craved. The yacht's dinghy would take them directly to the quay. Their ship was to sail that night.

Green sponged her clean; she dressed her, as though she were a child, in a pale blue linen dress that had miraculously been steamed and ironed, a matching hat, pale silk stockings and high heels, the clothing that would pronounce her 'upper crust' when she boarded. Georgina appeared, similarly elegant in darker blue. Only Jones wore the flannel trousers and jersey he had worn since Germany.

'Goodbye,' he said briefly, as Sophie stood for a few blessed moments on land, though that too seemed to heave and sway. Above them stretched the orange, rocky mountain of Gibraltar, the white huddle of buildings and steep narrow streets, the bustle of docks.

They had hardly spoken since Germany. Sophie realised she had hardly spoken to anyone, just as she had hardly eaten. It was as if her life was fading as they left the world she'd known for the past five years.

'I ... I hadn't thought ...' she began. There was so much she wanted to ask him, so much to say. But of course Jones was not travelling to Australia with them. She had grown so used to the four of them being together in the past month that she had not remembered, in these past shocked and seasick weeks, that his home was with Nigel. 'How will you get back to England?'

'Sail to Dover tomorrow, then perhaps catch the train. Though I expect Nigel will be waiting for me with the car at the docks. I'll wire him as soon as I see your ship sail.'

'I expect he will be there too.' She managed, somehow, to find her dignity, to find herself. She was Sophie Higgs, and she was going home. Home was the place where you belonged, after agonies like war. 'I will write to him,' she added, 'though he won't get the letter for a couple of months. I'll have to wait till we arrive in Cape Town to post it.' She owed James Lorrimer a long letter too. 'Jones, I have no words to thank you.'

He nodded. He didn't say no thanks were needed.

'Give Nigel my love. Tell him ... tell him everything. Tell him he was right, and that I know he was right. Tell him I send my love to Miss Lily. And that Green is extraordinary and a darling.'

'She is,' said Jones.

She looked at him sharply. But Jones had chosen England; Green had chosen Australia — had not even returned to Shillings after the war. Perhaps one day, Green would tell her why.

And, finally, Sophie had grown up enough not to press, if Green did not wish to tell her.

'Jones …' Suddenly she found herself hugging him, as if he were an uncle or a father. He kissed her forehead before he stepped away.

She forced back tears. 'I could never in a thousand years have imagined that when you opened the door for me that first time at Shillings …'

He laughed. 'If Nigel can be Miss Lily, I can be a butler. It's a comfortable role, you know. So many certainties. If only the world could be organised like a well-run household.'

'They should make you head of the League of Nations.'

He smiled and gave her a half-salute. 'Goodbye, Sophie.' It was the first time he had used her Christian name. 'I very much hope we meet again, and not just for Nigel's sake.'

'We will. Though it may not be for a few years. And thank you, again.'

Chapter 21

A ship is always an adventure. Not invariably a good one.

I advise tipping the purser well the day you board and then not again until you disembark, so he knows he must please you for a good gratuity.

Miss Lily, 1914

The ship was small and squat, her funnel black with soot: a freighter that carried only twenty-five passengers in acceptable luxury. A sailor dressed in a waiter's black trousers, jacket and white shirt showed the three women to their staterooms, facing the upper deck, each still with the label *Officers* above the door.

'There has been a mistake,' said Green quietly. 'I am sorry, Miss Higgs. I will see the purser at once about getting a room below.'

'Nonsense,' said Sophie. 'You told me you sometimes travelled first class with Miss Lily.'

'Only in the east, or where no one might notice. This means I will be expected to dine with you as well!'

'Excellent.' Sophie looked at Georgina for her reaction. The other woman nodded, looking preoccupied.

'Excuse me,' she said quietly. 'There is something I must see to.' She walked quickly down the corridor.

'Jones has arranged this,' said Green resignedly, watching the porter carrying her suitcase to her room. 'And probably Lily. Miss Lily, I mean,' she added hurriedly.

Sophie looked at her curiously. 'Did you call her Lily?'

'We grew up together on the estate,' said Green simply. 'Playmates. It would not have done for the younger son of an earl to play with a groom's son, but Nigel's parents probably saw no harm in his friendship with a girl. It was not as if I would ever be remotely marriageable for the younger son of an earl. I trained as a lady's maid with his mother and then, when she died, and Miss Lily ... appeared ... I worked for Lily. No one asked too many questions at Shillings, not back then, anyway, when people took loyalty for granted and never travelled beyond the next village. It might be different now. It probably is.'

'And your friendship continued,' suggested Sophie, suddenly liking her enormously.

Green smiled. 'Only in private.'

'But you didn't go back after the war? Excuse me if I am trespassing on something private.'

Evidently she was. Green's relaxed smile vanished. 'If you're wondering if there was anything between me and Nigel except friendship, there never has been. If you will excuse me, Miss Sophie, I will see to your things.'

The rooms were large and full of light, facing the sea, not the deck. Heavy mahogany furniture, a wide bed with a pink silk quilt; curtains drawn to give privacy to the occupants from those passengers who passed their windows on the narrow deck. Her wardrobe was already half filled with gowns. It seemed their trunks had arrived. And, thank goodness, the ship felt steadier than the yacht. Already her queasiness was diminishing.

She let Green unpin her hat, then knocked on Georgina's door. 'Come in!'

Sophie opened the door — no one locked doors at sea it was as much an unpardonable lapse of manners as locking one's door when visiting a private house. The room was the twin of her own. 'There are champagne and canapés in the dining room,' she began. 'Or would you rather —'

She stopped, at another knock on the door. She expected the waiter again or perhaps a stewardess. Instead it opened to reveal a woman in the brown silk of a well-to-do farmer's wife, a boy of about four in a sailor's suit holding her hand, looking scared but with his chin held high.

Georgina was already in tears. 'Timmy,' she whispered.

The boy ran to her, his arms locked around his mother's waist. She held him as if she would never let him go.

Nor did she need to now, thought Sophie, blinking her own tears away. Timothy was home.

And Georgina trusted her.

Chapter 22

Lettuce must be folded, never cut, but conveying a large leaf of lettuce to your mouth is ungainly. The secret is to fold it with your knife into a tiny parcel on your fork.

Miss Lily 1914

She could feel the change as the engines beat deep inside the ship, the water washed along their hull. A sea change, she thought, suddenly understanding the term.

For her world was suddenly different. This was not the world of war, of love and espionage and confusion. Nor was it yet home, which would have changed, as she had changed too. This was a place apart, timeless, only this small ship and its contents, the sky and sea, at least until they reached Cape Town.

Such a different ship from the vast luxurious one that had brought her to Europe. She had been a child then, unformed. Yet then she had dressed herself and now she stood as Green efficiently wrapped her in pale green silk lounging pyjamas with matching scarves, the latest fashion for afternoon strolling.

'Will you join me on deck?' She smiled at Green's hesitation. 'No one here knows you're working as my maid, not out of uniform and in first class. I hope you will eat with me — I'd much prefer that to the stuffed shirts at the captain's table. We can we have a table to ourselves. Georgina will want to eat with Timothy.'

'Children eat earlier,' said Green.

'A table for three, then.'

'Are you sure, Miss Sophie?'

'Yes. If you call me Sophie. And I can't keep calling you Green in public.'

'Lily calls me Greenie.'

'May I?'

Green ... or Greenie ... nodded.

It was cool on deck. A steward brought thin cups of hot beef bouillon and cracker biscuits. Sophie ate and drank. Her seasickness had vanished.

They did not talk at first. There was too much to talk about; it would take a lifetime, perhaps, to speak of what had happened in the past couple of weeks, and much else too. A maid and mistress's relationship is often longer and closer than one between spouses, thought Sophie. Greenie fiddled with a box-like gadget, hanging from a strap around her neck, like binoculars. 'A camera,' said Greenie. 'Jones bought it for me.' Was there a faint blush? 'I thought I'd try to take a photograph of Gibraltar from the sea, but I've no idea if I'm doing it correctly.'

'There'll be somewhere to develop films in Cape Town,' said Sophie idly.

'I think I'll wait and set up my own darkroom when we get to Sydney. If you have no objection,' she added hurriedly.

'None,' said Sophie, then realised she was returning to her father's house. But surely he and Miss Thwaites would not mind turning one of the attics into a darkroom. Her father would probably enjoy the technical challenge.

And she would see them soon. For the first time in years she let the longing for her family, her home, her country to envelop her.

Soon.

The seagulls dived and squawked. Small grubby boys yelled and waved on the shore. She waved back. Clouds floated like small mushrooms in the sky.

The ship changed course and Gibraltar was gone.

She bathed, slowly and luxuriously with rose-scented soap, before dinner, then changed into a new creation, dark blue jacquard shot with thin silver silk threads, knee length, for the first night at sea was never formal. The purser showed her, Georgina and Greenie to a small table by the wall. She was glad not to have to make conversation with one of the officers or, even worse, the captain, though he had a kind and sensitive face, if too thin. But the captain's table required formal manners. She needed a holiday from manners.

She glanced at the menu, suddenly ravenous, gave her order, then tore off a piece of roll, still warm and deliciously crusty, buttered it, nibbled, then asked, 'How is Timothy?'

'Wonderful. Incredible. Thank you. I … I don't know how to thank you.' Georgina gazed at her roll, not at Sophie, as if even meeting another person's eyes might bring on tears of joy or relief.

The waiter slipped soup in front of them. Sophie waited till he was out of earshot. She kept her voice low. 'I've been thinking. Once we are in Australia I will be extremely easy to find. If Emily tells William you have come to Australia with me, well, even if we do not both live in my family's home, your connection with me will make you vulnerable.'

She took a mouthful of soup. Cream of mushroom. Wonderful, if a little heavy. She thrust away the echo of Dolphie's voice, talking of wild mushrooms in the woods. 'You will be harder to find — impossible— if you and Timothy leave the ship at Adelaide, then take the train to Melbourne. They say Melbourne is quite civilised, though I have never been there. I can arrange for a house to be rented for you under yet another name. You should be unnoticeable there, unless you go into society.'

'I was thinking much the same,' said Georgina quietly.

'You could be a widow,' said Greenie, and Sophie was glad Georgina showed no sense of affront that a maid might suggest a life for her. 'And if I may be so bold … adopt an older girl, six or seven perhaps, an orphan. That way if an investigator looks for a single woman with a son Timothy's age, they won't take any notice of you. That is, if you do not mind the idea of taking in a stranger's child.'

'I think I'd like it,' said Georgina. 'An intelligent girl, who would like to go to university. Do archaeology perhaps. I have always been fascinated by archaeology.'

'I am sure they'd be happy to make that a condition at the orphanage,' said Sophie dryly. 'Intelligent girl, between five and seven, must enjoy archaeology.'

The soup was replaced by fish, anonymous and white under a green sauce, fresh, though the fish course would be smoked later in the voyage, unless this ship kept tanks on board, as it well might, with so few passengers. She found Georgina staring at her.

'Have I got sauce on my lip?' she asked flippantly.

'No. I have just never known anyone to enjoy food as much as you seem to be doing tonight. I don't mean you are a glutton. Until tonight you've eaten far too little. But you seem to ... to pay attention when you eat.'

'Miss Lily said —' said Sophie and Greenie together, then stopped, and laughed at each other.

'Who is this Miss Lily? Will I ever meet her?'

'Maybe,' said Sophie cautiously. 'She's not Australian. But when you've been in Melbourne for a couple of years, and if no one has come looking for you, I think we can assume Emily has not betrayed your trust and we can all meet again.' She glanced at Greenie. 'Miss Lily might even visit us.'

'Possible,' said Greenie non-committedly.

Georgina twisted her napkin absent-mindedly. 'And if an investigator does find me? Tries to snatch Timothy?'

'We'll make sure neither of you are alone. A secure house, and a car with lockable doors. You will need a chauffeur and a housekeeper, possibly a married couple. A gardener too, and a tutor for Timothy. I'll ask my father to discreetly make sure they know you must both be protected at all times.' Her mouth twisted. 'Sadly there may be as many unemployed men with combat experience looking for work in Australia as in England. I don't think finding people to defend you will be a problem. And with a good car and a capable chauffeur you can drive all the way to Thuringa, if all else fails. Your husband might guess you are there, but we can make very, very sure he cannot get to you at Thuringa.'

'But the law ...'

'He will have to prove Mrs Wattle is his wife. How can he do that in a strange country, where a dozen friends will swear she grew up with them, went to school with them? The constables at Thuringa will be ... accommodating. I suspect my father is also on good terms with the police commissioner in Sydney. Business often requires it.'

'But William is an aristocrat.'

'And we are the colonies. A title is revered, but the police know which side their bread is buttered ... and who may provide the jam. You will be safe,' said Sophie firmly. 'I promise.'

'And I do too,' said Greenie quietly.

A tear ran down Georgina's face. She politely ignored it, took a bite of fish, swallowed it. 'My friends call me Giggs,' she said. 'I'd like you to call me that, if you don't mind. Both of you.'

'Giggs?'

'For Giggles. I was Giggles. Emily,' said Georgina with satisfaction, 'was Podge.'

'Excellent,' said Sophie. 'Though I had better not refer to her that way for a few years, in case she decides to get revenge.'

'Did you have a nickname?'

'Not till I went to France. Soapy.'

Georgina raised her wine glass. 'To Soapy, Greenie and Giggs!'

'And may the world deal justly with us,' said Greenie. 'Or we'll kneecap them from behind.'

Sophie suspected she was not joking. The waiter brought roast pork. And caviar, cheese, chocolate ice cream and fruits to follow. Delicious. All of it was wonderful.

And she was going home.

Chapter 23

I wish I could tell you love lasts forever. It does not.

Miss Lily, 1914

JUNE 1919

HANNELORE

It was good to sit in the sunlight, sipping Helga's mix of wine and milk and woodruff. The swans ducked and wriggled in the lake, not at all as graceful as the swans Miss Lily urged them to emulate, so many years ago.

Dolphie sat next to her, in his Freikorps uniform, though he would exchange it soon for civilian clothes and a new position in the promised government.

'Sophie should be on her way home now,' she said. 'I wonder if she left from Naples, or went back to France or England.'

Dolphie did not reply.

'I have been thinking. You were right to say what you did. Sophie would not have left us if she thought we needed her. But she would not have been happy here, no matter how much we wished it. You said what you had to say, to make her leave.'

Again, he said nothing.

'I need to apologise to you.'

'There is nothing to apologise for.' He looked at the swans, not at her. Only she, who knew him well, saw the sorrow in his face. Yes, this uncle of hers would always do his duty, at whatever cost to himself.

'Do you think she believed us, about Ypres?' she asked at last.

Dolphie smiled wryly. 'Not for a moment.'

Chapter 24

To keep the nails clean, and the cuticles soft, press them into the flesh of half a squeezed lemon, twice a week, then rinse with rose water.

Miss Lily, 1914

The sea turned from blue to green and became an ocean. The sky grew grey and the ocean did too, and white wave tops danced about the ship. Yet this time Sophie did not feel seasick.

She and Green had the deck mostly to themselves, as icy drips of spray and rain splattered the awning. But the deck chairs were sheltered, and the air smelled of salt and baking pastries, not of putrefying wounds or cordite, the ever-present stink of the big guns, which had still not vanished from Europe.

Georgina spent most of her time on the lower deck with Timothy and the other children on board — nine of them, four near Timothy's age, including two boys. The mother of three of the youngsters in first class had sailed to England when their father volunteered, to be nearer to him on leave, only to find that he had been transferred to Palestine. He had been shipped back to Australia months before, but it had been harder for her to find a civilian ship. It had been four years since she or their children had seen him.

The other boy in first class was travelling with his grandmother. His father had died two days before the ceasefire; his mother died in the influenza epidemic. His mother's mother, an Australian, had come to fetch the boy to his new home. His face still had the hollowness of shock, despite his laughter as they played table tennis or quoits on deck if it was not raining, or skittles and word games in one of the cabins if it was too wet or windy on board.

The other children were in second class, but Georgina and Sophie persuaded the captain — who in truth cared little either way — that the best way of keeping the youngsters from annoying the older passengers was to let them play together, despite the differences in class, and use the lower deck both for games and the basic lessons Georgina gave them in reading and copperplate handwriting in the early afternoon. Green even joined them to teach geography lessons sometimes, not just about the places the ship would pass, but fascinating lands like Mongolia with its shaggy ponies, and South America where boa constrictors could eat a man.

The children might yawn at writing 'See Spot run', but by the end of the first week even the four-year-olds could draw a 'boa constrictor'.

And every evening, at dinner, Georgina's face grew gentler and happier, as the distance between the danger and herself and her son grew further

Sophie and Green's only companion up on deck was Mrs Falteringham, the elderly widow of the Reverend Falteringham, who had left retirement to be an army chaplain, lying about his age as so many had to do their duty to their country or their fellow man. The Falteringhams had been once to Australia on their honeymoon '... such an interesting country, my dears. Albert always watched when the Australians played cricket at Lords. And the kangaroos!'

Mrs Falteringham believed she sailed in grief and fortitude, to fill her remaining years with memories of her husband, but with every day of the voyage she seemed to grow younger and gayer. Sophie suspected she would live at least another thirty years, freed from the constraints of being a clergyman's wife.

She sipped whisky, strictly on doctor's orders, until dinner ('For my heart, you know, my dears.') and the best of port after it, again medicinally, for only the lower class of woman ever drank port and that diluted with lemonade. During meals she did not drink at all, for the reverend had been a teetotaller, as his widow maintained she still was, except as pertaining to those doctor's orders.

Instead, she ate, steadily and profoundly, perhaps from subconscious joy at an abundance of food she had to neither cook nor serve. Eggnog with the tea and biscuits brought to her cabin at daybreak; a breakfast of porridge, with cream and sugar ('The doctor has ordered me to build myself up.'), kidneys and bacon with scrambled egg; and toast, stewed fruit, more toast, fresh fruit carefully peeled with a small silver knife. This lasted her till it was time for morning tea, coffee or bouillon, with a small amount of whisky added to whichever of these she chose, and the small cakes and the sandwiches that kept the passengers entertained till luncheon.

It was the longest time Sophie had ever spent relaxing. She had been too young and too excited on her voyage to England in 1913 to even understand the concept of relaxation. But there, watching waves and clouds and the strange flying fish, whole hours could go by without exchanging a word.

It was almost as if in the quiet of the sea, the predictability of ship and sky and white frothed waves, she found the core of herself again. And with that strength, she found she could talk to Green.

It was their sixth day on board. They sat on the side of the deck sheltered from the wind, wrapped in coats, and blankets over their knees, cups of steaming bouillon in their hands, a plate of small crustless sandwiches on the table between them: chicken and watercress, lobster butter, cucumber and cream cheese.

Sophie sipped her bouillon. It was beef today, very clear and very good. 'You travelled a lot with Miss Lily?'

Green nodded, raising an eyebrow in a gesture that was suddenly so reminiscent of Miss Lily that Sophie felt once again the pang of loss.

'Where did you go?'

Green sat back, ready for the interrogation she must have known was coming eventually. 'Japan was the first place. Her ladyship had died, and Nigel had inherited the title then. His lordship sent me a telegram saying that a position as lady's maid had become available and the Shillings agent would arrange all the details. My mother got it into her head that Japanese were cannibals. You should have heard her wailing! But of course we couldn't refuse his lordship. I travelled all by myself, that time, terrified and too scared to let on I was terrified. It hadn't occurred to the agent that even though I'd travelled with the countess I'd never been further than the South of France before, and that with a retinue of other servants.'

'What was Miss Lily doing in Japan?'

'She had made a friend, a Miss Misako. Miss Misako had been one of those Geisha women, a famous one.'

Sophie remembered the highly erotic books they had studied back at Shillings, and Alison's horror at the sight of them. Darling Mouse, dead for years now. They must have come from Miss Misako.

'At first I thought I was supposed to be Miss Misako's maid. I suppose I should have been shocked when I found out I was there for Nigel, and that Nigel was now "Lily". But I'd known her all my life,' said Green simply. 'It just seemed right. Maybe being in a foreign country made the strangeness more natural too.

'Miss Misako had already taught Lily how to move her hands, her neck, her body in graceful ways. That's really how most people tell a man and a woman apart, you know, the way they move, or sit. But Lily needed me to show her how a European lady dressed and did her hair. She couldn't very well come back to England in a kimono.'

Sophie grinned. 'I suppose not.'

'But even after we came back to England we'd only spend part of the winter at Shillings, me and Lily and Jones, then we'd travel again. Jones and Nigel would return, just the two of them, for a few weeks to check on the estate. I took a holiday when Nigel was at Shillings, but never very far away, in case Lily needed me in a hurry and we had to set off again.

'Had to?' asked Sophie carefully. 'The three of you didn't just travel for pleasure?'

'Sometimes we did. Like the time we spent autumn in Venice — it smells something horrid, but, oh, the light is lovely. Mostly though,' she cast Sophie a brief look, 'we travelled as a favour for people Lily knew in government. Egypt, Palestine, Russia, almost everywhere, except India or the North West Frontier. His lordship wouldn't go back there.'

Once again Green seemed to find nothing strange in talking about the one person who was two, Miss Lily and the young man assaulted and left for dead as a novice lieutenant. 'We were useful, you see. Men are always suspected of being spies. But the charming Miss Lily, with her maid and chauffeur? Miss Lily was more likely to be invited to dine than have her room searched. And Lily could persuade the man in the moon to confess how he keeps the stars in the sky.'

Was that how Miss Lily knew James Lorrimer? Had they worked for him, or just had a similar passion to stop devastating war between England and Germany, a war that would destabilise the Middle East and even India, Africa, China and Japan, and so many other countries who might see that the colonial empire builders were not just vulnerable, but might even be defeated.

Should she ask? She had no real reason to know, especially now she was travelling beyond the world of wars and espionage. She forced herself to change the subject.

'So it was always you, Jones and Lily, or Jones and Nigel?'

'Sometimes if Nigel was with us, I'd travel as Jones's wife. But yes, the three of us working and travelling together, for all those years,' said Green.

'Please, tell me to mind my own business if you want to. But why didn't you go back to Shillings after the war?'

'Jones,' said Green.

'But you ... he ...' Sophie tried to find the words.

'Don't get the wrong idea about Jones, just because he ... understands ... about Miss Lily. Jones likes things nice and proper. He asked me to marry him the third week in Japan. I said no then. He asked me twice more in the next few years.

I kept saying no, and he married someone else. A nice proper girl, Edna. It was hard for him when she died.'

'But you are … were … lovers again?'

Green nodded. 'I like men,' she said simply. 'I like Jones. Love him, even, maybe.'

'Then why didn't you marry him?'

'Because I'd have been a wife. No more travelling in the east with a couple of children at my skirt. I'd have had to wait out the war at Shillings, like so many other women waited. I want my own life, not a slice of Jones's.' She gave a grin that did not quite work. 'Jones knows who I am. He accepts it. Not that he has a choice.'

'But surely Nigel could have got you a better job than the one you had. Or given you a pension and a cottage at Shillings …'

'No,' said Green.

'No, he didn't offer?' Surely both duty and friendship would have meant Nigel would have offered Green far more than just a good reference as a lady's maid.

'No, I didn't want to live at Shillings. I did find out during the war that Nigel had settled an annuity on me. I don't have to work if I don't want to. But …' she met Sophie's eyes, 'things happen in wartime. Things you don't expect. I couldn't go back to a cottage in an English estate. I needed a new life. I admit my first attempt with Miss Pokeme wasn't the best of choices.'

'Miss Pokeme? You're joking.'

Green shook her head.

'Poor girl.'

'Ha!' said Green. 'You try getting up at two in the morning because she wants her chocolate creams from the library. Or did she leave them in the car …'

'Greenie, excuse my asking this. Has Nigel —?' The words would not form themselves.

Green looked at her shrewdly. 'Has Nigel had affairs with women? Yes, a few over the years. But he's never had a woman he's loved in England — I'd have known if there were. Nor has he had any love affair that's lasted more than a few months, and never with a woman who knew about Lily, except Miss Misako. He's never asked anyone to marry him before you either. Lily had made a life she was happy with.' The words 'and now Nigel will need to do the same' floated unsaid across the waves.

'Are you going to tell me more about why you didn't go back to Shillings after Belgium, if I ask you very, very tactfully?'

'Not even if you ask every day from here to Sydney.'

'Then I won't waste our time.'

They sipped their cooling bouillon. 'Does Miss Lily know James Lorrimer?' Sophie asked finally. She had often wondered whether these two very different but highly significant people in her life knew each other.

Green said nothing. Sophie laughed. 'You've just answered me. You'd have said no if they didn't know each other. So Miss Lily ... investigated ... for James Lorrimer.'

Again Green said nothing. But this time she smiled.

She owed James a letter. And Nigel too. There was no hurry, for they could not be mailed till they arrived at Cape Town — the ship could send a wire in an emergency, but not a confidential letter. She wanted both written while the events and emotions were fresh in her mind, though, and once written those memories and emotions could be left behind.

She went to her cabin after luncheon, having watched with admiration as Mrs Falteringham ate smoked salmon on brown bread, cock-a-leekie soup, fillets of brill; quails à la financière; roast pork (the chef seemed to believe the human body needed pig at least three times a day), asparagus, prunes in bacon, cherry pudding and cheese. Sophie herself had eaten well, but the salmon, quails, pudding and cheese had been more than adequate. She was plumping out, as Green had clearly intuited she would: her dresses no longer hung loosely.

She nodded politely to the captain as they passed in the corridor. He had made it tactfully clear that while he respected her wish to eat privately and not at his table, he knew who she was and, more importantly, who her father was and what place his corned-beef empire played in the prosperity of the shipping line that owned the ship he captained.

The steward had made her bed and tidied the room, and left fresh biscuits in the jar by the bed. She missed the flowers and chocolates that had filled the cabin on her voyage to England, but of course there would not have been time to have them ordered for her. Nor did anyone, except Mr Slithersole perhaps, know when she was sailing, until Jones had sent the telegram to say she had left.

She sat at the small writing desk, took a sheet of the ship's fine linen paper and dipped her pen in the ink well.

Dear James,

I am writing this at sea, so it will be a month or possibly much more before you receive it, but I do not think there is anything of great urgency in what I have to tell you.

To begin with: I am well, safe and undamaged, as are all who travelled with me. We saw violence, but no more than one might expect at such times. The innkeeper and my business colleagues believe the violence will decline and orderly government will prevail, though they may have been over-optimistic, as peace would mean prosperity for them.

I think they are also too optimistic about how long it will be for Germany to settle. There is enormous bitterness, not just in the aristocratic class but in everyone I spoke to, about the 'betrayal' of Woodrow Wilson's ceasefire agreement and Clemenceau's ruinous demands when it came to the Treaty.

There are too many competing factions in Germany for a settled government to come easily, I think. But I am also reasonably sure that whatever comes next will not be more soviets. Like the English, the people of Germany want food, jobs and security. Politics is only relevant when it helps them achieve these.

I fear the most unsettling element in Germany's future will not be a return of Uncle Alec, which no one seems interested in, much less to want, but the economic repercussions when Germany begins to pay the wartime reparations to France. That is going to make a hard situation desperate and hunger will turn to starvation. But, even then, I think Germany will turn to the military, not to the Bolsheviks, for leadership.

I also have the feeling, as a businesswoman — please excuse the indelicacy of my describing myself in those terms, but it seems I truly am one — that whatever happens politically will not impede Germany's economic recovery. As Napoleon said of the English, they are shopkeepers at heart, or possibly factory owners, like me. Both Germans and the English like to believe that forest and green fields are at their heart, but in reality, it is their factories.

I did try to find Lady Mary the day before I left, but she is on a 'friendship tour' to Russia. That in itself is telling, but it is also something you probably already knew. The Worker's Friendship Club she introduced me to before the war became a refugee relief station, and still is. I didn't find anyone I knew there, and the few who ever worked there that I still know are doing other innocuous things, like studying economics at Oxford.

That is all I can think to say. If you have more questions, I would be happy to answer them, and not just because I too would enjoy our continued correspondence. If you wish, I will continue to write to Lady Mary, but I would be uncomfortable pretending any enthusiasms for bolshevism, and she is unlikely to bother with me unless I do. I am not quite sure how a factory owner's daughter can play at being a Bolshevik without giving the factories to the workers. Somehow I don't see my father countenancing that. I would, in fact, like to leave war, soviets and many of my memories behind, and with every league we sail I feel them further away both physically and from my life.

In fact, I am happy. I am going home and, yes, I know that home too will have changed, as I have changed, but I still do not think that my feeling is an illusion. I have a most unladylike eagerness to persuade my father to let me take a position in Higgs's Corned Beef and I still feel that corned beef — and its potential new canned companions — contribute much to the happiness and security of the world. It is of course impossible to weigh up the

relative contributions of war and espionage on one hand, and corned
beef on the other, but at the very least, believe corned beef can hold
its own when the good of the world is finally accounted.

Thank you for trusting my opinions enough to ask for them,
James. It means more to me than you can know.

I remain yours always,
Sophie

She studied the letter, blotted it then slipped it in an envelope. There was nothing she felt she could add. If anything did occur to her, another letter could be sent with the first. She would probably write to James again anyway, about the adventure of seeing Cape Town, and perhaps observations on the passengers that he would enjoy. An innocuous letter. One from a friend.

Time for the next letter.

Dearest Nigel,

You were right and I was wrong. James was wrong too, if that
gives you any comfort. Dolphie did write that letter to bring me to
Germany, and he did wish me to be his wife, bringing the Higgs
fortune with me. Though, to do him justice, I don't think that
my fortune was his sole motivation. If he had agreed to live in
Australia, I would have said yes. I hope I do not shock you or hurt
you by saying this for, after all, you too found the concept of living
in Australia impossible to consider.

I am writing this, as I am sure Jones has already told you, on
board ship with Georgina, who I have come to like very much
indeed and is now reunited with her little boy, and Green, who is
now 'Greenie' to me too, and we do have the most delightful chats
about Miss Lily. Do not blame us. We both love her very much
indeed and, apart from Jones, there is no one else we can talk to
about her.

I wish I could say I miss England. But every mile ... or is it
league or knot ... that we travel sees me closer to home, to the scent
of gum trees and a horizon lit by sunset hills. Greenie mentioned
you had been to Australia, by the way, though she has not yet told

me any details. Perhaps I will leave that tale for you to tell, because I miss you and <u>must</u> see you again sometime, even if my life must be across the world from yours.

I think, on reflection, this may be a love letter. Not one where the hero and heroine end up in each other's arms, perhaps, the conventional happy ending, but possibly a contented ending, as we write to each other across the ocean, leading separate lives that fulfil us. I wish you every possible happiness, darling Nigel.

Please give my love to Miss Lily too. I miss you both, more than I can say.

Love, always: many, many kinds of love,
Sophie

Chapter 25

Ships, no matter how small, vast or leaky, always have a fancy-dress party. It is best to have a headache that night, or be forced to dance with a man who feels he can behave like a gorilla because he is dressed as one.

Miss Lily, 1914

Mrs Falteringham gave a cocktail party, with small meatballs on sticks and creamed watercress in pastry boats, caviar on buttered toast, and plenteous champagne, because the ship's doctor told her champagne was strengthening. She forgave Sophie and Georgina for failing to join her bridge table. Green she regarded with well-founded suspicion, as a woman — rather than a lady — and not a bridge player either.

Sophie dreamed, not of gunfire or dying men or fruitless journeys in the night, but of factories with slightly sloping, well-drained concrete floors that could be washed with jets of water every evening, and factory canteens with comfortable chairs along each table, and labels for products other than corned beef.

The ship stayed a week at Cape Town, though neither Sophie nor Georgina took advantage of the time to take more than day trips into town, buying the obligatory carved elephants and ivory beads, as Sophie belatedly realised she should arrive home with gifts for all those people she hadn't seen for years. She did at least have a Parisian cloak, never worn, that would be perfect for Miss Thwaites, if wrapped in tissue paper as if she had never considered wearing it herself, and Cape Town provided a wooden box of the most excellent cigars for her father, as well as an ivory and ebony chess set that he and Miss Thwaites might play together. Each piece was an African animal, from the king of the beasts, the lion, to giraffes for bishops and monkeys for pawns.

Timothy delighted in a daily donkey ride, with Mrs Brown, the nanny he had been staying with in England, clapping as he rode past her. She seemed devoted to him. She had been recommended to Georgina by chance acquaintance on the voyage from Ceylon, and had then gone to Georgina's father's home and from there, before the story broke and everyone was watching Georgina's actions, to a small house she had rented under another name within a day's train travel of London.

Mrs Brown made no reference to Timothy's father, Lord William. This was possibly tact, but Sophie thought that it was more likely because she was a person who disliked thinking about potential unpleasantness and so focused on each day as it unfolded. Sophie envied her the ability, a little, but would not have accepted it if the gift were offered her.

'I have two mummies,' Timothy told Sophie proudly as she helped him off one of the rides. 'One is real mummy, and one is looking-after-me mummy. I'm not supposed to mention two mummies,' he added, 'in case other boys are jealous.'

'That sounds a good idea,' said Sophie, taking his hand to lead him to the stall where Georgina was haggling over a small carved collection of animals he had fallen in love with.

'Mummy, are there elephants in Australia?'

Georgina glanced at Sophie enquiringly. Sophie nodded. 'Yes, but not wild ones. In zoos.'

Timothy considered. 'Could an elephant live on a farm?'

'I suppose so. A big farm,' said Sophie.

'Do you have a big farm?' asked Timothy artlessly.

Sophie grinned, knowing what was coming next. 'Yes.'

'Mummy says we might not live with you but we will visit. If you had an elephant, we could visit it too.'

'But it might get lonely.'

'Not if we visit it a lot.'

'What do you think about dogs, cats or guinea pigs?' put in his mother.

'It depends on the kind of dog,' said Timothy cautiously.

'Any kind of dog,' said Georgina, smiling.

'Rash,' whispered Sophie.

Georgina smiled, and shook her head. 'We'll visit some puppies when we reach Melbourne. You can choose the one you like best.'

'Really?' He hugged her, hard. 'You are the best mummy in the universe. Did you know the universe is so big anything can fit in it?'

Georgina nodded.

'Did you know that dogs need friends and lots of room to play? Will our house be big enough for two dogs? And an elephant?'

'Just be grateful he doesn't want a boa constrictor,' muttered Sophie. They were still laughing as they climbed the gang-plank to the ship.

Green vanished for three days, with Sophie's permission. Sophie noticed the ship's engineer was not at his usual table for those days either. Green returned, looking very slightly smug as she set out Sophie's evening clothes for the last night before they sailed for Australia.

'Engineers know how to handle their equipment?' asked Sophie dryly.

Green looked startled, then laughed. 'I wondered if you'd notice,' she admitted. 'Do you mind, Miss Sophie?' The miss was an admission that Sophie did have a right to mind, as her employer.

'Not if it doesn't frighten the horses,' said Sophie, quoting Mrs Patrick Campbell, she who had spoken of the deep, deep peace of the double bed after the hurly-burly of the chaise longue.

'I've managed for thirty-five years with no scandal and no gossip,' said Green calmly. 'Rose-scented soap or gardenia?'

'Rose tonight. Thirty-five years? You started early.'

Green grinned. 'The butcher's boy and a haystack.'

'Was it prickly? Oh,' as Green doubled up with laughter, 'that was not meant as a pun.'

'Yes to both,' said Green. 'You've a run in your stockings and a stain on your white collar. I'll see to them tomorrow.'

Chapter 26

When, port by port, you begin to think, We are nearly there,
then you know the place you are headed for is truly home, either
physically or in the heart.

Miss Lily, 1914

Flowers in her cabin on the day they left Cape Town: roses, with love from Nigel, Lily and Jones, which she cried over, a little, then laughed and showed Green, who had flowers from all three too. So wonderful to have someone to share Lily and Nigel with.

Orchids from Mr Slithersole, and the largest bouquet structurally possible, containing every kind of flower the Cape Town florist might have available, from her father. She could hear Dad's voice say, 'Just put everything in! Nothing but the best for my little girl.'

He sent chocolates too, a four-pound box that she shared with Timothy, one each morning and afternoon, and with Mrs Falteringham, who had now switched to champagne, one glass at mid-morning, one at lunch, one pre-dinner and two as she dined. 'The doctor says champagne suits my constitution better. I have been wondering,' she added thoughtfully, 'if I might take a little house in Melbourne rather than return home to my sad memories. They say Melbourne is quite civilised, and the warmth would be good for my arthritis, the doctor says.'

'I am sure he is right,' said Sophie. Mrs Falteringham would join a bridge club within a week, be chair of the ladies' flower-arranging sub-committee at church and give little suppers, enriched by champagne and caviar, for surely there were doctors as compassionate and clever in Melbourne as on board ship.

Caviar on toast four nights in a row at dinner. The purser must have bought a large tin that must be used up. Fruit cups that held strange shapes among the familiar oranges and apples for dessert. A choice of chilled bouillon or hot at mid-morning, and small cakes, each identical under different gaudy icings, at the captain's tea dance in the afternoons. Sophie did not dance — had not danced, apart from the waltz with Dolphie just a few short weeks earlier, since the beginning of the war. So many of the young men she had danced with having gone forever. It would be impossible for dancing to ever be memory-free again.

This voyage was for looking forward, not back.

Timothy saw a pod of whales, leaping with flapping glistening flukes. It took days to persuade him that not even the river at Thuringa was suitable for a pod of whales. But the sight tempted him to the ship's library, and a book on whales, and Georgina settled with deep joy into teaching him to read from a book's text, instead of simply words on a slate.

And then, finally, a thin line between the sky and sea, and then a thicker line: cliffs and rocks and trees. Australia, though their first port of call at Fremantle was still as far from home as Germany was from England. Part of her wanted to dash down the gang-plank and hug the nearest gum tree, or sit on the dock and listen to Australian accents, almost the same as Sydney's. But the ship was only refuelling there overnight, its cargo destined for Sydney. A few passengers left, presumably replaced by others, who were also heading east.

Sophie was sitting at her desk writing a final postscript to Nigel, to be posted with new letters to James, to Ethel and Sloggers, to the Dowager, to her Goddaughter, little Sophie, now growing up among her aunt's family, and to others she had worked with. She looked up as Georgina burst in.

'Giggs, darling, what is it?'

'He's here,' said Georgina shortly. 'My ... William.'

'But that ...' Sophie had been going to say impossible. But, it was all too possible. It would only have needed a telegram from Emily to send Georgina's husband not to England but to

Fremantle, where she and Georgina, and his son, must make their first landfall in Australia. He need only have bribed someone at the port to show him manifests, and to keep an eye out for Miss Sophronia Higgs thereon.

Did British divorce laws apply in Australia? Would Australian laws force Georgina to return to this man here too? They had to presume they would.

'Did he see you?'

'No. But he must know I'm here.' She took a deep breath. 'He's not just visiting — I saw him go into a stateroom on the other deck. He'd been gazing at the children. Thank goodness Timothy was with Mrs Brown.'

Sophie nodded slowly, thinking. 'He can't be sure which child Timothy is, not today at any rate. A strange man can't ask each child their name, not straight away, anyway. The first thing to do is keep the boy out of sight tonight.'

'But tomorrow! Even if Timothy stays in his room till Adelaide someone will comment on his absence. I … I should have changed his Christian name too. But it would have confused him …'

'And William would still have been able to work out which is your child. He only has to see the way Timothy looks at you. We must deal with William tonight.' She pulled the bell for the stewardess. Her mind raced. It was as if every nerve that had quietened down since France was alive again, her brain working a thousand times faster than before.

The steward knocked and entered. 'Would you ask Miss Green to come to my cabin please?'

'I have a plan,' she added as the steward left.

'Sophie, what —?'

'It is best that you don't know it. Do you trust me?'

'Yes,' said Georgina.

'Can you do what I ask? Utterly and absolutely?'

Georgina stared at her. 'Yes,' she said again, at last.

'Let William see you. Let him see which is your stateroom too. Just a glimpse, if possible, but try to let him see you are scared. Try not to meet him, but if it's inevitable, don't tell him

154

Timothy is even here. Don't say anything — just run to my cabin and lock the door. My cabin, not yours.'

'Yes, but —'

'He's not going to make a public fuss. Not when he doesn't need to. I imagine he'll have a court order and people to enforce it in Melbourne, when he can tell them exactly which child is his. Giggs, darling, I promise you will be safe,' said Sophie clearly. 'Today is Wednesday. It was always on Wednesdays that he beat you, wasn't it?'

'Yes,' said Georgina flatly.

'Tell me the details.'

'But …'

'I need details,' said Sophie softly.

'I would undress and get into bed, early. The nightdress had to be silk, low-cut back and front, and sleeveless.' The words flowed, as if suddenly undammed. 'I'd wait, in the darkness. Always in darkness. It was as if what happened in the dark did not exist. William would come in and explain my crimes. I was not allowed to talk, to defend myself. And then —'

'That is enough,' said Sophie gently. 'Ah, Greenie, excellent. Giggs, darling, go out to the deck. Sit in a chair and watch the scenery. If he sees you … when he sees you … come back here as quickly as you can.'

'But what if he tries to stop me?'

'He won't try force you in public. But Greenie will be with you as soon as she and I have finished here. I doubt he will do anything with her there.'

'He will order her away!'

'And I will not go,' said Greenie.

'You don't know William,' said Georgina desperately.

'I once made a general eat the guts of a dog he had shot,' said Greenie calmly. 'Then I shot him too.'

'Go,' said Sophie softly. 'It will be all right.'

Georgina left, still looking terrified. But that was just as it ought to be. That too was part of Sophie's plan.

Chapter 27

A woman loves her son. A man owns him.

Miss Lily, 1914

The three friends sat at dinner, pretending to eat consommé royale, fillets of Nile perch with sauce béarnaise, quail in bacon, which must surely have been frozen, unless South Africa or Australia had quail too, steak in red wine sauce that Green said must surely be hippopotamus, it was so large and tough, though none of the three of them managed to laugh. Sophie's nerves tingled.

Mrs Brown and Timothy had eaten earlier with the children and were now safely tucked up below decks. Sophie had paid a waiter a large amount of money to stand a surreptitious watch over their door, and another to fetch her or Green at once if anyone disturbed their cabin.

Lord William sat at the captain's table, laughing. He had been drinking whisky earlier, and alternated whisky and wine with his meal. Bad form, thought Sophie. Lord William had been in the colonies far too long. He did not look at their table of women but seemed strangely excited, as some men were the night before they went 'over the top' to win a foot of soil from the enemy, or die.

'You're sure he saw you go to Sophie's cabin?' asked Green quietly.

Georgina nodded, lifting the same spoonful of meat to her mouth over and over again.

Then suddenly Lord William was with them, as the waiter served coeur à la crème with strawberries. 'May I join you, ladies?'

'No, thank you,' said Sophie politely. 'I am afraid we prefer privacy. Nor have we been introduced.'

Lord William laughed, confident, handsome. 'But Georgina can introduce us, can't you, darling?'

Georgina said nothing. She stared at the table, as Sophie had instructed her.

'No word for me, after so long?'

Georgina remained silent.

Sophie rose, Green and Georgina following her example. 'I believe I am tired. Will you excuse us?'

She heard him chuckle as they wound their way through the tables, felt his eyes on them as they left the dining room.

The night was filled with the usual shipboard noises: the change in engine mutter as they moved out from Fremantle Harbour; the creak of hawsers; laughter on deck; and a faint hiccup from Mrs Falteringham with the unmistakeable tittup of her sensible heels as she made her way to her own cabin.

The sounds of the docks retreated. The ship rolled slightly as it headed further from the shelter of the river's harbour. Sophie lay in her briefest silk nightdress, waiting. It must be midnight, at least. Surely he would come ...

The door opened. Sophie turned quickly, pressing her face into the pillow.

'You didn't really think you could escape?' he said softly. 'Where is my son?'

Sophie said nothing.

He laughed quietly. 'You will tell me everything tomorrow. But tonight ... you know what tonight is, don't you?'

She did not move.

'Punishment,' he said. 'I am going to have to punish you for many, many nights. Punishment for running away. Do you know how embarrassing that was? For stealing my son.' The softness had gone from his voice. If one could shriek in whisper, this was it. 'A wife belongs to her husband! A son belongs to his father! You are a thief twice over. Three times a thief. A wife does not steal her husband's reputation. You know what I have to do, don't you? You know what you deserve?'

Still she stayed silent.

'It is my duty! A man's duty to make his wife obey him. You have felt nothing,' he said quietly, 'like the punishment you will receive tonight.'

Clothing dropped on the polished wood floor. Trousers, she thought, underpants, coat, tie, collar studs, shirt studs, shirt, undershirt. No sounds of a one-legged hop to remove socks. A true gentleman, Miss Lily had said, always first takes off his socks.

The sound of socked feet towards the bed. A hand drew back the sheet.

The whip's first bite across the back of her neck was fire. Its second was so much pain that her body felt only shock. On the third lash, she screamed.

'Shut up! Do you want the whole ship's company to hear you?' He grabbed the pillow to shove over her face.

The light flashed on. He turned as Green clicked photo after photo, holding up her small square box. Sophie screamed again, louder, again and again, holding the sheet up to cover her silk-clad breasts, but letting the marks of the whip and the trickles of blood show on her back and shoulder.

Lord William moved towards Green, careless of his nakedness. 'Get out of my wife's room, you —'

Sophie screamed again. William stopped, and turned to look at her properly. 'What the ...?' he swore.

'Get out! Get out! Help! Help!' shrieked Sophie, carefully channelling terror.

'Murder!' screamed Green. 'He's murdering her! Help us someone, please!'

She stepped calmly between the naked William and the doorway, as he tried to fling himself out, then kicked him carefully between the legs, then once in each kidney as he fell. He screamed. 'Lily taught me that,' she added to Sophie. 'Won't even show a bruise tomorrow morning.' She grinned, excitement gleaming, then cried out along the passageway again. 'Please, please, someone help us!

The purser flung open the door, the captain behind him. 'Miss Higgs! What has happened?'

'That man,' sobbed Sophie, carefully letting her bloody neck and shoulder show as her nightdress slipped off her shoulder. 'I was asleep. He attacked me. Tried to kill me!'

'I did no such thing,' blustered William, suddenly aware that he was naked. 'Pass me my clothes, damn you!' He scrambled up, attempting dignity while holding his hands cupped over his genitals. The whip lay, like a bloodied black snake, on the floor next to him. 'I am Lord William FitzWilliam, only son of Baron Lynley. I believed this was the stateroom of my wife.'

'There is no Lady FitzWilliam on board,' said the captain coldly. 'This is Miss Higgs' cabin!'

'I tell you I saw her! I am not in the habit of lying, man.'

'Fetch the men,' said the captain quietly. 'Try to make as little further disturbance as you can.' He looked William up and down, then said, 'With your permission, Miss Higgs?' as he removed the spare blanket from the chair, and tossed it to William to cover himself. He gestured to the bloody whip on the floor. 'This is the way you usually greet your wife?'

'What happens between a man and his wife is no business of anyone else,' said William.

'But this lady is not your wife, and this is my ship.'

'He tried to suffocate me. He tried to kill me!' sobbed Sophie, glad that four years of tragedy meant tears could be called upon at very little provocation.

'Murderer!' cried Green.

'A murderer on my ship,' said the captain. 'Miss Higgs, I will send the doctor to you.'

'Thank you,' said Sophie, hiccupping a little. Green moved to her and put her arm around her, avoiding the wounds.

William seemed to have found himself again. 'There is no proof of any of this. If you try to take this further, who will a magistrate or jury believe? Two hysterical women and the captain of a small unimportant ship? Or a peer of the realm?'

'They will believe the photographs,' said Green, still holding the sobbing Sophie. Damn, it felt good to sob, and not just because the red weals from her beating hurt.

'What photographs?' demanded Lord William.

Green picked up her camera, then moved carefully out of his reach. 'Photography is my hobby. I was trying to see if I could capture the lights of the port from the deck when I heard Miss Higgs scream. I must have kept pressing the button automatically,' she glanced at the dials, 'as it seems all the film has been used up. It was a new roll too.'

'Photographs?' said Lord William incredulously.

'Photographs,' said the captain thoughtfully, glancing at the whip and then at Sophie, and realising, perhaps, that the third of their usual party of three was not in evidence.

'I have a feeling they are not the kind of photos most people are used to. You were quite … excited,' said Green calmly. 'I got at least a dozen good shots of you with the whip. The newspapers will be interested. Especially *because* you are a peer of the realm. Though I expect parts will need to be blacked out for the front pages and for the more sensitive members of the jury.'

Lord William stared at her, all expression gone, at Sophie, the blood running down her arm, as she met his eyes, at the captain, who seemed even angrier at the possible bad publicity for his ship.

Two hefty sailors emerged from the dimness of the passageway.

'Take him to the brig …' began the captain.

Lord William suddenly brushed past him, dropping the blanket. I hope they burn it, thought Sophie with a shudder, after it has touched his skin.

'Do not worry. He cannot escape —' The captain's words were cut off by a yell: 'Man overboard!'

'Excuse me.' The captain ran into the night. Sophie heard the click as the life buoy was unhitched, a faint splash as it hit the water, ropes scratching as the ship's boat was lowered.

Sophie clutched the sheet around her, wincing as it touched her skin. She had not expected this. Ridicule, possibly a short time in the brig or prison before influence got him released, then blackmail — a promise to leave Georgina and Timothy alone until Timothy was twenty-one, or the photos would be copied for the English press, and the American, which was keen on the peccadilloes of English aristocrats. She had not planned Lord William's suicide.

But it would do. Just one more life, after so many millions lost ...

I should feel more, she thought. She didn't.

The doctor arrived, with antiseptic, bandages, brandy and discretion. The ship's boat returned. But they brought no man with them, nor a body.

Chapter 28

*Always breakfast well. If each day is an adventure, you need to be
fortified. If it is not going to be an adventure, at least a boring day
will have begun enjoyably.*

Miss Lily, 1914

'What now?' asked Georgina, her voice still blank with shock but
her body absorbing the scrambled eggs and bacon and a serving
of the potato and cabbage slice included at each breakfast since
they changed chefs at Cape Town, as well as croissants with
guava jam and several cups of extremely hot coffee. 'Are we
really safe?'

'Leave it all to the ship's authorities to inform whoever needs
to know of his death and how it happened. I am sure they will
try to keep any scandal out of it. Emily will, as well, in case it
touches her husband's career. An accident, no more.'

The captain had already outlined that approach to her,
avoiding publicity both for his ship and Sophie Higgs.

'But his parents ...'

'Are a long way away, and can prove nothing, not with the
captain himself as a witness.' She took Georgina's hand. 'You
were not here, were never here. Mrs Wattle has no connection
to Lady Georgina, nor has Timothy Brown and his mother.
In three months' time you will write a short, formal letter of
condolence to his parents, assuring them that you and your
son are well and hope to see them in the near future. I will
arrange for it to be posted from New York, just to add to any
confusion.'

'But I don't want to see —' began Georgina.

Sophie held up a hand. '"Near" may mean six months or sixteen years, when Timothy has taken his majority and is off to Oxford ... unless by then he wishes to have an elephant ranch in Australia. But there is nothing his grandparents can do to take his title away from him.'

'The estate is entailed.'

'Then Timothy inherits that too after his grandfather's death,' said Sophie. 'And there is nothing they can do to change that without the heir's agreement and Timothy, of course, is too young to even begin to break the entail.'

'What if they try to get custody?'

'It will probably take them some time to find out you are not in America. William's family can hunt for you there, if they wish. If they do discover you have come to Australia with me — though I doubt either Emily or their son would have told them that, as they'd need to have given a reason for you fleeing across the world a second time rather than meet him — then by the time they begin legal proceedings you will be living with the most respectable Jeremiah Higgs and his daughter — no need for the Melbourne hidey-hole now — and on excellent terms with the chief justice, who comes to dinner on Fridays.'

'Does he really?' asked Green.

'Not yet,' said Sophie. 'I will think of some other ... suitable friends ... we will acquire too.'

She'd had 'suitable friends' procured for her since childhood: not true friends, but arranged by her father. Possibly they might still be suitable. Probably most were married. Or widowed. It was even possible, as Miss Lily had once tactfully suggested, that once her prejudice against them was put behind her, some might indeed become true friends. 'But Giggs, I think ... if William's parents prove to be good eggs and don't hound you, you need to let them meet Timothy one day. They have lost their only child, you know. Beast or not, he was all they had.'

'They hardly knew him, I think,' said Georgina quietly. 'He was sent to boarding school from six years old, then university and then Ceylon. I think he was just the perfect son they imagined.'

'Then let them continue to think so. Let them believe he stumbled overboard in a tragic accident, that you came to Australia to keep me company after my, er, health broke down after the rigours of war.'

'You're as healthy as a hunter fed on oats,' said Green, neatly eating asparagus omelette.

Canned asparagus, thought Sophie. Interesting. How much profit would there be in canned asparagus. Possibly a lot ... 'William's parents don't know that. But they deserve to know their grandchild ... if they don't try to take you over, or him. And if they are good people, he deserves them too.'

Georgina nodded, whether in agreement or to change the subject Sophie didn't know. 'I have a life,' she said wonderingly. 'I can make a life. For both of us.'

'You have indeed and you will,' said Sophie, wondering what she would make of it. Georgina and millions of other women, widowed and needing to make their own lives, instead of supporting their husbands. Women who had children to feed and clothe, and no pension or husband to help them, their husbands lost to the 'shell shock' and other mental problems that were not officially war injuries so not entitled to a pension. Other women, who suddenly might get degrees, and even enter a few of the professions, teachers, scientists, doctors, librarians, lawyers. Women who might be more than mothers, daughters, wives.

And manufacturers of more than corned beef. But she had to convince her father of that.

Five more days, she thought. I will see him and Miss Thwaites in five more days.

Chapter 29

*I prefer the old-fashioned 'farewell' to 'goodbye'; the latter is too
final. Fare ye well …*

Miss Lily, 1914

JULY 1919

She stood on the deck, letting the southerly wind whip her hair
into tangles. She knew the scent of that wind! The metallic scent
of the Southern Ocean, bringing cold even up here; the perfume
of sun-drenched gum trees and hot rocks — even the waves here
had a known pattern and the sky a blue found nowhere else.

It is the sky that tells us we are home, she thought. The way
the clouds flow, the smell of wind, the colours of the sea.

She had dressed carefully for her arrival: nothing too formal
or too French, but stylish enough so that Jeremiah Higgs
knew he'd received value for his money, that his daughter
was returning a lady. Wouldn't he love Georgina's title? And
Timothy, who was a viscount now. Her father would dine out
on it for weeks … my daughter's friend, Lady Georgina … I
took my daughter's friend and her son out to the headland to
fly kites. That little viscount … do you know he'd never flown a
kite before in his life …

At first the land was too far away to make out details without
binoculars. They only came closer to shore as they neared Sydney
Harbour. Suddenly, there were the Heads, high and protective,
the gap between them looking too small for a ship to fit through.
And yet she did, and the pilot boat that had appeared too.

She resisted the urge to yell to Georgina and Green and Timothy and the unflappable Mrs Brown, who had heard of their change of circumstances with scarcely a smile or look of surprise as if she had always expected the gentry to manage their own affairs in the end. 'Look!' she wanted to say. 'That's Manly Pier! And the ferries! And that's the island with the cannons in case the French or Russians invade!'

Except of course the French and Russians had been allies in the last war, not enemy nations as they had been in colonial times. She settled for, 'Timothy, over there! Pelicans! A wondrous beast is the pelican. His beak holds more than his belly can.'

'Sophie!' protested Georgina, laughing. 'That is ... indelicate.'

'I am indelicate!' They passed the quay, the ferries docking. A tug helped them turn into the pier. She stood by the rail and hunted among the waiting crowds. Too tall, no, too fat, no, not the right shape at all ...

And there she was — Miss Thwaites, looking totally gloriously Miss Thwaitish, grey-and-white haired, her dress shorter and a new coat ... or new since 1913.

But where was her father? Had he gone to buy her flowers or to make sure the motor car was waiting? Miss Thwaites had written he had finally agreed to buy one. Next to her was a young man with one arm, waving, waving, waving with the other at a girl further down the deck who must be his English bride. On Miss Thwaites's other side an elderly man slumped in a wheelchair, hardly visible under a blanket.

Her father.

Sophie stood still, glad he could not see her face. Miss Thwaites had said he'd had a stroke, but 'only a small one'. She'd written '... his heart is troubling him' but not how much. She had said he was tired and missing her ...

And Sophie had not listened. She, who had been so proud of finding out who she was and what she wanted, had not cared to truly think of those she loved most. They had always been there, everlasting, ever stable, and would be whenever she was ready to come home. But they were not. Miss Thwaites was growing old. Her father, possibly, no, probably, was dying.

The ship neared the pier. She forced herself to smile, to wave, saw the moment Miss Thwaites saw her, smiled too, touched her father's arm with so much love that Sophie sobbed, then choked it back. At least he'd had Miss Thwaites with him, to love him.

He waved back, for a second the vigorous man that she had known, his face glowing as if suffused with electric light.

'Your father?' asked Georgina gently.

'My father,' agreed Sophie, scrubbing her eyes ruthlessly with her handkerchief.

Georgina gazed at the crumpled man in the wheelchair. 'It is good you have come home.' She put her arm around Sophie's shoulders and kissed her cheek. 'Life goes on, Soapy,' she said softly. 'Both good and bad. Everything changes.'

'I ... I know.'

Next to her Green, back in servant mode, surreptitiously squeezed Sophie's gloved hand.

Chapter 30

Bread and milk, for invalids

Make this in the bedchamber in a silver chafing dish by the fire so the scents tempt the appetite.

1 glass milk, with the cream not removed or, if necessary, added again

1 tbsp sweet butter

2 slices bread

Heat the milk on the hearth. Then toast the bread on the flames till golden on each side; butter, and cut off the crusts. Slice into small squares.

Place the toast in the warmed chafing dish; pour on the milk, and serve at once, smiling. A little sugar, pale honey, or cinnamon or nutmeg can be added.

Miss Lily, 1914

Sophie sat beside the bed, her father's hand in hers. Papery, rabbit boned, the veins too prominent. The room smelled of lavender and carefully aired sheets and cigars. The latter worried her most. Her father had only smoked in the library or dining room before.

'Cousin Oswald is doing well?' She had tried to get her father to take a nap, but he wanted to keep talking, her hand in his, whispering out all of the last five years' news for his daughter that he could cram into an afternoon. He knows how little time he has left, she thought. How much time I have wasted.

No. Her life in the past five years had not been wasted. Jeremiah Higgs had invested both time and money well when he sent his daughter to England. And he was carefully calculating the return on that investment now.

'Oswald's a good boy.' The words were faintly slurred. Spittle gathered at the edges of his mouth, impatiently brushed away. But although softer his voice was surprisingly firm. 'Works well with Maria now he's back again.'

Miss Thwaites had written that she had taken over much of the responsibility from her father, with Cousin Oswald in the army overseas. Sophie had not realised quite how much authority her former governess was still wielding.

'Miss Thwaites is the manager of Higgs's now?' she asked tentatively.

A smile, such a familiar one she could have wept, except that joy in seeing him still outweighed the shock that this man must have such a short time still to live. 'Maria holds my proxy as chairman of the board. A manager looks after day-to-day decisions. That's Oswald, since he's been demobbed. The chairman ...'

'Dad, I know what managers do,' she said gently. 'And chairmen and boards. I set up hospitals and ran them, remember?'

'Properly?'

'Very properly. They are still operating. You taught me well.'

A faint laugh. 'Didn't mean to.'

'I'm your daughter,' she said lightly. 'Dad, I want to run Higgs's Corned Beef. If I'd come back with a husband, you'd have offered it to him.'

'Ha. Only to a good one. Not that Overhill fellow.'

She had almost forgotten Malcolm, the boy she had thought she loved, wanted to marry. 'The only men I have considered marrying in the last two years would have been excellent managers. But I will be a better one.'

A gleam in his eyes. 'You're very sure of yourself, miss.'

'Because I am your daughter,' she said again, grinning back at him.

'What about Oswald? Can't turf the man out of his job, not after serving his country. Besides, he's done good work.'

'I know. Cousin Oswald should stay as general manager. Dad, I want Higgs to mean more than corned beef. The market for that is still sound, but the army contracts are coming to an end and, as things settle down in Europe, there'll be less of a demand for canned beef. There are even some men who say they'll never open a can of it again after having little else in the trenches.'

'Heresy,' said the man who would not allow corned beef into his household. But he grinned weakly too. 'So what do you want to do about it?'

'We have the machinery, the market contacts. But people want luxury these days. Affordable luxury, something to confirm the war is past and life is good. I'd like to start with a canned fruit cup.'

'What's that when it's at home?'

'If you're posh, it's a fruit salad served in crystal glasses before the meal. If you're not, then it's just fruit salad with maybe a dollop of custard. But the good thing about canned fruit cup is we can put whatever fruit is cheapest at the time into it, as long as we keep it reasonably similar every time. It doesn't need pre-cooking either, like jam would or soup, so we can pretty much use the same equipment. The fruit will cook inside the cans, like the beef does.'

'And after your canned fruit salad, Puss?'

'How did you know there'd be an after that?'

''Cause you're my daughter.'

Why had she thought that this would be a battle? Jeremiah Higgs had obviously come right round to wanting this without her help. Miss Thwaites had shown him how well a lady managed not just a household but a business. Perhaps, too, he had accepted he would not get a son-in-law within his lifetime. And, possibly, he had learned to be proud of all his only child had achieved in England, France and Belgium, even if she had the misfortune to be female.

'Tomatoes,' said Sophie. 'Miss Thwaites wrote to me about the soldier settlement blocks planned near Thuringa. But they sound too small to support a family decently, unless they can find a crop that brings in proper money. Tomatoes would do that. Again, they'd cook in the can.'

'Tomatoes, eh?' he looked thoughtful.

'Maybe asparagus too, though you can get a tomato crop in the first year, but it takes four for asparagus. But asparagus would be worth planting, because soldier settlers will make more per acre from it — maybe ten or twenty times what they'd make from tomatoes. We'd make more per ton too. Might even pay us to give loans to put in asparagus, with a contract to buy the first five years' crops. People will pay luxury prices to eat asparagus all year round, just like aristocrats can thanks to their hothouses.'

'Sounds la-di-da to me. But people like la-di-da. Learned about asparagus in England, did you?'

Once more she saw the Shillings hothouse, saw Miss Lily show her how asparagus must be carefully picked up in the fingers. 'Yes.'

He lay back, his hand suddenly limp in hers. She felt momentary fear, then realised he was simply tired. 'Think I'll have that nap now. Have a talk to Maria, Puss. You can work out things between you. Glad you are back ...' His eyes shut.

She waited till his breathing grew deep and even, just for the pleasure of seeing him. She knew now to store good memories while you could. His false leg stood where it always did, by his bed, even if he would not wear it again. Roses sat in a bowl on the bedside table. For her, knowing she would spend time in this room, or for him?

Miss Thwaites waited for her in the library, sitting at the desk. She stood as Sophie entered. 'I apologise for appropriating your father's seat. Of course it is your place now.'

'Miss Thwaites, darling, that is still your desk. I'll get another one.' She stepped over to hug her ex-governess. The hug lingered.

Miss Thwaites moved to one of the chairs by the fire. Sophie had once thought her the most graceful woman in the world, before she met Miss Lily or, for that matter, Queen Mary. Sophie sat opposite her, warming her feet.

'You've changed more than I thought you would have,' said Miss Thwaites at last.

'War tends to do that.'

'Not just the war. You are … beautiful, Sophie.'

'I was taught how to be.' She took a deep breath. 'I want to be part of the business, Miss Thwaites.'

'Your father hoped you would.' Miss Thwaites's voice had suddenly lost all expression.

'Do you want to retire from it?' asked Sophie carefully. 'If you've taken on the responsibility just because Dad was ill and Cousin Oswald away, you can give it up now, today. Or at least next month, when you've eased me into your role. But if you want to stay …'

Miss Thwaites met her eyes. 'What else do I have? I'm not your governess any more. I am not your father's wife, because even though he is free to divorce now, it would take three years, and he will be dead. And when he is dead I will have nothing.'

'You have this house and Thuringa and me, for as long as you live, because you are my true mother, not the woman who bore me.'

Miss Thwaites put out a hand. 'Sophie —'

Sophie grasped it. 'I am certain my father has made sure you'll be a wealthy woman after his death, though knowing Dad he has probably made it an annuity so your poor feeble female brain can't waste it, despite your running the business for the last few years …'

Miss Thwaites laughed through her tears. 'Yes. An annuity. But Sophie, my dear, I want to work. Not good deeds, though I hope I will keep doing those, but, well, I have found I enjoy the cut and thrust of business. I loved listening to your father talk about his triumphs. Now I have found how heady they are — but no one else would employ me, not a female and not at my age, and I only really know corned beef.'

Sophie widened her eyes in mock outrage. 'Don't you dare set up in competition to Higgs's!'

'I promise I will not set up a rival corned-beef operation.' Miss Thwaites wiped her eyes. 'It is so good to laugh again!'

'Will you stay as chairman, with Oswald as general manager?'

'But what about you?'

'I will be president, which is a useful title that can mean anything we three wish it to be. To begin with, I'd like to use the surplus factories to can a luxury fruit cocktail, and then, well, we can discuss those later.'

'How do you know we have surplus factories?'

'Because the war is over, and demobilised men won't want to be reminded of corned beef for a while.'

Miss Thwaites looked at her thoughtfully, then smiled. 'I think we may enjoy this.'

'It will be more fun than Latin verbs,' said Sophie lightly. 'Will you stay in this house? It truly is yours as much as mine. If my father had divorced my mother,' that silly woman flirting her way across Paris, 'you'd have married years ago.'

'But he didn't,' said Miss Thwaites gently.

'Only because he didn't want the scandal to touch me. Or to confront the pain she caused him. Please, tell me truthfully. I need to stay here until … as long as my father needs me. But after that, would you like me to find another house in Sydney, and take my guests with me?'

'Truthfully,' said Miss Thwaites, smiling, 'I would like this to be a home for both of us. You … I have also always thought of you … as my daughter.'

This time the hug had tears on both sides. 'I didn't realise I'd had a mother till I was in England. Such a wonderful mother,' said Sophie, reaching for her handkerchief. 'I wish I could call you "Mother", but people would ask questions.'

'Maria?'

'May I? Really?'

'Of course. After all, you are quite grown up now. You even cry beautifully,' said Miss Thwaites.

'A learned skill. There is so much to tell you.' About Georgina, Nigel, Miss Lily, the Dowager. Everything, except how Nigel was actually also Miss Lily. That secret was not hers to share.

'Do you think Cook could make us crumpets and honey?' asked Sophie.

'I think so.'

'Then let's eat them in here and talk.'

Chapter 31

Dearest Sophie,

I am so sorry about the severity of your father's illness. Please give him my warmest wishes and tell him how grateful I am not just for the slow recovery of Shillings, thanks to my investment in his company and the wisdom of his daughter, but for his deep kindness when we met so many years ago. He is the best of men and has the best of daughters. If I thought it would comfort you, or please him, I would come out to Australia to say goodbye but, from what you say, there is little chance I would be there in time to say farewell.

Jones says he has received word from Green that she enjoys Australia and that you are well, and well dressed by an expert firm, 'even here in the colonies', though she assures him your undergarments and evening dresses are still ordered direct from Paris, as indeed they should be.

As for Shillings, we do well with the mechanical harvesters and tractors you purchased for us. The men compete happily for the chance to use them. I miss the horses lost to war, as well as the men who led them, as all of us at Shillings do. But this is a new world and we must accustom ourselves to it. Every decade brings a new world, of course. This one simply forced greater change on us than most.

I have made my first speech in the House of Lords, on the importance of the League of Nations, to thunderous indifference. I am not an able public speaker, I am afraid. The dinner table or drawing room is my métier, though the subject has not been to my

listeners' taste at dinner parties lately either. They would rather
believe that the League will make war impossible, despite Germany
not being part of it, it having no army to support it, nor even
the United States of America as a member. Meanwhile fighting
continues in Russia, in Africa, on the North West Frontier and
strikes and rebellions simmer. Perhaps my speech at least allowed
them to close their eyes and nap, for that is apparently what the
House is truly good for.

I wish you were here, not just from selfishness, but so that when
it snows you might make a snowman again, and eat cherry cake
and experience what was not possible last time you had Christmas
here nor during the war and its aftermath — a true country-house
Christmas with Yule log and pantomime and charades and carol
singing and feasting with friends. I miss you, Sophie, but believe
your decision to return was a wise one.

Speaking of your home, and Higgs Industries, I enclose a letter,
for its new president as Higgs's major shareholder, or rather its
major minor one. I have found it advisable to keep ammunition
handy, no matter how remote the chance it will be needed.

Jones does not send his love, being Jones, but would if he did
not feel it inappropriate.

From me, love always,
Nigel

Mr Jeremiah Higgs, founder and proprietor of Higgs's Corned
Beef, now officially Higgs Industries, died on 15 December 1919.

His funeral cortege stretched six city blocks, the horses
in black plumes, his daughter, Miss Sophie Higgs, her
companion, Lady Georgina FitzWilliam, her companion's
son, the Viscount Lord Timothy FitzWilliam, and Miss Maria
Thwaites in the car behind. Mr Higgs's friends spoke of his
enterprise, forward thinking and kindness. The women in his
life said nothing, as was appropriate at a funeral, and very few
noticed Lady Georgina freshening their cups of tea with small
nips from a silver flask.

Then it was over.

The cicadas sang as loudly as the choir as Jeremiah Higgs's body was lowered into the earth. The sky shimmered with the heat haze and the faint tinge of bushfire smoke about the Blue Mountains that meant an Australian summer; and every worker at Higgs Industries was given two days off work to mourn — and if they spent it sleeping or playing cricket or went to the beach, all the better, said the president, before she retired to the study with Green, Georgina and Maria to cry.

Women cry best together, thought Sophie, a skill few men had learned, just as they knew that tea was comforting, especially accompanied by crumpets with honey.

And that life went on.

Chapter 32

*Pockets are essential, not at your waist or hips, which will spoil
the line of your outfit, but tucked into petticoats, or, at court, your
train. Many a lady-in-waiting has been sustained by sandwiches
and brandy discreetly retrieved while the presentation queue
stretched for hours before the queen. I prefer petticoat pockets, but
what is secreted there is less accessible in public.*

Miss Lily, 1914

BAVARIA, GERMANY, DECEMBER 1919

HANNELORE

And life went on, it seemed, even when you assumed you had
lost it several times over. Her beloved Germany continued,
spluttering from crisis to crisis. But despite the political and
economic dramas that Dolphie was once more caught up in,
that made it seem as if the nation would split into the separate
kingdoms it had been until only the previous century, Hannelore
felt that her country would continue.

Aristocracy would too. The Kaiser might have fled, pushed,
rejected, but a prinzessin was still a prinzessin, not just in the
eyes of Dolphie's political allies, who naturally regarded high
birth with respect, but the others who called at the hunting lodge
now that order had been restored — or at least one's life was
not now immediately under threat from political assassination
or casual rape and murder.

She managed a walk out into the sunlight each day, feeble
as the winter sun itself, which managed only half an hour of

snow-drenched light — all she could manage too. She wore fur coats that were fifty years old, perhaps, that had been wrapped in linen bags in the attic to keep them from moths, forgotten by an aunt or even great-aunt. She also wore Sophie's bank draft, tucked in a pocket in her underwear.

Dolphie had not spoken of it, or of Sophie. Hannelore knew he had hoped Sophie's fortune might re-establish them, after his marriage to her. She would feel no shame at using his wife's money and nor would Sophie — a title and a fortune were a fair and well-established exchange. But to have that money thrown carelessly on a shabby bed by a woman who would not marry him must humiliate him deeply.

And of course, he loved her. Who could not love Sophie?

But the bank draft was hers. A man able to forge a career in this post-war world could afford pride. Hannelore could not. She also had her duty.

And so she planned, as she sat rugged up on the steps of the lodge, or huddled by the fire in the one small room that could be kept warm. She thought of Sophie. She thought of Higgs's Corned Beef.

Slowly the way ahead grew clear. A life, a small way to help those whom she loved, which included her entire country, and, as Sophie said, all humankind.

And when I have done this, she thought, shivering despite the fur coat, the fire and the rugs, I can write to Sophie.

Chapter 33

A new decade should be exciting. I have never found the first year of a new decade remarkable. Perhaps I failed to notice.

Miss Lily, 1914

FEBRUARY 1920

SOPHIE

Sophie looked up at Cousin Oswald from where she sat at her desk, then took the plain white envelope he offered her.

'My resignation,' said Cousin Oswald.

'But why? Cousin Oswald, if I have said anything that might make you feel we do not value you —'

'Not value me!' The New Zealand accent was stronger, either from indignation or because he had served in a New Zealand unit during the war. 'Miss Higgs —'

'Cousin Sophie.'

'Miss *Higgs*, I admit your Miss Thwaites was invaluable during the war. Many women were invaluable during the war. But the men who served their country deserve their jobs again.'

'Cousin Oswald, your job is waiting for you. General manager of Higgs Industries.'

'With two women as my superiors! I would be a laughing stock.'

'Not as your superiors,' said Sophie evenly. I am doing this all wrong, she thought. He has come to confront me, and I am attacking back. Miss Lily taught me better than that.

She smiled at him, slowly, carefully. 'It is so good to be home, isn't it?' she said softly. 'No more mud. No more rockets in the night. I never want to see fireworks again.'

The smile was reluctant. 'Yes, well, I must say I feel the same.'

'Who have been our main beef suppliers?'

'We buy what's cheapest at the market,' he said automatically. 'Apart from what our own farms produce.'

'And the price of cattle will go down. How much can we afford to lower the cost of corned beef and still make a profit?'

'We can't,' he said flatly.

We, she thought. I've hooked you, Cousin Oswald.

'Then how about we use the factory capacity for other lines? There is a young man who badly needs a job, Cousin Oswald. You may even have met him in France. Johnny Slithersole.'

'Young Johnny? We met on leave in Paris.' He grinned. 'I reckon half the army met the other half on leave sometime or other in Paris. But we got to talking about home, and that led to corned beef.'

'I won't ask you what else you got up to.'

'I married her,' said Cousin Oswald, grinning.

'What? Why didn't Dad tell me you were married? Congratulations! I am so glad. What is her name? When will we meet her?'

'Her name is Gladys.' His smile was open and relaxed now. 'Couldn't tell anyone. Gladys was a VAD. Would have lost her job if anyone knew she was married. She's trying to get a berth to Australia.'

'Telegraph Mr Slithersole, and I'll telegraph the Earl of Shillings — between the two of them they'll have the contacts to get our Gladys on the next ship to Australia.'

'Cousin Sophie —'

'You won't really leave us, will you, Cousin Oswald? You would be in complete control of the corned-beef side of the business. Miss Thwaites will just have a general role as chair, like my father had.' Which had been, in fact, complete control — but only when Jeremiah Higgs felt like taking it. But appearances mattered now, more than the reality. Sophie could trust Miss Thwaites's tact when it came down to making decisions.

'Johnnie Slithersole will be in charge of the new lines — he's been setting up a canning factory for a village in Belgium. I'll be "research and development —"' a new phrase she had acquired via America, and wonderfully vague it was too " — and the title of president, everyone knows that the general manager is the heart of Higgs Industries, and you are general manager of Higgs, Cousin Oswald. I just inherited it.'

'But the investors?'

Were in fact only one man, who owned only ten per cent of the company, and so had no say in how it was run. But the opinion of the Earl of Shillings mattered, as Nigel had suspected it would. Sophie opened the desk drawer, and handed Cousin Oswald the letter in its embossed envelope.

Cousin Oswald opened it cautiously, a man not used to linen paper, with an earl's seal.

> To Whom It May Concern
>
> Miss Sophie Higgs has operated three hospitals, two refugee centres, and undertaken the restoration of the Shillings estate in the months before I was demobilised. Her business acumen is unrivalled. If our generals had her organisational skills, the war would indeed have been over by Christmas, or, more likely, never fought at all.
>
> It would be a pleasure and privilege to serve with her in any capacity whatsoever.
>
> Yours faithfully,
> Nigel Vaile, Earl of Shillings

'My word,' said Cousin Oswald.

Sophie grinned. 'Would your wife enjoy a few days in the English countryside at Shillings before she sails?'

Trevor Scales, manager of the Darlinghurst factory, was not as easily swayed. Nor would a title have impressed him. Sophie did not even try.

He stood, arms akimbo, built like an outback dunny, looking down at her in what was now decidedly her desk at the factory. 'A woman's place is in the kitchen. And what's luxury fruit cocktail when it's at home?'

'Delicious. I'm sorry you feel like this, Mr Scales.' In that moment she tired of playing games with sulky men. 'I will not insist on two weeks' notice.'

He stepped back in shock. 'You're firing me! A chit like you. We'll see what Mr Oswald has to say about this.'

Cousin Oswald would back her, of course. But for this to work she had to be able to give orders without the backing of someone whose only real claim to greater authority was the ability to grow a moustache, at least before the age of fifty.

The easiest solution was to fire Mr Scales. Now, and very publicly. There were lines of men who'd take his job in a trice, she thought.

But Trevor Scales had served at Gallipoli till he'd lost two fingers in a Blighty One, said a whisper that sounded almost like Miss Lily's voice. He won't find it easy to get another job, and certainly not one that paid as well as this. You owe him tact and kindness.

Sophie sighed inwardly, smiled, and began again. 'It is good to be home again, isn't it, Mr Scales?' She imagined Miss Lily's laughter as Mr Scales automatically smiled back.

Chapter 34

My very dear Nigel,

It was so good to get your letter. I am very glad you and your colleagues finally convinced the government to let the Irish hunger strikers go. Their cause is a just one, as you showed me in my ignorance all those years ago.

Thank you for your Luxembourg recommendation. I would never have thought of contacting them. I think the connection is going to be a useful one. I would very much value your advice again, this time on a business matter. It probably has not reached the English papers, but the Arbitration Commission here has informed women workers they should not receive the same pay as men do for equal work the commission says this is for their own good, as it would result in women being replaced by men. The National Council of Women in Victoria has asked that female public servants receive four-fifths of the male wage, instead of just over half.

I would of course like to give all the women in our employ equal wages, but Miss Thwaites pointed out that, although unjust, the Arbitration Commission had a point. Neither she nor I hire the factory workers, but depend on the factory managers to do so, and equal wages might deprive women who desperately need the work. Do you think four-fifths is an acceptable compromise?

It took a year for Sophie to visit each factory, unaccompanied by Cousin Oswald or Johnny Slithersole, and to convince managers and staff to treat her as a businessman, not a woman. One day, as Maria said, the term 'businesswoman' would not sound ridiculous. But just now the mere task of establishing herself as her father's heir took work, especially as she was taking Higgs Industries far beyond corned beef.

It took another year to set up reliable supplies of fruit for the new 'luxury fruit cup' line, travelling by ship up the coast of New South Wales and Queensland to deal directly with the farmers herself, instead of depending on the wholesaler markets in Sydney where neither supply nor price were under her control. The system of buying directly from the farmers had worked for corned beef, and she saw no reason to change it. By the third year she had her tomato supplies, and a new factory at Thuringa as the soldier settler blocks were taken up, their fences and their Spartan houses built, their crops put in, the wallabies and cockatoos and bower birds deterred, and the remnant after the January hail storms finally harvested. But the price per pound was good. The crop may have been far less than expected, but the profit was enough for the new farmers to survive, and hope for more next year.

The profit was enough for Higgs Industries, too — just enough. Sophie was glad the Luxury Fruit Cup had been such a success. It gave her the confidence to extend the loans to soldier settlers willing to take the long-term risk of planting asparagus.

The challenge of widening Higgs Industries beyond corned beef, as well as proving to the business world that she indeed ran the company and was not just a decorative adjunct for Cousin Oswald and Johnny Slithersole satisfied her intellectually, and emotionally as well. She was indeed what she had longed to be — her father's daughter. She was glad he had known it too, in the end.

Personally, she supposed that she was happy. The 'suitable friends' had melted into lives that did not mesh with hers. But she had Maria's friendship, conversations over dinner that might range from widows' pensions to Xenophon's retreat from Persia two and a half thousand years before, a curiously relaxing way of applying the strategy she had learned in the last war to ancient battles. She wondered if her father had found the same in Maria's company.

Green now took the position Maria Thwaites once had, existing in a never quite defined world between servant and friend. It would not work in most homes. It did in Sophie's. Green had even been to Persia, though she was tactfully silent about the reason why. She and Maria discussed the ruins of Babylon, the latest Paris fashions, and even, on quiet nights before the fire, stories of grandmothers knitting secret codes on Belgian railway stations, adding a knot for each carriage of troops. Maria Thwaites was a woman who understood how an organisation like La Dame Blanche might achieve so much, and yet be so forgotten.

Sometimes, in the candlelight Sophie almost felt she might look up and see Miss Lily sitting with them, or would hear her voice, rich in insight and amusement. Each time she felt the cold leagues of ocean between them. And yet even if she had stayed in England, would Miss Lily have been there? Perhaps if she had married Nigel their marriage would have banished her forever ...

Dinners with Georgina and Timothy were more lively. Georgina played well, not just piano concertos but music-hall numbers. Green taught Timothy to dance the polka, and country dances she had danced as a child and young woman at Shillings.

Georgina and Timothy and Mrs Brown still stayed at the house when they were in Sydney. But Georgina had taken with unsurprising ease to a managerial role at Thuringa, three times its pre-war size since Jeremiah Higgs had bought the Overhills' neighbouring property, Warildra. Mr Overhill, senior, was still MP for Bald Hill. His wife and son now lived with him at their Melbourne house to be close to Federal Parliament, still based there while the new capital city of Canberra was being built. There was no flaunting of Sophie's dinners and even breakfasts with the queen to Mrs Overhill on the rare times Sophie had time to visit the property now, nor the chance to impress her by introducing, 'My dear friend, Lady Georgina and her son the viscount.'

Indeed Bald Hill had seemed to quickly forget Georgina's 'ladyship', except when introducing her to strangers. She was Georgie to the stockmen, and Gina to the vicar's daughter. Australians had a way of using nicknames to make people their own. Timothy was Tim, his chief claim to fame not his title but his amazing ability for one so young to bat. He'd be playing at Lords one day, gossip declared, and none even thought of the House of Lords as they said it.

Sophie missed Giggs's company. She loved Timothy as well; he was questing and enquiring and, to her and Georgina's relief, nothing in temperament like his father, loving animals with a deep and fascinated gentleness. At times she woke, feeling her arms empty, admitting at two am that she would like a child herself. But how could she explain Sophie Higgs to a prospective husband, even if there had been one, which there was not. Theirs was a household of women, each of whom had their own reasons for not marrying, or in Georgina's, not marrying again, and none of whom quite fitted the role of a woman of the 1920s.

This was a decade of serious gaiety, not fulfilment in work. The young women of Sydney cast themselves into the new decade by flattening their chests and wearing jazz garters. They danced the Black Bottom to forget the boys almost every family had lost and the marriages one woman in three of them would never have. More than sixty thousand young men lost from one small nation at the end of the world.

Women danced in the new nylon stockings even a shopgirl could afford while jazz bands played, even if it meant a four-hour walk home after the trams stopped running, carrying their dancing shoes in brown paper bags. Polyester dresses aping silk, gaily pretending joy. Young people pretending war had not happened, would not happen, trying to forget, forget.

Sophie could not forget. Work saved her. Her father's challenge, to feed the world with good corned beef, now joined with canned tomato soup, chicken and vegetable soup — chooks at least survived on the miserable soldier blocks — as well as canned luxary tomatoes and Her Luxury Fruit Cup and, by

1925, canned asparagus spears, exported, via England, to sixteen countries.

Each time she wrote to Nigel she was proud of the achievements she could list. He, at least, understood that contracts did not just mean money for those associated with Higgs, but that new enterprises meant food and jobs for those who needed them.

Her world was strangely simple now, despite letters and telegrams and business dealings across the world; living once again in the house she had grown up in; working each day in the office with Cousin Oswald; and supervising her factories with young Slithersole, a century older than his father in terms of anguish watched and endured, happier here at the end of the earth, far away from the mud of the Somme.

In dreams, her feet still walked in blood.

Sometimes, after a 'push', twenty thousand killed, the laden ambulances rumbling back and forth in journey after journey, the operating theatre floor so slippery with blood and pulped flesh it seemed impossible that any man could be left alive.

And yet they had saved men. Many men. She must hold on to that. Move on from that ...

A choko factory ... there had to be something you could do with choko. Not chutney, that needed pre-cooking — and vats of boiling jam or chutney made for a dangerous factory. There had never been a death at Higgs, which no other factory could boast.

Mock Turtle soup, perhaps, with tarragon for flavour, cream for succulence and choko for bulk ... plans for choko blocked away four am memories more securely than dance clubs or ice-skating rinks or the flickering of phantom shadows at the pictures.

At other times she dreamed of waltzing with Dolphie in a forest, the music beating time with both their hearts — but monsters lurked among the branches. Despite the joyousness of the dance she was glad to wake. Often, sitting at her desk in what had been her father's office, or his study at the Sydney house, she imagined Nigel with her, or Miss Lily, held silent conversations with them, was comforted by Miss Lily's laugh, or Nigel's conviction Sophie Higgs could achieve whatever she determined she would do. Then once again she would turn to work.

There was always a job for an ex-serviceman at Higgs factories. A man could sweep a factory floor with one leg of flesh and one of wood, could check labels with a good hand and a hook, could breathe in the clear air of Bald Hill if his lungs would no longer survive the smog of Sydney, for even Sophie could not create a factory that did not make too much foul smoke.

And if there were no jobs she would create another factory and another. Sophie Higgs could not save the world, or ten thousand men from mustard gas.

But she could do this.

Friendship and the world beyond Australia came in letters during the first half of the 1920s, in Nigel's elegant hand — which was not quite the same as the writing in the few notes Miss Lily had sent her, and which she'd kept. Ethel sent letters that did not quite hide her envy at Sophie's freedom in the business world — her father and brother still denied her any role in Carryman's Cocoa — as well as details of her journeys on motorbike through England, Wales and Scotland, and even Ireland despite the growing violence. Sophie read the adventures aloud to her companions, but not the passages of regret. Hilarious screeds from Sloggers, at Oxford, letters she read out in full at breakfast. Even the first cemented Sloggers's place in Maria's and Georgina's hearts.

Darling Soapy,

Well, I am finally in residence! Oxford is full of demobilised officers with scholarships, moustaches and a mighty disdain for any female who dares to don the robes of an undergraduate. Most of them were on the general staff and the nearest they came to a Hun was a spot of lunch in Paris. I imagine we'll get the real soldiers in a year or two, when they feel up to creating new lives for themselves, the men with nightmares and that look of wondering what danger is over their shoulder.

Did you read that glorious speech by the Bishop of London, officially giving the church's blessing for higher education for women, but reminding us we are 'all destined to be the wives of some good man'? He didn't specify which man is to be blessed with five thousand well-educated wives or where he is to be found, so let me know if you hear of him. None of the blighters here is worth a second look. It is a good thing I actually want a career, though I have to admit, just sometimes, the thought of a career AND a loving husband would be nice. But then one can't have both, so the career it must be.

Fascinating philosophy lecture yesterday …

The letters from the Dowager Duchess of Wooten were written by her secretary — as her arthritic hands could no longer hold a pen — about the estate, the family, about darling little Sophie, whose exploits also reached her in Doris's carefully written notes. Increasingly the Dowager wrote as if Sophie shared the memories of long ago. 'Do you remember when Alison fell out of the tree? Such a to do …' Sophie did not correct her in her return letters, for who else had the old woman now to share her memories with? The curse of old age, as the companions of your youth left you. Did the Dowager still write to Miss Lily? She could not ask — misplaced words to the wrong people from a confused old woman might irreparably damage Nigel's reputation. But she hoped that, just perhaps, the Dowager still recieved notes from Lily, and that Miss Lily too could sometimes exist in letters to her oldest friend.

James Lorrimer wrote, as he had promised, impersonal letters that she treasured for the insights — and inside information — the newspapers could not provide, not even the English papers she now had delivered. Now newspaper would risk worrying its readers and advertisers by describing how the 1920 Treaty of Trianon had not just re-drawn the map of Europe, destroying four empires, the German, Russian, Austrian and Turkish, removing old boundaries, but had bred new resentment. 'We are still essentially at the November 1918 ceasefire,' wrote James.

'Too tired to keep fighting, but a long way from peace. France will not be satisfied with anything less than the destruction of all German industry and armaments, and as you saw, Germany has been left with nothing but dreams of revenge. One day those dreams will be made real, not this year, or next year, but in our lifetimes.'

Both Nigel's and James's 1920 letters described the Polish army finally turning back the Bolsheviks at the gates of Warsaw, and the Indian National Congress's vote to follow Mahatma Gandhi's policy of non-violence, a concept that Green, Georgina and Maria agreed was both deeply interesting (if it worked), while Timothy wondered if Gandhi had his own elephant.

The letters of 1921 were about how the billions of pounds demanded of Germany, plus the tax on German imports, had driven the Bavarian extreme nationalists and the communists into an alliance calling for union with Soviet Russia against the Western powers. Each man spoke of the same events, and the same political viewpoints, but neither mentioned the other's name. Had James Lorrimer only known Miss Lily, the useful 'cousin of the Earl'?

'Probably,' said Green, when Sophie asked her. 'Nigel told precious few about him and Lily. I doubt James Lorrimer was one of them.'

Sophie had thought that Green might be bored with sedate Sydney life, without even the challenge of claiming and expanding a business to occupy her. She waited all that first year for Green to resign. But Green seemed content, even happy. Perhaps her own nightmares were as strong or worse than Sophie's. Sydney might be limited, but it was a long, safe way from the land of war and memories.

A year passed, and another. Each day when the letters were brought to the breakfast table Sophie looked for one from Germany. None arrived, though Sophie's banker's draft had been cashed six months after she had arrived home. Sophie was sorry not to hear from Hannelore, but not surprised. She did not write herself in case a letter from a former enemy might hurt her friend or Dolphie in whatever life they had fashioned now. By the end of the second year Sophie stopped looking for a letter. The portraits James and Nigel painted of life in Germany were of a land where even a prinzessin would struggle to survive, and foreign friendships would bring perhaps deadly retaliation.

James even wondered — to her, at least, and in the discretion of a letter that would only be read far across the world — if Lloyd George truly believed that Germany could pay, as he claimed, or was he merely playing to the gallery — and which was worse. British, French and Belgian troops entered Germany to enforce repayment. Germany had offered to pay half what had been proposed, but at last agreed, rather than face continued occupation.

Skirts grew shorter and so did sleeves, which then vanished altogether.

Another year, and in 1922 the Irish were at last offered a free state. Twenty-four thousand fascists and Blackshirts marched on Rome, installing Il Duce, Benito Mussolini, as fascist dictator of Italy. In Britain in 1924, army, navy and air force reserves were called in to act against the national strike — which was in any case called off at the last minute when railway and transport unions refused to support the miners.

As James had predicted back in 1919, support for a soviet-style government had dwindled, but Britain remained rent by growing inequality and desperation.

There seemed so little to write to James and Nigel in return, from this land at the bottom of the world, where poverty meant your children would go without shoes or education, but anyone who could trap a rabbit or grow tomatoes would not starve, nor freeze in the mild winters, not even in a shanty made of kerosene tins or third-hand corrugated iron. Bungalows had sprung up like mushrooms around every train station, and these new 'suburbs' catered for the six-hundred-pound war-service loans with houses with an inside bathroom, two or even three bedrooms, on planned estates of quarter acres, where families could live in middle-class respectability without any servants, or even a gardener, though few turned away ex-servicemen who offered to mow lawns, plant a vegetable garden, or wash windows.

Why should James be interested in the first Country Women's Association conference, the first federal cabinet meeting in the new capital city of Canberra, although it was less of a city than a few buildings and farms nestled next to the small country town of Queanbeyan? That was the year Greenie ordered a radiogram, and they all gathered in the library to listen to Australia's first radio broadcast, audible (if crackly) all the way from Melbourne as Dame Nellie Melba sang in *La Bohème*.

Instead she sent James what economic analysis she was able to glean from her contacts in France and Belgium. Both countries were slowly recovering from war, and the contracts with Higgs extended. Herr Feinberg and his colleagues in Bavaria, however, had been forced to terminate their contracts. Two were bankrupt, Herr Feinberg managing — just — to keep on in a land where vast inflation could mean it took a wheelbarrow of marks to buy a loaf of bread.

The loss of the German contracts did not affect Higgs Industries — they had only ever been intended as a ruse to enter Bavaria, and Sophie had not seriously expected them to be lucrative. Politically, however, the German desperation, the insistent isolationism of America, and the determined short-sightedness of the Allies was worrying.

Nigel's early letters were of debates in the House of Lords; of the League of Nations; of discussions at dinner parties. But increasingly as the years passed his news became limited to Shillings, and its world. Miss Lily's intimate gatherings had gained her contacts and influence across Europe. Nigel Vaile, Earl of Shillings, attempting to be heard in the House of Lords after so many years of invisibility, belonged to no faction and was courted by none either. Perhaps, thought Sophie, he had simply lost the optimism that any effort of goodwill might influence the world. Like James, Nigel did not mention his personal life.

Sophie had no way of knowing whether this was because he had too little, or if, possibly, Miss Lily had truly left and Nigel was accepting his position as eligible bachelor. Each time she saw the crest on a letter at the breakfast table she was afraid, just a little, that the strong black-inked writing inside might announce his forthcoming wedding. But no such letter came. Instead, increasingly, his letters were on the minutiae of daily life at Shillings.

> My dearest Sophie,
>
> The vicar is undone! "Ethan", the champion spin bowler of his beloved village cricket team has been unmasked as none other than Green's cousin, the redoubtable Esme, barmaid at the Shillings and Sixpence. In an even worse blow to his pride, it appears the entire cricket team and all the pub's customers have known for years.
>
> The substitution was only discovered at an 'away' match when 'Ethan' was seen slipping into the Ladies' not the Gents' convenience. Esme has been stripped of her cricket whites — symbolically, of course — although Jones says the vicar may relent by next season, rather than relinquish the championship.

As the years went by she hoped more and more each morning that there'd be a thick white envelope with Shillings's crest in the letters at the breakfast table. A day with a letter from Nigel was brighter.

James's letters made her feel as if political importance belonged to Europe alone, with the United States of America an 'also ran' and Australia excellent only at doing what she too was part of: exporting food and minerals so 'real life' could exist elsewhere.

Nigel's letters simply gave her joy. She told him so. She did not admit, however, that at every post she hoped even more strongly there might be a letter from Miss Lily. At times, in this new world, she felt adrift with only the memories of her wisdom. Nigel Vaile, Earl of Shillings, lacked Miss Lily's confidence to instruct.

Her own letters in return to her correspondents also held little that was personal. She could not write of Green's relationship with a married importer of Rolls-Royce motor cars, nor her assurance that married men were safer, as their intentions were not honourable and their discretion assured. Nigel, James, Sloggers and Ethel would not be interested in the first prize Timothy and his cattle dog had won at the Bald Hill Agricultural Show, or how her household had joined the growing craze for crossword puzzles, with even Cook offering a solution for three down: *bird of prey, ten letters*.

The 'suitable friends' of her Australian life before the war were all neatly married, though due to the loss of a quarter of their generation of men, often to those twenty or thirty years their senior. They now seemed, despite her tentative hopes on her way home, even more limited in outlook; nor was Sophie, as a single woman, and a businesswoman to boot, with no sign that she would resign her position to her husband on marriage, a convenient guest to invite to dinner parties, tea dances, or bridge or mah-jong mornings, tennis afternoons, ice-skating parties or picnic excursions to the Blue Mountains.

Those she met in business were usually men; but it was their wives who sent social invitations, and not to Sophie. Her few social contacts were with the Slithersoles (Johnny married in his first year in Sydney) and Cousin Oswald and his wife, or large dinners or balls at Government House, to which Georgina was naturally invited. Sophie's presentation to the Queen entitled her to her own invitations too. She accepted, partly for business reasons, to make and further cement contacts, but also as a gift for her father. He had won her this position, and in return she would maintain it.

She had even lost the wish to charm the few single men she met. Lifting her eyes to them under her eyelashes, flattery then self-importance seemed too much bother. Most had self-importance enough already. She mostly kept charm for business. A contract for pineapples was worth fluttering her eyelashes and giving compliments. But marriage? The few times she met an eligible man — and there were very few of the right age who had escaped both war damage and marriage — she heard the echoes of the Blue Danube, as she soared in Dolphie's arms;

remembered the deep contentment of eating crumpets with Miss Lily or breakfasting with Nigel; the challenge of James Lorrimer's knowledge of the world. No man she met could equal those she'd left behind; and she was too focused on Higgs Industries and the welfare of many to settle for nursing a war-damaged man.

Living quietly with Maria and Green, letting Georgina run Thuringa, building her empire with fruit cocktails, canned tomatoes and asparagus, satisfied her.

And then, quite suddenly, it did not. Creating an empire was fulfilling. Merely running one was less so. And Higgs Industries now purred like the Rolls-Royce engine of Green's 'friend'.

She awoke one morning to find there was nothing she had to do that others could not do as well, or better. She packed, or rather, asked Green to pack, for an extended stay at Thuringa. She had not spent more than a few days there at a time since she moved home.

It was time to spend hours ambling on a horse between gum trees again; to see if she could still swing a billy of tea without dropping it; and to pause, and see what direction life might take now. Taking on the challenge of making chokos fashionable? Travelling to the United States of America, perhaps with Green, ostensibly to look at other manufacturing enterprises, but mostly for the adventure, which she suspected Green was beginning to hanker for too? Or to think about being wife and mother, though to do either of those one must have a husband in mind. But of the men who had courted her, none had felt like someone she could share her life with.

Her life, and not just his.

Chapter 35

She arrived at Thuringa in a new dark green Rolls-Royce Twenty, on an afternoon when the blue sky was hazed with casuarina pollen and the leaves were turning gold on the poplars planted down the mile-long driveway.

She spent the first two days simply riding — Georgina had kept the stables well stocked with most excellent horses. On the third day, too stiff to ride again, she breakfasted with Georgina and Timothy on the verandah, a leisurely meal as they looked out at the galahs pecking down through the tussocks, newly down from the mountains before winter, the cattle fat and decorative, the fences neatly dividing the land into rectangles.

Georgina grinned at her obvious enjoyment of the scene. 'More tea?' She lifted the silver pot. 'You should come down here more often. And stay longer.'

Sophie spread a slice of toast with honey from the hives old Joe kept up on the hilltops. I should send a pot of this to Nigel, she thought. It was paler than Shillings honey. It tasted of sunlight and gum blossom. Maybe Thuringa honey would even encourage him to visit Australia. 'I will now. I'd forgotten how peaceful it is.' It had been this, as much as the business empire, that had called her back from Europe. She had forgotten how strong her love was for this place. She blinked. 'Timothy, is that a snake in your shirt pocket?'

'Just a young python, Aunt Sophie. Did you *know* that pythons can grow up to forty feet long and eat a man?'

'I think only boa constrictors can do that. Yours won't grow to more than about about six feet.'

'And not in the house,' added Georgina.

'But we're on the verandah —' began Timothy.

'Time for lessons,' said Georgina firmly, angling her cheek for a kiss. Timothy spent most of each day with a tutor now, preparing for school in Sydney next year. No matter how much he loved farm life, the young viscount needed to experience the best approximation of boys his own class that the colonies could provide.

'He's a darling,' said Sophie, watching him run off, the small python now draped over his shoulder. 'You've done brilliantly with him. And with Thuringa. Thank you.'

'Thuringa has done well by us,' said Georgina. Sophie looked at her sharply. Perhaps Georgina too felt it time to change direction. But to where?

Georgina helped herself to plum jam. 'By the way, the McPhee property is on the market. Jock McPhee is getting too old to run the place and both sons died on the Somme. Are you interested?'

'Of course.' Higgs Enterprises still followed the policy of buying any good land available in the district — it was not just good business but also what one did for neighbours. They knew their fences would be kept up, their strain of cattle appreciated, the house lived in, even if by a stockman. Those who received the generous asking price with no haggling carefully closed their minds to the possibility that that stockman and his family might have dark skin.

It had been more than a decade since native workers had been chained on any farm in Bald Hill. Under Georgina's gentle pressure as patroness of Bald Hill Central School, children with dark skins were not just permitted to go to school, but any attempt to expel them on spurious grounds was firmly resisted.

'Might be worth having a chat to the McPhees today then, if you've nothing else on.' Georgina hesitated. 'I was thinking of going up to Sydney this afternoon to see the dressmaker before the May Day ball. But if you like I could postpone it and come with you.'

'Go and gallivant,' said Sophie lightly, reaching for the honey pot again. 'I am more than capable of negotiating with the McPhees.'

Which was how, finally, six years after Ethel's urgings, Sophie Higgs and Midge Harrison, nee McPherson, finally encountered each other in the McPhees' lounge room.

Midge had been one of the two friends with whom Ethel founded the wartime canteen in France. She and Sophie would undoubtedly have met earlier if Sophie had not been so busy, although the Harrisons' property, Moura, was closer to Biscuit Creek than Bald Hill, so the Harrison family did their shopping, schooling and memberships of clubs there. Midge had also been preoccupied: she was not just a farmer's wife, but herself a farmer.

If local gossip was accurate — and it usually was, in Bald Hill and Biscuit Creek — in the last five years Midge Harrison had made the decisions that had turned a cockie farm into one that was almost — if not quite — a squatter's holding, pedigree rams improving their stock, her own money buying whatever adjoining land became available. Georgina had met Midge several times at Country Women's Association meetings and church gatherings, and liked her, but, possibly regarding Midge's husband with a remnant of her aristocratic reserve, had never invited them to dine.

Midge was sitting on Mrs McPhee's purple-and-green-flowered sofa when Sophie entered; she had a cup of tea in one hand, a jam-laden scone in the other and a spark of property competition in her eyes.

'Er, have you met?' asked Mrs McPhee nervously. Having two rivals for her husband's land required etiquette she was not familiar with, especially as both were women and so, by convention, were to be entertained by her and not her husband, who, in true male fashion, was down in the gully repairing a fence just when he was needed.

Midge put down her cup and scone, stood, and held out her hand, man-like, to shake. A red hand shiny with scars. That is our badge, thought Sophie. Those scars from constant wartime infections say, 'I was there.' 'Midge Harrison. Mrs Harry Harrison,' said Midge, smiling. 'May I call you Sophie? I have heard so much about you from Ethel's letters.'

'I've heard about you too.'

They all sat, Mrs McPhee visibly relieved that battle was not to commence in her lounge room. There might even be gossip to pass on. 'Tea?' she offered Sophie.

'Yes, please. Milk, no sugar, thank you. The scones look delicious. How is Ethel? I haven't heard from her in months. She is a mutual friend, from the war, Mrs McPhee.'

'I haven't heard from her much either.' Midge ate her scone with a heartiness Miss Lily would have gently reproved. But then at Bald Hill eating enthusiastically was not a social solecism, but a compliment to one's hostess, thought Sophie. Miss Lily would have approved of Midge. 'The last letter said she's feeding half the children in Manchester with free school lunches and is trying to open a Marie Stopes Clinic there too.'

'*Ethel?*' Sex was the last thing Sophie would have associated with the large and energetic Ethel.

Mrs McPhee blinked, obviously hoping this was another Marie Stopes, not the notorious campaigner for women's rights and author of *Married Love*, and the provider of devices that ensured love did not too copiously procreate.

Midge grinned, winked, swallowed the last of her scone, then got down to business as efficiently as Sophie herself would have done in another five seconds. 'So, about this property. How about we buy half each? You have the half on your side of the river, we have the half on our side. It's roughly half and half.'

And Sophie was getting slightly the best of the bargain, as the creek flats she wanted were north of the river, and more valuable than the southern side. She nodded agreement. 'Only if I pay sixty-five per cent of the purchase price — though we split the conveyancing costs evenly.'

'Done.' Midge held out her hand to shake again on the deal. Mrs McPhee looked even more nervous, at both the female handshaking and the magnitude of business that appeared to have been completed without her husband present, and by women, over her tea and scones.

'I'll get the solicitor onto it tomorrow.' Midge stood. 'Thank you for the tea, Mrs McPhee. We are going to miss your scones, and you too. And thank you for letting us have your home. We will care for it, I promise.'

'Thank you from me too,' said Sophie.

Mrs McPhee saw them out, hesitantly, as if still unsure whether she should wait for her husband to come in and ratify the deal, but equally sure she knew no way of stopping either Sophie nor Midge.

Midge paused at her car, a stylish blue Riley. 'Are you busy tonight? Would you like to dine with us? Totally informal. We're on the phone line, if you'd like to ring Thuringa to say you will be late.'

'I'd love to.' With Georgina in Sydney she wouldn't be left in the lurch by her non-appearance.

'I'd better warn you, my husband, Harry, is totally deaf. The shelling, you know. But he lip-reads quite well and even when his conversation is a non sequitur in response to an imagined comment, it's interesting.' She smiled. 'He's a good man. Kind.'

'The best sort.'

'The best sort indeed. I am lucky,' said Midge lightly. 'There's a shortcut to our place, takes a full hour off the road journey. The track goes through the northern end of the McPhees', the part that will be yours. Now we've met I hope you'll use it often.'

'I'm sure I will.' She was suddenly aware she had made no new friends since coming home. Green was a friend now, and Georgina, and her relationship with Maria was a strange mixture of family and friendship. What else did she have, except business and Thuringa?

Midge showed it was indeed possible for a woman to have marriage, children, and a fulfilled life beyond the home too. Lucky Midge.

I am bored, she thought. But I am not bored with Australia. The war accustomed me to living with urgency and drama. I must simply accustom myself to the small challenges of peace. By making choko a desirable canned product? She grinned at herself.

She followed Midge's car along the road, then around the turn along a smaller but well-used track. Midge stopped at a gate. Sophie waited for Midge to get out — it was convention that the first driver opened the gate, and the second shut it.

Instead, a short man, but solid, with wide muscled shoulders, in old army trousers tied up by rope at his waist and ankles — an army trick to stop rats and mice climbing up your legs in the trenches — and the rags of a shirt ambled out of a bark lean-to and opened it for them. Midge leaned out and handed him a coin. Sophie quickly rummaged in her handbag. Bother! Only a penny, a shilling and pound notes, all too much or too little. She drove through the gate, pulled up and handed him the shilling, and received a well-spoken, 'Thank you, miss.'

His face was bearded, but the beard was trimmed, though his brown hair was shaggy, probably chopped off with a knife when it became inconvenient; his hands were dusty, the colour of rock, his eyes a startling dark olive green, like the trees above them. His bare feet looked calloused to leather.

'How do you know it's miss?' she found herself asking, smiling at him automatically to make him smile too. Say something he will agree with; ask a question he can answer.

Why was she using Miss Lily's lessons in charm on this man?

Because he is strong, she thought. Not just those shoulders, the muscles of his brown arms. This ragged man had an air of strength she had not seen in any businessman in Sydney. For the first time in years I feel as if I am a woman, not a business. 'You are more than corned beef,' Miss Lily had said. She had not realised the depth of that warning ...

'You don't wear a wedding ring.' The man's voice was serious, low and educated, as close to an upper-class accent as Australia produced. 'Besides, I have heard of you. Miss Sophie Higgs.'

He hadn't smiled back. She glanced at the lean-to hut, sheets of bark neatly fastened to a framework of poles, like an elongated tee-pee; he'd dug a trench around it, army style, to channel the water that flooded down the slope when it rained away from the living area. A well-made stone fireplace stood just outside the doorway, a billy made from an old tin can hanging above it. A couple of dozen rabbit pelts dried on the fence.

And then she saw them. Cross after cross incised on large rocks, small rocks, far too close together for bodies to be buried there. Surely this man was not making graves for rabbits?

He watched her. 'One cross for every man I killed,' he remarked, as lightly as if he were saying, 'The flies are bad today.'

'In France?' she asked gently.

'Gallipoli, then Belgium.'

'You counted every enemy?'

'And the men I ordered into battle. Death is death,' he said quietly. 'Every death must be remembered.'

The Riley's engine in front stuttered, stopped. Midge waited for her. Sophie suspected she had heard this story before, guessed it was being told again now. 'How many crosses have you made?'

'Five thousand, two hundred and seven.'

'How many more must you make?'

'I think another seven thousand should do it.'

She did not think that he was mad, though she knew she might be mistaken. It was war that had been insane. But she had not been mistaken in his strength. Had any other man the courage to count his dead?

She sat, her hands still on the wheel of her car, her luxurious car with its leather seats and inlaid wood and tiny silver vase with a posy of fresh roses in it. Suddenly she breathed war again, the tang of sulphur, the sweet stench of rotting flesh. The flies echoed the buzz of bullets under the belch of big guns. 'What will you do then?' she whispered.

'Give myself to God.'

Did he mean he would become a priest or a monk? Or kill himself? She could not ask.

Her car stalled — she had left her foot off the accelerator. He bent, without asking, and turned the crank handle for her. The engine caught again. He gave her a half-salute. 'You saved men,' he said. 'I killed them, and gave the orders that got them killed. Go well, Miss Higgs.'

He walked back towards the lean-to. Sophie could see another stone there, the chisel waiting to be used again, on seven thousand more crosses.

Chapter 36

Midge Harrison's house was weatherboard, like most in the district, and painted a yellow cream. It stood high above the river, with wide verandahs around three sides decorated by three red sheep dogs gazing suspiciously down at the sheep, who ignored them, noses down in the clover-rich Moura pasture.

They pulled up their cars out the front and each woman got out. Rambling roses covered the fences about the house, pruned to neatness on one side by the sheep, rampant on the other. The path up to the front door was bordered by roses too, orderly bushes with an understorey of recently trimmed English lavender.

A man in an ancient Akubra hat stood up from his cane verandah armchair as they approached, removing his hat politely. 'Sophie, this is my husband, Harry. Harry,' Midge's words were clearer now, rather than louder, 'this is Sophie Higgs from Thuringa.'

'Pleased to meet you.' Harry's hand was as warm as his grin, leathery as his boots. This was a true farmer, not a man who owned a farm or ran one. Sophie could smell the fresh sweat of him, the faint musk smell of man. She suddenly envied Midge, who would go to bed tonight with a man like this, a man with kind eyes and strong hands, as well as the self-confidence to have a wife who made the chief decisions for their farm.

She froze at her thoughts, then realised Midge and Harry were staring at her. She smiled, and followed them indoors, trying to hide her shock. She had not thought like this since … she tried to remember the last time? Not even with Angus, for that had been half pity, nor with Dolphie. She had wanted both men, but not with uncomplex desire. No, she had last felt like this the day before she had turned Wooten Abbey into a hospital. Had her body suddenly woken from the spell of war, the years when the men's bodies that she met were broken, and desire a distraction that must be swept away?

They sat in what Midge called 'the lounge room', though she too must have lived with 'drawing rooms' before coming to Bald Hill, and talked of breeding stock, and the chances of rain, and how old McGraic bayonetted the garbage bin near the cricket ground for an hour each Saturday afternoon, to keep in training for the next time they had to fight the Hun, and his efforts to get other men to join him.

'Any luck?' asked Sophie.

Midge shook her head. 'None. Everyone wants to put the war behind them. And as a mother of sons I say "thank goodness". The boys are staying with their gran tonight, which means she'll be spoiling them rotten making toffee and honeycomb.'

Sophie thought of Germany's fury and humiliation; of the assumption of both James and Dolphie that another war was inevitable. But she said nothing. Why spoil an evening and the illusion of peace forever?

The housekeeper served dinner. Midge McPherson might live in a prosperous cockie's house, but she obviously did not feel she needed to do her own housework or all of the cooking.

The meal was simple, as a guest had not been expected: a stuffed rolled rib of mutton, roast potatoes, roast pumpkin, roast carrots, boiled beans, a vast plenitude of extremely brown gravy, slices of white bread like doorstops and butter so pale it must be home-churned, followed by boiled golden syrup pudding, stewed bottled apricots and custard.

Harry ate steadily, as befitted a man who had worked with his muscles all day. He contributed little to the conversation, but seemed deeply pleased to see his wife talk to Sophie with enjoyment and animation.

'... and Anne still goes out to dig in Mesopotamia each winter. You didn't ever meet her, did you?'

Sophie shook her head.

'Married an archaeologist. Well, she is an archaeologist too now, even completed her degree, but of course all their papers are published under his name. She says it makes sense, as he is the one who needs the grant money or the academic position. They'd never give either to a woman.'

'Just like you're a farmer's wife.'

Midge laughed. 'I am a farmer's wife. I just happen to be a farmer too. And the mother of two junior farmers. Did you see the rams when you came in? We're finally seeing results from the breeding program. But you won't want to talk about sheep. You've only got cattle, haven't you?'

'Can't make corned beef from sheep.'

'Actually we do a fresh corned neck of mutton every Christmas, a "collar" rather. It's excellent, much better than a ham. You'll have to try it. But I don't suppose it would sell, if you canned it. You know Sloggers too, don't you?'

'Yes, of course. We worked together for nearly two years. You must have met her in France?'

Midge nodded. 'I hope she gets her tutorship. Can't wait to tell her I've met you. And you know Ethel is standing for election?'

'No!'

'That's what she said in her last letter. Only local government, but I bet she gets in.' Midge looked at Sophie critically. 'You should stand for election this year yourself.'

'Me? Why on earth?'

'Because otherwise we'll be stuck with old Underhill for another term. And this year there's a better chance of votes for a new candidate because we've finally got the multiple candidate system and compulsory voting. It means that women are going to *have* to vote, even if,' Midge mimicked in an affected, little girl voice, 'I leave things like that to my husband.'

'They'll still vote the way their husbands tell them to.'

'They might not if there was a woman standing. A woman who opened the factory that keeps so many local families afloat.'

Sophie smiled. 'So who should I stand for? Nationalist, Country Party or Labor?'

'I doubt any of them would have you,' said Midge frankly. 'You'd have to stand as an independent. Look, old thing, it would be *good* if you ran. Most women have never really thought about who to vote for. Having a woman candidate would make them sit up and look for a change. Edith Cowan got elected in Western Australia.'

'That was at state level, not federal! And I'm not Edith Cowan.'

Midge laughed. 'Don't underestimate yourself. This new preference system is going to make a real difference.'

'How?'

'No idea yet,' said Midge sunnily. 'It was just brought in to keep the Country Party from gaining power, but I have a feeling it's going to mean more than that. Will you do it?'

'I don't know,' said Sophie slowly. Midge was right — it would be a worthwhile thing to do, to show both women and men that the right to vote was not just something you used unthinkingly. Maria would be delighted to see the young woman she loved standing for the cause she had worked for, as a suffragist back in the 1890s.

'Do it,' said Miss Lily's voice in her imagination. 'You need a wider life than canning factories, and you know it.'

At the very least it would be a challenge. A good challenge, not like the war. Which reminded her ...

'The man by the gate. Who is he?'

'He goes by the name of John.'

'Goes by?'

Midge nodded. 'He knew Jamie McPhee in France, before Jamie died at the Somme. I think Mr McPhee knows his full name, and where he's from. Harry knew him too, which is how I know he changed his name after he came back from Europe, but Harry just says the man is entitled to his privacy and won't tell me what his real name is.' She turned to her husband and mouthed, 'John at the gate,' clearly.

Harry put down his spoon. 'A good man,' he said, in the slightly-too-loud voice used by the very deaf. 'Would have got a VC but there was no other officer alive to recommend him.' He paused and added, 'A great man.'

'A lot of the blokes who were over there go and have a chat with him now and then,' said Midge. 'The ones who need it.' She didn't add, 'The ones who might otherwise get drunk, and bash their families; stay drunk, and kill themselves; who wake up screaming every night but insist their wives tell no one.' 'He doesn't do much but listen, and give a bit of advice, but, well, I've seen men change after a yarn or two with John. He does good work, despite his appearance.'

'Was he a chaplain?' asked Sophie, thinking of all the crosses, then repeated it, mouthing it clearly as Midge had done.

Harry hesitated. 'Sort of. Army captain, but when the chaplain got blown to pieces all across the camp he took over the services for a while, till they found us another one. Blokes used to like his sermons too. "I'm not going to pray for victory," he told us once. "Those Germans over there must be praying just as hard for victory as we are. If God were going to hand victory to anyone, He'd have done it by the first Christmas. I reckon He has given us free choice, and it's free choice that has landed us all here, even if it's someone else's choice. So I'm going to pray for what God *can* give us: the ability to bear what's going to happen to us today and tomorrow, to stand by our mates and take pleasure in a cup of tea, if that's the only good thing we get today." You should have heard them.'

'They cheered him?' asked Sophie loudly and clearly.

'Better than that,' said Harry. 'They were silent and listened. And some of them even smiled.'

The three of them sat in silence too, remembering. 'Sometimes it doesn't seem real,' said Sophie at last. 'There was so much horror, something new, worse, every day. But you got used to it.'

'Except none of us really did,' said Midge quietly, as Harry tucked into his pudding, hidden behind his deafness again. 'I expect you have nightmares too.'

Sophie nodded. 'Standing up to my ankles in blood in the surgery. A child, in shattered pieces. Which is funny, because though I saw children who had died, or were wounded and dying, I never saw the one I see in dreams.'

'Maybe that one stands for all the others.' Midge began to gather the plates, then stopped as Harry reached for a second helping. Sophie noticed she didn't offer her own nightmares. Or Harry's.

'The man by the gate. John. Is he mad?' She had nursed enough shell-shock cases to know that the years of stress could make life unbearable, either for the victim, or his victims.

'No. Or yes, but not dangerous, if that's what you mean. The opposite, maybe.' She seemed to be trying to find the right word. 'Happier, as if he lives in today, not seven years ago, and so can notice the good things, like Harry can now. Like the fact that someone has darned his socks.' She grinned at her husband. He grinned back, though it was obvious he hadn't heard her remark.

'How does John live?'

'Forages a lot, I think. For rabbits, at least. Mr McPhee takes the skins to sell for him every few months. I suppose Harry and I need to do that when the McPhees leave.'

Then 'John' must be country bred, thought Sophie. Bullets to shoot rabbits cost money, so he must trap them.

'He gets tips for opening the gate when people use the short-cut for our annual ram sales,' Midge continued. 'I sometimes give him a twist of tea, or a cake if Mrs Brinton has been baking. There's a spare cake in the kitchen if you want to give it to him on the way back. Don't worry,' she added, 'he won't get the wrong idea. He doesn't seem interested in women.'

'I'd like to. Thank you. And I will think about the election.'

'Come again soon,' said Midge. 'You can meet my two beasts. They're not bad, for children.'

'I'd love to,' said Sophie. And meant it.

Chapter 37

There are only four people in the world who know what happened to me back then, and you are the fourth. I hadn't realised how much it helps, to have another person know — and believe — in the strange and horrible ingenuity humans can use to inflict pain and suffering on each other. Thank you for listening. And for believing.

Miss Lily to Sophie Higgs, 1914

The moon floated like a yellow duck across a black bathtub full of stars. Sophie left the top down on the car, smelling the gum trees, the faint hint of wallaby. Even now she relished the flavours of home.

The man called John must have seen the approaching car headlights. The gate was already open for her. He stood beside it, neither smiling nor emotionless. An almost-smile, she thought. She braked, then handed him the cake. 'A ginger sponge from Mrs Harrison.'

'Thank you for bringing it.' He met her eyes. 'You want to talk, don't you?'

How had he known? Because all at once she did, desperately. Six years pretending that life was good and safe because no one around her was being blown up, but ignoring that vast stain on her life, was suddenly unbearable. Tears that had been stored for years were now flowing down her cheeks ...

She stumbled from the car and sat on a rock by his fire, a glow of coals now; she found a tin mug in her hands. She sipped it, and faintly tasted sarsaparilla, just like the 'tea' Bill the 'drover boy' — her chief stockman's late wife — used to make for her.

She sipped, and found she no longer needed to choke back sobs, though tears still wet her cheeks. She looked at the man across the fire, silent on his rock, waiting for her to speak. She liked his face. She trusted it. But there was more.

'He lived,' she managed finally. 'Jean-Marie, the little boy from the village where I started the hospital. And Charlie, he was just a dog. Though I don't know why I say "just" because ... because a dog can give as much love as a person. The problem is that most of the time the war doesn't seem real, any of it, too melodramatic to have existed when it's so *safe* here, and then I see a man with his face scarred from the gas, and hear him cough, or that look in another man's eyes, and the whole five years comes falling down on me like a wave. I'm not making sense, am I?'

'The war didn't make sense,' he said. 'But what you did in it did. Remember that. You made sense. Your actions made sense. They were good and you did your best and you do your best now.'

She found the tears had stopped. Her hands no longer shook. She felt as if a boulder had been rolled away. 'Thank you. I ... I try to do my best.'

'I know,' he said quietly.

'How?' Her gesture took in the isolation of the gate, his hut.

'Because you cried for others, not yourself.'

She wanted him to put out his hand, so she could hold it. Wanted, suddenly, the comfort of his arms. Felt a stab of shame that she could turn comfort into desire, because his face was beautiful in the firelight, and her body suddenly, deeply lonely. She said quickly, 'Mrs Harrison thinks I should stand for parliament. Should I?'

He looked at her in the mingling of fire, star and moonlight, considering. 'Yes. You got used to doing too much in the war. We all did, all of us who spent too long at the Front. You have to tail off gradually. You'll find peace one day, but not if you try to grab it too soon.'

'Is that why you carve the crosses?'

He looked at her steadily. 'Partly. Some men think I'm some sort of a saint. They don't realise that what I'm doing is selfish. I'm winding down, so one day I will be able to begin a life again. Good luck with the election, Miss Higgs.' He hesitated, then said, 'And if you need to talk again, or cry, or just sit and drink billy tea, I'm here.'

'Thank you,' she said. Because it was a true gift he was giving her. Midge was wrong. She, who had been trained by Miss Lily, saw in the dark of his eyes, his nostrils widening to smell her, that this man was indeed interested in women, was deliberately here where there would be none in his life to complicate what he saw as the duty to himself and to others.

Offering her advice he might give to a man who'd been in the war could disturb that serenity, and yet he offered it to her. Generosity indeed. Nor would she betray it.

She lifted her hand to wave to him as she drove through the gate. But his back was already to her as he closed it.

Chapter 38

*A debutante's evening dress should have a neckline exactly three
inches below the collarbones. After marriage, it can be as low as you
wish, as long as you do not display so much that the man seated
opposite you finds it impossible to move his gaze from your bosom
to his soup. You must be ruthlessly honest with yourself, however,
about the first hint of crepe about your skin. After that, a chiffon
scarf, in flattering pale pink, will distract from wrinkles.*

Miss Lily, 1914

MAY 1925

HANNELORE

One does not open a factory if one is a prinzessin. Only Sophie
perhaps could have considered it.

A prinzessin might, however, write to a friend in Australia,
might even, just possibly, visit her there. Hannelore would have
been tempted if Sophie was just a little less intelligent. Dolphie
must find his place in this new Germany. It was essential that
no one — particularly a woman who ran an international
company — know exactly Dolphie's role in the lead-up to the
mustard gas attack at Ypres.

Sophie's bank draft had been with a Belgian bank and so could
only be cashed in Belgium. Before Hannelore had recovered
enough to do so Germany's reparations to France officially
began.

The mark was suddenly worth only a hundredth of what it had
bought the day before. Within a month the mark had depreciated

by a factor of a thousand. The already generous amount Sophie had given her suddenly become a fortune in bankrupt Germany.

Hannelore bought land, to begin with. Farmland, to grow food, and then the hunting lodge from Dolphie, for he would not accept money from her — especially Sophie's money — but he needed to look well, and live well, to get a position in the new government.

And then as the government stumbled, recovered, stumbled and recovered again, and Germany sank still deeper into poverty, she visited Dolphie's sister-in-law for introductions.

And started the factory.

She herself did not start it, of course. A prinzessin could not do that, not and retain her dignity and valuable mystique. A manager was suggested; an old factory site was purchased. Her role was to provide the money, to sign the papers.

She did not even know exactly what the factory produced. Not soup, of course — there was still little surplus food to can — but 'components' — metal fabrications that might differ from one week to the next, depending on what the larger companies they supplied needed.

Labour was cheap, but Hannelore made sure that her workers *could* live on their wages, because behind the factory was a farm growing cabbages and potatoes and corn, as well as raising cows and pigs, and each factory family was entitled to a share in its produce as part of their wages. Their children could attend the school at the Lake Lodge.

She desperately wanted to write to Sophie, to say thank you and to tell her the money had been well spent. She did not. That time in both their lives was over. She had no wish to hurt Sophie by making her remember. In ten years' time perhaps she might send a letter. Sophie might even write back. It was so very hard to lose a friend, but duty, after all, was duty.

A prinzessin could supervise a school, and did. It filled in her days and gave her purpose. It was not the purpose she had longed for, back in the days at Miss Lily's, when she had hoped to lend her hands to creating peace between the empires.

Teaching children who were not ragged only because their mothers were industrious with needle and thread, even cobbling boots from scraps of leather, was not the world of an empress. But sometimes, when a child showed her proudly a whole page of writing with only four spelling mistakes, she might even be content.

Until the weekend (such an unimaginable word for a prinzessin to use before the war, or that she nor anyone she knew might be bounded by a Monday to Friday work regime) that Dolphie brought a visitor to stay at the lodge — a discreet place, for extremely discreet discussions. A most interesting man too, who like them had hated war. A man like them who dreamed of prosperity for Germany, and peace.

A most wonderful man, indeed …

Chapter 39

*An oyster must be eaten whole. Cutting an oyster before you eat it
is as unthinkable as cutting your bread roll. Yes, Sophie, I know
you* can *think of cutting an oyster. That is why you must practise
eating them properly until it no longer occurs to you to approach
them with a knife.*

Miss Lily, 1914

'An excellent idea,' said Maria Thwaites, sitting on the edge of
Sophie's bed at the Sydney house, resplendent in a grey satin
evening dress, three long strands of pearls and a bandeau with
two feathers. She and Georgina had begun their friendship
with memories of English schools and woods and horse
rides. Now, with the income from her directorship at Higgs,
as well as the lavish annuity bequeathed to her by Jeremiah,
and most importantly Green's refurbishment of her wardrobe,
Maria enjoyed bridge evenings, opera at the Conservatorium
of Music, mah-jong afternoons and lectures at the university
at least once a month or even, with very little guilt, twice or
three times a week.

'Agreed,' said Georgina, in a mermaid-green crepe. With
almost a third of a generation of men lost, women across the
world were accommodating themselves to a life without marriage.
None of the women in this household had lost sweethearts or
husbands to the war, but a household of women was no longer
the curiosity it might have been before the war.

A single woman — unmarried or widowed — might even
have a social life. Not at dinner parties, perhaps, or not often, as
numbers of men and women must be equal at the table. But this

post-war world was lavish in producing new social events where women might comfortably outnumber the men, like the bridge and mah-jong parties, or afternoon tea concerts. Or the musical evening Maria and Georgina had just attended.

'I am sure your father would be proud of you,' said Green, handing around cocoa, a nightly chore she had taken on to make it clear to everyone, herself possibly most of all, that she was a servant, an employee, although admittedly one who would then sit in a comfortable armchair, her feet on a footstool, to sip cocoa.

Sophie laughed. 'Dad would have been horrified.'

'Nonsense,' said Maria briskly. 'You only knew your father as a child. Jeremiah,' it was sad that only after his death could Maria publicly use the Christian name of the man she had loved for nearly two decades, 'moved with the times. He was always deeply proud of you. If he were alive today, I am sure he would support you in this too.' She smiled. 'Especially as your opponent will be Mr Overhill.'

'You don't think the Labor Party candidate has a chance?' asked Sophie.

Maria shook her head. 'Bald Hill will vote National again, for Prime Minister Bruce if not for Mr Overhill. The main issue at this election will be jobs, and the White Australia Policy — keeping out competition from those who might accept lower wages or, possibly, run businesses more efficiently.'

'Not more efficiently than us,' said Sophie with satisfaction. Higgs Industries now paid premium wages. Other factory owners might complain, but Higgs was now so dominant in its field that no cartel of other Australian businesses could hurt it. She looked at the three of them. 'You should all be telling me I need to find a nice husband, not run for parliament.'

'Marriage is over-rated,' said Georgina softly.

'And unnecessary,' said Green, who now had recently come to yet another "arrangement", this time with a stockman twenty years her junior, both at Thuringa and during his occasional visits to the city.

'I always taught you that women have to choose,' said Maria. 'It's a rare man who can allow his wife a life as full as his own.'

Sophie wondered for the first time whether her father would have given Maria so much control over the factories if she had been his wife, not his mistress and the governess for his daughter. And yet, she admitted, her father was a man who saw women's abilities. As indeed, he had seen hers.

'Blue serge,' said Green. 'Laced shoes, but a sun hat, not a city hat, with a scarf embossed with poppies. I know just the thing.'

'For what?' asked Sophie.

'Campaigning, of course,' said Green patiently. 'You and your supporters go from door to door, asking for votes, shaking hands, kissing babies. There will probably be a meeting of candidates at the church hall.'

'How do you know all this?'

'Miss Lily was most active in supporting the right candidates at each election. I don't suppose procedures here in Australia are much different, even if the candidate is a woman and you have compulsory voting and those preference things.'

'And women are used to voting here,' added Maria. 'But your friend Mrs Harrison was quite correct. I doubt many women have ever truly considered how to make their vote matter. They vote as their husbands do.'

'Then their husbands will need to vote for me too,' said Sophie. Her friend, Mrs Harrison? But Maria was right. Even in that one afternoon and evening, Midge Harrison had become a friend. And this election would cement the friendship.

Chapter 40

The world will always be run by men, my dears. Has there ever been any civilisation where it has been different? Yes, a woman may be a figurehead. She may even change the world — but only if her influence is discreet. Cleopatra was one of the most famous queens — and powerless. Think of Queen Elizabeth, and how carefully she made it seem that she followed her council's advice. The more influence a woman has, the more discretion is needed.

Miss Lily, 1914

31 OCTOBER 1925

Midge organised the door-knockers, recruited from the Bald Hill Country Women's Association. Sophie privately suspected that most of the door-knockers were unsure about the advisability of a woman MP. They might not even vote for her themselves, in the privacy of the voting booth — and had probably assured their husbands of their true Nationalist Party allegiance.

But the Harrisons were admired; Higgs-owned properties and factories were the district's largest employers. And every woman who had been roped into the campaign could casually remark she had drunk tea and discussed women's rights with Lady Georgina FitzWilliam '… so lovely and unaffected and her voice is beautiful'.

Tomorrow evening Sophie would speak on the stage of the church hall with the other candidates. Today she would go over her speech with Midge. She had brought chocolates from

Sydney for her and the children, as well as ice cream, which she hoped was not melting in its canvas bag of dry ice in the back of the car.

She had also packed an old fruit box to give to John when she met him at the gate. He seemed almost like an old friend now, after opening and closing the gate perhaps twenty times for her as she drove to the Harrisons' and back, though since that first evening they had never spoken more than pleasantries. Nor had she given him money again. Coins seemed too cold, as if what he'd given her could be bought. Instead she offered food, which he accepted gravely, and with thanks.

Today's box held a loaf of fresh Thuringa bread, a pat of Thuringa butter, cheese, two cans of Higgs's corned beef and the bulk catering can of 'fruit cocktail', which at this season was mostly late apples, pineapple, jam melon with passionfruit that travelled by ship down from Brisbane, as well as an apple pie. She hoped the selection was not too lavish, either for the life he had chosen or in a way that implied a condescending 'lady of the manor' generosity.

The car rounded the bend towards what everyone now called John's gate. Yet for the first time he did not appear to open it for her. Instead a song floated up from the gully behind his shanty.

'Oh, Danny Boy, the pipes, the pipes are calling
From glen to glen, and down the mountainside.
The summer's gone, and all the roses falling,
It's you, it's you must go and I must bide.'

She had first heard the song in 1915, sung by a man whose hand had been amputated and who was recovering at Wooten Abbey. By 1917 it was being sung everywhere. She had hummed it herself: it was one of the few songs that made a man with shell shock weep, but with tears that healed instead of hurt. She shut her eyes and found herself singing too:

'But come ye back when summer's in the meadow,
Or when the valley's hushed and white with snow.
It's I'll be here in sunshine or in shadow —
Oh Danny Boy, oh Danny Boy, I love you so!'

She opened her eyes to see the singer coming towards her. He was bare chested, water gleaming on his skin. His hair was wet, and the shirt he carried in his hand. He must have been washing in the gully. He hesitated, but she kept on singing. And then they sang together:

'But come ye back when all the flowers are dying,
And I am dead, as dead I well may be.
Ye'll come and find the place where I am lying,
And kneel and say an Ave there for me.

'And I shall hear, tho' soft you tread above me,
And all my grave will warmer, sweeter be,
For you will bend and tell me that you love me,
And I shall sleep in peace until you come to me.'

John had been right. Last time she had cried for others. She hadn't really cried for herself since she had wept for her loss at her father's death. But now she did. She wept for all her loss: the dear friends who had died, like Alison and Dodders; and those who had chosen to leave her, like Angus. She wept for the loss of those she had loved, but known she must leave, like Nigel and, yes, Dolphie.

She rested her hands on the steering wheel, put her head on her hands, and simply sobbed. He waited, letting her, then said, 'Billy's almost on the boil, if you want a cup of tea. Real tea, this time.'

She did not want tea. She wanted peace and suddenly she had found it there, among the stones to the dead. But a cup of tea was as good an excuse as any to stay here longer. She nodded, scrambled out of the car and hauled out the box from the back seat.

'There's an apple pie,' she said, suddenly feeling foolish, her arms full of … things … when things no longer seemed to matter. And yet they did, of course they did. Souls and love could not last without feeding, many kinds of feeding, but one that included bread and cheese and even apple pie.

He took the old wooden fruit box from her. 'Excellent,' he said, hefting its weight. 'It'll make a kinder seat than a rock. And that big can is a good size for a billy of stew.'

'That's what I thought.' She was able to hold her voice steady again. She followed him to the fire, its flames almost transparent in the sunlight, only the coals glowing. The billy next to it did indeed need only nudging and two minutes brought it to the boil again.

He threw in tea then she watched as he did the traditional bushie's trick of taking up the wire handle in a twist of bark to make a pot holder and swinging it around his head three times to help it brew. He grinned. 'Every man who does that is boasting. Have you ever tried it?' He shook his head at his own question. 'Of course you have.'

'Bill showed me how. She was a drover, married to our head stockman. *He's* retired. Well, retired in that he sleeps in till six am sometimes. Their son Matt is head stockman now.'

'I've met him.'

Of course he had. Matt had been at Gallipoli, had lost an eye there, and so had survived the war. He was sent back home to live among the cows, but without the pension a white man would have got. What pain, injustices and memories had Matt asked this man to help him cope with?

John poured tea into an enamel cup. 'I'd offer milk and sugar, but I don't have any. And, no, thank you, that wasn't a plea for sugar.' Another grin. 'I probably eat better than any man in the district, with so many bringing me "a little bit of what the missus made last night".'

'Is your name really John?'

'You must know it isn't, or you wouldn't have asked. Though I suppose it is John, now. You were crying for yourself, this time,' he added.

Oh, this man knew people. Saw people, in the way that few did, in the ways Miss Lily had tried to show her.

'Yes,' she admitted. 'But I've no right to cry. I have so much.'

'What you have doesn't compensate for what you've lost. Who did you lose that you loved?'

She could not bear this. Had never been able to bear it, adding up the totals of the dead. Suddenly, here, as a currawong sent its long liquid cry down the gully, she was able to. 'Where should I start?'

'Tell me in order.' His words might have been the wind in the gum leaves, the question almost as often repeated as the gum leaves' song.

'Alison.' Alison — her first friend in England, companion debutante, dying in childbirth of infection because infection was all around: Wooten Abbey had become a hospital. Alison as much a casualty of war as any soldier was.

She talked of Alison, of the patients lost at Wooten and her hospitals, nurses, ambulance drivers she had known for such a short but vivid time, of darling stalwart Dodders, dead of influenza after surviving four years in ambulances on the front line. She slowly became aware that the greatest loss of all had been Miss Lily, and Nigel too. But even to this man she could not talk of them, or at least not yet …

And she realised suddenly that the shadows were growing and Midge would begin to worry. And yet she still couldn't leave. 'Who did you lose?'

'Besides ten thousand men?'

'You know exactly what I mean.'

'I do. But I am here as expiation, not to console myself.'

'Do they have to be incompatible?'

He looked at the ground. 'I never thought of that. That I might find comfort while comforting others.'

'Don't you have the right to comfort too? You did no more than any other officer in battle.'

'Exactly. No more, and no less.'

'You think every officer should pay for the orders he gave?'

'I only know that I must.'

She put down her mug. Neither of them had touched the pie. She said abruptly, 'I killed a man. Shot him. He was German and it was on a battlefield in war, and he would have killed me. And I was trying to save many lives and he was in the way. That is the nub of it. He was in the way and so I shot him before he shot me.'

'Just one,' he said. 'It's a small number in the abundance of war.' He did not look at her with shock, or disgust. 'You try to make lives better now. I do not see a crime, or sin. And no, you have not saved the world. But perhaps your conscience is a little too ... ambitious if you blame yourself for that.'

She took a breath. 'I drove another man to kill himself. A brute, who whipped his wife and lied and bullied. I didn't do it deliberately — I only meant to make sure he would stay away — but I didn't regret it. I still don't. Because, well, death is tidy, isn't it? I built up a scene that horrified him so much he could see no other way out and jumped. Should I be carving crosses on two stones? Would that absolve me?'

'It's not about being absolved. It's about remembering them.'

'I won't forget.'

'Then maybe you did what was necessary, and are still doing it.'

It comforted, a little, and a little was enough for now. 'You never answered my question? Who did you lose?' They both knew there was no family, no person probably in all Australia who had lost no one.

'My wife. She died in childbirth like your Alison, and I was far away pretending that gaining a meagre foot of foreign soil mattered more than her and the child who was my son. And my brother, who was my twin.' He hesitated, then very deliberately sliced the pie and took a hunk and bit it. He said, after he had swallowed, 'That is why I go on living, because while I live in some strange way he does as well.'

'And enjoys apple pie?'

'It is good pie.'

'Was his name John? I'm sorry,' she added quickly. 'I have no right to ask that.'

'Yes. His name was John. When I have a child, if I ever have another child, which is improbable, it will be his too. If I live to see that child grow up, I will see his features, not my own. And I'll give that child the love of two fathers, not just one.'

'When you have carved the twelve thousandth stone?'

He smiled. 'I don't know how long after that it will take me to love and marry and have a child. But, yes, after that. Perhaps.'

'It is a bit like saying when the war is over ...'

'It isn't over. It never will be. This is just a lull.'

Nigel had said much the same thing, and James and Dolphie had also. Perhaps they all meant different things, but nonetheless it chilled her. For she agreed.

'How many crosses have you carved now?'

'I don't actually count them. When there are enough, I'll know.'

'And then you'll go away?'

He nodded.

She wanted to say, 'Don't leave.' But she had no right to say that, to demand more from a man who had given so much. 'Bald Hill will miss you,' she said instead.

She wanted to say, 'I will miss you.' But she still spent less than half her time at Bald Hill; would spend even less if she were elected to parliament. John offered unconditional help to everyone, always at his gate. All she had to offer him — had ever offered any of her friends — was her time when she wasn't doing something else. Yet he'd said that she'd done good work. And she had ...

'I think that last stone won't be carved until I'm no longer needed.' He looked at her, then shook his head. 'No, you were right. I'll go when I am healed. I should admit it, instead of basking as an almost-saint.'

'You can do both. Heal yourself as well as others. Any nurse can tell you that.'

'And one has.'

'Not me. I was a terrible nurse but an excellent hospital administrator.'

He laughed. Suddenly he was a man again. And that was dangerous, because once again she felt as if she was a woman, one whose youth was leaving her, whose body had never truly known love. And just as the song said, 'in sunshine or in shadow', he was so beautiful. Perhaps, she thought, his body held the life of two men, his own and his lost brother's. His hands would feel warm ...

She stood up quickly. 'I must go, or Mrs Harrison will have sent out a search party. I promise not to take up your time when I pass back through here tonight. I can't promise not to deliver whatever Mrs Harrison sends for you though.'

He stood too. 'She's a good one.'

'She is indeed.' She hesitated, then held out her hand. He shook it, briefly, firmly. His hand felt like a small sun upon her skin. Then he walked to open the gate for her, as she cranked the car.

Chapter 41

Remember me, if there is space in your wonderful lives to come.
I will not be in your lives long. I have accepted that. But it would
be good to think that sometimes I am remembered.

Miss Lily, 1914

'Sophie, it's good to see you again. May I present my wife? Thebe, this is Miss Sophie Higgs. Sophie, my wife, Thebe.'

'Delighted to meet you,' said Sophie pleasantly. 'And to meet you again, Malcolm.' How could she ever have thought she wanted to marry Malcolm Overhill, whose face possessed all the intelligence of an overbred Hereford bull?

Malcolm drew her aside. 'I say, Sophie, you can't really mean to stand against the pater. It isn't done.'

'What isn't done?'

'Women standing for election.'

'It is being done. It is exactly what I am doing now.' She smiled at Thebe Overhill, who was looking politely furious that the ex-fiancée she had heard about was better looking, better dressed and far richer than herself, as well as accompanied by the now locally famous Lady Georgina and young Viscount Timothy FitzWilliam. Sophie gave Malcolm a farewell pat on the arm, then made her way through the crowd to the stage.

Midge hugged her at the bottom of the stairs. 'You will be brilliant. Go get 'em.'

'Chin up,' said Georgina.

Timothy shook her hand politely. 'Best of luck,' he said, as if she were going to a football match. Which was pretty much what it felt like.

Green gave her hat a surreptitious tweak. 'Perfect.'

'My darling girl,' said Maria, with such sudden, unexpected emotion that Sophie brushed two tears away as she ascended the stairs.

She sat, as the vicar introduced 'the man who needs no introduction, Mr Overhill, MP', Sam Upton, the Labor Party candidate (she noticed the vicar did not bother to add Mr to his name), and 'our own Miss Higgs' in accents that were both admiring and patronising.

She smiled. People clapped, not for any particular person but because that was the time to clap.

Mr Overhill spoke first. 'I can do no better than to echo our prime minister's words tonight! It is necessary that we should determine what are the ideals towards which every Australian would desire to strive. I think those ideals might well be stated as being to secure our national safety, and to ensure the maintenance of our White Australia to continue as an integral part of the British Empire. We intend to keep this country white, and not allow its people to be faced with the intractable problems presently facing many parts of the world.'

He added more. Sophie stopped listening, trying to remember her speech. Maria, veteran of the successful Australian women's suffrage campaign, had warned her not to read from it, but to meet the eyes of each person in the audience.

Which was impossible, she thought.

Mr Overhill sat, to great applause and a hearty 'Hear, hear!' from his son, on the opposite side of the stage from her friends. Her dear friends, who she was going to let down ...

'Miss Higgs? Perhaps you would speak second? Our rose between two thorns?' The vicar clapped her politely.

Sophie stood. She moved to the front of the stage, and smiled out at her audience. 'Ladies and gentlemen, thank you for being here together —'

'Speak up, lady! We can't hear you!'

'This is an important time for Bald Hill, and for Australia ...'

'Why should we want to hear her? Ducks on the pond!' It was the traditional cry that went up when a girl or woman entered the shearing shed, or any place exclusively for men, and meant all tools were downed until she left.

'Ducks on the pond! Ducks on the pond!'

This had been organised. Someone — either Mr Overhill, or even Malcolm or Mr Sam Upton the Labor candidate — had made very sure that no votes would be stolen by a woman tonight. And once the chant began others took it up, for the simple joy of joining in.

'Ducks on the pond! Ducks on the pond!'

'Shut up!' Suddenly Harry Harrison was beside her. He held up his hand and yelled, 'And it's no use your yelling at me because you all know I can't hear you!'

Laughter. The chant died away.

'You all know why I'm deaf too. Why Larry hasn't got two arms and Billo will be on crutches for the rest of his life. There's a lot of you here who know what it was like for us blokes there in the trenches.' He paused and gazed around the silent hall. 'Every one of you except our Mr Overhill, who never put foot in any trench unless it was a kitchen drain some poor bloke was digging for him. Well, let me tell you about this woman here.

'Sophie Higgs is like my Midge, my Rose. Sophie Higgs was there, in the middle of it all, not to fight but to pick up what was left of us afterwards. We'd go through weeks or months at the front but girls like my Midge and Sophie Higgs went through the whole sodding war there. They called them the roses of No Man's Land and, by God, and that's not blasphemy,' with a quick nod at the startled vicar, 'but it's the truth, they were our roses there.

'Any man who came back home from the war owes that home-coming to women like my wife and Sophie Higgs. Any woman whose husband, sweetheart or son came home should get down on her knees and thank these women, because without them we'd have lost the war by that first Christmas, and lost our lives, and even lost the will to live.'

He paused again and looked around the hall. 'I'm going to vote for her. I don't give a fig for women's rights. I just know that women like Miss Higgs and my missus are the best that life can give us. And if any man here only sees a skirt, and not a heart more courageous than any man's I've known, then he's a fool.' He stopped, kissed Sophie's cheek, then left the stage.

The hall was silent, straining. She had lost every word of the speech she and Midge had so carefully prepared. And suddenly it didn't matter, as she knew exactly what to say.

'Fellow Australians. Man or woman, black or white, that's who we are, that's what we fought as for the first time over there. We were Australians.

'Mr Overhill knows a lot about how they decide to run our country down in Melbourne. Mr Upton will tell you about workers' rights and I'll probably agree with him. If he knows anything about Higgs Industries, he'll know we have discussions with unions, not arguments, and it's settled when both of us agree on terms and not before. And this is what *I* know.'

She lifted her chin. 'I know how to fight. Not with a bayonet, like Mr Harrison and many others of you. I fought for my country with different weapons, the same as every other person here tonight did. Every single one of us fought the war too, tending stock to feed the army, making fruitcakes, knitting, keeping home safe so our men had a home to come back to — and so that I had and Mrs Harrison, and all the other women who survived our time on the battlefields.

'I promise you this — if you elect me I will keep fighting for whatever you tell me is important. Not for what matters to me, but for what matters to you. I will fight with every fibre of my being.'

She stepped back. Sat.

The cheering shook the hall.

Mr Upton's speech was an anti-climax after that.

Chapter 42

It has often been quoted that freedom cannot be given. It must be taken. Too many slaves cling to their slavery. It takes courage to be truly free. But sometimes the right person, the right words at the right time, can give that courage, for long enough for freedom to be real.

Miss Lily, 1914

SATURDAY, 14 NOVEMBER 1925

The Bald Hill electorate had five polling places but the actual vote sorting and counting took place at the church hall, long benches holding scrutineers from all parties, including from what was now known as the Women's Party.

Sophie sat, cautiously sipping sweet fruit cup — too much and she'd need to use the hall's stinking outdoor dunnies — but refusing sandwiches, scones, fruitcake, lamingtons, date and apple cake, more lamingtons, ham and cheese pie and still more lamingtons. The district had gone lamington mad since a lamington category had been added to the Agricultural Show.

She wished Miss Lily was here. For surely Miss Lily would approve, not just of her parliamentary ambition but of the efficiency of their campaign. Every house in the district had been visited by herself or her volunteers, and at every house they had been offered tea and cake, not mutterings that a woman's place was in the home.

Around her the crowd milled in two discrete camps, the Overhills' on one side, Sam Upton's on the other, but she was glad that her friends and the women who had campaigned for her moved freely from her to whichever other group they had traditionally been politically allied to.

Just as she was afraid the result of the vote would not be known that night — there was no way she would be able to sleep till the count had finished — the vicar's bell rang up on the stage. For some reason she never could remember his name, possibly because he had never seemed to give an honest opinion of his own, unlike the chaplains of courage and integrity she had known in France and Belgium. No wonder the people of Bald Hill needed the solace of John ...

She stood automatically as the vicar called them in to the hall, walked, trying not to shake, climbed the stairs and stood once more between Mr Overhill and Mr Upton.

'The results for the 1925 election for the Bald Hill electorate,' said the vicar portentously. 'Primary votes: Sam Upton, Australian Labor Party — twenty-nine thousand, eight hundred and ninety-one votes; Miss Sophie Higgs, twenty-eight thousand, four hundred and one votes; and Mr Maxwell Overhill — thirty thousand, one hundred and fifty-two votes.' He held up his hand as Mr Overhill's faction began to cheer. 'Which, when preferences are distributed, gives the seat of Bald Hill to ... Mr Sam Upton, MP!'

A small section of the hall seemed to fade away in shock. The Overhills *were* the Bald Hill electorate; the Bald Hill electorate belonged to the Overhills. The only question should have been: When would Malcolm take over from his father? Hands reached up to shake Mr Upton's hand, and Sophie's. But I haven't won, she thought. Why do they shake mine?

Women were hugging her. Midge, Georgina, Maria, Green, a dozen others.

'Wonderful, darling! You did it!'

'You showed them!'

'Old Overhill is spitting chips!'

'Votes for women!'

'But I lost,' said Sophie helplessly into the delighted congratulations swirling around her.

Midge stepped back. 'Darling, you didn't really expect to win?'

Of course I did, thought Sophie numbly. I always win. They cheered me, so I thought I'd win.

'It's the most incredible result for a woman in any federal election!' said Maria enthusiastically. 'Another two elections, or perhaps three, and there really will be a woman in federal parliament.'

But not me, now, thought Sophie. I didn't win! Even Maria didn't think I would win ... why did I even bother?

A strong hand grabbed hers. 'I can't thank you enough, Miss Higgs,' said Mr Upton. 'There was no way we'd have won a stronghold like this without you.'

'I ... I don't understand.'

'Preferences, girl! I got in on the strength of your preferences! You took away enough Nationalist Party voters to get my primary vote up, and your preferences got me over the line. All of the Labor voters who went your way gave me their preferences. You won this election for me, and I won't forget it.'

'I ... I'm glad. Congratulations,' she said belatedly.

'You've got it right at Higgs too. Workers and management sitting down and discussing things. That's what we need nationally, eh? Have to have a chin-wag about it some day ...' Mr Upton was borne away on the shoulders of supporters.

The Overhills and their cars had vanished.

'Champagne,' said Georgina firmly.

'Tea,' said Midge equally firmly.

'I ... I think I need to go home,' said Sophie desperately. 'I didn't sleep much last night.'

'Of course! I'll drive —' began Georgina.

'No, stay. Please.' Celebrate with all these women toasting each other, with teacups or fruit punch or, daringly, tasting champagne, because for some reason they all did seem to think this was a major victory. Which possibly it was. A victory for women, a seat won on women's preferences, the establishment of a major female voting block.

But she had lost, had lost, had lost …

'Sophie, are you sure?' asked Maria, worried. 'You don't look well. Mrs Harrison, your home is closer. Perhaps Sophie and I …'

Midge met Sophie's eyes. For a moment Midge looked unsure, and then she nodded. 'Use the shortcut,' she said, and turned to reassure Maria.

Chapter 43

There is so much comfort in the warmth of another person next to you.

Miss Lily, 1902

The fire still glowed by the hut at John's gate. Of course he must know that Midge would pass on her way back, and be ready to open and shut the gate for her. The stones with their carved crosses shone pale red in the firelight — whiter in the headlights. She turned off the car's engine as he stood. He knew I was going to stop, she thought vaguely as he walked towards the car, not the gate.

She sat, still in shock.

'Sophie?' It was the first time he had used her first name.

'I lost the election.'

'I thought you would,' he said gently.

'Did you vote for me?'

'I didn't vote. Don't vote. Not yet.'

'I thought I'd win. I really did. They cheered me. Cheered and cheered. Everyone was so polite and encouraging when we visited them. But they didn't vote for me. Or not enough of them.'

'But you almost made it.'

'How do you know that?'

He shrugged. 'Blokes talking. People move like a tide, sometimes. You can tell which way the water's flowing just by talking to a few. People around here wanted to say they liked you, admired you, so some of them voted for you, just as soon as they were sure there wouldn't be enough votes for you to win. They're not ready for a female MP yet.' He made no move to open the gate, nor to nudge the billy onto the coals. 'Sophie, why have you come?'

And she knew. Had been calculating, even as she told herself she should not do this, that this man's body was the only one that she could safely join; a man who had no 'honourable intentions' or designs on her fortune, who had no wish for a woman's life to join with his. No one would ever know of this, except for Midge and maybe Harry, who had already drunk quite a bit of beer with his army mates before she had even left. Maria and Georgina would assume she had stayed at Midge's place.

Had Midge guessed that she intended this, or thought that she simply needed an outsider's wisdom, a quiet place to reassess the world, and talk? She could trust Midge not to gossip. And even if she did, just now she didn't care.

She took a deep breath, and tried to keep the pleading from her eyes. 'I want to spend the night with you.'

'Why?' He might have been asking why she preferred brown bread to white.

'Because ... because four men have asked me to marry them, and only one of them ever kissed me properly, and only once, and I am twenty-nine years old and have never been with a man and tonight I need to be.'

'Sophie, don't be silly.'

'I'm not! Make love to me. Please.'

'I am convenient?'

He sees too much, she thought, but not enough. 'Yes. But that's not why I am here. You are sunlight after too many years of shadow. You are the scent of gum trees after the suffocation of offices and drawing rooms. I want to make love to *you* ...'

He said nothing. Did nothing.

'You don't want to,' she said in a small voice. 'Of course you don't want to.'

'Of course I want to. Too much. No, not *too* much, I just ... didn't expect this. Not yet. Not like this either. I'm trying to work out what to do.' He gave a half-laugh. 'You are champagne and feather beds and all I have is a sacking mattress.'

'That's what I need. Exactly what I need.' She tried to read his expression. Yes, he did want her. But she had known that ever since she met him. And the refuge he had chosen was one where the only women he was likely to meet were Midge and Mrs Morrison, both happily married. Was celibacy part of his vow to himself too — a necessary part of healing? Was that why he hesitated now?

'I'm sorry,' she said abruptly. 'I should never have intruded like this. I should go.'

'No. I just … need to readjust my world a bit.' But he smiled tentatively as he said it.

'You're sure?'

'No, of course not.' But the smile was still there, and more certain now. She thought she saw joy, then — unexpectedly — amusement. 'You know, I think I've worked out what we need to do first.'

'What?' she asked, still dazed.

'I think, to begin with, you need to come out of the car.'

Chapter 44

*Yes, I remember the first time I made love, which was not the first
time I had sexual relations, but four years after. And there was
nothing — nothing — similar about the two.*

Miss Lily, 1914

Firelight, shining through chinks in the bark wall. A mattress
that was literally covered in sacking and smelled like it was filled
with fresh gum leaves — and crackled like gum leaves too when
she moved on it. The hut floor was dirt, but swept clean and
hard. Cans were arranged on rough plank shelves, some with
labels, others well washed and holding what looked like seeds,
or dried berries, or rusty nails.

His hands were not rough at all, just calloused from the
chiselling.

She stood, shivering despite the warmth of the night, as he
undressed her, slowly, almost as if he were Green, giving her
a chance to protest and move away. He threw back a sacking
sheet, smelling of leaves and sunlight, and she lay down. He
covered her with the sheet to her waist while he undressed
himself, once more, slowly, so she might still have time to
object.

She didn't.

'You look like a woodcut,' she said softly.

'I'm sorry?'

'A book someone gave me, years ago, to teach me how men
and women … come together.'

He smiled, but still looked solemn, almost as if this were a rite
he must do well. 'So you know what comes next?'

'Only theoretically. And in fifty-six positions.' His skin was so white where his clothes had covered it.

'I think,' he said carefully, 'we will try only one first. Sophie, are you sure?'

'Yes. Are you?' She leaned on one elbow, looking anxious as he lay down beside her. He wanted her physically — Miss Lily's lessons had taught her that much and she had watched men in hospitals for almost five years too. But physicality was not enough, tonight.

'I'm sure. I think … I think perhaps I have carved my twelve thousand. I think it is time to do this too. I think … I think you are the most beautiful woman I have ever seen and this is the rightest thing I have ever done.' He stopped and kissed her.

This kiss went on. Hands joined and bodies too, legs twining. It was all as if it was that one long kiss, the first kiss, but there were hands as well as lips, and in unexpected places …

Pleasure, like a burning flame. She heard herself cry out, felt pain burn too, a tiny one, lost in the happiness. Then he cried out as well. She found the kiss had ended and she was wrapped in his body, his arms about her. Their breathing slowed. At last he said, 'Fifty-six, you said?'

'I'm not sure I remember them all.'

'Shall we try?'

'Yes, please,' said Sophie.

Later, much later, she heard a car. Midge, she thought. Then — she will see my car. See that we are not sitting around the fire, drinking billy tea.

She did not care.

He left her then, throwing on shorts and shirt; the car left, and he came back to her. She didn't ask if Midge had commented, if Harry had been awake. He looked down at her, uncertain for a moment, then smiled, and unbuttoned his shirt. 'I feel like a car that needs new brakes and four new tyres and will never be the same.'

She leaned up on one elbow. 'You make me sound like a car wrecker.'

'Cars can be put back together, maybe better than they were before. I'm just going to have to work out how to do it. I just … thought I knew how my life would be for the next few months, or years. And now suddenly I know nothing. How many of your fifty-six are we up to?'

'I've lost count.'

'Then we must begin again.'

Chapter 45

Love does not last forever. Nor do we. But love lasts longer, than a person.

Miss Lily, 1914

She woke to a kookaburra call.

And he was gone. The fire was warm, the coals still glowing under the ash, but no fresh logs had been added to it.

'John?' and then more loudly, 'John!' Perhaps he was relieving himself behind a tree, or wherever else he did it. Speaking of which …

There was a creek in the gully, but he wasn't there. She washed her face, between her legs. She turned and saw a black snake watching her, as if to say, I am a stick, ignore me and go on with life.

She stood and walked back to the hut. 'John!' she called. 'John!'

Still no answer.

He wasn't there. Of course he wasn't there. He had finished the twelve thousandth cross, and he was free to live again. Sophie Higgs was part of the life of John. And he was not John now. Or perhaps when he woke this morning he had realised he still was John, had to be John, but could not be in her presence.

He could not have gone far, not unless he had walked out to the road to get a lift. He had either fled, or must be near enough to hear her, but did not answer. She did not know which she dreaded more.

I do not even know his name, she thought. And then, a spurt of anger: he should not have left me without a word.

Another thought: he did not ask me here. Last night was my choice. Had she forced him, for charity, to lie with her? A vulnerable, war-damaged man? Once again physical willingness was not the point. Would he have chosen this if she had not been dazed and needy, after the first time she'd ever been denied something?

She was a child who had always got her own way, always. Had created her hospitals, dined with the Queen. Even her loss of Angus had been cut short by the possibility of a future with Dolphie ... and the loss of Dolphie made small by the wonder of coming home, taking up what she had wanted most since she was three years old — her father's empire. She'd been accepted as her father's equal, then strode on to make that empire greater.

She had taken everything she wanted. She had taken him last night, because she was lost and he was beautiful. Perhaps she had even thought he might love her, one of those 'underthoughts' you pretended to yourself you never had.

She sat on the fruit box — the fruit box she had brought there — by the dying fire. Who was she now? What did she want? What was she to do now? More factories? Find another dozen products to put in cans, make another few million pounds?

There was one thing she must do. She must leave here, quickly, because this was John's haven, and he could not return while she was there.

She stood and glanced at her watch. Ten past six. Maria would wait till eight, perhaps, then ring Midge to check she was there. If she wasn't, Maria would send people out looking, unless Midge told her about seeing Sophie's car. Please don't, Midge, she thought. If John had been there when she woke — if his hand had been in hers now — she could have faced explanations. She could not face telling her friend that she had driven John from his hut.

She felt, vaguely, that she needed to pack before getting into the car. You always had luggage with you for a journey. But she had brought nothing but herself.

The car started at the first turn. She hoped John was not far away, would hear the engine and know that it was safe to come back home. She opened the gate herself, drove through it, shut it and drove on.

Trees. The morning light. Happiness glittered somewhere, because last night she had been loved, even if it was for a few hours only. And it had been love, even if this morning John had fled from it. Joy, because last night had been beautiful and so was this morning: each leaf looked like silver was tipping the green. The election heartache of last night seemed less relevant to her life than boa constrictors. And after a bath and breakfast she would feel …

Something. She didn't know what yet. But feeling would come back. A life. Something, because this was morning, and 'something' always happened as the day went on. She did not even need to do anything for the day to continue, for the sun to climb higher, turn whiter, the wallabies retreat into the shade, the wombats to their holes. John could return to his hole now too. She would have to find some way to let him know she would never take the shortcut now. Maybe Midge could mention it, say she had decided to take the smoother, longer road …

She was blocking a thought, an important thought. John would have found a way to make her talk of what thought she was hiding from, but John was the one person she could not talk to. And she didn't want to think. Why should she think if she didn't want to? Just let the day take its course, and maybe by tonight she could bear to think again, let whatever was prowling around her mind out of its cage.

She turned into the Thuringa driveway. Maria ran down from the verandah, Green behind her. Green looked like she had been crying. Green never cried. 'Sophie!' Maria's voice shook.

'What's happened? Has something happened to Georgina? Timothy?' She stopped, as Maria held out a telegram.

'It was delivered last night while we were at the hall.' Maria's hand shook too. 'I telephoned the Harrisons as soon as we got home, but Midge said you were staying with one of the other campaigners who isn't on the telephone line. Midge was going to drive there as soon as it was light to tell you …'

So Midge had kept her secret. 'I haven't seen Midge yet. I left early.' She must have just missed her. Thank goodness she had missed her. She looked again at the telegram in Maria's hand, at Maria's expression. Somehow her own hand would not reach out to take the piece of paper.

'Sophie, I am sorry, I am so very, very sorry,' said Maria helplessly, pressing the paper into her lifeless fingers. There was no choice. Just as she had comforted herself with the inevitability that the sun would continue to rise today, so it was inevitable that she confront that piece of paper.

She took the telegram, then blinked twice before the letters stopped dancing and she could make sense of it.

> *Nigel diagnosed tumour yesterday stop surgery delayed four weeks to organise affairs stop small chance of success stop I cannot bear this stop come if you can stop Jones stop*

It was impossible, of course. Her mind would not accept it. The chill of her body told her it was true.

'I'm going,' said Green tightly. 'He shouldn't have to bear this alone.' Sophie didn't know if she meant Jones or Nigel.

The night before had vanished, as it should vanish, as it should never have happened. The news was too big for any other feeling. The sun could have danced and she would not have cared, would not even have noticed. Somehow, at the back of her mind, there was a shred of relief that this was so momentous that this was impossible that she *could* think of anything else, anyone else. Her world now must be Miss Lily and Nigel, all there had never been, all there *should* have been.

She could have sailed to England anytime in the last two years, and Higgs would have operated as securely without her. She could have asked Nigel to visit Sydney, but hadn't, in case it implied that not even a feather brush of world affairs would quiver if he was away from England and the House of Lords.

She, who knew that even peace was temporary, had somehow thought that Nigel, Shillings, Miss Lily, would be there forever.

Only four more weeks and Lily and Nigel could be gone ...

'Four weeks,' said Sophie slowly. 'But it will take six weeks at least to get there, even if we sail tomorrow.' I should have sailed months ago, she thought, instead of coming here. Should have walked with Nigel hand in hand among the apple trees, spent afternoons with honey and crumpets with Miss Lily. All the afternoons that now could never happen. 'You need a slow tailing-off of all the wartime urgencies before you can find true peace.' Who had said that, or something like that?

No, she didn't want to remember who had said it. It didn't matter now. Finally her need to change the world *fast* had gone, and all she wanted was the quiet of Shillings under a blanket of snow, and dear familiar arms around her.

Too late. She had been a fool. Or, perhaps, another casualty of war, putting loss so far behind her that she had left love behind as well. She had *known* she missed Nigel, loved Miss Lily so very deeply, and yet had not gone back to England, even after she had created her empire, and grown bored with maintaining it.

'I want to be on the next ship to England anyway,' said Green, her voice shaking. Yesterday Green would simply have made sure she was on that ship. Today ... the world had changed, today.

'Call Oswald. He'll make it happen. I ... I need Giggs.'

'She's still asleep,' said Maria. 'I thought you should see this first.'

'Wake her. I'm going to England,' said Sophie. 'And somehow I am getting there before Nigel has his operation.'

'You've just said it's not possible ...' began Green.

'It *ha*s to be possible ...' I am the demanding child who must always get what she wants again, she thought. But this is the most important thing I have ever wanted. Not important for the world, like mustard gas. Important for me.

She turned to Green. 'Call Oswald and arrange the passage for yourself. No expense spared, even if he has to lease a ship to get you there. Pack what I will need in England too, please. But I won't be on the ship.'

Green stared. 'Then how will you get there?'

'I don't know. Fly, part of the way. Car, yacht, ship, camel … I don't know. Whatever Cousin Oswald and the Slithersoles are able to organise, from one point to the next. I may not even know till I get there how I am going to get to the next point from wherever I am. But I am not going to sit on a ship eating pâté de foie gras while Nigel may be dying.'

She slammed the car door then ran up the steps.

Chapter 46

*Decisions made in haste are sometimes necessary. If haste is not
vital, do not make decisions swiftly, but let them brew.*

Miss Lily, 1914

She should pack, but Greenie would do that more efficiently. She
should do … something. Instead she stood, gazing out the window,
letting the tears and snot flow unchecked. She needed to be with
Nigel now, and half the earth stood in her way.

A knock. Maria Thwaites entered. 'Sophie. Sophie, darling.'

It was better in her arms. Like being six years old and having
a broken toe soothed and the whole world ahead of her and she
would never fail, and those she loved would never die.

'Sophie, do you really want to do this thing?' asked Maria
quietly.

Sophie stepped back, accepted the offered handkerchief, blew.
'Yes.'

'You love him that much?'

Them, she thought. I love them both. But instead she answered:
'Yes. I just didn't realise until now how much. I wanted other
things as well and thought it was the wrong kind of love … and
it was complicated.'

Maria looked at her closely. 'And now it's not?'

Sophie managed a smile. 'It is still complicated. But I've finally
realised that there is never a wrong kind of love. If it is, then it's
an "I want", not love. And complications don't matter. Or yes
they do, but can be sorted out. I'm good at sorting out.'

'Yes,' said Maria dryly. She looked at Sophie with the sympathy
of a woman who'd loved for decades privately, so the world did

not see, and who had lost her love, just when she might claim him. 'Flying is fastest,' Maria added carefully. 'But dangerous. I doubt you could fly all the way either. Not with fuel and repairs and spare parts. Not in four weeks.'

'I know.' Sophie also knew something of her own state of mind, she who had seen so many men so caught up in war's urgency that they felt they must do something, even if that something meant their death, rather than face loss they could not bear. She too had almost reached that state. Her body, her mind, felt back in 1917, flung there by failure and rejection and the probability of more loss to come. In 1917 you had to *do*, and keep on *doing*, or you might sink.

'I have a friend who will help you get part of the way,' said Maria with surprising matter-of-factness. 'We met in my suffragist days and have corresponded ever since. We have just talked on the telephone, about other aviators who might be of use to, or know someone in the right place. We cannot put together an entire journey for you today, but we can start you on it and trust that at the next stage, and the next, we can get you further.'

Maria looked at her searchingly. 'Sophie, you do understand ... if any one of those stages fails, you may be stranded for weeks or even months. A ship wouldn't get you to England until after the surgery, but at least you would be sure to get there.'

'There is not much point, if Nigel is dead,' said Sophie flatly.

'You aren't thinking clearly,' said Maria softly. 'Failing to survive an operation may mean he dies weeks after it, not during it. A ship might still get you there in time to be with him.'

'And it might not. That's not the point anyway. I need to be with him *before* the operation. To hold his hand, to smile at him, to tell him that he *will* survive. To make sure every doctor and nurse who get within a mile of him know how to avoid infection ...'

'You must love him so very much indeed.'

No, she thought. I love Miss Lily that much *and* Nigel, and Jones and Shillings and its people. And just now I do not particularly care for myself, nor my tomorrows if I must go on without them ...

Her body ached from the night before, part discomfort, part physical satisfaction and wholly loss. John had run from her, just as Angus had ...

Miss Lily had been right all along. Women could manage the world, but they frightened men when they did so too openly. Erase nearly all of us and all we did from the history of the war, she thought. Push us away when we seduce you, as she had tried with Angus and succeeded with John, sending the poor man running from her through the morning.

'I want to fly.' Leave it all behind, she thought. Leave the corned-beef empire, the women who had worked so hard for her election and felt it a triumph, not a loss. Leave myself behind. Leave John free. He would always give to those in need and she had known that ...

She was going back to the last time she had felt truly secure, at Shillings, in Miss Lily's drawing room, in 1914. Perhaps, this time, her life would go in the right direction.

'I thought that's what you would decide. My friend will be here in half an hour,' said Maria, her voice shaking just a little. 'She can get you to Darwin. We will arrange to have a banker's draft and other things waiting there for you and plans to get you on your next leg. She says to wear trousers and a jacket and a scarf for your hair. Riding boots. She has a spare helmet.'

'She?'

'Her name is Mrs Randolph Henderson,' said Maria and this time, as she held her, she cried too.

The plane landed with wings waggling in the back paddock, the last of the cattle shoved out the gate as the small craft circled, then sank through the air to the grass, running neatly across the tussocks and cattle dung.

It was not much of a plane, far flimsier than the aircraft Sophie had seen during the war. A fruit box was made of sturdier wood, and the fabric covering looked like it wouldn't provide much protection against even a gentle breeze.

The pilot climbed out of the small cockpit onto the wing, then jumped down.

Sophie had expected a woman her own age — dashing, white scarf and goggles, but of course this was Maria's friend. Mrs Henderson was possibly in her fifties, wearing tweed trousers and a matching long flying tweed coat that she must have had specially tailored, a pale pink shirt and pearls just showing under the collar. She stood by her plane as Maria strode towards her, followed by Moonbeam Joe carrying a jerry can of petrol and Sophie, who was empty handed.

Mrs Henderson had warned Maria that even the weight of spare underwear or toothbrushes would reduce the distance the fuel would take them. Gold, that looked so portable and useful, was far too heavy. Sophie wore woollen slacks, and matching jumper as well as socks and riding boots, the lightest but still warm outfit she had.

You could not begin a journey to England without luggage. It was impossible. So was a fifty-year-old woman piloting a bi-plane. So was Nigel dying ...

The hand that shook hers was firm. 'So you've decided to risk the flight? Good to meet you, Miss Higgs. Miss Thwaites has told me so much about you. We first met in the Suffrage League many years ago,' she added. 'Good times, those. We got things done.'

'You've been flying long?'

A sardonic grin. 'Long enough to be able to get you to Darwin. This crate will only go about three hundred miles before she needs refuelling, but she takes petrol and we can probably get that wherever we see a car. Two hops today, if we are lucky.'

Mrs Henderson met Sophie's eyes. 'My sons were in the air force. Their father too. Richard, my eldest son, was the only one to make it through the war. He and a friend flew their aircraft home — it took them three years. He bought this beauty in

March, one of the first off the line, then a month later he got pneumonia. He'd had a bout of mustard gas. His lungs were never up to much after the war ...' She took a deep breath. 'So this is all I have of them. I have been flying ever since Richard first took me up.'

And like me you do not care terribly if you die doing so, thought Sophie, still numb.

She hugged Maria. Green and Georgina had already left so that Green could make her connection with the steamer. 'You really will come to England if I need to stay there for a while?' she asked Maria.

'Yes. Oswald and Johnny can manage. We will see each other there,' Maria said, a little helplessly. One's chicken should not literally fly from the roost. Sophie had never seen Maria look helpless before, as if she had lost ...

Me, she thought. She has lost me, and somehow last night and this morning I have lost myself.

A million words to say, but none that could adequately say what she felt. Another hug. Mrs Henderson handed her a thin leather coat, and long leather gloves. She was already sweating, but she donned then obediently and scrambled up on to the plane and into the single seat behind the pilot.

It's just like being in a car, she thought, as they taxied across the paddock. A car could not fly, and nor could this beast ... then suddenly the fence was below them, the tiny craft climbing mountains in the sky, as if hunting for a cloud to play with. The wind had become a road and they were travelling along it. A bumpy road; they lurched and stumbled yet did not fall ...

Nor had the world vanished, because it was below her. All of it, everything she was flying from: Thuringa, its paddocks, and its river glinting like a coiling snake among the trees, the dolls'-house homestead, the speck that was Maria, two men on horseback, impossible to see who they were from up there ...

The plane made a sharp arc, dipping one wing so Sophie was sure that they would plummet. But the craft remained steady.

Bald Hill, the church hall, the factory and the abattoir, the cattle huddled in the paddock outside so like men waiting to go 'over the top': for the first time she felt a horror that all her fortune had been built on death and bleeding cattle.

But she was leaving that too.

And then the McPhees' and beyond that John's shack. No smoke rising from the fireplace. She panicked briefly at that, then realised it had only been two hours since she had left. The coals would still be glowing under the blanket of ash, when he needed flames again. She wanted to look away, in case she saw him. She wanted to ask Mrs Henderson to circle until she finally found him, unable to hide from this craft up in the air. She did neither.

If only he could know this plane was taking her away. She hadn't even remembered to tell Midge to give a message to him, but of course gossip would soon tell everyone in Bald Hill that Miss Sophie Higgs had left Thuringa in an aeroplane, bound for an earl's castle in England, for all the aristocracy lived in castles ...

There was the Harrisons' house set in the neat Moura paddocks, a doll's house with a verandah. She wanted to wave but there was no sign of Midge or Harry or their children, and they probably wouldn't see the wave anyway.

Then that too was gone. The world was squares of paddocks, rolls of trees, the river, mountains to their left, the sun to their right.

And she was flying.

At the red soil property of an old school friend of Mrs Henderson's they stopped for Thermos tea, and scones fresh from the morning's oven but already hard as cricket balls in the dry heat, spread lavishly with tomato jam to make them edible, then refilled the plane with petrol.

Between hugs, Mrs Henderson briefly explained their haste and that she would stop longer, 'So we can really catch up,' on her return. A visit to the lavatory — a long-drop dunny at the end of a long line of pear trees that each marked the site of a previous convenience ... and then they were in the sky again.

Clouds arrived. They flew under them, shaking, through them, shaking even more, then above them, with not quite so much shaking but a great deal of glaring light. There was no way to make conversation in the air, not with the engine noise, the wind and the flying helmets.

I am coming, Nigel, she thought. Coming to Miss Lily too. When she had lost her way in the past decade it had been Miss Lily's face she saw, her voice advising her, the scent of her powder, her smile in the Shillings shadow.

The telegram might say *Nigel*. But if she lost Nigel, whom she also loved, she would lose Miss Lily. No other love could possibly replace them both.

Another stop on what seemed to be an endless, featureless grey gravel plain, this time to refuel from a jerry can they were carrying in the back. Up again, flying below the cloud now, Mrs Henderson pulling levers, examining instruments on her control panel. Sophie would have liked to ask her what they meant, but the noise and wind made it impossible. Her face already felt raw from wind and cold and sun.

The horizon turned pink, then red. Sophie had been aware of a strangely straight line below them, like a black mark etched across the landscape. The Overland Telegraph Line. She supposed they were going to follow it to find Darwin. She was vaguely relieved. She'd had images of flying over north Queensland jungles juggling a compass.

There would be jungle enough to come.

The plane nosed downwards, this time onto red plains with wind-twisted, white-trunked trees, and anthills like castles. For five startled seconds as they neared the ground, a piece of the red earth turned into a kangaroo. The kangaroo leaped, and kept on leaping. The plane landed, taxiing in small bumps until it stopped.

Sophie looked for a house, a shed, a tent. None appeared. Nor did Mrs Henderson appear to see any need to explain their lack.

She stepped out carrying the cushion that had formed part of her seat and a couple of paper bags.

Sophie pulled at her seat too, and found it came free. She joined Mrs Henderson, now lying with her head pillowed on the cushion. No blanket, and even in November the night there was beginning to cool. But their long coats would keep them warm. Probably.

Mrs Henderson passed her the paper bag. Sophie took out a bottle of water, drank a quarter of it and then found a cheese and salad roll, dry except where it was soggy from the tomato, and an apple. They ate, quietly, Mrs Henderson staring up at the sky as it turned pink and then pale once more and finally darkened.

The first star pierced the darkness and then another.

'This is my favourite time,' said Mrs Henderson at last. 'Just looking at the night going on forever and knowing tomorrow I will be up there too.'

'It's beautiful.' The whole sky was jewelled now. The air smelled of hot sand and cooling breeze, and a faint tang of male kangaroo.

More silence. It was so good to be still, the ground steady below her, no engine noise. At last she asked, 'Where will we reach tomorrow?'

'There's a camp not far from here where they'll have petrol. Darwin by tomorrow night if we're lucky. The wet's started, you know. It may get a bit rocky.'

She hadn't known. Or rather, had not remembered, had not even stopped to consider. Should have.

'Thank you. You're taking a great risk for me.'

'No, don't think that. Today and tomorrow I am flying for a purpose. You've given me that, at least.'

'I'm sorry,' said Sophie softly.

Mrs Henderson accepted it. 'I was never one of those who waited, you know. Wives and mothers who said, "When the war is over ..." as if it was going to all be the same as it had been before. I did not cry when I said goodbye because I did not want their last sight of me to be tears, but proud and glad to be my husband's wife, my sons' mother. I knew even then that would be my final glimpse of them, waving from the ship. To have Richard back for those years was ... unexpected. A treasure. And he gave me the sky.'

They watched it again. The air grew still and colder. Each star might have been made of ice.

'Maria said you worked in Belgium for two years.'

'Yes.'

'Was it ...?'

'As bad as they say? Yes.'

'But they don't say,' said Mrs Henderson softly. 'They come back, those men, those women, and they think they are protecting us by saying nothing. But we can see it in their faces and hear it in their screaming nightmares and we must say nothing, pretend we do not see.'

'Keep a stiff upper lip,' said Sophie. 'Take it on the chin. Get on with life, man. All those things that men say. War is their great secret, even from themselves. If it wasn't, they could not do it again and again.'

'Like childbirth,' said Mrs Henderson, and Sophie wondered if she smiled in the darkness. 'That is a women's secret. Impossible pain, and yet we do it again and again.'

'I never have.'

'I hope you will, one day.'

Sophie lay still, watching the blinking stars. She had never thought of contraception. She who had proudly ordered cartons of Mrs Stopes's book for distribution at her factories. What if she had conceived ... Was it only the night before? Surely not in just one night ...

She would know in two or three weeks. Until then she would not think of it. Might not need to think of it. And there were jungles and storms and cyclones long before it might even be a possibility.

'I thought I'd left the war behind,' she said. 'I think suddenly it has caught up with me again. I feel as if I have to *do*, but don't know what.'

Mrs Henderson laughed. 'I'd say flying towards England is *doing* something.'

'I suppose it is. Almost as melodramatic as a war.'

Another laugh. 'Wait till you see lightning rip the sky open, or feel your wings sag under snow. The sky can beat any man's war for drama.' She added quietly, 'Every time the thunder batters I can feel that I'm with them, hear the shellfire they must have heard, pull up courage enough to keep my hands on the controls ...'

You need another life, thought Sophie. I need one too.

At last she slept.

Dawn woke her; she was stiff and cold despite the coat. Mrs Henderson was already pouring the last of the petrol into the plane.

Another camp where the men obviously knew Mrs Henderson and her story, for they treated her with rough kindness, accepting her money, refuelling the plane and filling the jerry cans, brewing them tea so strong it almost dissolved the enamel mugs, sweetened with sugar that was almost an equal measure of sugar and bitter ants. They had been lugging great rolls of wire for the Overland Telegraph. 'The natives cut it for fish hooks, or belts to carry their knives. It's a job replacing it.' The man who spoke had the far-off look of yet another who still lived in the land of war; he had taken this job, perhaps, for the silence.

'Can't blame them,' he added. 'It's a bit like paying them rent, I reckon. But can't say that to the money-wallahs down in Adelaide.' He tipped his hat to Sophie politely, then fetched a large grey item that might have been a stone or a johnnycake cooked in the ashes. But Mrs Henderson ate it, so Sophie did the same. It satisfied the hunger, so was — probably — johnnycake, not rock.

They flew on, towards grey cloud mountains that turned purple and then black. The plane bucked like a frightened horse for half an hour, so badly that Sophie shut her eyes and dreamed of Nigel, Miss Lily, crumpets and honey, Maria, the river at

Thuringa, the Shillings orchard, her whole life's experience of love ...

And suddenly they were down, not crashed but landed, in a paddock with a shed that looked as if it had been built to house a plane with wings that could be folded back, a Gypsy Moth F60.

And it had.

Chapter 47

When you are young you do not realise that you will love many times. When you are older you will know that no matter how many you love, one love cannot replace another.

Miss Lily, 1914

Two hours later Sophie was in a bed with sheets, her stomach filled with tough steak and dripping crisp roast potatoes and queen of puddings, none of which sat easily in a stomach that had been whirled as if in a vast copper with the laundry. But the pillow was soft, a breeze riffled the humidity and even the sudden tenor roar of rain that began as if a giant had clicked its fingers and stopped as abruptly could not stop her sleeping. She dreamed of men's faces, men she loved. She had left men she had loved. Now she was going back to one.

She woke to a cup of tea in a china cup on a doily, the doily on a tray and the tray held by a maid in correct black uniform. 'Breakfast is in half an hour, Miss Higgs. Will I bring your bath?'

She bathed, quickly, found the maid had washed her undergarments and even had them dried, as efficiently as her hostess the night before had provided her with a nightdress and toothbrush.

And now breakfast, on a sunny verandah with a view of a grey sea that looked unhappy about the clouds that swirled above. Three women sat at the table already, eating bacon and eggs and toast with guava jelly: Mrs Henderson, coatless, the pearls revealed as very fine indeed; Mrs MacIntosh, in her fifties too, perhaps, and whose acceptance of her friend's unexpected appearance testified to their deep and long-standing connection; and a young woman Sophie's age, perhaps, for her face consisted only of her eyes, blue but lashless, two holes for nostrils and a lipless mouth in place of red scar tissue. Other damage was perhaps hidden under her brown leather flying helmet.

Sophie forced herself to smile equally upon them all, and not to let her eyes linger.

'Miss Higgs, do sit down,' said Mrs MacIntosh. 'This is Miss Eugenia Morrison, who will take you up to Calcutta in her seaplane.'

'I can't say how pleased I am to meet you —' began Sophie.

'Maybe I'll take you.' The young woman's tone was both hoarse and graceless. 'We have to establish the terms first. Your bloke in Sydney said you were the one who had to agree to them.'

'Yes,' said Sophie cautiously. Johnny Slithersole and Cousin Oswald had been given authority to pay whatever was necessary for this journey. What terms did this woman want?

The bright eyes in the shiny red face met hers. 'This trip's not going to be safe, or easy. In return — if we make it — I want to fly freight around the north, here and to the islands and New Guinea, and to Singapore too.'

'Whatever you want me to pay —'

'Not just money.' The words were rudely abrupt. They were also, possibly, painful to speak with so much scar tissue. 'I can't run a company. Not looking like this. I can manage the flying side but I need a partner to do the ... negotiating. That's where you come in.'

'All right,' said Sophie. 'I agree. Whatever you need. Money, manager, secretary and typist.' She would possibly have agreed, from pity and sympathy, even if Miss Morrison had not offered an exchange. 'Thank you,' she added to the maid, as her own plate of bacon and eggs, plus grilled tomato, weeping pale red, was placed in front of her.

She took a mouthful, then glanced at Mrs Henderson, spreading jelly on toast thick enough to bridge a harbour. 'I don't suppose you two would care to run it together? Higgs Industries would be the silent financial partner.'

A pause. Mrs Henderson put down her toast. 'A business? I have never thought ...'

Women do not do business, thought Sophie. Even when their men had vanished to war or death.

'They need air transport up here,' said Miss Morrison gruffly. 'Especially in the wet. Q.A.N.T.A.S. does well enough in Queensland and the outback, but we need a seaplane service for the coast and islands. Not just freight — medical supplies, food, a doctor.'

'It would be a ... valuable service,' said Mrs Henderson, tasting the words. 'Shall we discuss it when you return?'

Miss Morrison did not grin. Her scars obviously would not stretch enough for that. But her voice was an edge less angry when she said, 'I'd better make it back safely then, hadn't I?'

Sophie lifted her teacup. 'To safe journeys and returns. How did it happen?' she added bluntly.

Silence hung like she had flung a curtain across the room. One did not ask questions like that, especially at a breakfast table, especially when one was a guest. Miss Lily would not have approved.

Or possibly she would. Because this woman's wounds were ripping at the heart of each one of them, yet they were saying nothing.

Miss Morrison looked out at the sea. 'I was a VAD. A plane came down — it was 1917, near Poitiers. I got the pilot out, then it exploded. I managed to get my arm across my eyes, which saved my sight. The pilot wasn't so lucky. But he manages.'

'You still hear from him?'

'We married. He looks after the house; I pick up what work I can ferrying freight. Or people. But his face is even worse than mine, so he can't front a business either.'

'You call yourself Miss?'

A shrug. 'I am myself. Why should I take a man's name?'

The thought had never occurred to her. 'Good point.' She took more toast.

Another almost invisible grin from Miss Morrison. 'No questions about our route? The dangers?'

Sophie matched her shrug. 'You're the expert. I'm the cargo. Would you pass the jelly, please? It looks delicious.'

Across the table Mrs Henderson was crying, silent tears of loss and hope she wiped away with a delicately embroidered handkerchief. Mrs MacIntosh took her hand.

Lives went on, thought Sophie, but only if you worked hard to make them do so.

Chapter 48

If travel had all the familiarity of home, there would be no point in travelling.

Miss Lily, 1902

The seaplane bobbed at its mooring.

Sophie hauled herself aboard and glanced around the interior. She calculated that the plane could seat six, although the rear area was now filled with boxes and what her nose told her were jerry cans of fuel wrapped in oilcloth. At least this plane had a cabin, wooden panelled with cushioned seats, and a basket of what might be lunch — or tools in case of a breakdown.

Miss Morrison nodded briefly, her scar twisted in perhaps a smile. She didn't speak — Sophie was sure now that speech itself hurt. She wondered briefly about the communication between a husband and wife, both speechless, faceless, with only one who could see. It could either be distant, a matter of convenience for two outcasts. It might also be deeply close, a communication of touch of the whole body, man and woman coming together, as she and John ...

The engine stirred, then roared, a far deeper note than the Gypsy Moth's had been, cutting back the thought she had refused to think ever since that morning, that she had hoped not just to find him with her, but to go together from there to ...

The plane surged forward in the water, erasing all but blue-green bubbles rising up the windows, and Sophie's sudden terror that Miss Morrison might have decided to dive rather than fly, and end their lives in one dramatic downwards swoop.

Then all at once the nose was up, not down. They were above the water … no, down in it again … then with a waggle of wings firmly headed skywards, as bumpy a road as any paddock trail. The Moth's erratic airborne swerves had seemed bird-like. Every time this more substantial plane lurched, she thought they would fall …

She glanced down to see a too-white strip of sand on one side, mud and mangroves on the other, the turbulent green sea. Australia was now behind her once again, further away with every second. The place she loved, where she belonged, and she was leaving not just because she had to, for Nigel's sake and Jones's, but because she could not bear to stay. Once more she needed to find another Sophie Higgs and knew she would not find her there.

And yet …

She was singing. At first she thought the engine's roar drowned out her voice, then realised that there was a hum accompanying her, the music made by a mouth that could no longer sing.

'Oh, Danny Boy, the pipes, the pipes are calling
From glen to glen, and down the mountainside.
The summer's gone, and all the roses falling,
It's you, it's you must go and I must bide.'

Now she had gone, John could return to his gate, knowing he need not face her, and her importuning him, again. No one in Australia truly needed her, as Nigel did, and Lily perhaps, if she could ever be found again, and Jones. Those who loved her could now come to England sometimes too.

'But come ye back when summer's in the meadow,
Or when the valley's hushed and white with snow,
It's I'll be here in sunshine or in shadow —
Oh Danny Boy, oh Danny Boy, I love you so!'

She no longer trusted love. It was too easy to love an image your own heart created, as she had with Malcolm, Angus, Dolphie, and yes, perhaps, with John too. Or had she simply loved the peace he gave her?

> *'But come ye back when all the flowers are dying,*
> *And I am dead, as dead I well may be,*
> *Ye'll come and find the place where I am lying,*
> *And kneel and say an Ave there for me.'*

If she died on this journey or for some other reason did not return, perhaps John would carve a cross for her, if he forgave her, and forgave himself, for breaching the asceticism he had chosen.

> *'And I shall hear, tho' soft you tread above me,*
> *And all my grave will warmer, sweeter be,*
> *For you will bend and tell me that you love me,*
> *And I shall sleep in peace until you come to me.'*

But she would come back. Not to him, for that was not possible, but to her land, the river and its sunlight. When at last she slept in peace, it must be there.

Chapter 49

'She is a lovely lady.' Does that mean, literally, that she can be loved? I think so.

Miss Lily, 1914

Time passed. Nights and days under gunfire, shelling … nothing had prepared Sophie for the terror of sitting in a lurching, staggering box juggled by winds as the monsoon screamed around them.

Surely after the fiftieth lurch her body and mind would accept that this time she was not going to die as they plunged to the ocean below? But even the fifty-first time there was still a real possibility of death.

She did not want to die.

She did not want to fly either. But after the first landing near Surabaya, thirteen hundred miles from Darwin, and well within the limits it seemed of this strange craft, where they would refuel the next day after sleeping cramped in the bobbing plane, there was a choice of going on or going back. But going back meant flying too. Nor would her pride let her show cowardice in front of Miss Morrison.

They made Batavia the next day, once more sleeping in the plane to avoid having to hand over identification papers and go through port formalities. Singapore next, another eight hundred and sixty miles measured in lurches and terror as well as by the map, where she longed to say, 'Let's stay a week, in a proper bed after a wonderful scented bath.'

After Singapore they flew into the ground.

They had been staggering through a storm, Sophie's eyes closed, for there was nothing to see but grey or black or driving rain, and if she kept them shut she might pretend that if she looked again there might be blue sky. She took the crash and shudder for yet another bolt of lightning, the first seconds of fall for what Miss Morrison had muttered was an 'Air pocket,' as if any pocket could be miles deep.

They kept on falling, lurched, drifted, Miss Morrison doing frantic hand movements on the controls.

And then they crashed.

Or landed, as the case might be, but this was a landing with the plane suspended in a tree and upside down, not right-side up in the sea. And rain still pelted all around them. She was conscious of that, for possibly three seconds, then blackness.

She woke to find herself on a stretcher in a hut. The rain had stopped, though the air still felt thick with moisture. Children with dark skin and long shorts peeped in at the door giggling and then ran off. And then, impossibly, a woman with tanned but English skin, a faded flowered dress, sandals, and a voice that could cut ice. 'Ah, Miss Higgs, feeling better now? The boys have nearly got your crate repaired.'

'I ... where are ...?'

'Luckily you landed near the Mission. Mrs Hartley Bentleigh.' A firm handshake. 'My husband is having so much fun. He was a chaplain in the war. Says it's quite like old times again. He and the boys have mended the wing and carried the whole bird down to the lagoon. Miss Morrison says there is enough room to take off from there. A sporting lass, isn't she?'

'Er, quite.'

'I'd offer you tea, but we've had no supplies since the rains began. I can offer you a glass of coconut milk. No? I suppose I should be checking you for concussion but I never was good at that kind of thing.'

'No concussion.' Which Sophie had enough experience to know was not true. She was nauseated and her head felt as if it would split and be welcome to do so. She did not even wish to know exactly where they had landed. 'The ground' was information enough. 'Perhaps I might just rest until … until Miss Morrison is ready.'

'Of course, my dear.' Mrs Hartley Bentleigh strode out again, leaving Sophie to wonder if she had been a delusion.

And then she slept again.

They left the next morning with, miraculously, a break in the weather too. Sophie promised to send a cheque to the Mission ('So good of you, my dear') with a note in her pocket telling her exactly what denomination was required, and where the Mission was, information she did not have the strength to absorb just then.

They flew again.

Rangoon, where a blank-faced man of unknown race and magic hands worked on the engine while his companion laboured on the superstructure, and between them had the women flying again within a day. The rains and wind held off as they flew across the water to Calcutta.

And landed — once more sinking down into the water before they rose to bob on the surface. Miss Morrison turned to her, as if they had completed a shopping trip into the city and back, shook her hand firmly and managed to say, 'I will telegraph your offices about setting up the transport company.'

'I think Mrs Henderson probably already has, but yes — I'll telegraph my Sydney office to make sure you're getting all you need as soon as I get to England. I promise we will do all we can to get your business going.'

She glanced outside at the busy port. Large ships, small ships, strange vessels … did Miss Morrison expect her to get out now and swim to shore? Even as she thought it the aviator climbed out onto the wing and a smart white cutter drew up to them.

'Ahoy there!' The young man wore impeccable white flannels and a solar topi. 'Miss Higgs? Ah, *you're* Miss Higgs.' He turned from Miss Morrison's ruined face with relief. Miss Morrison stayed expressionless, though her hands clenched. How often does she endure that? wondered Sophie.

'We've been watching for you with binoculars from the balcony of the Consulate. Good old Higgs's Corned Beef, eh? Cornerstone of the empire, corned beef. They're holding the train for you.'

What train? She had thought that there at least she might need to arrange the next part of her journey herself, but it seemed her employees — her friends — worked even more capably for her than she had realised. Instead of asking the man for details she turned to Miss Morrison, hesitated, then hugged her, hard. A second later the hug was returned. 'We are going to meet again,' said Sophie shakily. 'When we are on the ground and we can talk, and I can meet your husband. And you will stay with us and we will talk about a million plans and ... and life ...'

'Yes,' said Miss Morrison, and kissed her cheek with lips that had vanished years back and yet still kissed.

Sophie waved to her, and the cutter wound its way across the harbour.

Chapter 50

Travel is adventure. It is not always a good one. Adventures rarely are, at least while one is experiencing them.

Miss Lily, 1914

The train was long, and full of freight, but seemed to have as many passengers on its roof as there were crates of goods inside, except on her carriage, which had been tacked onto the end, like a mouse that had bitten a snake and didn't know how to let go.

Her carriage was definitely not a usual part of a freight train. The inside was panelled with mahogany except where it was satin or gold velvet or Persian carpet or polished bronze. There were fifty-six lamps, in carved marble, bronze and alabaster — she counted them as she lay in the great, white-pillowed, four-poster bed. Whoever had designed this carriage had the same concept of 'restraint' as Genghis Khan.

A servant in white jacket and trousers brought her tea and chilled mangoes, the cheeks already neatly sliced, and strange small stews in silver dishes or anchovies on toast at times that never seemed to fit with any mealtime she knew about. But she was too tired to do more than smile and sleep with the curtains drawn to keep out the new scenes she had no interest in.

Perhaps it was the aftermath of the crash, or the withdrawal of whatever desperation and anguish had led her to this wild journey. And yet she realised, as she lay there in sheets that were changed each morning while she bathed behind a screen in scented water with soap of the same perfume, and towels as long and soft as mermaid's hair, that she had swept across a landscape just as thoughtlessly once before, though admittedly not across the world — just two countries, and to save ten thousand, not a single man.

Her presence wouldn't save Nigel. It had been a momentary need to justify this journey to herself and Maria to ever claim it might. She had not even thought deeply what her presence might mean. Just that Jones had asked for her. She trusted Jones.

And so she ate and slept and bathed, and ate again.

Sometime, in the cold recesses of an early morning — which meant she was far north on the Indian coast to be this cold — her carriage was attached to a goods train. When she woke properly and peered through the curtains all she could see was grey desert and funnelled bare hills, quite like the desert she and Mrs Henderson had slept in only a week ago.

A telegram lay on her breakfast tray, if rice simmered in chicken stock with small soft grapes might be called breakfast. She picked it up.

Orient Express booked stop luggage arranged stop Mr Lampeen will escort you stop love from us all Maria Thwaites stop

So this train, whose destination she hadn't even ascertained, must be crossing Central Asia and the Middle East to Constantinople. And luggage would be good. At the moment she washed her underwear every evening and her nightdress each morning and longed for Green. She did not want to give her underwear to the steward to wash. It might offend him. It might not return either.

A volley of shots fractured the morning, if it was morning. Her watch had lost all meaning — she had no idea how many time zones she had crossed. The shots were answered, reminding her that she must now be on, or near, the North West Frontier, where Nigel had been raped, beaten, left for dead. Where he had met her dad.

Her father had lost his leg on the North West Frontier. Nor was it any safer today, according to its rare mentions in the newspapers. But the shots had sounded far away and the area was secure enough for a freight train line to exist — blowing up or removing a train line should be simple enough for determined men.

She peered between the curtains again; she saw the same grey hills closer, this time adorned by a black goat; and then the goat was gone.

She lay back, for the first time wishing she had a book to read. On any other train one could ask the steward for an English language newspaper, but not when one's carriage was tacked on the back of a freight train and one had no idea what country, much less languages, were around them. The steward had not even spoken when he had brought her breakfast.

Somehow, it did not seem to matter; or, rather, it mattered deeply that it did not matter. The train carried her; trains, unlike planes, could not deviate from their course, and Mr Lampeen was awaiting her with luggage.

She would trust the minions of the empire her father had created, and she had extended, under the umbrella of the massive British Empire itself. And wait.

Mr Lampeen wore a too dark, too narrow suit, a thin moustache and perfumed hair oil, and drove a car of elderly magnificence. He spoke little and likely had few English words to speak, but did not want to lose face by admitting this lack. Sophie accepted his 'Miss Higgs!' and 'The car, Miss Higgs,' 'The luggage is on the train, Miss Higgs,' and 'Good journey, Miss Higgs?' and, after their drive from the city outskirts to the central Sirkeci Station, with a brief stop en route for Mr Lampeen to send several telegrams in two directions so her friends could keep up with her movements, followed the steward into the polished carriages of the *Orient Express*.

Her berth smelled of lemon polish, of tea and biscuits and starch and the hint of mothballs. The seat was soft leather, and shone; lamps glowed softly.

'Mademoiselle Higgs?' A soft voice, speaking Parisian French. 'I am Eloise. Lady Georgina arranged for me to attend you on this journey. Will you dress for dinner, or take it here?'

'Dress?'

Eloise, neat in black dress, black stockings, black shoes, black hair and very white skin and hands, put down the small jewel box she had brought into the compartment and opened the wardrobe. She selected a gown in a soft burnished gold and held it up for Sophie's approval.

A dining car. People. She would like to be near people again, among them, not travelling past them. Not to speak to, but to listen, to be back in her familiar privileged world. And this was Nigel's world too, and Miss Lily's. A dining car, a maid, brought her closer to them.

'The dress is perfect, Eloise.'

How had Georgina and Green arranged this miracle? For the dress would most certainly fit, as would the others hanging next to it, and the coat, the most glorious coat of soft leather with a wide shawl-like collar and cuffs of mink at sleeve and hem. She opened the jewel box. Pearls, but not the old-fashioned short string like Mrs Henderson's. Was Mrs Henderson now camping by the Overland Telegraph Line again, gazing at the jewel stars or already plotting her new enterprise and new life with Miss Morrison?

These pearls would loop in two waist-long strings. Extraordinarily expensive — which one must not mention but keep in mind — and, moreover, so evenly matched that only the most well-connected of all jewellers could have obtained them. In Paris, certainly, and by wire from Australia. On top of the velvet-lined case a mundane telegram said simply, *Thank you stop travel well stop love Georgina stop*

She heard Miss Lily's words, from so long ago. How had they gone? 'One must always wear something given with love.' Perhaps not quite those words, but that was their meaning.

These clothes, these pearls, were procured and given with love.

A bath, with rose-scented soap. She let herself glide into the dining car, her body swan-like even with the slight lurch of the train, as she was used now to far more severe turbulence. The *Orient Express* was almost like punting on a small still river.

She sat, at a table for two but already set for one, for her. She did not wish to make small talk on a journey as long as this. Starched tablecloth, starched napkin. Silverware that gleamed. A menu …

She chose.

A glass of champagne. Oysters, though she ate only two of the six, knowing the staff would consume the leftovers, turtle soup, turbot with green sauce, chicken 'à la chasseur' of which she ate only a mouthful too. The steward offered red wine with the fillet of beef and château potatoes but she declined; she ate three mouthfuls of beef and some of the potatoes. A chaudfroid of game animals was presented next, which suddenly made her think of John's rabbit stew, so that she sent it back untouched, lettuce salad with small hearts of radish and strips of orange peel, a chocolate pudding that she ate slowly, letting each spoonful spread across her tongue, then scraped the bowl, deliberately disobeying the manners taught her by Miss Thwaites and Miss Lily.

Passengers gazed at her discreetly. They were wealthy, mostly elderly; one younger man had the look of an ex-officer who had declined in standing and become either a card sharp or a gigolo, investing in a first-class fare to look for his next prey. He smiled at her. She kept her face blank.

Three women, of three generations, who might have been visiting the battlefields of Palestine, having lost loved ones there. Had it been the daughter's husband, fiancé, and the other two were there to comfort her? Or a son, brother, grandson?

At another time she might have joined them for coffee — or wished that someone had brought her an invitation to join their table. But just as her body reminded her it needed rest and sustenance to recover from the early terror and continued stress of this journey, her mind seemed cast back to 1917, as well as the events of just over a fortnight earlier.

So much had happened that she needed all the time available to process all that had occurred. She must catch up with her life before she arrived at the inevitable challenges of Shillings and England.

She declined coffee; she stood, knowing her dress, her pearls, her poise were perfect, even if her hair was not quite — she had grown too used to Green's fastidious care. Shorter hair was ostensibly less work and certainly dried faster, but long hair could be pulled back in a simple chignon, even by an amateur like her. Somehow a bob always had a stubborn lock or two that wisped away from the rest, and Eloise was not Green who alone, it seemed, knew the magic for keeping Sophie's hair neat after it had left the attentions of her comb and lavender spray.

She walked back to her compartment and knew that with the grace Miss Lily had taught her no one had even noticed her hair.

The bed had been made up. Starched sheets, a soft pillow. She sipped cocoa from a cup of fine china emblazoned with the railway's crest and presented on a silver tray. And then she slept.

They changed trains at Belgrade the next day, though her new compartment was almost identical to the first one. Porters and Eloise took care of her luggage. She wore her new coat and felt stares again as she swept across the station platform. The mink hat even covered her sub-standard hair.

Belgrade to Vienna. The train wheels on their tracks below her sounded like a heartbeat: an irregular one, just like the lives beating all around.

Dark, light; dark, light; her body had lost all sense of time. She slept when her bed was made up, crisp linen and feather pillows. She did not dream; or did not think she did. It was as if her life had emptied so that dreams could no longer come. She ate when the steward ushered her to the dining car, and enjoyed the ritual, because eight-course meals meant she was approaching the 'civilisation' that required them, the land where Nigel waited.

She knew the food was good too, even though she could not remember its flavour after she had swallowed it.

The only food she truly tasted was when she breakfasted alone in her compartment, off a tray: scrambled eggs with smoked salmon; croissants with English marmalade, which was not at all how one should appreciate either, but was how she liked them, and no steward on the *Simplon Orient Express* would argue with the strange tastes of a passenger; and milky coffee, this time with the curtains open, letting herself be drawn back into the world of Europe — bare forests of dappled trunks above a tapestry of dark earth or gleaming snow, and women in black — black scarves, black shawls, black stockings, black rags wound about their feet, bearing loads of firewood on their backs. She imagined their feet, cold and bleeding, their hands bleeding and splintered too.

Theirs was not the simplicity of John's life, where he had wood enough for warmth and food and peace, and no responsibility except to the dead, which admittedly was enough to crush his soul. These women had children, grandchildren, elderly parents waiting for the firewood back in cold cottages. But one could not stop the *Orient Express* to share its luxury; nor could she stop her life to share its privilege.

She had created jobs and decent working conditions. She had done her best ... except, of course she hadn't. This journey in itself was a personal indulgence that cost more even than the pearls she wore even at night to keep them safe aboard the train. It was a maid's job to guard the jewellery and she was afraid that Eloise might feel slighted to be denied that role, but the pearls linked the Sophie of a fortnight ago to the one who would arrive in ... what? ... two days, perhaps three, in England.

She pulled the bell for Eloise. 'May I have a newspaper, please?'

'Of course, Mademoiselle Higgs.'

'Thank you.' She gave her a smile of apology. 'I am afraid I have been most ungrateful of your care. I am ... tired, you see.'

'But of course, Mademoiselle Higgs.' A look that said, 'If you are not going to make me your confidante, which is the right of every lady's maid, then I will not unbend for you.'

Sophie sighed as Eloise left the compartment. She would tip her well in Paris ... except she had no francs; nor did she wish to waste time establishing a line of credit at a bank. Perhaps the manager of the bank she had used back in 1919 was not even there.

Ah, well. Whoever had hired Eloise must arrange for her to be well tipped.

She lunched in the dining car and dined there too, focusing now on her graceful hands, the perfect poise of her neck, subtleties she had let slip as a factory owner or at Thuringa, as well as the long meals she had dispensed with in her Australian life, where four courses — soup, fish, meat, pudding — followed by tea with petits fours, was considered a banquet.

Does Nigel still eat like this at Shillings? she wondered, nibbling game pâté on thin toast. In the immediate post-war period they had dined simply, one course and fruit from the estate, the sugar ration kept for the cherry cake Mrs Goodenough religiously made every four days for Sophie. But Nigel would be ill now ...

Where was the tumour? Jones could not have given that detail in a telegram to be read by so many. Surely not in his brain, or he would not be able to tidy the estate affairs before his operations. Or would he, if the tumour had been diagnosed early?

Please, let it not be his brain, she thought. Or ...

No, there was no place in the body she could think of where a tumour that might kill you could be acceptable. Why couldn't tumours be confined to portions of the body one could do without, as so many were doing now — legs or arms or even faces ...

She shook her head in apology as the waiter brought the soup. Some parts of the body should remain inconspicuously doing their duty. She no longer felt like eating.

Chapter 51

*There are times when time vanishes like steam from a teacup, and
others when it sits upon you like London fog.*

Miss Lily, 1914

The change of train at Vienna brought a most handsome man
in a short German jacket and with hair of perfect oiled neatness
into her compartment. He presented her with a buff envelope
that contained a wire and three more envelopes, filled with
many French francs in small and large denominations, a wad of
German marks which she suspected had very little value, and two
hundred English pounds in one pound notes. She would have to
sleep on them for security. Eloise might have been chosen simply
for her availability and skill with stain removal and ironing. She
might also have been a staunch companion for La Dame Blanche
with Green, and thus trustworthy not just with pearls and cash,
but with one's life. Lacking information, caution still seemed
advisable.

The envelope also contained a telegram, written with a happy
disregard for expense:

*Darling Sophie comma all here relieved and delighted you have
arrived safely in Europe stop all well here stop Green arrives
Southampton 6 January stop is bringing your luggage but has
arranged for all necessary to await you in Paris stop do not continue
to Calais as a flight from Paris to Shillings will avoid wasting
time with paperwork at a port stop Mrs Henderson has arranged a
surprise for you in Paris and all other arrangements have been made
comma but phone Jones from Paris to tell him when to have a field*

cleared for landing comma as the time of your exact arrival will be
uncertain stop all send their love to you stop Timothy has painted a
portrait of Thuringa and given it to Green for you stop please give
his lordship our very best wishes from all who love you in Australia
and my best regards to Jones stop love always Giggs stop

It is real, she thought, looking out at the snow-covered hills, the tops of rows of grape poking above them, the almost black-green of stands of pines. I am going to arrive at Shillings in less than three weeks from Jones' telegram. It is really happening, and I am here and almost there —

The train stopped so abruptly she almost fell from her seat. She stood and looked out into the corridor, a row of heads peering from doors. The steward appeared with an almost realistic expression of unconcern.

'There is some small snow on the track,' he said in English. 'It must be dug away; an hour only.' He repeated the message in more fluent German, and then in French.

'Harrumph,' muttered the occupant of the compartment next to hers — sixties, balding, portly, played bridge and spent meal-times discussing Mesopotamian archaeology with his slightly younger and only slightly less corpulent male companion. 'That means there's been an avalanche. We might be stuck here for days.'

'I heard of a train that was halted for nearly three weeks ...' said the matron beyond him, whose pearls were almost as excellent as Sophie's.

Sophie retreated to her compartment. One hour or three weeks: snow at least waist-high outside, the nearest town an unknown distance away, one week to Nigel's surgery, and absolutely nothing she could do to change the situation.

Chapter 52

When your heart and mind are battered, a solid training in good manners can be a comfort. Good manners mean you can keep going without thinking, for a while.

Miss Lily, 1906

HANNELORE

The schloss was snowbound, but it was warm, a tribe of servants dedicated to adding wood to each fire, working their way up the castle, and then beginning the routine from the bottom again. The luncheon had been pre-war: caviar en croute, soup, oysters, trout, neck of venison, roast goose, roast pork with grapes and apples, anchovy savoury, Bombe Imperatice and dessert of nuts and cheese. The jewels on necks and wrists and earlobes rivalled the collection in the Tower of London, Hannelore saw with amused pride.

Germany still struggled. But at last she and others could see its way back to greatness.

The men conversed, and the women gossiped; or perhaps it was the other way around. Then it was time to change to dine once more, a process that would take two hours, leaving time for champagne before dinner and thus filled in a winter's day.

She found Dolphie in her room, smoking a thin cigar. He gestured to it. 'Do you mind?'

'You know I don't.' She gestured to Liesl to leave. 'An hour to dress will be plenty,' she assured her. 'The diamonds I think tonight.'

She was glad she had not tried to sell her jewels. They had been almost worthless towards the end of the war, and in its aftermath. Too many tiaras going begging and who in Germany would buy them? And even if someone had had the money, it had not been a time to advertise one's status.

Now, once more, it was.

'So?' she asked Dolphie.

'Ernst has asked me for your hand in marriage.'

'Ah. I thought he would.' It irritated her only faintly that, despite all she had achieved, her fate was still negotiated by men.

'Do you want to marry him? He is rich — I checked — and the title is good. I know you like him.'

'Yes, I like him very much.' She sat in the chair by the fire — the schloss was well served by its fires and porcelain stoves, but in Germany in winter there were always draughts too — smoothing the velvet of her gown. 'But, no, I will not marry him.'

'Are you sure?'

He means I will soon be too old for marriage offers, she thought, except from widowers who already had an heir. 'I do not think it would be fair to him.'

Dolphie raised an eyebrow.

'Dolphie, in that ... that time we do not speak of ...' she took a deep breath, grasped courage while keeping her hands still and graceful in her lap '... they used a bayonet to rape me. I do not think it likely I can bear children. Either the pregnancy would fail, or I would die.'

He kept his face expressionless. She was grateful. She could not have borne sympathy or compassion, even though she knew he felt both.

'I see,' he said, when she assumed he had managed to steady his voice. 'So you will never marry?'

'I'm not sure I would want to marry anyway,' she admitted. 'But my probable barrenness does seem to fix the matter.'

'Ernst might accept adopting one of his illegitimate offspring. He seems ... potent,' said Dolphie. 'These things can be arranged, as you know.'

Yes, she knew. Knew that Ernst had mistresses, would continue to after his marriage, even though she believed he felt true affection for her, and certainly respect. They would holiday in Greece or Italy. Or even, possibly, in Australia, to see the kangaroos, if ever she felt she could ask forgiveness from Sophie.

Once far away from Germany she would be announced pregnant, but in danger of miscarriage, the doctors warning her not to travel. The mistress would give birth, be given a house and pension, and stay where she'd been put while the baby grew up as the uncontested heir.

Australia would be quite suitable for that and it was large. She need not even go within a thousand miles of Sophie, much as she longed to meet her again. And Africa was large and suitably remote, as well. She and Ernst would return with babe in arms, and if it was a girl they would do it all again. Better, perhaps, to have a girl first, for there would be fewer murmurings and careful investigations of the child's resemblances.

Possible. Quite simple. Ernst might even agree, both because he liked her and because the marriage would give him status. But she did not wish to do it.

'Please tell him no with my deepest regrets. Tell him if I married anyone, it would be him.' She smiled. 'Which is the truth. It just matters less than it sounds.'

'I will tell him after dinner.' His voice changed tone. 'I have been offered a position at the embassy in London. Nothing major. But it could lead to ... contacts. Now you have decided about Ernst, I can ask — will you be my hostess?'

She had last seen London as an outcast, the friendships offered there drawn back as soon as war was declared. Except for Sophie's.

She was not sure she wanted to face London again. She was sure, however, that it was her duty. To establish Germany in the minds and society of England, to make contacts that would further their cause. To work for peace, and for peace to be kept.

'Of course,' she said and pulled the bell for Liesl to come and dress her.

Chapter 53

I remember a Christmas I spent in a shepherd's hut, shut off by the snow, with a single companion, and we dined on hard cheese and stale bread. We looked out at the stars and for the first time I understood the concept of heavenly peace. It was the richest Christmas I had had.

Miss Lily, 1914

In one hour and twelve minutes exactly, according to her watch, the train was free and snuffling on its way again, slowly at first, then the snuffle changing to a reassuring roar. The engineers were piling in coke, to make up time, or possibly because further blizzards were expected.

It felt both strange and deeply right to be following this particular Stuttgart route again, the one she had taken when she had left Europe nearly six years earlier. The same trees, snow-clad now, icicles like small daggers hanging from branches, instead of meadow flowers and curious deer. Gingerbread villages belched comfortable-looking smoke from stone chimneys; a girl in a shawl to her ankles herded geese who might be heading either to a warm shed or to the dinner pot.

Had Dolphie married? Surely he must have found himself a more amenable heiress by now, one who would sit at home and breed his heirs and let him rebuild his life using her fortune. Was Hannelore married too?

It had been an unlikely friendship, Sophie reflected, two young women far apart in background, yet flung together in the strangeness of both Miss Lily's lessons and the equally odd, if more conventional, peculiarities of a debutante season. Perhaps it was that … isolation … that had drawn them as close as sisters, though as Sophie had never had a sister, the comparison was possibly not apt.

At any time in the past six years she could have asked Mr Slithersole to enquire about the Prinzessin von Arnenberg from their Stuttgart and Munich customers. Even in post-war Germany the affairs of a graf and prinzessin must be food for gossip, even if it was 'Poor things, in such poverty now' or 'The prinzessin? She married a korporal and has had twelve children, including triplets and three sets of twins. She breeds poodles now!'

She had not because … because …

Because Europe was the land of war, the land she had left, and she had foolishly imagined her past could be left behind just as easily as the continent. When things were … settled … with Nigel, whatever settled might mean (she refused to countenance the word death) she would enquire …

Another change of trains at Stuttgart. She longed for still ground, truly still — even the gentle roll of the *Orient Express* was tiresome now. She wanted no new countryside passing around her, no transient people. She wanted the familiar and those she loved, and Mrs Goodenough's cherry cake. Jones would undoubtedly tell Mrs Goodenough when she rang him from Paris. Two hours' flying time would give her sufficient time to bake one.

What would Nigel say? Had Jones even told him she was on her way? Would he fold her in his arms …?

Perhaps it had been only Jones who wanted her there. Perhaps Nigel had found another love. Maybe Miss Lily had returned to live at Shillings for the final weeks. Perhaps …

The snow lay behind them now. Tidy rows of cabbages lined what had been churned battlefields. Acres of mud were still black-brown, but this time they were fenced and enclosing pigs. Even the dead, blackened forests seemed to have vanished, either as firewood or because living with such visible skeletons was unendurable. The dead forests had perhaps been disposed of just as the crosses tidied the human mess into the ground.

I will be weeping next, she thought. And then: I cannot bear this. To see Nigel for a week, then see him die. To know that she would never eat crumpets with Miss Lily or feel the warmth of her gloved hand …

They approached Paris in darkness. She did not sleep; and then she did, so deeply that she dreamed Eloise was knocking on the door for long minutes before waking to discover it was real.

'We reach Paris in half an hour, Mademoiselle Higgs.'

Time to bathe, to dress once more in clothes suitable for flying, trousers in soft green and rust tweed, and matching jacket, a burgundy silk blouse, lightly frilled, the leather coat, its furred hem almost sweeping the floor, the hat, leather gloves that matched the long aviator boots that none of the aviators who had helped bring her here had worn, but which looked dashing …

And of course, the pearls. Thank you, Mrs Henderson, for showing me the perfect accessory to wear when appearing from the sky.

A silver powder compact, with mirror, in one pocket, lipstick in another. Strange to think how these two necessities for a stylish arrival had been unthinkable not so very long ago. Everything else was packed into a dark green leather trunk and passed to a porter.

'May I wish you a bon voyage, Mademoiselle Higgs?' To her surprise, Eloise looked genuinely sad to part. Or was she simply hoping for a larger gratuity? Sophie handed her a sandwich of francs and was rewarded with a '*Thank* you, Mademoiselle,' and even a curtsey, rarely seen since before the war.

The brakes squealed. The train huffed, instead of surged. Men scurried on a platform in the smoke-hazed dawn.

The train stopped. Footsteps sounded heavy along the corridor, and then a voice: 'Sophie lass, where are you?'

Sophie opened the door with a bang. '*Ethel!*'

Chapter 54

The true structure of our lives is friends.

'Midge telegraphed me,' said Ethel, solid in a pink suit and white stockings that made her legs look like substantial cottage cheeses. Apart from the shorter skirt she looked almost exactly like the eighteen-year-old girl Sophie had met in the war, capably organising one of the largest canteens near the Western front. 'Said you'd need company. Nay, you don't have to explain anything. Midge has done that.'

'But how did you get here?'

'Same way as we're getting back to England. My nephew George runs an aeroplane company between Paris and London, but he's taken the day off to bring me over and take us both back. Put Mademoiselle's trunk in the back, *see voo play*,' she added to the porter, in French that was as Yorkshire as it had been during the war.

'I ... I can't say anything except thank you. I do need help.' She had never said those words before, she realised. Never asked for help. Help to get to Ypres, help to learn the right manners, but not help for herself.

Ethel twinkled at her. 'Midge said you were full of good ideas, but other people had to carry them out for you. Luckily I'm an organiser *pa eggsallence*.'

It took Sophie a second to realise the last two words were meant to be French. 'Thank you again. A million times thank you. First of all I need to make a phone call.'

'Righty ho, got it all fixed. Monsewer in the ticket office over there has a telephone.' Ethel guided her through the crowd, a milling sea even at this time of the morning, effortlessly parting its waves to let Sophie through.

Sophie gave the operator the number, waited, drinking tea from the Thermos Ethel had — of course — provided, sweet enough to power a beehive, and eating a cheese and pickle sandwich which brought back enough good memories to steady her voice when the phone rang again.

She picked up the receiver. 'England for you, Mademoiselle,' said the first operator. 'Putting you through to Shillings now,' said the next and finally, a voice saying, 'Shillings. His lordship's residence.'

A man's voice. Not Jones.

'This is Miss Sophie Higgs. May I speak to Mr Jones, please?'

'Mr Jones is not available, madam.' The voice made it clear that telephoning one of his lordship's staff was not acceptable.

'May I speak to his lordship then?'

'He is not available either, madam.'

'Then who is?' demanded Sophie. 'And who are you?'

Silence on the other end. The voice spoke again with a degree of caution. 'I am Cutler, Mr Vaile's butler, madam. Shall I see if he or Mrs Vaile are available?'

Mrs Vaile? For one heart-wrenching moment Sophie thought Nigel had married. No, no: his wife would be a countess, not a Mrs.

Who were Mr and Mrs Vaile? And why weren't Jones or Nigel available?

'Never mind. I am calling to let Nigel —' (take that, Cutler the Butler) '— know that I shall be arriving at Shillings by plane in about two hours.' It was more likely three, by the time they were in the air, but better to have them ready too early than too late. 'You will need to make sure the field below the orchard is clear of stock so the plane can land.'

The voice was more confident now. 'I am sorry, madam, but that is not possible. The zebras are in that field.'

Zebras? 'Zebras? What in the name of Harry —?' The old wartime oath was not ladylike, but impossible to hold back. 'What are zebras doing in the field below the orchard?'

'They would eat the roses in the garden,' said Cutler's refined tones. 'And the hippopotamus will be in the orchard. It is due this morning.'

Jones must be giving refuge to a madman. It was the only possible explanation.

'If the zebras are in the field below the orchard in two hours' time, they will likely be squashed by my plane,' said Sophie sweetly. 'The same goes for camels, rhinoceroses and aardvarks.'

'Mrs Vaile felt a rhinoceros might endanger the guests. You *do* have an invitation to Shillings, Miss Higgs? Henry has just brought the household book and I cannot find your name in it. Mrs Vaile does know that you intend … *wish* … to attend?'

'I have never met Mrs Vaile and his lordship has made it clear that Shillings is my home whenever I wish. See to the zebras, Mr Cutler.' She clanged the receiver down. Take that, she thought. She looked at Ethel, who grinned.

'Zebras?'

'I think Jones may need rescuing,' said Sophie lightly. Protectiveness rose like an angry tide.

Zebras, camels, Vailes and a butler putting on an accent of not quite refinement … she'd have them all in order by lunchtime.

She took a final bite of cheese sandwich, feeling finally exactly like herself. Bring on the hippopotamus! 'Let battle commence,' she said to Ethel. Grinning, they strode out to the waiting car.

Chapter 55

I prefer a cup of tea before battle, rather than brandy, whether the battle is on a war front or in a drawing room. Tea clarifies and strengthens. A piece of fruitcake is an excellent addition.

Miss Lily, 1914

The aircraft was the most substantial she had seen yet. An aisle ran between six seats, not including the cabin for the pilot and co-pilot, and there was a rear chamber for luggage. Nephew George, however, was an unlikely pilot — at least a foot taller and wider than Ethel, which must have made him the most valued forward in a rugby scrum, if heavy cargo in a plane.

The seats were narrow, but cushioned; the wood trim was pale and polished. Ethel settled herself in beside Sophie, her backside almost contained by the seat. 'La-di-da, isn't it? Not like the kites in the war. Even has a girl serve tea and scones these days.'

'Not a pannikin of cocoa and corned-beef sandwiches and two cigarettes?'

Ethel gazed out the window as the plane began to taxi. 'They were good days, weren't they? Nay, you know what I mean. They were bad days but we knew what we were doing. Clean up the generals' messes and feed the boys and try to spoon them cocoa if their faces were blown off. These days ...'

'Midge said you were standing for election to local council.'

'Lost,' said Ethel briefly.

'Me too. Mine was a federal.'

Ethel grinned. 'I know. You even got half an inch in *The Times*. Colonies to have Female MP?'

'I assume they didn't even bother to announce I lost. You're still running the clinic?'

'Got some good women to keep that afloat. I've been getting an allotment project off the ground, if you'll excuse the pun. Pushing blokes with scarred lungs out in the fresh air, and growing fresh vegetables for kiddies who live on bread and treacle. Every little bit helps, as the old woman said when she spat into the sea.'

The plane swerved upwards, the smoothest take-off Sophie had experienced so far. But of course, George must make this plane flight pleasant enough for people to want to do it again and to tell their friends. 'Flying to Paris? Darling, you must try it. You can get there in time to have lunch and buy a hat and be home for tea. I bought this one the last time Horace and I were over there ...'

'Another sandwich?' offered Ethel, rooting in her capacious handbag as if digging for parsnips.

'Please.' There had been no time for breakfast.

'Can do you a ham and pickle. Here, you finish what's in the Thermos.'

'You don't want any?'

'Not till they work out how to put a bathroom in these things.'

'A hole, so it all drops,' suggested Sophie.

'I told George that but he says a long drop would spoil the aero-whatsits.'

'Aerodynamics?' She had not spent two days in the company of Mrs Henderson without learning some useful phrases, even if Miss Morrison had contributed little.

'That's it. Should have gone back at the station. I keep telling George he needs to build an airplane station too, one with toilets and where you can buy a cup of tea and a rock cake. The rock cake might make the passengers a bit heavier but that toilet could also make them lighter. He said he'll think about it.'

'Is his business good?'

'Enough to keep him flying and out of working at Carryman's Cocoa. Luckily he's got a younger brother whose heart heads to chocolate rather than the sky.'

Ethel's father evidently still did not consider a girl a useful heir. Though possibly if Ethel had children ... 'You're not tempted to get married? Excuse me, old thing — put it down to colonial bumptiousness.'

'I don't mind. Nay, not for me. If it's a choice between a man and a motorbike, I'd rather have the bike. One gives me freedom and the other would take it away.'

'Girls?' asked Sophie discreetly, under the noise of the engine. The wings waggled, as if shocked by her suggestion, and they changed direction. She could see the coast below them, grey water and grey sails, seagulls scattering, jealous of these apes with wings who had taken to the skies.

'Nope,' said Ethel cheerfully. 'That wasn't an offer, was it?'

'Of course not!'

'Well, it takes all sorts. Especially now. Well, I suppose it always did, but people are more open about it these days. What are you going to do with this Nigel fellow once you get there?'

'Be there for him.'

'Yes,' said Ethel patiently. 'But as what?'

'Friend. Nurse. I truly don't know.' And she had carefully pushed that question aside throughout her journey. 'Whatever he needs.'

'He didn't give you a hint when he asked you to come?'

Sophie flushed. 'He didn't exactly ask me. His secretary did. And best friend.'

'Ah,' said Ethel, carefully noncommittal.

Sophie suddenly thought of her two other journeys, to Ypres and to Munich, impulsive, dramatic, and without full understanding of where she was going, or even why. This dash was even more dramatic, its ending less dangerous, despite the zebras, but even more unknown.

No, it isn't, she thought. Whatever happens in the next week, or weeks, there will be Nigel or Lily, who I love, and Jones, who I trust, and Shillings, where I am myself more than anywhere except home.

Ethel peered across Sophie and out the window. 'The good old white cliffs. You'd better go up front and give George directions.'

'Hasn't he got a map?' Sophie asked in alarm. She wasn't sure she could recognise the roads to Shillings from the air.

'Of course he has,' said Ethel patiently. 'But you'll need to tell him where to land. And help him look out for zebras too.' Her grin appeared again. 'I'm looking forward to seeing those zebras.'

'So am I,' said Sophie. And found she meant it.

Chapter 56

When does friendship begin? Liking someone enormously at first sight is no guarantee that you will stay close. Acquaintanceship may slowly ripen. The only test of true friendship is time.

Miss Lily, 1914

Hedges, their covering of briar and brambles bare now in winter, showing the old stones beneath. Cold cows on cold grass, and reproachful sheep. Why did the merinos at the Harrisons' look disdainful and these merely reproachful? It must be the merinos' long noses. These sheep did not know they were part of an earl's estate ... and there was the Shillings and Sixpence and the home farm ...

'That field! The one just past the house, with the —'

'Zebras,' said nephew George. 'Miss Higgs, I can't land there. I might hit one of them.'

'What happens if you do?'

'I have no idea. I've never landed on a zebra. Or any other animal,' he added hurriedly. 'I imagine it would flatten the zebra and damage our undercarriage.'

'Land,' ordered Sophie. 'I'll pay if the plane's damaged. Zebras run from lions — I bet they know how to escape from a plane too.'

The zebras stared up as the plane circled, as if wondering if it was a new variety of vulture. Sophie peered down at the rose garden, but there was no sign of a hippopotamus, just bare bushes, heavily pruned among the —

Palm trees? Surely not. Except they were.

The rear of the house was crowded with vehicles, at least twenty of them. As they circled again a man in a toga and laurel wreath and, presumably, gooseflesh unless he was wearing several layers of woollen underwear, wandered out of the front door carrying a bottle of champagne.

'Land,' Sophie ordered again.

The wings waggled. The plane dropped. The zebras left in an explosion of hooves just in time. Nephew George brought the plane to a halt before the hedge.

'Well done,' said Ethel encouragingly, hauling herself to her feet. 'I'll give you a hand to unload the luggage while Sophie makes her entrance. I'll be up later, lass.'

'You're staying?'

'Wouldn't miss it,' said Ethel cheerfully. 'Brought a bag just in case. But I'll make myself scarce if all is not ginger peachy with his lordship.'

'Thank you,' said Sophie. And meant it. Troops in reserve were always useful. Especially one as resourceful as Ethel.

She stepped out of the plane and straightened, feeling her fur coat blow back in the wind, and settled her hat at the correct angle. The scent of Shillings. Cold grass and old stones and lichened apple trees and ... zebra dung.

'I say, is that your crate?' A young man, not the Roman, but who looked vaguely familiar. He wore normal dress, plus fours and a striped vest under a tweed jacket, a champagne glass in one hand and a bloody handkerchief around the other.

'No, a friend's. What happened to your hand?'

'A zebra bit it. Nasty beast. One was just trying to have a chat.' He drank the rest of the champagne then let the glass fall into the grass. 'Is that a costume? An aviatrix shouldn't come as an aviatrix. Not done.'

'I'm not an aviatrix and I'm not in costume. Should I be?'

'Well, it's a costume party, after all. "Tutankhamun Returns". Don't think an aviatrix quite fits the theme, but then I never was one for history.'

'Surely his lordship isn't having a party now?'

The young man looked at her more closely. 'Not his lordship. Claude Vaile and Beatrice.'

The cousin. The one who would inherit when Nigel ... if Nigel ...

'How is his lordship?' asked Sophie quietly.

He looked at her with concern. 'I say, are you all right? He's not well, I gather. I haven't seen him yet this visit — only arrived an hour ago. Vaile says this party is to cheer him up.'

'I can't think of anything less likely to,' said Sophie crisply. 'You're not in costume yet?'

'And I won't be. Rank hath its privileges.'

And then she knew who he was. 'Oh, I am so sorry. I should curtsey, should I? Or is that only if we are formally introduced? I have lost all my manners in the colonies. And I don't know how to curtsey in trousers.'

The Prince of Wales laughed. 'Shall we pretend the zebras introduced us? And call me David.'

'I am Sophie Higgs, Your, er, Royal Highness.'

'I said to call me David.' He looked at her with interest. 'Nigel has spoken of you. I was sorry I never met you on my tour of the colonies.'

'You made quite an impression,' said Sophie dryly. He had also, if rumour was true, left possibly a hundred illegitimate children behind. But that rumour was almost certainly unfounded.

Or at least exaggerated.

'I'm glad you're here. All this —' The injured royal hand gestured at the zebras, two chilly-looking camels among the apple trees, and a pair of Cleopatras smoking gaspers in the leafless rose garden, still unadorned by a hippopotamus. Perfectly pleasant, and pleasantly perfect, just as a prince should be. She supposed he had been taught well. '— it's all jolly bad form. I didn't know it wasn't Nigel's do until I got here.'

'You're not a friend of Mr Vaile and his wife?'

'No,' said the prince. 'Though I do enjoy a good party.' He looked at her sideways and repeated, 'Jolly bad form in this case, however. There is a dinner tonight, and a ball tomorrow night.'

'And Nigel has surgery in a week's time.' A week and one day, she thought. I got here!

'That soon? I say. I'm sorry.' His eyes gleamed at her. 'Anything I can do to help, just yell.'

'I will, Your Royal Highness.'

'I said call me David.'

'I know. But just then you were being a prince.'

He laughed. 'I can tell why Nigel is so keen on you. I'll just linger by the front door and have a cigar.'

'So you can watch what happens next?'

'You really are a clever girl.'

'Always,' said Sophie. She strode past a pair of mummies, dressed in bandages except for their patterned socks and shoes, six Julius Caesars, who did not seem to know that Tutankhamun was ancient history to him too, and a bifurcated camel, sitting on the heads or tails of their costumes, gaspers. A mermaid in a mink stole lay, hiccupping gently, on the lap of yet another mummy. Well, a pharaoh's garb would be chilly in an English winter.

All the guests seemed well lubricated. None gave her more than a cursory glance. Planes and aviatrixes, it seemed, were not worthy of comment. They seemed more interested in the Prince of Wales, following her with amusement. It was as if all the frantic idiocies of post-war England were gathered here at Shillings, an obscenity of past glories while their master was at the point of death. She had read of parties like this. Australia even had its own version, as brittle, if less sumptuous, and none, as far as she knew, featuring zebras. The war had cracked people's lives and the safety of their worldviews, and so they danced and played faster and faster to ignore the cracks.

For a while.

This is not real, thought Sophie. Not just the costumes, the false pillar façade on Shillings Hall, but the gaiety, put on like a bandeaux of gilt and feathers.

She ran up the steps to the front door just as it opened.

Cutler the Butler was tall, lean and had appalling teeth. Good teeth were a necessity for a butler, and if not natural should be acquired by his employer. 'I am Miss Higgs,' Sophie announced.

'I am sorry, Miss Higgs. Mr and Mrs Vaile are not at home. Nor is his lordship.'

'But I am,' said Sophie.

Mr Cutler's elbows widened subtly, blocking the entire door. 'I said, Miss Higgs, that —'

'Would you prefer that I go through the window? Actually ...'

She turned and hurried back down the steps before he could call a footman to manhandle her — not that she couldn't handle a footman or two, but it wasn't fair on the boys to leave them clutching their male parts for the next two days just because Cutler the Butler was an ass.

She strode around the house, past the library, from which emanated a gaggle of voices and someone screaming 'Dahling!' and, yes, a fire was lit in Miss Lily's small drawing room, glinting through the curtains. Sophie rapped on the glass with her knuckles.

Nigel's voice said faintly, 'What the dickens ...? Jones, would you mind?'

Jones's large hands appeared, followed by his body. He stared, his face cracking in a grin, and opened the window, then gave her a hand as she clambered inside. 'Miss Higgs,' he whispered. '*Sophie.*'

She stood on tiptoe and kissed his cheek. 'I'm here. It's all right.'

She looked at Nigel, who was not all right. Who sat on Miss Lily's seat by the fire, in flannels and a beard. A beard! His skin was pale, his eyes shadowed, widening in shock. 'Sophie!' Impossible to tell what he was feeling.

'Sophie,' he said again, as if he were tasting the words. And this time she heard joy, and the small ice dagger of fear that she had propelled herself where she was not wanted melted.

The door opened. 'There she is!' said Cutler the Butler. 'Excuse me, your lordship, she insisted.'

A woman appeared behind him, middle aged and fighting it far too hard, dressed in a long purple tunic embroidered with gold thread and beads, purple stockings, sandals and an over-supply of probably paste diamonds. A purple toga-ed man with a gold-painted laurel wreath came panting up beside her. Ah, thought Sophie, Mr and Mrs Vaile. Who should not wear purple, not with those red-veined cheeks. Her eyes were drawn back to Nigel. Nigel, who seemed to see only her. Nigel, beginning to smile.

'What on earth is happening?' demanded Claude Vaile, following his purple-clad wife and Cutler into the room. 'Cutler, get this woman out of my house!'

Curious faces crowded in behind him.

'Your house?' The voice from the doorway was quiet. The crowd turned towards the Prince of Wales. 'My dear chap, this is Nigel's house, remember? Your dashed zebra bit me,' he added.

'I ... I am so sorry, Your Highness,' stammered Beatrice Vaile. 'We have an intruder.'

'I am not an intruder,' snapped Sophie, glancing back at her. How dare they? Nigel had looked so small, so lost.

'You have not been invited,' stated Beatrice Vaile, her face turning almost as puce as her costume.

'I invited her.' They were the first words Nigel had spoken except her name since she'd clambered into the room.

'This is my party,' snarled Beatrice Vaile.

And suddenly the world locked into shape again. And the future. Because suddenly Sophie knew exactly what she could do for Nigel, and Jones too, and Shillings.

Sophie grinned. 'But as this will also be my house tomorrow,' she said, winking briefly at Nigel, 'I'm afraid I fail to see how you can be throwing a party here.'

Nigel stared at her, startled for a split second before his grin matched her own. 'Will it be?'

'Of course it will.' She turned to the purple tunic. 'Nigel and I are getting married by special licence tomorrow.'

'You are not!' barked Beatrice Vaile.

'We are,' said Nigel, not at all apologetically. 'Jones, dear chap, would you mind seeing to the ... necessaries? And tell Mrs Goodenough we need cherry cake. And Miss Higgs's room made ready for her.'

'The guest rooms are all taken,' snapped Beatrice Vaile.

'They can leave,' said Sophie. 'Now. In fact I wish the whole lot of you to leave.'

'But they were invited!'

'Not, I think, by the earl.' The prince's voice was friendly, and his smile implacable. 'Come on, Vaile, there's a good chap. You can see Nigel isn't up to this.'

'But I ... we —'

'I'll tell you what: I'll get my bagpipes. That will bring everyone together by the stairs. You can tell them the party's off.' The Prince of Wales gestured to the butler. 'You'll find my pipes in my luggage. My man will show you where they are.'

'I ... yes, Your Royal Highness,' said Cutler breathlessly. The heir to the throne of Britain outranked his mistress, and had been bitten by her zebra.

'And then get rid of the zebras,' Sophie called after him. 'And the hippopotamus.'

'It was indisposed,' said Beatrice Vaile, still in shock.

'I hope it recovers,' said Sophie brightly. 'Now could you all make a noise like a bee and buzz off? Apologies, Your Highness,' she added to the prince. 'Of course I didn't mean you.'

'Naturally not. But I'll buzz anyway. This way, children.' The Prince of Wales sauntered from the room, leaving a faint scent of expensive cigar. The rest followed, dazed, except for Jones.

'Nigel?' said Sophie.

Chapter 57

The most wonderful events of life are never expected.

Miss Lily, 1914

She stepped across the room. It was a small room, but the distance seemed greater than any she had ever walked before. She kneeled next to Nigel, feeling the fire warm on her face. 'You don't have to marry me, you know. I just said it to get rid of all those people — and to disrupt their plans.'

'I know. I invited my cousin to stay two weeks ago. I thought he should get to know the place. But he and his wife seem to think it is nothing more than a place to entertain. He's even planning to cut up the barley field for suburban villas.'

'Who is going to live in villas out here?'

'He says those who can no longer afford to keep up larger places. He might be right.'

'He's not going to get a chance to find out,' declared Sophie.

'Sophie, darling, he is my heir. Even if we marry, he will inherit the house and title when I die.'

'Which will not be for a long time,' said Sophie fiercely. 'And not if you have a son.'

'I think this may be where I leave,' said Jones, who had been seated on the window ledge.

'I think it might be too,' said Sophie. 'Could you see about that marriage licence, please?'

'And your room. And the cherry cake,' said Jones. He smiled, but Sophie could see the trails of tears on his face. 'I knew you would come,' he added. 'And get here in time.'

'Green will be here on the sixth of January.' Sophie smiled tremulously back at him. 'I hope you can keep her occupied.'

'I am sure she found ... occupation ... on the ship,' managed Jones, trying for urbanity.

'And I am sure she would prefer the occupation to be you,' said Sophie. 'Just don't make the mistake of expecting her to marry you this time. But I had better mind my own business.'

'I will leave you to mind it,' said Jones, his voice almost steady, but from tears or laughter Sophie couldn't tell, as he left and closed the door. She kept her gaze on Nigel. He looked surprisingly vigorous for a man about to die.

She told him so.

He smiled. 'A medical irony. I have a chance of life if they operate now, and none if I do not. But yes, I feel decidedly alive, despite the gathering of the family vultures. Just deeply tired. But not nearly as tired as I felt before Miss Sophie Higgs climbed through the window. I seem to remember you entering the house trailing leaf mould once before.'

'Well?' Sophie took Nigel's hand. Frail, but warm. She had always loved these hands, both Nigel's and Miss Lily's.

'I fell in love with you twelve years ago. I asked you to marry me seven years ago, and you refused. What has changed now? Except my probable death,' he added.

'You are not going to die!' she ordered him. 'Not for decades! I forbid it utterly.' She lifted his hand to her cheek. 'A lot has changed. I wanted to build an empire, and I did. I needed Australia, and found it once again. But mostly ...' She hesitated.

'Miss Lily?' he offered, watching her face.

'No. Never. You were right all those years ago when you thought I was someone who could accept her — be married to you both. I love you both. But your life seemed so neat back then, just you and Jones —'

'I told you I was not a homosexualist.'

'That wasn't it either. Your life seemed — tidy. I would have been just a bit added on. Oh, a valued bit,' she added, as he seemed about to protest. 'A giver of political dinner parties, influencing people and policies. An extremely successful lovely lady, just as Miss Lily trained me to be. But I wanted more than that.'

'And now?' he asked cautiously.

She grinned. 'Now I have crossed from Australia to England in three weeks, passing through a monsoon and a small air crash and an avalanche. I have evicted your heirs and their zebras and charmed the Prince of Wales. I have built my father's business into an empire spanning three continents with far more than corned beef. I am eminently capable of making sure I have my own future. Or rather, our future, made by both of us, whatever it shall be.'

She took a deep breath. 'And I love you. Will always love you, and Miss Lily, for richer and for poorer, in sickness and in health, and death is going to have to battle damned hard to part us.'

It was as if long-extinguished lights began to glow again. Nigel grinned at her. 'In that case, will you marry me this time, Miss Higgs? In weighing up the advantages and disadvantages of any prospective marriage, I should point out as well that I am thirty years older than you, but on the plus side, you are not likely to have to put up with my decrepit old age.'

'I most certainly will,' said Sophie. 'And I will be emptying your bedpan when you are a hundred and ten. Or supervising the emptying of it. I have had a lot of experience in getting men to live against the odds.'

'I am sure of it,' said Nigel softly, and there was something of Miss Lily's amusement as well as her confidence in his voice.

'Nigel, I love you. I want to marry you. I want to murder your relatives and bury them in the rose garden, but I will be content with knowing that they will not step foot on Shillings again while you breathe. But here are two things I have to tell you.'

He looked at her carefully. 'Very well.'

'I am Australian. It's not just that my business is there, and my friends. I need to be there for part of each year, six months perhaps, to be truly myself.'

'Of course.'

It was so simple. Perhaps it had always been that simple, and she had refused to see. 'And I would like my husband to come too, for at least part of that time.'

'I will agree, but it might be completely meaningless. I am ... unlikely to survive, Sophie. You have to know that, no matter what you choose. If I do live, I may be an invalid for the rest of my life.'

'You can be an invalid on board ship and in Sydney and at Thuringa.'

'Yes, I can, can't I? And will, if that is what you wish. What is the second thing?'

She held his hand tightly and met his eyes. 'Three weeks ago I slept with a man. Just once. It is the first time I have ever ... And you need to know this because it is possible ...' She could not go on.

'That you might be pregnant?'

She nodded, dumbly.

'I think that would be most wonderful,' he said quietly.

'You truly don't mind?'

'About a possible child? No. Sophie, the tumour is in my abdomen. If I survive the operation, it will mean I will not be able to father children. And, yes, before you ask, I could father a child now.'

'You're sure?'

He laughed. It was so good to hear him laugh. He stood, a little shakily. She stood too as he put his arms around her waist, then kissed her, warm lips, warm skin, a body she had never felt against her and yet somehow had known forever. A long kiss, his hands clasping her closer, and closer still.

At last they moved slightly apart. Her face stung a little, from his whiskers. He sat, pulling her down onto his knees. 'I could show you how ready I am to father a child here and now, on the rug,' he said softly, 'but we are too likely to be interrupted. And you are not sleeping in your own room tonight, or if you are, I will be with you.'

'Nigel —' A wail like a thousand bunyips crying in chorus interrupted her.

'Ah,' said Nigel, 'His Highness's bagpipes. We should be free of infestation by tea time.'

'Crumpets?'

'Always crumpets,' said Nigel gently. 'But Sophie, this man you ... slept ... with — do you love him?'

'I ... I never considered whether I did or not. It was an impulse, and then your telegram arrived, and whether I loved him or not became irrelevant. He is lovable. But he is also a hermit, a good man, but never recovered from the war. He spends his life carving crosses for those who died.'

'And yet he slept with you?'

'I seduced him,' admitted Sophie. 'And am ashamed of it. He was regretting the whole thing the next morning.' She could not quite admit that John had fled, rather than face her.

'So you don't want to marry him?'

She shook her head. 'I want to marry you. For many, many reasons.'

'You're sure?'

She pulled back from his shoulder and looked him in the eyes. 'Nigel Vaile, I have just broken what may be a world record to get here to marry you. I have flown through a bloody monsoon —'

'Sophie! Your language!' He hugged her in delight.

'I have been corrupted by the colonies. You will have to train me all over again. Unless I manage to corrupt you too. I have been shaken on trains and eaten far too many bowls of turtle soup. I want a bed that stands still.'

'I am not quite sure I can promise a still bed,' said Nigel.

She stared at him. 'I have never known you to speak like that.'

'I have never been engaged to be married before. I find it a heady if unexpected experience. One is entitled to speak with frankness when one is engaged.'

'Are you sure?'

'Definitely. And there is even more licence for unbridled behaviour after we are married.'

'That sounds delicious,' said Sophie, as the prince's bagpipes burst into 'Scots Wha Hae'. She could faintly hear Beatrice Vaile having hysterics somewhere down a passageway.

'Hark the herald angels sing,' said Nigel irreligiously. 'I did promise you a Shillings Christmas one day, didn't I?'

'Then you'd better come out of this operation prepared to host one,' said Sophie. 'We'll set up Shillings so you can recuperate here. I am extremely good at setting up hospitals.'

'I know. Sophie, if you have a girl —'

'If I am pregnant. I am only a few days late.' She flushed. 'It's probably just due to the travelling and the change of time zones. My body doesn't know when or where it is.'

'Then we must let it know. And make a baby in the next week. And if it is a girl, or if we do not have a child at all,' he smiled, 'as I said, the title is entailed, and the house. But luckily my father and brother broke the entailment to sell all but the house and gardens and the Home Farm.'

'But you own the entire estate!'

'Exactly. I bought it back with the profits from investing in your father's business. Which means most of the estate is mine to dispose of as I see fit. My cousin does not know this, by the way. He lives on his army pension.'

'Ah, that explains Cutler the Butler. Quickly acquired?'

'I believe so. Possibly a repertory actor who once played a butler in the provinces. My cousin will inherit only the title, house and Home Farm. He will be bankrupt within a month trying to pay for the upkeep of the house and grounds. I would very much like it if you would buy them from him.'

Sophie smiled at him. 'Of course, whether we have children or not.'

'And you will see that it is looked after?'

'I will.'

'I'd have left the estate to Jones, but my cousin would have contested it and probably won, insinuating scandal. Part of which,' he added, 'would have been true.'

'He can't contest a will made in your wife's favour. And, anyway, I can afford better lawyers.'

'You have also managed to get the Prince of Wales on your side.'

'That should help.' She winced. 'Does His Royal Highness play the bagpipes often?'

'Sadly, yes. But he is a good chap, Sophie.' Nigel smiled. 'I first met him in France, sitting bare bummed next to me on a plank above a lavatory trench. We were both there some time — dodgy tummy from bad water — and got chatting. He would have liked to be on the front line, but His Majesty wouldn't let the heir risk his life.'

'I liked him too.' Though it was hard to imagine the slight figure — and slightness of character too — as a king. 'Can we really get married tomorrow?'

'I believe so.'

A voice boomed in the hallway. The bagpipes ceased. 'That will be Ethel,' said Sophie.

'Ethel?'

'I knew her in France and her nephew flew me here from Paris this morning. She'll be my bridesmaid.' It was lucky Green had included a white sheath dress in the wardrobe Eloise had delivered. Or, she reflected, perhaps not luck at all, but hope.

And hope had been fulfilled. She leaned back in Nigel's arms again. 'I'm not too heavy?'

'Never.'

'Ha. You won't say that after your incision. I will cuddle you most carefully on the other side then. We are going to be happy, Nigel.'

'I know,' he said.

For whatever time they had together.

Chapter 58

*I hope my girls will find total fulfilment. I have accepted at last
that I will not.*

Miss Lily, 1912

Night, the scent of burning apple wood and the gentle flicker of
firelight on the polished posts of the bed, though its curtains and
canopy were long gone, on the gleaming silk carpet and on the
sweaty glow on Nigel's skin.

'Oh my,' said Sophie, panting and lying back against the
pillows.

Nigel grinned and let himself slide back down beside her.
'Well?'

'Very well, my lord.'

'Was it as good as with that other chap?'

Sophie laughed, and raised herself up on an elbow to look at
him again. 'I thought that was the kind of question a gentleman
would never ask.'

'And one to which a gentleman always wants the answer.'

'I am not sure you are a gentleman in bed,' said Sophie primly.

'You haven't answered my question.'

She felt a stab of disloyalty. 'The time before was ... nice.
Good, a kind of love, even though it wasn't really if that is
what you meant. He was comforting me as well as making love,
I think.' Nor did John have decades of Japanese woodcuts and
professional instruction. And there had been times tonight when
she had felt the ... expertise ... displayed as much as the love. She
settled on, 'That was ... that was ... incredible.'

'You cried out four times,' he said smugly.

'A gentleman shouldn't count.'

'Of course he should.'

'You seem so ... expert.'

He laughed softly, still smug. 'You thought I wouldn't be?'

'Yes,' she said frankly. She had even been prepared to show him what to do, to have to encourage him to do it, with the remembered lessons of Miss Lily's book. Except, of course, Miss Lily had given that book to her.

'It's true I've been celibate for more than a decade.'

'I was celibate for twenty-nine years.'

He kissed her to quiet her. 'My first teacher was Japanese. Misako.'

'I know. Green told me about her.'

'Did she now? I must find out what other secrets she has shared.' He lay back on the pillows, his hand holding hers. 'Misako was what you might call a courtesan, but that calling has been refined there to an art unlike any in the world. Misako taught me how a woman can be beautiful. She taught me other things as well.'

'Ah, I see. Like that thing where you ...' She finished her sentence with a descriptive gesture.

He grinned, obviously exhausted, ill and happy. 'And much more. Sophie, if I live ... they have to cut through the nerves. But there are many, many ways to please a woman. I don't want you to think —'

'Shh. We love each other and will find many ways to live that. Let's wait for the days ahead to discover what they'll be. Did you love Misako?'

He looked startled. 'Why do you ask? How did you know?'

'Your tone of voice ... and I know you, and Miss Lily. You are so very good at love, and I don't mean its fifty-six positions. You would not have spent so much time with her if you hadn't loved her. Did she love you?'

'I think so. Yes.'

'Why didn't you marry her?'

'Because she was forty or so years older than me, spoke no English and thought Europeans were barbarians. Except for me.' The smugness was back and the tenderness. He pushed her hair back from her forehead and kissed it, then her cheeks and lips, gently, softly. 'She said I was naturally civilised. I only needed teaching.'

'Is she still alive? I should thank her,' said Sophie lightly.

'She died when I was here in England, about fifteen years ago. I wish I'd been there, or at least been able to say goodbye.' He smiled. 'I would like to have told her I was getting married too.'

'I wish I could have told my father you and I are getting married. I think he'd have been glad.'

'Despite the age difference?'

'Perhaps because of it. He knew you, trusted you, admired you, or he'd never have sent me to Shillings. He might have thought any cousin of yours could keep me in line. Which you have, more or less, you and Miss Lily.'

Silence, beside her. 'I love Miss Lily too,' said Sophie quietly. 'She's with us as well.'

'Yes. I was afraid you'd have preferred to forget her, here and now.'

'Never,' said Sophie. 'I wish Dad could see me married by an archbishop. And in the Shillings church!'

'He insisted. It appears I have to sign the licence myself, and so he offered to bring it down, though he will have to dash off afterwards. The advantages of being a peer of the realm about to undergo a major operation.'

'Oh, and Nigel, I should have told you — Ethel has rung up some friends. Rather a lot of friends. I invited a few people too.'

'Then they can all come to a late luncheon. There was a ball planned for tomorrow night. Mrs Goodenough has disposed of much of the Vailes' banquet but I imagine we can still feed fifty or so. David has invited himself too. He said it should be interesting.'

'Perhaps too interesting. Some of the people may be ... unconventional. Not top drawer.'

'Excellent. He will enjoy it thoroughly. He is hoping to pipe us into the church.'

'Oh dear. The hens at the Home Farm probably won't lay for a week. I asked the Slithersoles and James Lorrimer and his aunt too. I hope you don't mind.'

She had also sent telegrams to Australia, to Thuringa, to the Sydney house, to Cousin Oswald, to Midge and to the Dowager Duchess of Wooten, bedridden, but perhaps little Sophie could come in her place, if her aunt or even dear Doris could bring her. She had sent telegrams to Mrs Henderson and Miss Morrison, announcing her marriage as well as assuring them of the help of Slithersoles Senior and Junior in their business venture. She had considered sending a telegram to the mother who had left her as a six-week-old baby, but that woman lived in Paris — close enough she might even attend with an earl, a prince and an archbishop on the menu. Best keep her forgotten and out of their lives.

'Ask the world,' said Nigel.

Sophie lay back again. Her hand held his, tightly. 'One more confession,' she said.

'A few other lovers you forgot to mention?'

'Of course not. My other premarital experience is limited to two kisses, from two different men. Though they were extremely interesting kisses.'

'I won't ask for details then. What is this other confession?'

'I called your surgeon too. Nigel, I'm sorry, I know I have no right to interfere.'

'Actually, you do,' he said gently. 'From tomorrow you will be my wife, my next of kin, my legal guardian jointly with Jones if ... necessary ... and my heir.'

'Also I hope jointly with Jones.'

'Actually I haven't worked out the details of that. I will need to sign a new will after the ceremony. So will you, for that matter. This is all a little unexpected.'

'We can work it out together. How about joint ownership of the estate, but all profits after expenses, staff pensions and necessary improvements go to Jones? And if something happens to me — well, you'll get my presidency but I would like my people to inherit some stake in Higgs as well as keep their positions.'

'I am marrying a businesswoman, aren't I?'

'Who will ensure the ongoing prosperity of Shillings. Nigel, I didn't ask for details about your condition — he wouldn't have given them to me without your permission, even if we had been married today. But I persuaded him to perform the operation here.'

'What? Sophie, it's major surgery.'

'There will be an anaesthetist, the best equipment possible, two assistants for the surgeon and a doctor and four surgical nurses to stay in the house afterwards. Mr Ffoulkes, your surgeon, has himself agreed to spend his Christmas holidays here, with his family. His wife in particular is looking forward to it,' said Sophie dryly. 'Christmas at Shillings, with an earl, even if he is upstairs in bed. Luckily they only have one daughter. She's twelve, so is unlikely to be noisy. Nigel, I told you — I am very, very good at creating hospitals.'

'But why, Sophie? I would prefer to be at Shillings, I admit, but I accepted that I might well die away from here years ago. I certainly knew it during the war.'

'Because I *am* good at hospitals. Surgeons usually do an excellent job — it is not their work that kills people, but sepsis afterwards. And it happens all too often in hospitals, the infection carried from person to person and who knows how else. That's why the post-operative survival rate in my hospitals was so high. Small wards, lots of washing and I kept a very close eye indeed on where the doctors put their hands. I could control the nurses' hygiene but it was harder to persuade a man.'

'I expect you managed,' he said wryly.

'Yes. And I'll manage this time too. Boiled white gowns for everyone, boiled scarves over their hair, and boiled gloves, each time anyone comes near you until the incision has healed. Boiled sheets ... everything.'

'Thank you.'

'No discussion? Argument? Protestations of "Am I going to be hen-pecked like this all through my marriage?"'

'You are a swan, not a hen,' he reminded her.

'I almost remember to be, most of the time. But swans peck too.'

'I knew exactly who you were when I first realised I wanted to marry you, twelve years ago. You know, there are more ... interesting ... things to do right now than discuss hygiene.'

'Really?'

'Definitely,' said Nigel, and began to do them.

Chapter 59

I do not attend weddings. They are too painful — you know why.

Miss Lily, 1912

The dress was white, knee length, shot with silver, and had silver beading at the hem and sleeves, ending in a froth of snowy rabbit fur.

Jones had found a long veil in the attics and the maids hand-washed it, bleached it, and resecured the tiny diamonds on its headband. It smelled of starch, and the apple wood from the fire in front of which it had dried overnight.

Mr Slithersole arrived, carrying a box, his wife in floral mauve and extreme excitement, his daughter trying almost successfully to look nonchalant.

'From his lordship,' said Merle breathlessly, as she handed a small flat leather case to Sophie in her dressing room. Merle was Green's niece, who had no experience as a lady's maid.

Green would have to train her, Sophie decided, in case Miss Lily reappeared. One maid could not be expected to attend both husband and wife, or whatever she and Lily were to each other. Wife and wife ... no, that was not correct. Words didn't matter, Sophie decided, where there was so much love. And ... complications ... could be worked out.

She opened the lid, and stared.

The case contained a necklace of diamonds, presumably hastily retrieved from the bank vault in London and cleaned. Sophie watched herself in the mirror as Merle put the necklace around her neck, small stones and one long pendant shape matching the earrings.

'Jones told me to put a little rose oil on the comb, Miss Higgs. He said it will keep your hair neat.'

So that was how Green had managed it. 'Thank you, Merle.'

She waited while the veil was draped. Traditionally the bridesmaid helped with the veil, but Ethel was greeting the wedding guests at the Shillings and Sixpence with champagne from the Shillings cellars as well as the pub's excellent ale — the district would be gossiping about that for years. And, besides, while she would trust Ethel to feed an army, and command it, she was not sure her fingers could manage the delicacy of tulle.

She looked at herself in the mirror and saw a bride. Saw a swan, a true graduate of Miss Lily's skill. Saw Alison, the morning of her marriage, and felt tears sting, for her, for all she had loved who had gone, for Nigel, who might leave her so very soon, just when they had begun ...

Oh, Danny Boy, the pipes, the pipes are calling,
From glen to glen, and down the mountainside.
The summer's gone, and all the roses falling,
It's you, it's you must go and I must bide.

No, she would not let him go! She had lost too much, and so had he. They deserved time together. And she would fight fate itself to make sure they had it.

Cars lined the muddy lane outside the church. The zebras peered, fascinated, over the fence, like horses in striped pyjamas, giving strange high-pitched then low-pitched cries. While the Vailes and their guests, the caterers, Cutler the Butler and even the palm trees had been dispatched by supper-time the previous night, the zebras were still in residence.

Jones handed Ethel from the Shillings car, massively glorious in shimmering pink, which clashed only a little with her red face and hands, then held his hand out to Sophie. She took it and held it tight as she stood up, then put her hand on his arm. Small burps of music came as the Prince of Wales, resplendent in his kilt, prepared his bagpipes.

'Doris!' She hugged her former maid, and stared at 'little Sophie', her Goddaughter, eleven years as shy and awkward looking as her mother. She embraced her, trying not to cry. 'All you have to do is hold up my veil at the back, and then go and sit back with Doris. I ... I want to ask you a million questions but probably won't get a chance to. Soon though.' She pressed a kiss to the soft cheek.

'Sophie!' A tall woman in an excellent green satin ensemble strode from the church.

'Sloggers! How wonderful!'

'You look wonderful too, old bean. I won't hug you in case I mess you up but you need to know.'

'What?' asked Sophie, suddenly terrified. Nigel had collapsed. The archbishop hadn't arrived. The licence needed documents that were back in Australia ...

'A jazz band has arrived! Six of them, and a singer. They say they are supposed to play this afternoon and refuse to leave.'

'There was to be a house party — Oh, never mind. Ask them if they can play us out of the church. Better explain it to the Prince of Wales too.'

'That is the prince? Gosh.' Sloggers sounded interested, but not deterred. She strode over to the piper.

She saw David listen, nod, then he began to play. He walked, as possibly only royalty could, step, step, step, each perfect, bagpipes bellowing around the church.

'Good luck, old thing.' Ethel bent and kissed her cheek, then began to walk towards the church, not perfect at all.

Jones wiped the smudge of lipstick Ethel had left off her cheek. 'This is one of the most wonderful moments of my life,' he said quietly, offering his arm to Sophie. She rested her hand on his arm.

'You wait till Green gets here,' said Sophie, to ward off tears for them both, as they followed Ethel, young Sophie clutching the veil in case a tornado might unexpectedly rip it away.

Sophie, turned, and winked at her. They entered the church, smiling.

Step, step, step ...

The bagpipes swung into what was probably the wedding march. Sophie, young Sophie, and Jones began to walk up the aisle, following Ethel, who looked like a pink ship in full sail, holding a vast bunch of pink roses that did not quite match her dress. All around them surprisingly well-dressed women — though admittedly two were dressed in men's coats, jackets and ties — stood and cried as per tradition into handkerchiefs as Jones kissed Sophie's cheek at the altar and placed her hand in Nigel's.

'Dearly beloved ...' began the archbishop.

Beloved, thought Sophie. Once I thought I never could be loved. I was corned beef, valued for money, indulged because I was the only child my father had to indulge. But I have been beloved all my life, and am beloved now, and so is Nigel ...

Outside the zebras sang their dismay that the bagpipes had ceased.

'The hippopotamus has arrived,' said Jones.

Sophie turned, champagne glass in her hand. The jazz musicians, who had given an original but beautiful rendition of Mendelssohn, were now playing just outside the big drawing room, in fur coats and fur-lined boots arranged somehow by Jones.

The Slithersoles foxtrotted, dazed and happy; fourteen-year-old Miss Victoria Slithersole and then young Sophie danced with the Prince of Wales. Both would be floating on the experience for the rest of their lives, and spent the rest of the afternoon together, exchanging notes on the wonder of it all. Ethel clumped around the dance floor with the vicar, who was trying not to look put out at not performing the marriage service for the Earl of Shillings. Women danced with women — inevitable when nine out of ten of the guests were female. How had so many of the women she'd worked with managed to get here today? Ethel must have worked miracles. But then, she always did.

But the hippopotamus?

'What have you done with it?' she asked Jones.

'It's in the hay shed at the Home Farm. I was afraid it might be chilly in the rose garden.'

'When can we return it? And the zebras?'

'I'm afraid they were not on hire and return,' said Jones grimly.

'Really? Were the Vailes planning on turning Shillings into a wildlife park? No, I don't want to know. May I have the honour of the next dance, Jones?'

He looked startled. Admittedly, he had long been Nigel's secretary, not butler, a position now held by a young man named Hereward, whose handless left arm was kept discreetly tucked inside his jacket — the Vailes had evidently preferred a butler with bad teeth to a hero with one hand. But Sophie suspected the butler role, and its social limitations, still lived in Jones's heart.

'It's a Charleston,' she added. 'It would be bad for Nigel to attempt it.'

Jones grinned. 'Very well.'

It should not have surprised her, of course, but Jones was excellent at the Charleston. They even did an encore. And across the room Nigel sat in conversation with Ethel, Sloggers and Dr Marie Stopes, and met her eyes with joy, and love.

Chapter 60

May you have joy, my dear. I know I have encouraged you to find other fulfilments in your marriage, but may there be joy too.

A letter from Miss Lily to Lady Alison Venables, 1914

DECEMBER 1925

They made love only once the night before the surgery. Sophie was glad. Their first and even second nights together had been a garden of paradise, where nightingales sang and even the air was champagne.

But as the week progressed something almost frantic had accompanied their love-making, as if Nigel was determined to show that, despite age and illness, he could be a lover too. Or perhaps, she thought, lying on her side next to him, his arms about her, he simply knew this would be his last week of sexual pleasure.

And for her? Just then she did not care. Or at least would not think about it.

Nigel trailed his fingers from her shoulder down her breast, her waist, over her hips. She shivered. 'Your body is so beautiful,' he said softly.

'So is yours.'

'I've never found it so.'

'What?' She rose up on one elbow to see his face more clearly in the firelight. 'I love your body. Oh. Would you rather it was a woman's body?'

'If you are asking would I turn my body fully into a woman's if I could, then no.' He pulled her down again, fitted her against him. 'With my body, I thee worship,' he quoted from the marriage service. 'I love women's bodies. I love your body. I love loving it this way, with mine. But when I look into a mirror ...' He shook his head. 'It has never seemed as if the reflection is truly mine.'

'Except when you are Miss Lily,' she said quietly.

He didn't answer. The fire snickered as a log fell. Firelight flared brighter, showing his body more clearly, which *was* beautiful: a tragedy that he did not know it.

And tomorrow that beautiful body would be torn, not ripped by war, but deliberately.

And that was why she was there.

Sophie sat in the small drawing room with Jones, as the winter sun spread morning light through the window from the icy garden. Neither spoke. Upstairs the surgeon and his team were operating on Nigel Vaile, sixteenth Earl of Shillings.

She longed to be there, but she was, after all, not a nurse or even a VAD. She had done all she could with personnel, equipment, sterilisation. But organisational skills could only help so far.

The vicar had called; it seemed he had forgiven her for usurping him with the archbishop. He and the Mothers' Committee would maintain a prayer vigil until the evening, he said. Sophie managed to thank him, and not cry. Four children had arrived, each bearing posies of dried summer flowers, with holly for greenery. Each had been given a mince pie and a shilling and a kiss on the cheek, even if one small boy had indelicately scrubbed it off.

It had been strange to be called 'your ladyship'. Stranger still to think of Nigel being carved like a leg of lamb ...

No, she would not think of it. Bad enough that he must live it, without her sharing it. She must think of good things, so she could meet him calm and competent and focused on his recovery.

It had been two hours now. She had held his hand till his last moment of consciousness.

'Luncheon is served, your ladyship,' said Hereward, carrying a tray.

'I do not think —' began Sophie.

'Mrs Goodenough insisted,' said Hereward, placing the tray on the piano and putting the bowl of chicken soup, fresh rolls still steaming in their basket and butter on the table by Sophie, and the some on a side table for Jones.

Impossible not to eat, when they were so kind. The soup had every vegetable obtainable in mid-winter, and barley, thick and comforting.

'Please thank Mrs Goodenough,' said Sophie a little while later, as Hereward took the empty bowls away.

'Yes, your ladyship. I will serve coffee in here, your ladyship.'

Not a question. He had learned command in the war, and Sophie had also learned when it was time to obey.

She and Jones drank the coffee. Finished the coffee. They waited.

Keep him here for me, Sophie silently prayed. A few years, only, or a lifetime.

Their marriage had begun on a whim crossed with so much desperate urgency she had not truly evaluated what she must have subconsciously intended when she began her journey. But she knew now, after only a week of marriage, that this was right. Was very nearly everything.

What was that phrase Lancelot had used of Guinevere in 'Le Morte d'Arthur', that Miss Thwaites had so laboriously instilled in her, that Nigel had quoted when he proposed? *In thee I've had mine earthly joy.*

Please, she prayed, let me have more than a week. Let Nigel live.

Hereward brought in the tea tray. No cherry cake. What perfect tact. Cherry cake was for happy days. No cream sponge. Fruitcake, dark and sustaining, and small cheese and cress sandwiches. She drank two cups of tea, dutifully ate a slice of fruitcake and two sandwiches; she watched Jones drink and eat exactly the same. They exchanged a look as they simultaneously put their plates down. They needed strength.

They waited.

A knock.

Sophie reached automatically for Jones's hand. Servants did not knock. 'Come in.'

A nurse. Her heart began to beat again. If it had been bad news, the surgeon would have brought it. 'Mr Ffoulkes said to tell you all is proceeding well, your ladyship.'

'How long now?' Sophie managed.

'Mr Ffoulkes is putting in the last stitches, your ladyship. Half an hour perhaps? I will fetch you.'

Sophie waited till the nurse had left, then rang the bell for Hereward.

'Please ask Mrs Goodenough to have coffee and a good meal ready for the medical team in about half an hour.' She had no idea what they might like to eat, or rather, the knowledge was buried somewhere, but was not retrievable right now.

'Yes, your ladyship. If I may say, your ladyship, we prayed for his lordship at the servants' dinner. We will keep praying.'

'Thank you, Hereward. We … we are praying too.' She waited till the butler had left, then held out her hand to Jones again. 'We can wait outside the room.' The chairs were hard there, but she did not want to make a fuss and ask for armchairs. 'I'll meet you up there.'

She washed her hands in 'midwives' water' — water that had been boiled for half an hour with rosemary and lavender. Others would touch Nigel with gloved hands, but she needed skin to skin, and hers must be clean. She was careful not to touch the door or banisters, or even her skirt as she sat next to Jones.

And waited.

The door opened. Mr Ffoulkes came out, taking off his mask.

Sophie stood, and found no words.

'Ah, Lady Nigel. Successful,' said Mr Ffoulkes, sounding weary, self-important and sympathetic all at once. 'The tumour was discreet. We removed it all.'

'His pulse? Breathing?'

'His pulse is a little uneven, but strong. You may go in.'

But she was already moving, stood by the hospital bed, saw his white face, the regular breathing, in, out, in, out. His beard had been shaved off that morning, as had the hair on most of his body. Sophie had even had them shave his head. She had learned in the war that hair carried infection, unless it was the lice that infested hair that carried it. She was taking no chances.

She used her foot to move a plain wooden chair from the corner of the room over to the bedside. The room smelled of Lysol and blood and intestines, a smell she had never thought to have to bear again. The chair too had been boiled in a copper, carried here in gloved hands. It was the only other furniture in the room. Even the floor was scrubbed wood, the carpet taken up, new pipes installed to hold hot water warmed by the fires in the rooms on either side, so there should be no chill but no smoke or ash or firewood either.

She sat, found Nigel's hand under the sheet, held it. Watched him breathe. Keep breathing.

In, out, in, out ...

A minute, an hour, or a month passed. The beam of sunlight on the scrubbed floorboards began to dim. She found a nurse standing next to her. They had been introduced, but the name had fled. The nurse felt Nigel's pulse, counted it with the watch on her belt, nodded to herself and then, when she remembered Sophie understood, to her. 'Steady enough,' she said.

'I know.' Sophie had seen patients with far worse vital signs survive. And those with better, die, but that had been from sepsis, gangrene ... 'When does he need more morphia?'

'When he begins to show signs of pain. It is difficult to know how long the anaesthesia from the operation will last.'

She had known that too. But procedures might have changed in seven years.

In, out, in, out ... The most boring activity two people can manage in bed, Nigel had told her, is in, out, in, out ...

He was going to live. He had to live. If she had to stand in the doorway and wrestle death, he was going to live.

He breathed. And she breathed with him.

Mr Ffoulkes came to stand with her under the bright electric light. Sensible Miss Lily, to prefer the gold light of candles. The surgeon did not deign to check Nigel's pulse himself. 'I believe the tumour was cystic,' he informed her. 'Not cancerous.'

'I'm sorry, I don't understand.' Leg amputations, brain surgery ... she had no experience of cysts or cancers.

'It means that if he recovers there is a good chance the growth will not return.'

'Oh. Good. Thank you, Mr Ffoulkes. I hope they have given you a good dinner.'

'Excellent, thank you, Lady Nigel. His lordship's port is ...' The surgeon hesitated, obviously realising that this was not the time to praise the port. Not a socially subtle man. But what man of empathy could spend his life cutting up the bodies of living people either? Either a saint, or one who could turn off fellow feeling.

She did not care particularly which he was, as long as his technique was good.

She slept in the chair, her arms and head resting on the bed beside Nigel's. Twice he became restless. The nurse must have been listening next door because, before Sophie could call, she came to give him his morphia. A different nurse the second time, and then a doctor, one of the assistant surgeons, who pulled back the wound dressing, checking for swelling, haematomas, though Sophie had checked for those shortly before.

She woke again at dawn, to find Nigel watching her, his face inches from hers. He smiled, the barest movement of his lips. His eyes closed again.

In, out, in, out. Both breathing and pulse were stronger now.

She left the room, called for Jones, hugged him, cried in his arms for thirty seconds, then left him to take her place, white gowned and white gloved, while she went to bathe and dress and eat, and then return.

Nigel woke enough to smile again as she came in, woozy from the morphia. His first word to her was, 'Bedpan.'

She held the bottle, not the pan; she was relieved to see him urinate, even if the urine was blood tinged. She put it aside for Mr Ffoulkes and the nurses to examine. Nigel lay back, exhausted by the effort.

'You're going to live,' she said. 'It was a cyst, not cancerous. No infection.'

'Early days,' he whispered.

'Are you in pain?'

'Not yet.' The faintest of smiles. 'Once your soul has lived in agony, the body's pain can be ... a distraction. Almost welcome.

'Please don't die, Nigel. I need you. I love you!'

'Then I had better live,' he whispered.

'Shh.' She dropped a kiss on his dry lips, held up water for him to sip. Water was important after surgery, another law she had learned in France that English doctors did not seem to know.

Mr Ffoulkes arrived, smelling of kippers, accompanied by a retinue of two assistants and a nurse. The nurse took Nigel's temperature, looked startled. 'Half a degree low.'

'No infection! Excellent! We'll have you playing golf in no time, old chap.'

'Never,' whispered Nigel. Mr Ffoulkes ignored him. An earl who was a patient was still only a patient. No attention need be paid him.

There was no fever that night either. Nigel dined on clear chicken broth, spooned by Sophie, rich in bones and the juice of vegetables, then apple juice. 'Cut down the morphia by half, beginning tomorrow,' she instructed the nurse.

The nurse looked startled. 'But Mr Ffoulkes's patients —'

'In half,' ordered Sophie. She had seen too many men struggle with addiction and daymares as they tried to wean themselves off the stuff. Nigel would have the regular dose of morphia to help him sleep at night, but each day the dose would be cut in half again.

Still no fever on the third day. She helped Nigel stand for a few minutes, again without Mr Ffoulkes's knowledge or permission, and another of the reasons she had wished the surgery and recovery to be in a house she controlled rather than a hospital with its own regimen. Once a patient stood up things seemed to 'fall back into place' as one VAD had described it in France. If the stitches were placed well, they'd hold.

They did. A little swelling that afternoon: the wound needed draining — more morphia for that, but when Nigel woke, his pulse was stronger than ever. 'What's that music?'

'Carol singers. I gave them permission to sing in the hall.'

'What a lovely sound to wake up to. And your face too.'

'I could telephone His Royal Highness if you'd like a change in repertoire.'

He laughed, winced. 'What is for dinner?'

'Clear chicken soup, or beef consommé, and port wine jelly for dessert.'

'That sounds almost delicious. Sophie, are you ...?'

'Pregnant? I don't know yet. But there has been nothing to say that I am not.'

The singers below burst into 'Unto Us a Child is Born'. Sophie caught Nigel's eye and they laughed.

If he could laugh, then he would live.

On Christmas Day Mr Ffoulkes presided over the Shillings dinner table with oysters, cream of onion soup, a tranche of turbot with sauce Albertine, venison in red wine, roast goose with chestnut stuffing, roast potatoes, parsnips and carrots followed by endive salad, anchovy toast, pudding, chocolates, nuts, crystallised fruit, mince pies and petits fours.

Upstairs Sophie, Nigel and Jones shared the servants' meal of turkey with stuffing, and a small pudding especially made for them by Mrs Goodenough, in each portion of which they found tucked a silver ring, even Nigel's extremely small one. It was the first solid food he had eaten. Sophie waited anxiously, but he asked for brown bread with his soup at suppertime, so she judged all was well.

Mr Ffoulkes departed on Boxing Day. This had been an experience his wife would dine out on forever, and his daughter too, but Nigel was so obviously recovering that there was no need for him to remain, though, as Mr Ffoulkes reminded them, he was only a telephone call away.

The two surgical assistants would stay to supervise, remove stitches, continue the watch for haematomas or fever. The nurses stayed too, though Sophie insisted on bathing her husband, helping him dress in one of the soft white cotton nightshirts embroidered on the collar that she had ordered for him, as near to a nightdress as a man could wear without comment.

On New Year's Day he walked to his own bedroom, leaning on Sophie on one side and Jones on the other. Sophie slept next to him that night, waking often to listen to his breathing, in, out, in, out, subconsciously careful not to jostle him in her sleep.

Five days later Green arrived, with trunks. Jones blushed when Sophie asked him at breakfast the next morning how he'd slept. It was good to hear Nigel laugh again.

From then on Sophie's dress improved enough for Nigel to remark on her outfit each morning; he made suggestions to her and Green, as he watched the bathing, hairdressing and selection of dresses from their bed with gentle, wistful eyes.

On 19 January she woke and watched him sleeping — the dose of morphia had been lowered till it was almost non-existent, but he still slept much of the time — then swung her legs over the bed. Dizziness swept over her, so for a second she wondered if a surgical embolism might be contagious, and then she managed to reach for the chamber pot before retching. She covered it quickly with a cloth, turned and found Nigel had lifted himself to sit against his pillows. He raised an eyebrow.

'Pregnant,' said Sophie. 'No, don't you dare try to kiss me. My breath must be foul.'

'Champagne?' he offered, grinning.

'No celebrating till I'm three months along. I don't want to tell anyone either. Just in case ...' For this would almost certainly be her only pregnancy, if this man was going to live, as she was now sure that he was. If she lost this child, she could just bear it — but not if the world sympathised with her. Though of course they must tell Jones ...

Green entered with the tea tray, looked at the chamber pot, and smiled.

And Greenie, of course, as well.

Chapter 61

When we teach the young, we imply that life is simple, and can fit the rule we show them. It is not, of course. The more one knows of life, the more complexity one finds; difficult, sometimes, but always fascinating.

Miss Lily, 1911

FEBRUARY 1926

The letter arrived with Maria Thwaites, beloved, darling Maria, beautifully dressed in a brown suit that said 'Paris, not the colonies'. Green's influence was pervasive.

'I feel I have known you forever,' Nigel said in greeting, a Nigel standing, dressed in flannels and waistcoat again, his hair regrown to an acceptable length, but thankfully without his beard.

News of home, a packet of dried gum leaves for her to smell and use to remind Nigel of his promise they would travel to Australia, perhaps not this year but certainly when the baby was a year old.

The letter was from Midge, the first she had received from Australia since she'd left. Thank goodness for telegrams. This letter was on quality stationery and she had used good ink too, but the paper was slightly yellowed, the paper of a woman who ordered her stationery from Sydney once a year, just as she ordered her linen and whatever food stuffs the Bald Hill store did not provide, like crystallised fruits and sherry that would not choke a brown dog and toilet rolls, gardenia soap, oil of cucumber for the complexion and a lipstick that was neither blush pink nor sunset orange.

Darling Sophie,

(Midge's handwriting was still copperplate, the girl's hand she had been using since she left school to create a canteen with Ethel and the still unknown Anne, at sixteen.)

First, a thousand million congratulations on your marriage. You have no idea how Bald Hill is buzzing — you almost won an election and then married an earl! They cannot wait to see him. I believe lots will be drawn on who gets to ask you to tea first — after us, of course.

We are all well, including my family, all at Thuringa, our sheep and your cattle. A hundred friends send their love or regards, and a sack full of letters will undoubtedly arrive for you soon.

Now for the difficult part of this letter.

The morning you left we were woken by John at six am. Well, I was woken — Harry was already making porridge in the kitchen (send a man to war in France and he learns how to make porridge. But I am procrastinating. Sadly the only friends who understand that word are now only available by letter, apart from your Lady Georgina.) So, to stop procrastinating.

John seemed odd. Elated, embarrassed and I am not sure what else, but as I saw your car by the gate the night before, I hazarded a guess.

I emerged in my dressing gown, as Harry couldn't understand quite what he wanted. It turned out to be coffee, proper coffee, which he suspected correctly we would have as grounds, not in a bottle, as well as fresh bread and butter if I had it, eggs and perhaps a jar of jam?

I have never known John to ask for anything before, nor to appear anywhere except at his gate. But I gathered up his requests while he refused Harry's offer of porridge. He then strode out of the garden, along the paddock, and back up the hill towards the gate.

That is the last time anyone has seen him.

The district knows by now that he has left, though it took several weeks for the knowledge to percolate, as you and I and Harry are the only ones now who regularly use that gate to reach each other's houses.

This means I am the only one who has put three pieces of information together and added them up to what may well be seven. I must stress that no one else seems to have thought to try the same arithmetic. Georgina still believes you stayed the night with one of the volunteers, and hasn't thought to ask who it was. I doubt she ever will.

I know this seems like nosy neighbouring, but I care for you and John very much, in different ways. The third time he was not at the gate I went into his hut. His clothes, what there were of them, were gone, as were his plate and mugs and billy and blanket. I did however see a note, at the back of the table. I enclose it here, as, just possibly, it was meant for you.

Of course I may be barking up the wrong tree entirely, in which case apologies, especially as you are so wonderfully married and Georgina tells me even expecting an heir, if the baby happens to be of what society insists is the superior sex. You may not even wish to see this, supposing my deduction is correct. But I admire and value John too, and so this has not been tactfully disposed of, as perhaps it should have been.

My dear Sophie: whatever happened that night, do not think I judge you, blame you or will even try to understand unless you care to tell me. You are my darling friend, and have my love and admiration forever.

Love, and from Harry too, and our best wishes to Nigel, Midge

PS Ethel sent me photographs of the wedding. You looked divine and she looked like Ethel! I warn you, I may yet visit, on the pretext that we need to look at rams.

Sophie put the letter down. The only other item in the envelope was a scrap of brown paper, folded many times. She had not even noticed it next to the thick cream writing paper.

The writing looked as though it had been scratched with a rusty nib and blobby ink, but the hand was good and legible:

Darling Sophie, I have gone to find you breakfast. Today the world begins!

The world lurched instead. It had never occurred to her to look at the table. It had never occurred to John, possibly, that she would not fetch mugs from the table when she woke, to make a cup of tea. But he would bring her coffee ...

He had not fled. He had not left her. He might, even, in time, have loved her; and the child she carried might possibly be his. A child he would cherish. What had been his words? Any child he had would be his twin brother's too.

She had hurt him. Not in the way she had thought — by breaking what she had assumed was a vow of celibacy — but by bringing him to the world of peace, and then abandoning him. Was she stealing his child from him too, and his brother's?

Where was he now? Had he gone to find another gate, one with no memories of her, to carve another thousand crosses? Or had he truly resumed his life or gone to find it?

She could not speak of this to Nigel, to Maria or Green or anyone. The child she carried must be Nigel's. She could trust Midge to keep any suspicion otherwise to herself. Legally, the child of marriage was the husband's. There was nothing she could do to right this; nor did she even know how to begin to know what was right.

She could not stay still. She had to walk; up a hill of gum trees among the singing magpies; down gullies dusted with ferns. But, given that neither of these was possible, she could, at least, walk down to the apple orchard.

Someone — probably Jones — had set a chair, blanket and cushions under her favourite apple tree that morning. There was still no blossom to fall in soft pink and white rain about her shoulders, nor the song of bees, but at least it wasn't snowing, nor was there a chill wind. She could imagine them, there in the soft sunlight, in a few months' time.

She sat, tired from both emotion and pregnancy and the watchfulness she still kept on her new husband's health. It felt strange to rest. Stranger still to want to rest, to focus on this new life growing within her. Of all that she felt this, perhaps, was the most profound:

War took life. Women created it.

I will not let war's insanity take my child, thought Sophie. Then smiled, at herself, and the instinctive tigress nature of a woman, at the knowledge that when war came again — *if* war came again and this child she held were required for war service — then she would be helpless, as uncounted mothers had always been.

And fathers. This child was Nigel's, in law as well as love. And yet ...

A snowflake fell, slowly dancing in the breeze, till it rested, finally, in her lap. So much for a clear, fine day. She touched it gently. Perfect, as if sculpted. It somehow clarified confusion. She looked up and saw a single puff of snow cloud in the pale blue.

She stood, and made her way to the library; she sat, and gave the operator a phone number. The call was returned surprisingly swiftly. She picked up the receiver. 'Shillings.'

'I have the number for you, Lady Nigel.'

'Thank you. Is that you, James?'

'Sophie, are you all right?'

'Happy and healthy and becoming the size of the Albert Memorial. I'm breeding,' she added laconically.

'Congratulations! And Nigel? He must be tickled pink.'

'Recovering well. He and Jones have gone to inspect the new haymaker at the Home Farm. I think the Claude Vailes are going to be discommoded for many years, even if my child turns out to be a girl. James, may I ask a favour. A ... discreet one.'

A pause. The line crackled. At last he said, 'If I can.'

'I need to know the name of an Australian captain who served in either France or Belgium. All I know is that he was one of a pair of identical twins. His twin's Christian name was John, and he was killed. His brother survived.'

A laugh from the other end of the line. 'You do know that John is the most popular male name in the English-speaking world?'

'Yes.'

'What other information do you have?'

'He has been in Australia for at least the last five years. No scars or distinguishing features. Brown hair.' She tried to think. 'Good teeth. Well educated, I think. James, I know this may be impossible —'

'Actually, it is easier than you think. The names of those who enlisted will be in alphabetical order. My assistant merely needs to find two identical Australian surnames, and then check whether they have the same birthdate. I will call you back.'

'It will really be as simple as that?'

'I think so.' Another pause. 'I am glad you are happy, Sophie.'

'And you?'

'Busy. The world keeps hiccupping instead of turning smoothly. But women in your condition should not be bothered by venality and stupidity.'

'As bad as that? I'm sorry, James.' But he was right. She already felt a Jersey cow's calmness. Was this why for so long women had been presumed to have no interest in politics? Because they were usually pregnant and preoccupied with life and death, not transitory chatter? 'Thank you, James.'

'I will call as soon as I have your information.'

Of course he would. She said softly, 'Be happy.'

'You know,' he said, sounding surprised, 'I think I am.'

'You enjoy quietly re-sculpting the world, James. You always have. Only boredom would trouble you.'

'You are right, of course. Goodbye, Sophie.'

'Goodbye, James.'

She let the receiver rest in the holder and sat, trying to make sense of too many emotions and so remove them from the forefront of her mind before her husband could read them in her face.

Sophie, Maria, Nigel and Jones still dined in the library each night, instead of in the dining room, where the chairs were too hard and straight. Whatever arrangement Jones currently had with Green — Sophie was fairly sure there was one — was kept discreet, Green presiding with Mrs Goodenough and Hereward at the servants' table, not upstairs with them.

Nigel was pale after the day's outing, his feet up on a stool, dining from a tray while Sophie and Jones ate at the small table drawn up by the fire. Apple wood ... Sophie longed suddenly for the scent of gum trees, a billy boiling on the flames. She resolutely did not think of a brown face across the fire.

She glanced at Nigel, spooning his chicken soup, served every night as it was considered an excellent restorative for invalids, and pregnant women too. She had not told him of her query. Nor did she intend to. It was the first secret she had ever kept from him. There were things he did not know about her, of course, but this was the first where she had made the decision he would not know.

Unless, one day, he asked. Until then, there would be no reference to any other possible father of this child she carried.

The baby gave a sharp kick, as if it heard.

'What are you smiling at?' asked Jones.

'Your Godchild just kicked me.'

'My Godchild?' asked Jones carefully.

'Of course,' said Nigel. 'Who else? Speak to your Godson sternly, please, and tell him not to kick his mother.'

'Behave yourself,' said Jones, grinning at what Sophie had named the Bump.

They think you are a boy, thought Sophie. What if you are not? They will still love you, but every time they look at you they will think, If only she had been a son. And you will know it, consciously or not. She met Maria's eyes, and knew she was thinking the same thing.

Sophie smiled and laid her hand on the Bump once more. And I will expect you to run a corned-beef empire, she told the baby silently, and I'll have hysterics when you sail to Paris at twenty-one to become an artist.

Hereward cleared the soup plates away, brought in snipe on toast for Sophie and Jones and beef jelly for Nigel. He would have mashed potato with an egg, after that, and then stewed apple. He ate soft foods with enjoyment now, preferring them to roasts that must be finely chopped or chewed till they were soft and had lost their taste, and had very little pain.

She had ordered a lamington roll for pudding, to be served with ice cream, in memory of home. Nigel could eat that too.

Home, she thought. Australia is still home. But tonight there was an apple-wood fire, Nigel, Maria, Jones and lamington cake, and a few sharp kicks from the Bump, as if to say, 'Do not expect me to be any more biddable than my ancestors.' And she was content.

Chapter 62

I have never found life simple, though I have longed that it might be. Would I find it boring? I do not know.

Miss Lily, 1912

James's phone call came tactfully at three pm, when invalid husbands might be expected to be napping and Maria had left to arrange flowers in the church with the Ladies' Guild. Maria planned to stay until Sophie had fully recovered from the baby's birth, but Sophie could see with amusement that inactivity had begun to bore her. Maria Thwaites too, it seemed, had always wanted to run a corned-beef empire, and now missed doing so.

Sophie shut the library door before she picked up the receiver. 'James?'

'I have found your information. Or rather, not found it.'

'I don't understand.'

'Two hundred and fifty-seven sets of Australian twins enlisted. Of these, sixty-three sets of twins were both killed — a high number, but not when you understand that in most cases they served together. Only five pairs of twins had one killed, and one survive. None were called John. Of the five survivors, one is in an asylum in England and has been since 1917; one had both hands amputated in '16 — you did not mention such an injury; one married a French widow and runs her farm; one is headmaster of a school in Western Australia, and has worked there since his return from France. The last is on a disability pension.'

Which might just possibly be him, even if the name John had been meant to mislead ...

'What is his name?'

'Joseph Angelsleigh. He and his brother enlisted in 1918, but had the bad luck to run into a nasty cloud of mustard gas. Joseph survived, but his face and hands are too scarred for him to undertake normal work; hence the disability pension.'

She kept her voice steady. 'An Englishman then? Or a New Zealander?'

'I had those checked too. I also checked triplets — four sets of triplets enlisted. There are no survivors who fit with the description you gave me. Sophie, may I ask why you want to know?'

'No.'

'Ah, so that's the reason,' he said.

Trust James to understand exactly. But she could also trust him never to mention it. Except to her. Perhaps if he wished to ask another favour sometime, like dropping into another German revolution. Which she was never going to do again.

'Sophie, I've heard that sometimes men believe they are not the person who went to war. Possibly the person you are looking for fits this category.'

'You mean they feel "What happened then was not possible, so it couldn't have happened to me?" That makes sense. Sometimes I feel like that too.'

'Maybe this man does as well, and he feels it so strongly his mind has broken down.'

Which meant that she had taken advantage of a man so broken in mind that he had been easy prey — and a reason not to add to the burden of responsibility that he carried. Ten thousand lives, all on his shoulders. A man mentally damaged by war must not carry a new unwanted life, as well, she thought, with deep relief.

And yet if he was *not* damaged, surely she must tell him about the child. Or he would hear, perhaps, that the Countess of Vaile, who had been Sophie Higgs of Thuringa, had a child nine months after they had been together. *Someone* must know his real name; Harry, for starters. Once she knew that, she might

337

find out where he might be ... But Harry was uncontactable except by mail, and it was impossible to commit this to paper.

She managed to speak, at last. 'Thank you, James. I am more grateful than I can say. If ... if you can think of any other way of locating an Australian captain who now calls himself "John", could you let me know?'

'I will endeavour to do so, but, truthfully, do not see much hope of success. It is so very easy for a man to be someone else these days, for any number of reasons, and a surprising number are. I would say give my best wishes to Nigel, but suspect he does not know of this enquiry.'

'No. Thank you for that too, James.'

'I am yours, always,' he said dryly.

'You should get married,' she said, the comment made before she had realised that it had slipped out.

He laughed. 'This is where I should say — there have only ever been two women I could marry, my dear late wife and Sophie Higgs. Truthfully, indeed, there have only been two women I have liked and respected, and known that if we were married I could lead whatever life I needed to, and they would carry on and lead theirs.'

His first wife had taken ill when he was in South Africa and died some years later, she remembered.

'I do love you, Sophie. But my aunt and I do very well.'

If she had been a man, she assumed he might have added, 'And I find companionship quite nicely elsewhere.' But she was a respectable married woman now. And an aristocrat, which transcended even womanhood. 'Take care, James,' she said instead. 'Enjoy overworking and keeping us all safe.'

'You overestimate my abilities,' he said ruefully. 'Look after your heir, Sophie.' And hung up.

For a moment she thought he meant hair. So James too assumed her child must be a boy, because so much depended on just that happening.

She rested her hands on her belly. 'I wish there was a third sex so you could surprise them all,' she whispered to the Bump.

'But you'd be awfully lonely. And I promise ... if you are a girl I will never, ever let you feel second rate, or patronised by English aristocrats or Freudians or schoolteachers or Oxford dons. You will be you, and male or female will not matter.'

And maybe, she thought, you will help me make a world where that is so.

Chapter 63

Love and the acts that make the world a better place are life's deepest pleasures. It is the times when one can do neither that are hardest to bear.

Miss Lily, 1914

It felt both odd and right to have Maria at Shillings.

She and Nigel became friends almost at once. Maria Thwaites might even have become a 'lovely lady' if she had met Miss Lily before the war, Sophie thought, watching them chatter across the dining table, opposite her and Jones.

But Miss Lily's passion for giving women power in a world where it was held by men seemed to have vanished with the war, just as Miss Lily herself no longer appeared. Perhaps Nigel/Miss Lily believed women would forge paths in their own rights now, as indeed they were already doing …

'But progress is so slow!' declared Maria. 'We had such dreams, back in the 1890s. We truly thought women would vote for education, women's hospitals, even to disband armies. And yet it seems almost all women simply follow their husband's lead at the ballot box.'

'We have Lady Astor,' murmured Nigel, relishing his potage Crécy, a change at last from chicken soup. 'And you have had some success in Australia.'

'One woman only. Though Sophie did make a true difference in the last election. Perhaps I am too impatient. As a student of history I should know that social progress happens slowly. Only war or earthquakes are quick.'

'The last one did not seem particularly fast,' said Jones, sitting back as Hereward took his plate.

'I'm sorry. I didn't mean —'

'No, I spoke facetiously.'

Sophie smiled. Jones the butler would never have used the word facetiously, although he undoubtedly had known it.

'War is a series of things that happen too fast to evaluate them,' Jones went on. 'Which is why, perhaps, they are so ineptly fought. We'd have lost the war within months if the Germans hadn't been as inept as we were.'

'And if the British Empire hadn't had the backing of the female fifty per cent of the population whose abilities had been crabbed, cramped and confined,' added Sophie.

'Hamlet,' said Maria dreamily. 'Sophie, would you care to go up to London to the theatre for a few days? If you don't mind, Lord Nigel.'

'Of course I don't mind.'

'I'm sure Sloggers or Ethel would love to join you. I'd rather stay here,' said Sophie. Which was true. She needed to be near Nigel, to be able to check every hour at least that he was still living, his warmth still available to hug and be hugged.

She was also, she realised, scared to leave. Shillings had always been a place of refuge, for her as well as for Miss Lily, cut off from the currents of the world. Even the war that had taken its sons, and two of its daughters, had not impinged its violence directly on its fields and cottages. The men who had come back shattered in body or mind had found a strange peace here too, settling not into just the ancient rhythms of the land but the new challenges of tractors and mechanical harvesters and ditching machines.

Nigel has given them a future, as well as a present and a past, she thought, as Hereward brought in the stuffed pike, a hideous fish caught by the vicar and presented with pride and which, like any gift of love, must be accepted. And surely sauce soubise could make even pike delicious. Sophie tasted it. Or, at least, good as long as one focused more on the sauce than the fish.

Hereward removed the fish plates; he placed a roast saddle of mutton before Nigel to carve and the dishes of vegetables in front of her. Dinner at Shillings had always been served by the butler before, with portions offered to each diner, not en famille where the host carved and the hostess distributed crisp potatoes, parsnips in butter and brown sugar, Brussel sprouts done to a crispness without even a hint of sulphurous overboiling, the gravy boats and mint sauce passed along the table for each to serve themselves. But Shillings had a family now, and would have as long as Nigel lived. For this to continue — the security of tenants, the care of land, the eye of the manorial lord who made sure a short-sighted child was given glasses, and a bright one encouraged to serve an apprenticeship or even study at university — the baby within her must be born.

She did not dare do anything, even as mild as travelling to London, that might jolt the life inside her. Shillings needed a son ...

And if it got a daughter?

She would consider that when the time came.

Chapter 64

Did you know that every family that knits Fair Isle jumpers has
its own unique pattern? I have sometimes wondered whether every
now and then a child rebels and says, 'But I want to make my
own.' Are they regarded as disloyal? Do their neighbours whisper
and say, 'She doesn't think her grandmother's pattern is good
enough for her!' or do they praise her and say, 'A new happy
complexity of wool has been added to the world.'

Miss Lily, 1914

She had not been put upon this earth to knit. To bear a child,
incredibly, yes. But booties and matinée jackets? Others could
knit those. And they were. Maria Thwaites had knitted her way
across the Atlantic. Green knitted rompers and combinations that
she promised had no war codes twisted into them whatsoever.

Instead most mornings Sophie visited the farms, or cottages,
with Maria or Nigel or Jones, and sometimes with all three,
asked after the health of pigs, the egg-laying capacity of hens,
enquired whether the last calf was a bull or heifer, as much for
the physical and social exercise as to let those on the estate know
they were still the Shillings community. A few business matters
were handled by letter or telegram or telephone, but the Higgs
empire, not currently expanding, was comfortably tended by the
Slithersoles Senior and Junior, and Cousin Oswald.

Sometimes Nigel did not wake till late. She knew some
nights were restless. At those times he still needed morphia.
The previous night had been one of those. Sophie waited till he
had been bathed and dressed by Jones and Nurse Taylor, then
sat with him while he ate a soft-boiled egg broken onto lightly

buttered torn white bread and drank coffee made with milk and a small dash of whisky to ease the pain he would not admit he had but that the lines on his face proclaimed.

After breakfast he half dozed while she read to him, not the newspapers but old books from the library, Mrs Gaskell and other purveyors of escapism from the century before. Nigel declared the old norels gave such hope for the future, because at least today's dreams and social consciousness were so much better than the past's.

Nigel was going to live to see the future. Some of it. He would die, one day, as all do and must, but before that he would live and see his child grow up.

After lunch he slept, properly, while Jones and Maria found their own tasks. Sophie curled up on the sofa in the drawing room — how impossible it would have been to put her stockinged feet up on the silk coverings even a decade earlier — and read *The Forsyte Saga* — Nigel had no taste for modern literature.

'Breeding' was a restful occupation, she thought, for her at least, at this time and place and with the luxury for it to be so. She placed one hand upon her stomach as she read, to feel the baby's kicks. Most emphatic ones. She smiled. Temperament was decided in the womb, it seemed.

The drawing room door opened. 'A visitor, your ladyship,' said Hereward. 'Are you at home?' He offered a card on the silver salver.

Sophie inspected it. Lady Boniface FitzWilliam. So this was Georgina's mother-in-law, the source of her unspoken fear that had kept her in Australia, where the Higgs connections meant her late husband's family could not claim her son. Her letter of sympathy to her late husband's parents had been met by a solicitor's demand sent via the misleading address in America that she, and the heir, return. Georgina had not replied. But she was mentioned too often in the social pages of the *Sydney Morning Herald* for society in England not to discover where she now lived.

Sophie put the card down, considered, then nodded.

'I am at home. Tea, please, Hereward.'

'Yes, your ladyship.'

Sophie stood as the woman entered. Good furs, excellent pearls of an old-fashioned length, the long hemline old-fashioned too, though the dress was new. 'Lady Nigel, please excuse my calling on you unannounced, not introduced, and uninvited.'

'Not at all,' said Sophie meaninglessly. 'Do sit down.'

They sat. Lady Boniface's rigid back did not touch her chair.

'I hope it was not a tiring journey,' said Sophie, as Hereward carried in the tea tray, followed by a footman with a tray of edibles. 'Milk, sugar?'

'Black, please. I lost the habit of milk out in India. Such unreliable supplies.'

'A crumpet? Bread and butter? Or cherry cake? Mrs Goodenough's cherry cake is very good.'

'Lady Nigel, you must wonder why I am here.'

'Possibly not,' admitted Sophie. 'You are here about your grandson?'

'Yes, I ...' To Sophie's horror the elderly woman began to cry, still stiffly upright, her face impassive. Sophie waited ten seconds, then threw convention out the window and kneeled beside her. She proffered a handkerchief. Lady Boniface took it, wiped and blew.

It was time for frankness. 'Do you and your husband intend to attempt to gain custody of your grandson?'

'I ... I ... Of course not!' Lady Boniface looked at her with genuine shock. 'My husband ... is not himself these days. Indeed, he is barely aware of his surroundings. He has been like that for the past two years.'

She unconsciously clenched her kid-gloved hands. 'Lady Nigel, if you will pardon the indiscretion, you will be a mother soon. I ...' She stared at the silken lilies on the carpet. 'My arms are empty,' she whispered. 'I have not held my grandson as a baby. I ... I wish only to hold him as a child. I will not intrude on his mother's choice of upbringing, will even travel to Australia if she will permit —'

'If she will permit.' How power had shifted for Georgina.

'Please,' whispered Lady Boniface. 'Timothy is the only child of my blood that I will ever see, ever hold again. Please.'

Sophie took the old hands firmly in her own. 'You must visit us when we return to Australia. We might even introduce you to a kangaroo, as well as your grandson. But,' she laid her hand upon the swell of her belly again, 'I believe I would like my friends to be at the Christening. Our wedding was so hurried, due to my husband's operation. I will ask Georgina if she and her son will come to England. I think now, perhaps, they will.'

'And she will let me see ...' she spoke the word almost reverently '... Timothy?'

'I am sure she will,' said Sophie quietly. 'She loves her son, but she will not withhold other love from him.'

'She sends me a photograph twice a year. She is ... most dutiful,' said Lady Boniface, who knew that Georgina had not been dutiful. Who might, or might not, know that she had also been battered and demeaned as a wife.

But that was beside the point now.

'He is a lovely boy,' said Sophie.

Lady Boniface looked at her eagerly. 'What is he like?'

'He enjoys flying kites, as high as possible. And he is an excellent rider. Quite fearless. Too fearless ... but don't worry, we are very strict about the horses he is allowed to ride.' She thought it might be tactless to mention his passion for pythons and boa constrictors — or that sending a solicitor's letter was not the best way to entice her daughter-in-law to visit. But that, presumably, had been the doing of her father-in-law, not the woman in front of her. 'Timothy enjoys poetry too. His mother reads him one poem each night and he has even written a few of his own. Very intelligent for his age,' she offered.

'Poetry?' The tremulous voice held incredulity. And then, more firmly: 'Poetry. It would be ... interesting ... to have a poet in the family.'

Sophie laughed. 'He is eleven years old! A bit early to choose a career yet.'

'He will have the estate, of course. But our agent is excellent, if his tastes run to … poetry …'

Or staying in Australia, Sophie thought. 'I think your grandson will be so excited at taking his position in society, as well as an estate of his own, that you will see plenty of him in the years to come. But you need to meet him as soon as it can be arranged.' She glanced at her watch. It would be four in the morning in Australia. 'I will send a telegram tonight, Lady Boniface. Do you have the telephone connected?'

She shook her head. 'No. But I will be at the Dorchester in London for the next week. Perhaps you wouldn't mind contacting me there?'

'Of course,' said Sophie. 'If we have the Christening in early September, there will be plenty of time for Georgina and Timothy to travel to England.'

She did not add that Georgina must at times have been desperately homesick, kept away by the fear of further legal action, even if it was eventually fruitless, by her late husband's family. That too need never be referred to again.

Timothy must have his family and Lady Boniface would have her arms around the boy while he was still small enough to accept a hug, and not just patronisingly pat his grandmother's cheek. But even that, she realised, would be relished by this old woman.

'I hope you will be one of the party,' said Sophie. 'And it will be a party.'

'A child is the greatest blessing,' said Lady Boniface.

Even when he grows up and behaves like your son, thought Sophie. 'And now will you try some cherry cake?'

'I would love to,' said Lady Boniface.

Chapter 65

*My dearest friend, I have no words to comfort you on the loss of
Alison, except this crumb: a child has been born.*

Miss Lily to the Dowager Duchess of Wooten, 1915

The last weeks passed as if they'd been lined with lead. She could
not reach her shoes; had to lurch on the bed like a stranded
whale for Green to fasten them.

Was she the only one to count the weeks, or did Nigel count
them too? A child by John — or whatever his true name was —
would be born three or even four weeks before one sired by Nigel.

If she had never slept with John, they could have been sure.
If she had never slept with John, there might be no baby at
all ... although if Marie Stopes was to be trusted — that deeply
scientific woman — then she might have been at a fertile time
with Nigel too.

Impossible to know what would have been best. Impossible to
change it too.

The labour pains began either two days late or three weeks
early, on a Sunday morning, so mild she thought at first they
were the usual discomfort — it had been impossible to find a
comfortable position to sleep in for more than five minutes for
the past month. She and Nigel now slept in different rooms,
for he needed uninterrupted sleep, and knowing she must not
disturb him interrupted hers.

On the fourth contraction — or possibly the twentieth, for
they were indeed still only mild — she decided it was safe to lie
and wait for Green to bring in her morning tea.

They were about twenty minutes apart by the time Dorothy crept in to add wood to the fire, saw her mistress was lying awake and tiptoed out to inform Green.

Green arrived ten minutes later, tea tray in hand.

'Drink it yourself,' said Sophie. 'I'd better have an empty bladder.'

Ladies did not have bladders. Women did. Women who had worked in hospitals understood about them.

'How far apart?'

'Twenty minutes. I'm serious, Greenie darling. Sit down and drink the tea. I feel like company.'

'Not his lordship?'

Suddenly, deeply, she wanted Miss Lily, potentially only down the hallway, and yet unreachable. 'Let him sleep for now. This may take a while. Don't tell Maria yet either.'

They might try and convince her, yet again, to go to hospital. Women who ran hospitals knew that survival, of both mother and child, in childbirth was almost twice as high with a midwife, especially one who used the old remedy of hands and instruments washed in boiled rosemary and lavender water, though whether the herbs or the boiling were most effective, Sophie did not know. Possibly no one did. Why bother with scientific investigation of a womanly remedy?

Green settled back in the armchair, glanced consideringly at Sophie, then put her feet up on the footstool. She sipped, and nibbled a Bath biscuit. 'Once the household knows I expect I'll be on my feet till the heir is delivered. And for an hour at least afterwards.'

'Probably. You do realise it may be a girl?'

'A girl will be *your* heir,' Green reminded her. 'Your father's will left everything to you and your children in perpetuity. And his lordship can leave his personal fortune where he likes.'

'There is that,' said Sophie, then gasped as a stronger contraction grabbed her.

Green finished the tea, stood and brushed off some crumbs. 'I'll call Mrs Addison.'

Mrs Addison had delivered the district's babies for twenty-four years and lost only two, and one of those had been six weeks premature, and the other ... No one had spoken of the other, except to mark its resting place with a headstone. The baby's mother now had four other children.

Yes, Mrs Addison was the person to be trusted now.

Ten hours later and she wanted to strangle Mrs Addison. If she said, 'Doing well, lovey,' one more time she would kick her.

'Time for the sacks,' said Mrs Addison calmly.

'What ... are ... they ...?' muttered Sophie, before adding a long scream. As it ebbed she felt soft and woolly balls, impossibly hairy, one placed in each hand. They felt like they were filled with sand, with marbles in each one. They felt in fact like ...

'Squeeze them tight, lovey, and think of every man in England when you do,' advised Mrs Addison.

Sophie squeezed. And screamed. And laughed, and kept on laughing, squeezing, gasping ...

The door opened. 'Is —?' began Jones.

'Out,' said Green, Sophie and Mrs Addison in unison.

The world diminished. Pain, then slightly less pain; impossible pain, and even more ...

'Now push. That's it. You're doing well, lovey.'

'Push!' said Green, grasping her hand and one of the woollen balls.

She pushed. And pushed. And felt ...

'A girl!' said Mrs Addison, not quite hiding her disappointment. 'You're doing wonderfully, lovey. Now for the afterbirth. Push one last time for me.'

A girl. Poor Nigel. The Vailes would triumph eventually then ... She pushed, felt something slither, then pushed again.

'Mrs Addison?' said Green. Even more urgent agony and Sophie's scream split the ceiling.

Or should have, but did not. Another push, and then another ...

'A boy,' said Green calmly, wrapping the second child efficiently and putting him in Sophie's other arm, across from his sister. And then she sat on the hearthstone and sobbed, her face in her hands, crying for life and death and for the future.

And Sophie held her children while Mrs Addison did ... things. Then called to Jones and Nigel, 'You can stop listening at the door. You have twins, a boy and a girl. Babies and mother are doing wonderfully, aren't you, lovey? Just give us a few minutes and you can see them.'

Sophie stared at the tiny faces, the boy so much smaller than the girl. Surely he would have Nigel's blue eyes? The baby blue was far lighter than his sister's. Perhaps both would have her hazel eyes.

Perhaps they would tactfully mostly resemble her. Or ... was it possible, just possible, to have two children by two men at the same time? The larger girl conceived first, born first, her birth triggering her brother's, small as a three-week premature baby would be.

'He's so tiny,' whispered Sophie, in awe and weakness.

'But a bonny boy,' said Mrs Addison firmly. 'Twins are often early and a little small. We'll need to keep him warm, your ladyship, and sunlight for an hour each midday too. Nothing like sunlight to strengthen the bones. Feed him every two hours. Ah, I've seen it often. One twin takes all the feeding and the other is the runt of the litter, meaning no offence, your ladyship. He'll be as tall as his father before you can blink, and in the football scrum.'

She hoped he wasn't. All that hope and love and labour just to play football. But then men enjoyed getting muddy, hit by others — as long as there were no trenches, mortars or poison gas involved.

Mrs Addison looked at her proudly. 'Shall I ask his lordship in?'

'Yes,' whispered Sophie. 'Ask their father to come in.'

Night. Firelight. The babies slept in the nursery, watched over by Nurse (who had apparently lost her other name with her profession, but who Maria had decided met all the modern criteria for nursedom) who had promised to bring them in to Sophie as soon as they stirred, despite her risking the ruination of her figure by old-fashioned breastfeeding, instead of offering them hygienic bottles every two hours to the minute.

Sophie opened her eyes. Nigel sat in the armchair knitting a bootie.

Sophie watched him unseen for minutes. At last she said, 'One bootie isn't much use between four feet. I didn't know you could knit.'

'I learned on the North West Frontier. The Scots knit before battle. Or they used to.' Nigel put the bootie down. 'I've knitted twelve so far. And two matinée jackets. But I don't knit in public. It might … confuse things.' It was the first time he had even discreetly alluded to Miss Lily since their marriage.

'They are perfect, aren't they?' said Sophie sleepily.

'Naturally. Clever Sophie, to produce both a son and daughter.'

'If I'd really concentrated, I might have made it triplets, with a spare for the heir.'

Nigel's mouth twisted. 'Speaking as one who spent his youth in the uncomfortable position of being a spare, I'm glad you didn't.'

'Perhaps our son will want to be a stockman, or take up country dancing professionally.'

'Can one be a professional country dancer?'

'I am sure our son will do whatever he sets his mind to,' said Sophie. 'And our daughter may love estate management *or* breed zebras.'

Nigel smiled. 'Why should they not be both and more? Neither of their parents let their sex or others' expectations determine who or what they are.'

'Except for you. Sometimes. But then your road has been far steeper than most.'

'Nor is there any end in sight. One hears,' said Nigel carefully, 'of clubs in Berlin where men dressed as women dance. But I do not think I would care for those.'

'I should hope not. What will we call our magnificent offspring?'

'Your choice. Your labour and your choice.'

'No preferences? Really none?'

Nigel shook his head. 'As long as neither name occurs in the Vaile family tree.'

Sophie was silent. Nigel kissed her cheek. 'Well?'

Oh, Danny Boy, the pipes, the pipes are calling ...

'Has there ever been a Daniel in the Vaile family?'

'No.'

'Then Daniel it is.' Danny Boy, she thought. 'And for the girl?'

'Rose.'

Sophie laughed, then stopped when it hurt. 'I thought I was being allowed to choose the names.'

'You can.'

'No. I like it; I like them. Daniel and Rose.' A Rose for Lily, whose name must not be spoken. And for all the roses who had been there for the Anzac boys, she thought, remembering Harry's speech during the election campaign. The roses of No Man's Land, the roses who did not return, the roses who won a war, even if men would never give them the credit.

John might approve of the name Rose. There had been no further word from James Lorrimer about his possible true name or whereabouts. She must accept that he had vanished; and that he had chosen to. She glanced at Nigel, his face gentle and intent as the door opened, and Nurse carried a baby in each arm, each one murmuring a little, tired of waiting. They already knew they only needed to make their desires known, these so deeply wanted children. No need to make a fuss.

'Stay while I feed them,' said Sophie to Nigel. And Nurse — who had evidently been well briefed by Maria on Sophie's tendency to make up her mind and have the world follow her decision — did not even twitch her lips at the temerity of a male watching this rite of motherhood.

353

Chapter 66

Every birth is a new beginning. Though every day, or hour or minute may be a new beginning too. And every beginning is an ending of what was new the moment before.

Miss Lily, 1914

Darling Sophie,

It is in every newspaper! Our very own Countess of Shilling has had twins! I don't think there is anyone from Sydney to the back of the black stump who doesn't know of the great event.

Darling, I am so happy for you, and your Nigel. I will also add, very quietly indeed, that friends who count the weeks don't count. I am at the centre of a wide gossip ring, and I can promise there has not been a breath of anything but delight. You are merely expected to produce the earl, the offspring, and a vast garden party as soon as it is practicable to travel such a long way with Rose and Daniel. I love the names, by the way.

It is impossible to say how delighted I am. The only thing that will make me happier is to see you again. Harry sends his regards, which is man talk for 'love'.

Love from all of us, and especially me,

Midge

PS Ethel says Nigel is a 'good egg'. I trust her judgement! He must be nearly good enough for you.

No news of John. And Midge would tell her if she knew of him, especially as she guessed the children might be his. Possibly she had already found out his real name from Harry, but 'John' might now have a third name, and a new and unknown refuge.

I must not think of him, she thought. It is not fair for Nigel, nor the children, all of whom deserved certainty.

The Vailes sent a stilted letter of congratulations. Sophie resolved that she would keep the Vailes from ever visiting her children, not only because they were unlikeable, but in case they came deliberately bearing chickenpox or measles. She would not put juvenile germ warfare past that lot.

They never had collected their zebras, which still grazed in the field, their coats grown conveniently shaggier. The hippopotamus though had been rehomed in the London Zoo.

Small knitted garments arrived, sent by every female she had worked with, including Doris; a matinée jacket from Her Majesty, which had needed a consultation with Nigel to find the correct response; a large toy zebra from the Prince of Wales; and a crocheted blanket in complicated baby stitch from young Sophie. More letters arrived: weekly ones from Midge; from Ethel, Sloggers and Dodo at Oxford; from Lady Mary in London whose acquaintance she had renewed; from women she had worked with in Belgium and France; from Mrs Henderson, telling in detail of vast sunsets as their new airline carried supplies across the north; and a postcard of a didgeridoo from Miss Morrison, saying simply, *We've done it. Thank you. Eugenia M*.

Georgina arrived too, with Timothy, who had taken photos all the way from Australia, and needed to show her and Nigel every one once Green had taken him up to the attics to show him how to develop the film. Georgina left him at Shillings while she made a first cautious visit to the Dorchester to see Lady FitzWilliam.

She returned with a deep peace in her eyes, and plans to visit, 'just for a few days', the estate Timothy would eventually inherit. Sophie suspected the days would become weeks, the visits longer and more frequent and that, within a year, both mother and viscount would be in residence, creating the bonds that held Shillings together as a community, and the estate benefiting a great deal from Georgina's talent for management.

Business wires and letters sat on Hereward's silver salver and then the breakfast table almost every morning now, Cousin Oswald and the Slithersoles Senior and Junior having evidently decided that the business of birth was completed and the business of corned beef, fruit cocktail and other products could be resumed.

Mostly little was needed except her agreement. Sophie had, however, noted Martinus van der Hagen's Nutricia NV baby food company in the Netherlands, and now Mr Clapp in America was selling his versions too. As she knew from the Shillings apples, any blemish made fruit unsaleable, and carrots too. There was not just a market for the new canned baby foods but a plentiful supply of a cheap yet nutritious raw material that would otherwise be fed to pigs or wasted.

I am thinking of small jars, she wrote, *each holding one meal's serving of mashed apple, pear, or a combination of potato, carrot and puréed pea, called 'Baby's Vegetable Medley' or 'Baby's Fruit'. This would mean that, as with Her Ladyship's Fruit Cup, we could alter the contents according to the harvest.*

We could begin with a trial factory here, near Shillings, preferably before Miss Thwaites goes home, so she can supervise the build and first production runs and then take her experience back to create one at Bald Hill.

I hear the soldier settler blocks are proving a sad disappointment to many of the hopeful demobbed veterans and this would give them another market to help them survive. Once again I must emphasise that while these factories must of course produce a profit, it should be no more than three per cent, with a further five per cent for future capital investment, thus giving the highest price possible to the growers. There would be, of course, the usual Higgs working conditions in the factories.

I do not think the French or other European nations would be potential major markets, but if we perhaps put 'Under the Patronage of the Earl of Shillings' on the labels for an American market, Mr Clapp may find us serious competition.

No, there was no need to travel to London, or Sydney or Thuringa. Life was here. And yet ...

But come ye back when summer's in the meadow,
Or when the valley's hushed and white with snow.
It's I'll be here in sunshine or in shadow ...

Home was still the hush of midday in a gum forest, or the insane shriek of the cicadas. It was Harry Harrison yelling at the sheep dogs while the flock moved in a grey wave across the hill. It was pelicans landing like unsteady seaplanes on the river, the shrill of mosquitoes in the night and stockmen whose skin might be black or white, and women with rough hands who called her 'darl' and who had voted for her.

Shillings mattered. It was an unalterable part of her life now. But for her heart to be truly fed, she must see home.

Chapter 67

Social rules are both senseless and eminently meaningful. To know them is to show that you belong.

Miss Lily, 1914

'David insists on coming,' said Nigel, emerging from the library, a box in his hands, 'but he says it must be in London as he can't get away.'

Sophie sighed. If the Prince of Wales was going to attend the Christening, it would need to be a formal affair. They should even open Vaile House, which had been rented for the past twenty years, the tenant inconveniently dying only a month earlier, leaving time for renovations but not enough for a new tenant, giving them no excuse not to celebrate in style.

She needed a social secretary. She smiled. Georgina could find her one. After all, Giggs had never officially resigned her position, even if she had never actually been paid a salary either.

Georgina and Timothy were up at the FitzWilliam estate again, but surely Georgina could still find her a secretary, or at least advertise for applicants to come to her for vetting. They would need a month to move the household, and the guests must be given at least a fortnight's notice, even in these informal days. The new secretary had better have exquisite handwriting, as she wasn't going to write out two hundred invitations, nor would she inflict that duty on Maria, who had accepted an invitation to visit Sloggers, tutoring at Somerville College in Oxford.

And dash it, she would have to ask Emily, if the celebration was to be in London. Emily had already sent her two invitations to dine, knowing it was impossible for her to accept, but still conferring the obligation on the Countess of Shillings to return the invitations. Emily played the game well.

And Emily would need to put up with bluestockings and archaeologists — Midge's friend Anne was pregnant, was returning next week and would therefore be in England for at least a year or even two — and an extremely long royal performance on the bagpipes.

'If you can put up with the formality, I can too,' she said. Because one day, only eighteen years away, Rose would make her debut just as her mother had done, or possibly not just as her mother had done, but according to whatever conventions one was following at the time. And Daniel would perhaps hunt the ballrooms for an acceptable wife for Shillings. No, a loving life partner: that sounded better.

But for those events to happen, the children's parents must play their roles too. Australia must be part of their lives, but at least a few social seasons were inevitable, beginning with this.

She looked at the box in Nigel's hands, then at his amused smile as he held it out to her. 'What's this?'

'Traditional, darling, on the birth of the heir.'

Sophie stared at the most opulent tiara she had ever seen, larger even than Queen Adelaide's. 'You didn't buy this.'

'Of course not. It's been in a bank vault.'

'Do you think it might go back there?'

Nigel laughed. 'Tomorrow, if you are sure you don't want to wear it for the party after the Christening.'

'Never. Why not sell it?' That tiara would buy mechanical harvesters for all of Southern England.

'I can't. It's part of the entail. The entail can only be broken if the current earl and his heir agree — once the heir is over twenty-one.'

'I profoundly hope that in twenty-one years Daniel signs away every ugly stone of it. Any other traditions I don't know about? Wearing a crinoline for a year after childbirth? Doing a Lady Godiva around the village?'

'Just the Christening.'

'The vicar will be thrilled.'

'By the archbishop, as it will be in London. Darling, it will be expected.'

'And you of course never do the unexpected. No, you are correct. Sometimes one has to do the right things. Or the silly thing that society thinks is right.' She would manage, she thought.

And manage quite easily. It seemed she had absorbed the lessons of the Dowager Duchess of Wooten, who had guided her through her debutante season, extremely well. The Dowager had never seemed incommoded. Sophie realised now that it was because she never was.

The admirable Miss Pinkley, bless Georgina and her ready understanding of who was required, took Sophie's twelve or so scribbled names and, after adding dozens more, wrote out beautiful guest lists. Sophie waved these away without even reading them, after making sure the guests she did want had been included.

She did, however, consult Mrs Goodenough about the menu for the luncheon after the Christening. It would be an indoor luncheon buffet, unthinkably informal before the war, but at least it meant she didn't have to worry about precedence if the Prince of Wales didn't turn up, or arrived just as the affair was over, as he was notorious for doing.

Mrs Goodenough glowed with the joy of feeding royalty, as well as the cream of London society, though Sophie suspected that 'flotsam' would describe many of the guests better — butterflies who fluttered from one function to another. But butterflies were decorative, she had to admit.

It still seemed strange to order the menu in her own home, after so many years of Maria or others taking care of the task. She and Mrs Goodenough decided on caviar on toast; glazed ham decorated with candied satsuma slices; game pie; boned stuffed goose; and silver hotplates with curry and yellow rice, and small dishes of what Jones referred to as 'the fixings' to eat with curry. Sophie had toyed with vast centrepieces of corned beef, but relinquished the inspiration reluctantly. Besides, for many there, it would bring back memories of battlefields ...

She included two new Australian dishes for sentiment; vast pavlovas, their meringue skirts named for the divine dancer, laden with whipped cream and strawberries and passionfruit she had imported specially. (Although Cousin Oswald had told her firmly that the pavlova had been invented in New Zealand and not by a shearer's cook turned chef in the west.) And small individual lamingtons would be served with coffee, those chocolate-and-coconut-coated sponges named for Lady Lamington, much-admired wife of the deeply disliked ex-Governor of Queensland. Sophie approved of lamingtons. The coconut kept your fingers from getting sticky; though naturally at the Christening they would be eaten from plates with cake forks.

Miss Pinkley supervised the opening of Vaile House; Jones managed the hiring of extra staff for the month the family would be in residence there; Green took care of matters sartorial; and Nurse packed whatever paraphernalia would be needed to move the babies and the nursery. Jones even drove the car.

London had not changed. Fog hung, yellow as pus, wisping between houses, sitting as if it had conquered the town, thicker than mustard gas, though slower to poison and kill. Cars burped exhaust fumes, outnumbering horses now, the scent stronger than manure.

Poor sparrows, thought Sophie. They had lived so well on horse droppings and undigested corn. What could feed on car exhaust?

Vaile House felt like a hotel: sumptuous, tasteful, temporary. They would let it again after the Christening, Sophie decided, unless Nigel objected. But entertaining at Shillings sometimes would be necessary now, if she and Nigel were not to be labelled eccentrics, damaging their children's prospects. Although with the Higgs fortune and the Vaile titles, possibly four dinners a year and an annual charity garden party would suffice.

Yet once they were settled, the move to Vaile House was almost imperceptible: waking up beside the same husband, in an almost identical bed, in a similar room, to the same face bringing the same morning tea. Mrs Goodenough had been transported along with the rest of the household so even breakfast was the same, the two boiled eggs on torn-up white bread that Nigel consumed as a matter of course, her own kedgeree. Maria Thwaites, frowning the same gentle disapproval at the same newspapers ...

To her surprise what she had thought of as merely convention was one of the most meaningful experiences of her life: to hand each tiny child to the archbishop, to see the Prince of Wales, surprisingly small in this large space, holding the Godfather's candle, and Jones too beside him, with Georgina and Ethel as Godmothers, for as she had explained to Maria, her place as Sophie's true mother meant she was grandmother, and needed no other role to bind her to the children.

The archbishop came to luncheon. The Prince of Wales piped the guests in but, thankfully, two tunes sufficed. The twins peered at the bagpipes, Rose with interest, as if already wondering how they worked, Daniel with joy at anything that so effortlessly made so much noise.

The prince promised to play for them again as soon as they wakened from their nap.

Sophie floated. A rose-coloured dress, embroidered in deeper pink on one side, a slash of silver beading on the other, her hair newly shingled with Green standing sentry to ensure not a quarter inch too much or little was shaved off the back of her neck, rose shoes, with silver flowers on the toes and tapping heels, a silver bandeau with a matching rose above her temple, and the fashionable length of pearls Georgina had given her.

'My dear Emily, that *dress* — you look divine!' And have put on weight. What had Giggs called her? Podge. That was it. And Nigel says your husband is still stuck in the government position he was in seven years ago. Even your wiles can't shape a better career for him ...

'You look wonderful too. And so young. And so does your husband. No one could ever think him old enough to be your father,' said Emily, with sugar-filled grace.

'No one ever has, Podge darling.'

Emily's smile froze slightly. 'So clever of you to produce an heir so quickly and conveniently.'

'We tried extremely hard,' said Sophie sweetly. 'It was great fun. And of course,' she added, unable to resist, 'Nigel had access to all his cousin's woodcuts. A knowledgeable man is irresistible.'

She passed on, leaving Emily's mouth in a perfect O, like a goldfish's. But Emily's dress had been extremely good, partly concealing the new mass of her bosom. Green must find out where she had obtained it. She'd glimpsed Green peering from an upstairs window, evaluating every ensemble. 'Do you mind very much not attending?' Sophie had asked.

'Goodness no. Wouldn't touch that crew with a barge pole. You can do a lot with a barge pole,' Green had said reminiscently, though without specifying if it was in the arts of love or war.

'Sloggers, I absolutely adore that hat! Lady Boniface, how lovely to see you. Thank you so much for being here today.'

Oysters in crisp bacon coats were circulated on silver salvers, as was the champagne, and whisky for the old buffers, and the Prince of Wales cocktail ordered in his honour — champagne based but with a decided kick.

Now and then she caught Nigel's eye above the crowd and smiled, both of them concealing boredom interspersed with genuine delight.

'How wonderful to see you ...'

'The Honourable Miss Mary Macintosh,' whispered Miss Pinkley.

'... Miss Macintosh. So delighted you could come. Please do make some time for the buffet.'

The room had more knees than any she had seen in London — their owners wore short beaded or fringed gowns — but the women's faces were strangely the same, with rouge and lipstick and powder, and the jewels familiar from years earlier, or at least post-war good copies.

'They are divine musicians, aren't they, Sir Marmaduke? Yes, I do agree that modern dances are not like those in our day, though I have to say *your* day will last a hundred years at least!'

'Excuse me, we haven't met. And Ethel is too busy hatching another scheme across the room to introduce us. I am Anne McHenry.'

Sophie turned to see the Honourable Anne, the third in the canteen trio with Midge and Ethel, now married to an archaeologist — no, an archaeologist herself. She of all people must stop categorising women by their husbands' careers.

Sophie examined her — a scarred face, brown skin, a firm handshake. 'I am so pleased to meet you at last. Look, there is no way of having a decent conversation in this crush.'

Anne laughed. A good laugh. 'I would never say such a thing to my hostess, but agree entirely.'

'Come to lunch, tomorrow, with Ethel too, if she is not engaged already down at the East End. You will like my husband, and adore the twins.'

She turned again, caught in the tides of the crowd.

'Ah, my dear Comrade Sophie!' Lady Mary greeted her. The elderly peer looked much the same as she had more than a decade earlier, when she introduced her to the Workmen's Friendship Club during her debutante season. That club, of course, had been charity, not bolshevism.

Hadn't it? Had she let the affairs of the world pass by her for far too long, as she focused on cans and tomato markets?

'Heard about your sterling work getting the Labor chappie elected. Well done, my dear! We must get you on the strike committee.' Lady Mary took out a small leather-covered notebook, with a silver pencil attached by a ribbon. 'Are you free next Tuesday?'

'I will have to ask Miss Pinkley,' extemporised Sophie.

'Ah, this mad social whirl. It will be different after the revolution!' said Lady Mary.

Oh dear. 'Quite. Lady Mary, have you met Ethel Carryman? Lady Mary, Ethel's doing sterling work up north, and managed a miracle of a canteen in France. Ethel, Lady Mary runs a soup kitchen in the East End — it's a wonder you have not met.'

A smile to excuse her as she met the eyes of another guest, remembered from her season. 'Colonel, I do hope you approve of the curry.'

'Quite as good as Bombay, my dear. The memsahib approves of your chutney too. So hard to get a mango chutney in England.' His nose was the shape and colour of a plum and his walrus moustache was stained curry or tobacco yellow. Ah, there was Georgina talking to Anne's husband and a man with the brown skin that suggested he was also an archaeologist; Timothy had found young Sophie and was explaining Australia's varieties of snakes in great detail. 'Some of them are not poisonous at all.'

'You look beautiful, Sophie dear.'

He had strategically placed himself in a corner. A small almost dance-like few steps and they could talk almost privately. Sophie made a note of the manoeuvre. 'Thank you, James. You're looking well.' He was: hair a little thinner; his eyes amused, as if he saw what lay below this social posturing, but had compassion enough to keep it — or at least its players — safe.

'Bored with being wife, mother and countess yet?'

She laughed. 'Of course not.'

'You will be.' He looked at her intently. 'Both you and Nigel. You have your heir, and Shillings and Higgs Industries are thriving. I predict you will be bored extremely soon.'

'And you'll have a job for me?' she asked lightly. 'I'm not planning on travelling anywhere, except to Australia.'

'The ... task ... I am thinking of is closer to hand.'

'I don't understand.' Was he talking about Lady Mary? The 'comrade' had been a shock, but she had always been eccentric, and good hearted.

James smiled. 'I think you will know what I mean by the end of this afternoon. Perhaps I'll call on you in a month or two.'

'Of course, we would love to see you at Shillings. Come and stay, and your aunt too. But I really can't see —'

'You will,' said James calmly. 'Ah, Winston, my dear chap, just the man I hoped to see.'

'Sophie?'

Her world stilled. She turned.

Hannelore, thinner, but still square and short, her hair still in a chignon, not bobbed, in a dress of blue lace and truly excellent diamonds, even better than her own, though she would not wear diamonds at a luncheon. But she was not a prinzessin, and Hannelore carried them well. She always had.

'I did not think you knew I had been invited,' said Hannelore, with a swan's grace and a smile perfect for the occasion. Only her eyes were watchful. 'I have been most careful to be on everyone's guest list this year. Your secretary is excellent at her job.'

'Is ... is Dolphie with you?'

'He sends his apologies. I am his hostess these days, for his embassy work here in England. Herr von Munster accompanied me in his stead.' Hannelore waited for Sophie's response.

And suddenly there was nothing but joy, and friendship. 'I am glad. So glad,' said Sophie, taking Hannelore's hands. Scars, almost invisible, under blue lace gloves, just as her own hands were scarred, and Anne's, Sloggers's, and Ethel's. 'What have you been doing?'

'I have a factory, most profitable, though it is not like your factories. I will not even try to thank you for giving me the means to start it. But it is managed well while I am here, as I am sure yours are managed excellently also. I am enjoying London ...' Hannelore laughed at the look on Sophie's face. 'Oh, no, I have not changed that much. I am not here for the parties or, yes, I am here for the parties. I am truly working, Sophie, working at last as we dreamed so many years ago. Working for *peace*.'

'For the League of Nations?'

A shrug, as if that earnest but powerless organisation might make any difference, as so far indeed it had not.

'No. For true peace. For our country to be prosperous again, to take its place in Europe. A united Europe, free of Bolshevik rebellions, an alliance of strong governments and able people.'

'It is a wonderful dream,' said Sophie carefully.

'We need to dream it to make it real. We must talk,' said Hannelore, kissing her cheek. 'Come to the embassy. I have met a man.' She laughed at the hopeful expression on Sophie's face. 'No, not that kind of man. This man is a leader, one who will finally lead us to peace.'

'And I will find him at the German embassy?' asked Sophie, smiling. Cracked pieces of her life were finding their right places again. Her friendship with Hannelore could not just be healed, but strengthened, and an alliance made. Peace in the world that now contained her twins was the best of all ambitions.

'No, for that you must come to Germany. But we can talk of his ideas. His name,' breathed Hannelore reverently, 'is Hitler. Herr Adolph Hitler.'

Chapter 68

*I dream of many things: a world of peace; a world where all
can show what is in their hearts and never be condemned. And
sometimes I dream of something I have accepted is unattainable but
still grieve that I will never have, for I will never be a mother, nor a
grandmother.*

Miss Lily, 1912

The guests had gone.

Sophie sat in the quiet nursery, next to the cribs where their
babies slept, Daniel with a milky smile as if the world was
love; Rose with fierce concentration, as if sleep too demanded
unrelenting focus.

The door opened. Miss Lily entered, as beautiful as the
moment Sophie first saw her, her face half shadowed in the late
summer dusk through the window, perfect, swan-like.

She wore pale pink silk, fringed at the knees and elbows ('After
forty a woman's elbows should only be seen by candlelight, my
dears,' she had said so many years earlier). A matching chiffon
scarf was draped gently around her neck. A new dress, thought
Sophie, recently ordered from Paris. Her hair was fashionably
shingled, a style that could convert from a man's hairstyle to a
woman's in skilled hands like Green's. Green, back at her old
duties and, Sophie imagined, greatly contented.

Sophie smiled from her chair by the cribs. Happiness began
to glow, like a small sun that must never be contained. She
held out her hands. Miss Lily took them, the bare scarred
hands in her silk-gloved ones, then she drew up a chair to sit
next to her.

'I hadn't known if you would want me to be part of this,' said Miss Lily finally.

'I love you. I will always want you with me. And these are our children.' She bent over to kiss the lightly powdered cheek.

'But as they get older?'

'We'll find a way. They are our children, after all. They will be intelligent, compassionate and change the world.' She laughed softly. 'Or maybe all mothers feel like that.'

'I doubt it,' said Miss Lily dryly. 'Most parents want their children to be inconspicuous, change nothing and be an extension of themselves.'

'Normal is deeply overrated then.'

'I have always found it so,' said Miss Lily.

Sophie watched the even breathing of her children. 'What world are they going to grow into? I lost track of it while I was pregnant. But it is seeping back now. The Austrian revolution, the strikes, the Bolsheviks.' Her voice broke slightly as she whispered, 'I don't want them to grow up in a world of war. Anything but that.'

Miss Lily was silent. At last she said, 'Once I thought that keeping countries from preparing for war was a way of ensuring peace. I was wrong. If we had been better prepared, the war would have been shorter.'

'But we have the League of Nations now. And Hannelore's Herr Hitler, working to move Germany away from the Prussian militarists to true peace and prosperity.'

'We can hope our children will be safe,' said Miss Lily gently. 'But mostly we can give them joy now. Show them the beauty of the world, of books, of music. Teach them love and friendship. Those last, in spite of war.'

Sophie shivered. 'You make it sound as if another war is inevitable.'

'There is still war, Sophie. Even if it is not here, and now. You have always known the Great War has never entirely ended.'

Daniel smiled in his sleep. Did babies dream? If so, his dreams were good. And here and now was good as well. More than good.

They sat in silence, side by side, as outside the mid-summer sun collapsed, as gracefully as if it had been taught by Miss Lily, into the sea of London's smoky yellow sunset.

The curtains fluttered, as dusk brought a breeze. Nurse would shut the window for the night in a little while, but for now, the room was theirs and the children's. She could almost hear cows lowing back at Shillings, in the meadow where once a zebra bit the Prince of Wales, and the swish of owl wings, hunting.

Rose stirred, her eyes opening. She gurgled, a notice-me demand.

'So like her mother,' Miss Lily murmured.

Sophie stood, bent and picked up her daughter, then laid her in Miss Lily's arms, such expert arms, cradling the baby's head, just as she would cradle its future.

'Meet your Aunt Lily, Rose,' whispered Sophie. Was 'Aunt' the best compromise they might find? Her eyes met Miss Lily's and saw a joy too deep to speak.

This, at least, was peace.

Jackie French AM is an award-winning writer, wombat negotiator, the 2014–2015 Australian Children's Laureate and the 2015 Senior Australian of the Year. In 2016 Jackie became a Member of the Order of Australia for her contribution to children's literature and her advocacy for youth literacy. She is regarded as one of Australia's most popular authors and writes across all genres — from picture books, history, fantasy, ecology and sci-fi to her much loved historical fiction for a variety of age groups. 'Share a Story' was the primary philosophy behind Jackie's two-year term as Laureate.

jackiefrench.com
facebook.com/authorjackiefrench

MEET MISS LILY AND HER LOVELY LADIES ...

BOOK 1 – Out now

A tale of espionage, love and passionate heroism

Inspired by true events, this is the story of how society's 'lovely ladies' won a war.

Each year at secluded Shillings Hall, in the snow-crisped English countryside, the mysterious Miss Lily draws around her young women selected from Europe's royal and most influential families. Her girls are taught how to captivate a man – and find a potential husband – at a dinner, in a salon, or at a grouse shoot, and in ways that would surprise outsiders. For in 1914, persuading and charming men is the only true power a woman has.

Sophie Higgs is the daughter of Australia's king of corned beef and the only 'colonial' brought to Shillings Hall. Of all Miss Lily's lovely ladies, however, she is also the only one who suspects Miss Lily's true purpose.

As the chaos of war spreads, women across Europe shrug off etiquette.

The lovely ladies and their less privileged sisters become the unacknowledged backbone of the war, creating hospitals, canteens and transport systems where bungling officials fail to cope. And when tens of thousands can die in a single day's battle, Sophie must use the skills Miss Lily taught her to prevent war's most devastating weapon yet.

'The story is equal parts Downton Abbey and wartime action, with enough romance and intrigue to make it 100% not-put-down-able'
Australian Women's Weekly on *Miss Lily's Lovely Ladies*

DANGER CIRCLES EVER CLOSER TO MISS LILY AND HER LOVED ONES ...

BOOK 3 – April 2019

Amid the decadence and desperation of Berlin in the 1920s, a band of women must unite to save all that is precious to them ...

With her dangerous past behind her, Australian heiress Sophie Higgs lives in quiet comfort as the new Countess of Shillings, until Hannelore, Princess of Arneburg, charms the Prince of Wales. He orders Sophie, Nigel — and Miss Lily — to investigate the mysterious politician Hannelore insists is the only man who can save Europe from another devastating war.

His name is Adolf Hitler.

As unimaginable peril threatens to destroy countries and tear families apart, Sophie must face Goering's Brownshirt Nazi thugs, blackmail, and the many possible faces of love.

And then the man she once adored and thought was lost reappears, and Sophie will be confronted by the girl intent on killing the mother who betrayed her family: Miss Lily.

The third book in the Miss Lily series, *The Lily in the Snow* is a story filled with secrets and explores the strength of friendship and the changing face of women in this new Europe.

'If you've sped your way through The Crown and are looking for another historical drama fix to sink your teeth into, *The Lily and The Rose* is going to fast become your next obsession'
New Idea on *The Lily and the Rose*